MORNING SONG

"A splendid and uplifting read. . . . Kimberly Cates has brought her storytelling skills to a new level as she explores the dark recesses of the human heart. She weaves a beautiful story of love, redemption, forgiveness and passion."

—*Romantic Times*

"Cates always writes an emotionally entertaining story, and this one is no different. The characters are marvelous, and the plot . . . keep[s] the reader on the edge of their seat in anticipation."

—*Rendezvous*

"Cates has created a headstrong heroine who is also lovable, and a hero who is guarding a secret so touching it will bring tears to readers' eyes when finally revealed. A sweet yet sensual romance."

—*Affaire de Coeur*

"A finely crafted story. . . . Hannah Gray, her nephew Pip, and hero Austen Dante, will pull readers in deeper and deeper until the satisfying end."

—CompuServe Romance Reviews

"The perfect entertainment for a stormy summer night."

—*Minneapolis Star Tribune*

"[A] delightful romance."

—*Southern Pines Pilot* (North Carolina)

"Cates writes eloquently and emotionally. Her complex, riveting plot makes this a one-sitting novel, impossible to put down!"

—*BookPage*

MAGIC

"A magically written, otherworldly romance that readers will find enchanting. . . . Fast-paced and fun to read."

—Amazon.com

"Cates uses Celtic lore and Irish tradition laced with humor and shimmering sensuality to produce an engaging, well-written story."

—*Library Journal*

"Fun to imagine. . . . Cates' books always have an enchanting quality."

—*Southern Pines Pilot* (North Carolina)

"The joy of fairy tales and the everlasting beauty of true love make *Magic* wonderful. It's a tale full of belief in everything good, heroic, chivalrous, and mystical."

—*Romantic Times*

STEALING HEAVEN

"Kimberly Cates has the talent to pull you into a story on the first page and keep you there. . . . *Stealing Heaven* is a finely crafted tale . . . a tale you won't soon forget. It can stand proud beside Ms. Cates' other excellent romances."

—*Rendezvous*

"Stunning in its emotional impact, glowing with the luminous beauty of the love between a man and a woman . . . *Stealing Heaven* is another dazzling masterpiece from a truly gifted author."

—*Romantic Times*

Books by Kimberly Cates

Lily Fair
Briar Rose
Magic
Angel's Fall
Crown of Dreams
Gather the Stars
To Catch A Flame
Only Forever
Morning Song
The Raider's Bride
The Raider's Daughter
Restless is the Wind
Stealing Heaven

Available from Pocket Books

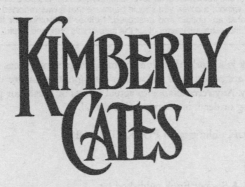

KIMBERLY CATES

LILY FAIR

SONNET BOOKS
New York   London   Toronto   Sydney   Singapore

An *Original* Publication of POCKET BOOKS

A Sonnet Book published by
POCKET BOOKS, a division of Simon & Schuster Inc.
1230 Avenue of the Americas, New York, NY 10020

ISBN: 0-671-02822-7

First Sonnet Books printing November 1999

10 9 8 7 6 5 4 3 2 1

SONNET BOOKS and colophon are trademarks of Simon & Schuster Inc.

Front cover illustration by Ben Perini
Tip-in illustration by Gregg Gulbronson

Printed in the U.S.A.

The Prophecy

IT WAS A PERFECT NIGHT to become immortal. White wind swirled in from the Irish Sea, whispering the secret glory of an army of heroes stretching back to the dawn of time. A druid moon pulsed above land no invader could ever tame. Shimmering like silver lace, a path of light wavered toward that mysterious sphere, as if daring any man with the courage to step onto its insubstantial plane to climb skyward into legend.

A journey that for some men was easy, touched as they were by the fiery hand of fate. But for others . . . treacherous, insurmountable, a cruel jest that left pride in tatters and a deep well of bitterness where souls used to be.

Conn the Ever Truthful, high chieftain of Glenfluirse, stood at the arrow slit of his castle, salt wind stinging his weathered cheeks, a restless light in his hooded eyes. He should be rejoicing, drowning in the revelry of the warriors he had led into battle. Men even now drinking and bellowing across his vast table, recounting tales of valor to their adoring wives.

He had won. Enemies in full retreat. More pleasing still, he had heard the whispers again between his fledgling bard and aged druid. Soon now. Soon all Ireland would know Conn as the Undefeated One. It was a sobriquet any chieftain would lust after. One that would ensure his name would be marked as indelibly on the landscape of Ireland as the Slieve Mish mountains that hunched their giant shoulders skyward. And yet even that glorious title would not be of his own earning but, rather, the careless gift of another man.

Fintan MacShane. Conn turned, his gaze finding the warrior despite the confusion. Tall, powerful, with a spear caster's broad shoulders, Fintan sat in a corner with his wife, oblivious to the fact that half the women in the hall would gladly have shed their husbands and rushed to his bed to claim they had sampled his unique magic. Or that any warrior would trade all he owned for the gift fairies had placed in Fintan's hands. The gift of never missing a spear cast in battle, despite the fact that he was stone blind.

Battle after battle had been won because of Fintan—his skill, his courage, his ability to lead men. Conn had been dragged along upon the tails of his glory. Yet Conn had taken some small comfort in the dark of his own chamber, bitter pleasure that it would not matter if Fintan's name was etched into the heavens beside the very stars. For Fintan's wife, beloved as she was, had been barren. No son or daughter would ever mark the blind spear caster's acts of valor. Fintan's seed would die, even as Conn's sons thrived.

Yet even that comfort was to be denied Conn. The fairies again had worked magic for Fintan. His wife, long past the age of childbearing, swelled with the babe both had longed for. Even now, they whispered together as if they were newly wed, desperately in love, Fintan's hand caressing the child through Grainne's gown.

Bitterness welled up in Conn, poisonous frustration

he hoped no one present would see. But at that moment, the bard rose, resplendent despite his youth, his clarsagh in his arms, a grim reproach in his eyes as he cast a glance at Conn. "I shall tell a tale of Fintan." The bard's mellifluous voice filled the hall. "Fintan whose place is already marked among the stars."

Conn winced, knowing he could ill afford the bard's disapproval, or that of the men Fintan had dazzled yet again this day with his skill. Conn's jaw almost shattered with the effort it took to force a smile to his lips as he swaggered back to the trestles, taking up a tankard.

"Fintan!" he roared, saluting the spear caster. It mattered not that the man could not see it. The other warriors did. "May your name live forever, and your son live long to praise it!"

But despite his efforts, the bard still stared at Conn, seeing far too much, peering into the deep, secret well of his hate. Shaken, Conn fought to distract the bard by shouting out in a hearty voice.

"Druid!" He summoned the dark-robed holy man in the bard's shadow. "Use your divining arts for the hero of this day! Tell us what manner of warrior Fintan's son will be."

A relic from a vanishing age, the druid glided across the room in a sweep of dusty robe, as if he belonged to a realm beyond the physical world and his feet did not touch the earth. Fintan's wife looked up, a hint of alarm in her eyes, one hand curving over her babe as if to shield it—from the ugliness of war yet to come? Or from the dark power of predestination?

"Whist, light of my soul." Fintan chuckled, obviously sensing her reaction. He drew her hands away. "Do you not know there is no power on earth we need fear? Nothing ill can happen to this child," he murmured. " 'Tis a child of destiny, given to us by enchantment."

He smiled, so certain, so arrogant in his gift, as if immortal already. Conn's hate for him was superseded only by his need for Fintan's skills.

A hush fell over the chamber, even the stone walls seeming to hold their breath as the druid closed one long, white-fingered hand over Grainne's vulnerable belly. A gasp tore from the man's lips, and he yanked back his fingers as if they had touched fire. Grainne cried out, eyes wide as she peered into the druid's ashen face.

"What is it?" Fintan demanded, sightless yet sensing the sudden terror in his beloved wife's heart.

"The babe," the druid murmured, low, as if he had aged a hundred years from that single touch. "It is a daughter."

"You are a fool if you believe such news will dismay me, druid!" Fintan scoffed. The spear caster turned from the old man to his wife. He cradled Grainne closer. "A daughter of yours is finer than any other man's son."

"Fintan, there is more. The child . . ." The druid cast an agonized glance from the parents to Conn, and what Conn saw in those ageless eyes turned his blood to stone. "The child will be the downfall of the chieftain. She must . . . she must be put to death the instant she draws her first breath."

"Nay!" Grainne screamed denial, clutching her belly. Fintan rose, weapon in hand, as if terrified the druid would cut the babe from her womb.

"You are wrong, druid," the warrior growled. "No man is more loyal to the chieftain than Fintan Mac-Shane." A low murmur rose from the crowd.

"It is not a question of loyalty, Fintan," the druid pleaded. "It is her destiny—"

Fintan spat on the floor beside the old man. "Destiny? Bah! If any man dares touch my child, I vow that act will be his last." The blind spear caster turned toward Conn, unnervingly as if he saw him. "I have fought for you. Bled for you. Tell me now, my chieftain, what has my blood purchased? Where does your faith lie? Do you trust in the oath of Fintan MacShane that no child of his will do you harm or in the blathering fear of this old man?"

Conn stood, frozen, knowing that the future lay in his hands. How often had he dreamed of holding some weapon over Fintan's head, of possessing real power instead of merely the illusion of it. Now he could destroy Fintan in one devastating blow, but one slip, one stumble, and all hope of being called the Undefeated One would be gone.

Distasteful as glory might be when given as another man's charity, it was still far better than no glory at all.

Conn sucked in a steadying breath. "Fintan, lay down your spear. May the gods curse me if I were to murder the only child of a man I hold as a brother."

"But you must listen," the druid pleaded. "Great disaster. I saw it when the babe leapt beneath my hand."

Conn shrugged. " 'Tis a girl. What danger could a girl child be? What weapon could she wield save the beauty of her face? Once the babe is born, I will send her off to a nunnery, where the sisters shall raise her as if she were royalty. When she grows to a woman, I will call her back to court and wed her to a man strong enough to ward off any curse."

Grief and gratitude warred in the faces of Fintan and his wife.

"But to surrender our babe!" Grainne sobbed. "I cannot bear it!"

Fintan gathered her in his arms, his voice rough with grief, resignation. "It is a gift Conn has offered us. The child's life. Love, there is no other way."

Three days later, screams rose from the chambers of Fintan, the hands that had cast countless spears clinging to his wife's as she brought their babe into the world. For one night, the beautiful child lay in her mother's arms, her father's fingers stroking her silky cheek.

At dawn, Fintan gathered his daughter in his arms, strode from the chamber of his grief-stricken wife. In the shadow of the druid's hut, the warrior faced Conn. "Your word she will be safe."

"Do you doubt me? They call me the Ever Truthful," Conn said steadily, hiding resentment, bitterness, and the tiniest flicker of triumph. This time it was *he* who held the mighty Fintan's fate in his hands.

Fintan surrendered his child to the horseman waiting beside a standing stone. "Her name is Caitlin," Fintan said, his voice rough with grief. "Caitlin of the Lilies, for she is lily fair."

Disbelieving, Conn leaned over to peer at the girl-child's face. He froze, staring at the most beautiful babe he had ever seen, a child otherworldly, like the Christian angels he had heard about or the fairy maids who had enchanted countless mortals, luring them to their distant kingdoms.

For an instant, Conn quailed, fearing that the girl had her own brand of magic. But he shoved the thought aside. No, she was but a mortal child. A mere girl. No threat to a chieftain cunning as he.

Conn watched as the rider and child disappeared into the dawn. Problems such as the one this girl presented must be handled delicately. Delicately, he mused. He needed Fintan's strength and skill to gain his own place in the annals of legend. And even a high chieftain dared not challenge the wrath of fairy magic. Let the child live, for the present. Then, the instant Fintan's usefulness was past, Conn would know what to do.

Conn glanced at Fintan's face, sightless eyes following the daughter he would never touch again, the warrior's rugged face streaked with unmanly tears.

Aye, it would be simple enough to unravel this coil in the end, Conn reasoned. Even legends had to die.

Chapter

1

❦

THE WILD IRISH HILLS seethed like a giant's cauldron, a baffling mixture of rugged stone, lush green meadow, and lacings of mist broken by patches of sky that glittered as bright and blue as a fairy's wing. Even the trees seemed human, digging their roots like fingers into earth pulsing with the passion and pain of a land at war with itself.

Legend claimed the Tuatha de Danaan, the fairy folk who had once ruled the island, had lost a great battle but defeated their mortal enemies in the end by melting into trees and hillsides, stones and streams, fleet red deer and the most cherished reaches of people's memories.

Now, another battle was being fought for Ireland—a war between druid gods of earth and saints' God in heaven. Yet, though Caitlin of the Lilies had been raised within the holy confines of the Abbey of Mary of Infinite Mercy, and though she loved the sisters there—their gentleness, their faith—she understood a truth they could never comprehend.

No matter how many saints hallowed Irish ground, no matter how many monks inscribed manuscripts of impossible beauty upon the island's seaswept shores, Ireland would always have a pagan heart.

She could feel its steady throb no matter how determinedly she bent her head in prayer, the voice of the land calling to her, wild and sweet. *You can never be like the rest of them, Caitlin of the Lilies, for you belong to me.* She had fought it, sometimes feared that indefinable *something* that made her different from all the others. In the end she had surrendered to the invisible barrier that separated her from the practical world of the nuns. And yet never once in twenty years of life had she been able to deny that it existed.

Whatever spell had been cast upon the night she was abandoned at the druid altar was real. And never had she felt its pull more strongly than she did today. *Her* day. The day twenty years ago when Reverend Mother had found her, a newborn babe wrapped in the robe of a chieftain.

Caitlin glanced back at the walls of the abbey, knowing that there were plenty among Reverend Mother's pious flock who disapproved of her yearly pilgrimage to the block of stone with its ancient writings. They charged her to spend the day fasting and in prayer. To resist her shameful link to things heathen. Yet how could she do as they bade her? It was the one time in the year she had something to hold, something to touch, to assure herself that the voices in her dreams were real . . .

She shivered in anticipation, her bare feet light on the cool moss as she raced through the trees, certain the yearly offering would be there. She could almost feel it—the cool stem of one perfect lily between her fingers. She could nearly smell it, the fragrance whispering sweet possibilities. The precious knowledge that someone beyond the abbey walls still cared for her.

Whoever had abandoned her had not forgotten her. And somewhere in the wide world Caitlin had never seen, a mother, a father, a whole family might wait to claim her.

She could not suppress a sting of guilt, a sense that she was ungrateful. No mother, real or imaginary, could have loved her more than the mistress of the abbey. And yet, had not Reverend Mother been the one first who guided her steps along the path to the druid stone, with a secret sorrow, a wistfulness shadowing the nun's mist-gray eyes, as if she knew that this was where Caitlin belonged, no matter how much Reverend Mother might wish otherwise?

Caitlin felt a twinge, but she promised herself that after she delighted in the lily and the wondrous imaginings it always brought, she would go to Reverend Mother's cell, show her the perfect flower. She would lean against the older woman's knee as she had every night since childhood and wrap herself tight in real love that never faltered. *Love that should be enough*, a voice inside Caitlin whispered.

Nay, she would not tarnish this day with regrets or self-recriminations. Reverend Mother always wished her to feel joy on these journeys. From the beginning, she had understood the questing spirit in Caitlin, the restlessness of a young girl who had never seen the wonders of the world that lay beyond the abbey.

How many times had those prayerful lips curved with indulgence as she told Caitlin her own memories of the outside world? The great fortress where she had grown up, favorite daughter of a mighty warrior. The thrill of cattle raids, the adventures spun by bards about the hero Cuchulain. She had said other things as well, confided her regret over the heartbreaking rift between her and her beloved father when she had refused to marry any one of a dozen suitors, choosing instead the life of a nun. Reverend Mother had hinted quietly of different dangers other nuns spoke more plainly of, wickedness and sin, horrors so unspeakable the women had fled to the abbey to escape them.

Yet, in spite of all the tales she heard, Caitlin had fashioned the Irish wilds into an innocent girl's dream where all women were brave and every man a hero, and each year a perfect lily drew her closer to that magical realm.

Caitlin grimaced. Not that she had had much success imagining the bold, handsome heroes. From the beginning, the abbess had told her it was possible that one day she would leave the abbey, that it was even possible marriage might be her destiny.

Yet the only example of a man Caitlin had ever seen was Father Columcille, a wrinkled gnome with a bulbous red nose and rheumy eyes she had watched with great interest as a child, certain they would pop out of their sockets at any moment.

In the end, the men in Reverend Mother's tales had become creatures elusive and mysterious, as deliciously fantastic as the pagan gods Cuchulain had fought. But it did not matter if they were real or not, Caitlin thought with a toss of her head. It was *her* world, *her* imaginings, and today was the one day in all the year she could venture beyond the abbey's stone walls to taste the magic of that world just a little.

She rounded a tussock of heather, the trees thinning, the sun falling across her in great bars of light. Suddenly she slowed her steps, uncertain why. Did she feel the reverence in this old and holy place? Was she hoping perhaps this time the mystery of her birth might be revealed? Or was her hesitation something more simple? The knowledge that once she walked through the last archway of oaks and crossed to the great slab of stone to claim her lily, the enchantment would be over for yet another year?

One hand smoothed a cascade of raven locks. The other settled the folds of her simple robes about her, but no power on earth could ever tame the exhilaration sparkling in her fairy-blue eyes.

Intent on making the delight last as long as possible, Caitlin fastened her gaze on the ground, carefully placing her bare feet in an effort to avoid spring's first blossoms that scattered the seldom-used path.

Her fingers tightened in the rough cloth of her robes, and she caught her bottom lip between her teeth as she glimpsed the base of the massive stone. Ever so slowly, she let her eyes trek up the gray surface, past intricate carvings she could not decipher. Sucking in a deep breath, she raised her gaze higher, to the broad top of the druid altar, the rugged cradle in which her lily had always lain.

Caitlin froze. She could not speak, could not breathe. There, upon the altar, lay a man, his dark lashes pillowed against high-slashed cheekbones. Did he sleep? Or did he lie there in some sort of fairy enchantment? Part of the magical spell that had bound her from her birth?

He might have been Cuchulain, called back from the land of heroes, so powerful was the long sweep of his body, rugged planes and hollows, corded muscles barely disguised by the linen of his shirt and the thick wool folds of the garment wrapped around him.

Hair the sleek brown of a stag's coat was threaded with strands of fiery red that snagged the sun. The waves glowed rich and thick against the tanned planes of a face as fiercely beautiful as any peregrine's. His nose, an arrogant blade, was strong as the shortsword bound at his waist, his cheekbones carved in a high, proud arch. But it was his lips that held Caitlin transfixed. Lips impossibly soft, unspeakably sensual, unbearably masculine, above a stubborn jut of jaw. The mouth of a poet, a bard, captured in the face of a warrior.

She swallowed hard, drinking in the sight of him, certain that if she gazed at this man for an eternity she could never have her fill. One glimpse, and her world had altered utterly, forever.

Was this what the lilies had promised? The mysteries that had always surrounded her? Was this, then, her destiny? This man?

Or *was* he a man, built of bone and sinew? Was he mortal at all? She trembled at the thought. Could it be possible that he was something far different? An offering from the ancient ones who had melted into the trees and the mountains, setting Ireland aglow in countless shades of green, feeding the island with the life in their souls? Could this magnificent creature be woven of that beautiful magic? For her?

The thought was terrifying in its sweetness. Yet could this encounter have any meaning besides fate? Every year, there had been a lily waiting for her on this day. Now he lay in its place . . .

Filled with wonder, she reached toward the hard column of his arm, but it seemed wrong, a cold way to begin an enchantment. Moved by an instinct she barely understood, she leaned toward him, felt the heat of his breath against her own cheek. He was real, she thought numbly. Real.

Closing her eyes, she pictured his awakening when she brushed the hot satin of that poet's mouth with her own. Summoning up her last bit of courage, Caitlin lowered her lips to his.

A roar shattered the clearing, a flash of sinew and hard, grasping hands catching her in a bruising grasp. She tried to scream, but in a heartbeat, she was sprawled on her back on the stone, a crushing weight pinning her down. Caitlin struggled, a shriek rising in her throat, but a hard hand crushed down on her mouth, stifling any sound.

Balling her hand into a fist, she swung with all her might, catching her attacker on one high cheekbone, her knee driving instinctively for the vulnerable flesh between his thighs. With a grunt of surprise and pain, the beast rolled off her. "Hellcat, you all but unmanned me!" a rough voice snarled.

Her vision cleared, and she found herself staring into a face as fierce and pagan as any warrior god the druids had ever dreamed. She felt a horrible sense of loss. The sleeping hero she had found vanished forever.

Green eyes pierced her so deeply that she could not breathe. "I thought your Christian God said to love thy enemy," the man sneered with a scornful glance at her habit, "not knock him senseless."

Caitlin scrambled back, her legs so tangled in her robes she could not get to her feet. "Wh-who are you?"

"They call me Niall." His mouth hardened further still. "Niall of the Seven Betrayals."

What kind of man could he be? One whose very name proclaimed his infamy? Caitlin's gaze flicked to his, and she saw her revulsion register in those fierce green eyes. His lips curled in the harshest smile she had ever seen.

"You are wise to be wary of me, madam."

She hated him for sensing her fear, hated herself for letting it show, no matter how well founded that fear might be. Drawing the tattered remnants of her pride about her, she tipped her chin up in what Reverend Mother always called her fairy queen expression—one that, at the moment, made it evident she wanted nothing more than to command some minion to cut off his head.

"Did you steal my flower?" she demanded, incensed as if he had robbed the treasure of Tir naN Og itself.

If nothing else, she had set him off balance. "Steal?" he echoed. "A flower? What the devil for?"

"It is supposed to be there. On the druid stone."

"Let me assure you that if I ever decided to turn thief, I would not waste my time stealing an accursed *flower*. Why the blazes should it matter so much to you? I cannot begin to guess." His eyes flicked down the coarse homespun of her clothes, and he laid one powerful finger alongside his jaw. "Then again . . . perhaps I can. Meeting a lover, are you? I wonder if your abbess would approve."

"I—I am not! She would—" Caitlin cut off her stammerings, her cheeks burning with embarrassment and indignation. She wanted nothing more than to slap the smug expression off the man's face.

"So you *are* from the abbey. You might be of some use to me yet." Something in his voice terrified her. "I have ridden three days without sleep searching for the abbey of Saint Mary's. Could not find the accursed thing. Finally fell asleep on that rock of yours. Perhaps it was fate. Now I will not have to stumble about, searching, any longer. *You* can show me the way."

Caitlin stared in disbelief. This warrior, intimidating enough in a chance meeting, was far more frightening seeking the abbey. And he wanted *her* to lead him to the walls?

She shuddered, thinking of the sisters who had raised her—so gentle, so compassionate, so trusting in the protection of their God. She reeled from the sudden realization that all the things she loved about them left them terrifyingly vulnerable.

She struggled to keep from imagining what sort of damage this giant of a man, this warrior, could do to a flock of defenseless women. "What business could you possibly have at the abbey?" she demanded.

Disgust and impatience sparked in the warrior's hard eyes. "I come to claim a wench."

Caitlin crossed herself. "G-God help her."

Niall gave a snarling laugh. "She will need far more help than your puling God can offer."

"Wh-who . . ." The question snagged in Caitlin's throat, a hard, barbed thing. She knew before he spoke, felt it—a horrible sinking in the pit of her stomach.

"They call her by some absurd name. Caitlin of the Lilies."

"Nay!" Caitlin gasped, foolish childhood dreams crumbling into nightmare. "That is impossible!"

Holy Mary, why had she not guessed? Why had she not suspected that what the other sisters had warned her of, feared, was true? That the lilies were sweet poison, luring her to disaster instead of a fragrant path to some wondrous destiny?

Terror drove sudden strength into her limbs, her hands tearing loose the tangled skirts as she scrambled to her feet. One last glimpse of that implacable face burned itself in her memory, then she ran, back to everything she had loved yet so long taken for granted.

But no matter how fast her feet flew, Caitlin knew the truth. The abbey walls could not bar a man like that forever. Tears streaked her cheeks, hot, hopeless, sick with certainty. Even Reverend Mother's love could not protect her now.

Caitlin felt countless eyes upon her as she ran through the rickety gate, the bevy of sisters gaping when she dragged the heavy bar across it as if an invading army marched against the abbey. Caitlin winced as the aged wood barrier groaned beneath the bar's weight, the gate in danger of tumbling down of its own accord. Sister Luca, a plump woman who often nodded to sleep over her prayers, dropped the bundle of carrots she had been clutching and hastened toward her, alarm in her moon-shaped face. "By Jesus, Mary, and Joseph, child, what has happened?" she asked, brushing the dirt from stubby fingers. "You look as if a horde of devils is at your heels!"

"N-not a horde." Caitlin shuddered. "One is enough!" She was shamed by the tears that stung her eyes, but she could not stop them. "Wh-where is Reverend Mother?"

Luca's cheeks went white. "In her chamber, I think. But she had some private meditation to attend to. She asked not to be disturbed."

Caitlin cast a glance back at the wooden gates, half expecting to hear the thunder of a battering ram, the bellow of the devil's voice, at any moment. A man of the sort she had found in the druid grove would be wise enough to follow her to the abbey. And once he found it, he would not be thwarted by such a paltry barrier as the abbey gates for long.

Caitlin grasped the old nun's sleeve. "Whatever happens, Sister Luca, do not open the gates. You cannot let him in! I beg of you!"

"Let *him* in? A—a man?" The old woman crossed herself with fierce resolution. "Never, by the sacred blood of Saint Patrick!"

A little comforted, Caitlin wheeled, raced into the ancient stone building. She wound through chambers where she had skipped as a child, played hoodman blind, learned to recite her prayers. A place where danger had never even dared scratch at the window in the form of a childish nightmare.

Her hands shook. Her heart thundered. Reverend Mother would make everything all right. Forever calm, infinitely wise, she would think of some way to help her.

Caitlin rounded a corner, plunged into Reverend Mother's cell. She froze, the sight so blessedly familiar, the place so filled with peace, it seemed almost possible that the scene in the druid grove had been nothing but a wicked dream.

Fine-boned as the most fragile bird yet exuding incredible strength, Reverend Mother leaned over a humble wooden chest, holding something up into the brightest shaft of light from a sliver of window, doubtless so she could see it more clearly with her failing eyes.

Caitlin was stunned to realize that it was the robe she herself had been wrapped in as a babe: folds of white linen exquisitely embroidered with birds and horses, interlacing designs worked with threads of gold. Caitlin had thought it had been given away to the poor years ago, like every other worldly possession that came into the convent.

Reverend Mother straightened, alerted by the sound of footsteps that she was no longer alone. The saintly woman turned, her cheeks pink as if she had been caught in some dark, indulgent sin. Her eyes glowed, misty with memories, proud and a little sad. But the moment her gaze locked on Caitlin, she dropped the robe back into the little chest, the fragile folds tumbling in a disordered heap like a broken rainbow.

Brow creased with worry, the abbess crossed to her, framing Caitlin's cheeks in her callused palms. "Caitlin, child? Whatever is amiss? You look ill."

It was harder than Caitlin could have imagined, shattering the older woman's peace, but there was no help for it. "I—I went to the grove."

"Did you injure yourself? Parts of the path are rocky—"

"Nay. But my lily . . . it was not there."

Relief smoothed the creases bracketing Reverend Mother's mouth, a soft empathy gleaming in her mist-colored eyes. "I know you are disappointed, my dove. Perhaps some woodland creature ran off with it. You and I can go search for your lily together."

"Nay!" The idea of Reverend Mother going out into the woods, facing that beast of a man, was unspeakable. "There was something else in the lily's place." Caitlin was trembling now. She could not stop. A sob broke from her lips. "A monster—a horrible beast of a man. He grabbed me and . . ."

Reverend Mother paled, stricken as if someone had plunged a dagger into her breast. But she seemed to draw on her wealth of inner strength and faith to shore her up. She gripped the lid of the chest with one hand to steady herself. "Caitlin, you must tell me what happened," she insisted in a calm, bracing voice. "Everything, child. Did this man . . . touch you in ways he should not have?"

"Aye! He did! He did!" Caitlin saw the aged nun curl tight inside herself as if she had taken a physical blow. "Look at my arms!" Caitlin shoved up the sleeves, displaying the beginnings of bruises on her lily-pale flesh. "He grabbed me! He shoved me down onto the stone and—and he *bellowed at me!*"

The abbess went still, hope sparking in her eyes. "That is all? You are certain?"

"*All?*" Indignation shot through Caitlin. "No one has ever done such unspeakable things to me before! I struck him in the face. Kicked him. I got away."

The nun actually smiled! "Of course you did, my bold, brave girl! Thanks be to God." Reverend Mother gathered her in her arms, stroking her hair. "Whist, my heart, I have got you safe now. He cannot hurt you ever again."

Caitlin melted into that familiar embrace, wanting desperately to trust in its shelter as she always had before.

"Doubtless he was some wandering villain," Reverend Mother murmured with relief. "Some warrior who has already gone off in search of easier prey. Still, we must send word to the outlying farms so they can guard against him, and we must warn the other sisters. It is better to be careful."

"Wait, you do not understand. This man will not ride away. He came in search of someone." Caitlin swallowed hard, raised her tear-streaked face to stare into Reverend Mother's eyes. "He came for me."

The older woman stilled. "For you?" She said it as if she could not believe it. Said it as if, someplace in her heart of hearts, she had been expecting it forever.

Caitlin's stomach wrenched, all of this suddenly, terribly real. "He said he had come to—to claim a worthless wench by the name of Caitlin of the Lilies."

Stricken, Reverend Mother released her, then turned away. Her weathered hand stroked the exquisite folds of embroidered cloth that spilled out of the chest, the wondrous colors faded now but still beautiful.

"I always feared this day would come. Knew it would. The robe . . . it was so fine, the lily left for you every year. I tried to prepare myself. And to prepare you." She turned, an expression Caitlin had never seen before on her face, a fierce, almost feral love, the earthy love that made a mother fling herself before a charging stag to save her child.

"But this I promise you, Caitlin, my own. My soul will be damned before I let some cruel brute drag you away from here, despite the claims of fate and destiny!"

Relief spilled through Caitlin, and she clung to the tiniest thread of hope. She almost believed Reverend Mother *could* keep her safe, as long as she kept the image of the enraged warrior from her mind.

"Reverend Mother?" a timid voice interrupted from beyond the doorway.

Both Reverend Mother and Caitlin straightened, attempting to banish the signs of their distress.

"What is it?" Reverend Mother asked.

Sister Luca poked her head into the chamber, her lips trembling. "There is a man pounding upon the gates. I told him we are a cloistered order. No one from the outside world is supposed to be allowed within the abbey walls, but he says he brings word from the chieftain. If we refuse to allow him entrance, he will break down the gates. I—I am quite certain he can do it, may Saint Patrick preserve us."

"Do not be distressed by his threats, Sister. I will deal with this messenger. You will take our Caitlin out to the cloghan hut at the rear of the abbey grounds. Wait with her there until I send someone to fetch you."

"Aye, Mother."

Caitlin felt the warmth of Reverend Mother's hands against her hair, the quick, bracing kiss upon her cheek. Then the abbess was gone in a whirl of coarse habit and stony determination. Chilled, frightened for the first time in her life, Caitlin fled out the back of the abbey into the sunshine, to the small stone hut where she had played as a girl.

For a lone child, it had been transformed into the castle of the fairy king, the belly of some mythic beast that had swallowed her whole. More often still, the hut was a magic fortress where her imaginary brothers and sisters had frolicked under the watchful eye of the mother she had never seen.

Even long after she had abandoned such childish games, Caitlin had returned to the hut in an effort to stem the growing restlessness inside her. She had sought out the quiet of the stone walls, finding an ineffable serenity there, left perhaps by the first holy order to build on this site.

Always, Caitlin had loved the sense of peace that seemed to seep from the very walls, the feeling that here, nothing evil could touch her.

Closing her eyes, she recalled all the tales the abbess had told her, of miracles carried down by angels, astonishing feats of saintly magic.

She could use a miracle now.

With Sister Luca sniffling beside her, she fell to her knees, uttering the most heartfelt prayers she had ever said. *Please, make this go away, make it all vanish,* she begged the saints in the Irish heavens. *I did not know. I was a fool not to understand . . .*

A fool? No, too protected, too much a child to understand that the hands of fate were merciless. She had loved the glorious tales of destiny and bright mysterious futures Reverend Mother had spun. It had made Caitlin feel special to know that such a future waited for her beyond the abbey walls.

It had sounded so wonderful, so romantic, not to face a prospect that was lackluster and dull, the same as all the other women. She had cherished the thought that she was unique, held it close to her heart.

She had never suspected the price she would have to pay—that she could be torn away from a life she loved, flung onto a path she never wished to follow.

She had not guessed there would be terror, uncertainty. Had not known she would want to cling to Reverend Mother's skirts, hide in the blessedly familiar haven of the abbey forever.

But such doubts did not matter. Caitlin could feel her mysterious fate thundering toward her, a force that could never be turned away—certainly not by Reverend Mother, despite the abbess's vow. Caitlin trembled. Was there nothing, no one who could help her?

The wind threaded through the square stone door, whispering of other powers, the Tuatha de Danaan of the earth. Desperate, Caitlin pleaded with them. *Listen to me—if I belong to you. The lilies and the dreams, this destiny Reverend Mother spoke of. It is too real. Make it go away. I cannot leave here. Cannot leave her.*

Caitlin swallowed hard, whispering words she had never spoken before. "I am afraid."

Chapter

2

NIALL GLARED at the rickety gate, frustration and fury flowing through him so hot it was a miracle the wood did not burst into flame. By the blood of Cuchulain, he had spent a lifetime schooling himself in the ways of a warrior, endured countless wounds without flinching, passed tests of skill and bravery that would make any sane man tremble. He had girded fierce pride about his narrow waist as tightly as his shortsword and fought his own demon, impatience, with the fury and determination of a thousand Finn MacCools. But even a warrior could only endure so much.

Curse the girl to the bowels of her Christian hell! She had outfought him, outrun him, and slammed the accursed gate in his face as if he were some filthy beggar. If anyone at the chieftain's court heard about this day . . .

He grimaced, hating himself for the knot tightening in his belly. Who would guess that a man who sought out the most deadly heat of every battle could be unnerved by such a subtle weapon as mockery? But he had been forced to endure enough of that poison in his twenty-four years to last a hundred lifetimes.

The image of eyes azure-bright as Ireland's clearest

lake goaded him, and Niall's jaw clenched at the memory of the wench he had found in the wood. *Niall of the Seven Betrayals* . . . the mere sound of his name had made her dark-lashed eyes widen in horror and revulsion, her pink lips curling as if she had bitten into bruised fruit.

He should be used to inspiring such a grim reaction in strangers by now. He thought he had managed to bury his emotions over the years, hide the vicious sting such rejection caused him. But with this exquisite young woman, the wound had been new as a fresh sword cut.

Not that he could let that matter. He had learned in a dozen bitter lessons that lashing out in anger or pain would only make things worse. The only thing it accomplished was to give enemies a choice place to aim their blows. Nay, he had to hide his emotions, control them, never let anyone see—especially this raven-haired wench who had so unnerved him.

He banged on the gate again, splitting the skin on one knuckle, but he scarce felt the sting as a timid voice drifted through the barrier.

"A moment longer, sir. We are a cloistered order. Our abbess . . . she must decide what to do. It is unheard of to allow one such as yourself to enter. Only the terribly sick can pass through these gates."

Niall ground his teeth. It seemed he had spent his whole life waiting to be allowed inside—into the warm circle of someone's trust, maybe even into someone's heart. He had pounded at those invisible gates since he was a boy of eight, had grown to manhood battering scorn back with the blade of his shortsword and the strength in his own warrior's body. He had performed impossible feats for his chieftain, six quests in an effort to wash away the shameful legacy of the father who had left Niall with betrayal as part of his very name. With this last quest, Niall's prize would be won. A name cleansed of infamy, a future washed clean of his father's dishonor.

With the last drop of his blood, Niall had fought to reclaim his honor, but now . . . what would happen when the court discovered what his final quest had been? The ultimate test of his manhood, his courage, his loyalty to his chieftain? Fetching some wench from a convent? Niall winced. If there had been an army to bar the way, or some accursed dragon-beast spitting flame, it might have been a worthy task. But the only test to his courage and strength here was a rotted wood gate and a bevy of nuns who doubtless ran shrieking at the scratching of mice in the dark.

He could already hear the laughter back at court—the whispered jibes behind cupped hands, the triumph of his enemies, the quiet shame of his hard-won allies.

But worst of all was the faint suspicion Niall could not quite shake free, the dread that somehow he had been betrayed by the chieftain who had been more a father to him than his own. Niall suppressed an unwelcome chill. Was it possible that the ruler men called Conn the Ever Truthful had planned this humiliation of his great enemy's son from the very beginning? That he had been raising Niall higher and higher in power and royal favor only to dash him to the stones below?

Nay, Niall could not believe that. He shoved suspicion resolutely aside. There must be something more in this quest, something yet hidden. The chieftain was shrewd, renowned throughout Ireland for his honesty. And the only reason Niall had not starved as a boy was Conn's generosity. Generosity that would have extended even further, had Niall's mother not been mad.

Niall's hand shifted to the leather pouch affixed to

his waist. Whatever the truth was, it would be revealed soon enough in the letter Conn had pressed into his hand just before he left Glenfluirse. For an instant, Niall was tempted to dig the missive out, read it—either confirm or dash away his fears. But Conn had ordered him not to open it until the first night he and the girl were alone.

The gate creaked, yanking Niall from his dark musings. He felt an irritating surge of gratitude toward the grizzled nun swinging the portal open. Despite a mustache that many a whelp of a youth would envy, the woman regarded him as if she expected a hidden army to charge in after him, intent on ravishment. He should have been vaguely amused, but the fear in her eyes tugged at something inside him. Her expression reminded him of emotions Niall had known all too well, had fought to forget—what it felt like to be completely vulnerable, at someone else's mercy.

"I mean you no harm," he ground out, but the words sounded more like a challenge to battle than an offer of comfort.

The woman skittered back. "Th-the abbess will see you now. F-follow me."

He shook his head. He might as well have saved himself the trouble of trying to put her at ease. Few women had ever been anything but afraid of him, except for the mad ones who found something exciting about dancing with the devil.

In a rustle of robes, the nun fled before him, as if she expected him to take a bite out of her backside. At last, they reached a chamber furnished most simply, a lone woman standing in a shaft of sunlight from the arrow slit above her. He had faced armies of warriors that had looked far less resolute.

Niall glanced around, looking for the young woman

he was supposed to fetch, impatience firing inside him. Blast, he had no time for these womanish games.

"I come from Conn the Ever Truthful, high chieftain of Glenfluirse. He has commanded that I bring Caitlin of the Lilies to his court."

The abbess merely peered at him, unaffected as if he had delivered a clutch of rabbits from a nearby farmer.

Perhaps living with all these fluttery women had made the abbess a halfwit. "She has been under your protection, this woman?" Niall demanded.

"She *is* under my protection," the abbess said, her chin bumping up a notch.

"I come to relieve you of your responsibility. Your services are no longer needed." Niall dug a heavy leather bag from the folds of his shirt. "This is for your trouble." He dumped the pouch's contents onto the abbess's table, surprised himself at the riches that glowed upon the worn wood. Cloak fasteners of gold, torcs and rings, some studded with precious stones. Odd gifts for a nunnery.

"Return it all to your master." The abbess barely spared the trinkets a glance. "No riches on earth could ever pay me for raising this child."

Niall grimaced, aware of the tenderness between his legs. "I met one of your wenches in the wood. If she is any indication of the type of wards you are entrusted with, I understand your sentiments."

"You understand nothing." The abbess glared at him, her eyes burning with emotion. "Will he care for her? This chieftain of yours? Will he protect her? See that she is happy? In all these years, we have heard not a word from him! We know nothing of his plans for her. All her life, Caitlin has been loved. The abbey is her home."

Niall shifted his feet, uncomfortable with the intensity

in the abbess's features, a heart laid bare, love, grief, defiance, courage. An odd mixture he had not seen in the years since he had last looked into his sister's small face.

"A high chieftain is not required to confide his plans to a simple abbess or to one of his warriors. We are his subjects. We do whatever he asks of us."

"I have far more allegiance to Caitlin than to any distant chieftain. A loyalty forged in love, not duty or fear. I will do anything in my power to protect her."

Niall looked into her face, a sharp retort on his tongue. Yet truth was, it would be simple enough for the old nun to spirit the girl away into one of countless hiding places where he could never find her. Leave him stumbling around the countryside like the veriest fool, possibly to return to his chieftain empty-handed.

He wanted to rage at the woman, force her to his will, but he had stared into the faces of enough enemies in battle to know instinctively if their resolution would waver when he pressed them. This woman would let him cleave her in two if it would protect the girl. Something twisted in his chest. Loyalty—it had always moved him, perhaps because his own father's allegiances had shifted like the winds. From his chieftain and his wife to a woman who had driven him mad with lust.

Niall gazed into the abbess's eyes, wanting to offer her some small comfort. "You ask about the chieftain. I cannot tell you his plans for your fosterling. But I can tell you this. He is a good ruler. A just one."

The hope that flickered in the abbess's face was almost painful, edged by doubt. "You are his messenger. Of course, you would praise him."

He had stated the truth. Was tempted to leave it at that. If the old woman worried, it was her own choice. Yet he found he could not ignore the terror in her, the love.

It was harder to speak than he could have imagined. Why? he wondered vaguely. His lineage was no secret. His link to the chieftain had been spread around every campfire from Slieve Mish to the Irish Sea.

"I was the son of the chieftain's greatest enemy. After my father's treachery, his execution, Conn should have left me to starve. Instead, Conn brought me to his court. Made me his foster son. Every man around him argued against it, feared it, but Conn was more a father to me than the villain who sired me."

"That was generous," the abbess allowed.

"The chieftain was more than generous to me. He fed me, sheltered me, taught me to fight."

"But how can I trust you? Take *your* word? I have never looked upon your face until today."

"You can trust me because of the other gift Conn offered me. One far more precious than any of the others. A chance to redeem my honor."

"Your honor?"

"Conn gave me seven tasks. Seven quests to wipe away the stain of my father's treachery. I have performed six of them. Deeds I have bled to fulfill. Delivering Caitlin of the Lilies to his court is the final task Conn has assigned me. Can you ask for any better proof of the chieftain's intentions toward her than that?"

The abbess seemed to be wavering, torn. "But she is . . . is so young. She has seen none of the world. Knows nothing of life. She has never even looked upon any man save Father Columcille. You are a warrior. To send her off with you alone—"

Niall peered into the abbess's face, one that, for all its devotion and quiet goodness, was etched with lines and shadows left by the harsh edges of life. A stark reality both Niall and the older woman understood far too well.

"I will take the girl, whether you will it or no," Niall admitted, unflinchingly honest. "But this I swear to you by all you think holy. I will keep her safe." His eyes narrowed, fierce with resolve. "I would suffer the tortures of your Christian damned before I failed my chieftain."

Someone was coming.

Caitlin froze, listening to the measured crunch of footsteps, a wild panic jolting through her as she wondered if the approaching person brought deliverance or doom. The thousand prayers she had been uttering died in her throat, and she glanced at the round-eyed Sister Luca, who cowered in the farthest reaches of the hut, her terror echoing Caitlin's own.

Was the old nun's imagination running wild as Caitlin's was? Envisioning the warrior stalking toward the cloghan hut, his body too powerful, his muscles gleaming, rugged as the rock wall of a sea-dampened cliff? Even misted by her imagination, the intensity in his eyes seemed to burn away the very air until Caitlin could not breathe. Nay. Caitlin brought herself up sharply. Such dark fantasies were only making things worse.

She fought to hide the tremor that swept up her spine as a shadow fell across the doorway of the stone hut. But it was not the silhouette of a broad-shouldered man, but rather the rippling waves of a nun's garb.

"Sister Clare!" She gasped in relief, Sister Luca clumsily crossing herself as the young nun stepped forward.

"Is he gone?" Caitlin asked, more in desperation than real hope.

"No. He is with the abbess now. I am to take you to her."

A sudden urge to run struck Caitlin, and she all but

scooped up her skirts and fled. But Sister Luca reached out, patting her arm. "All must be well, or the abbess would never have summoned you. You must trust in God."

Despite all the convent's teachings, Caitlin was shamed to realize that she would far rather trust in Reverend Mother. She would die before she shamed the abbess by fleeing like a frightened child. Sister Luca was right. The warrior must be tamed to Reverend Mother's will, or she would never have risked summoning Caitlin.

Sister Clare and Sister Luca started forward, as if to mount guard on either side of her, the two nuns the most ridiculous and precious of sentries. Straightening her spine, Caitlin shook back her tumbled black locks. "I shall go alone. I would sooner be flayed alive than let that man think for a moment I fear him."

Sister Clare started to protest, Sister Luca let out a whimper, but Caitlin would not be swayed. She strode quickly out into the sunshine, winding through the banks of azaleas, wild rose, and yarrow that lined the garden path.

The building was dim after the glare of the sun, and Caitlin blinked, her eyes fighting to pierce the shadows as she made her way through the abbey by an instinct bred in countless childhood games. But even as she approached the familiar cell, her vision had not fully cleared. Silence emanated from the abbess's chamber— not the usual quiet serenity, rather a silence far too thick that pressed on Caitlin's chest. Swallowing hard, she forced herself to step inside.

He stood against the wall, hands clasped behind his back, face as unreadable as the ancient writings on the druid stone. Reverend Mother sat upon her chair, fingers folded in prayer. Shadow veiled them both.

"My child." A slender, capable hand reached out to Caitlin. She took it, comforting herself with the strength in it, the familiar warmth.

"Is—is everything settled?" Caitlin asked.

"Aye. It seems . . ." The abbess's voice broke a little. "You are to have an adventure."

Caitlin could not stop herself from backing away a step. "I do not understand."

"This man is the messenger of the chieftain who gave you into our care so many years ago, and he has come to reclaim you. Take you back to court."

Caitlin drew her innate regalness about her like a robe, praying it would conceal the terror thrumming inside her. "I thank you for bringing your chieftain's offer, Niall of the Seven Betrayals. And I am sorry for your trouble, trying to find me. But—"

"You! The wench from the woods!" Recognition flared in those fierce eyes, the great hulk of a man suddenly seeming uncomfortable as if someone had thrust a bunch of nettles down the back of his shirt. "*You* are Caitlin of the Lilies?"

"Aye." Caitlin shifted uneasily, remembering all too clearly the feel of those hard muscles, the strength in those large hands, and the rage in him when she had escaped his grasp. A man as fiercely proud as this one would not deal well with the humiliation of being bested by a woman. She swallowed hard. "Please thank your chieftain for his concern, but inform him that I choose not to return to court."

"The choice is not yours to make," the warrior ground out. Caitlin sputtered in outrage, but he merely plunged on. "Now, gather whatever belongings you can in the time it takes me to ready my horse, and leave the rest behind. We depart at once."

"At once?" The words slammed into Caitlin's stomach like a fist, and she glanced at the abbess, feeling betrayed.

Yet Reverend Mother looked as stricken as she felt. "Surely you cannot mean to leave so soon."

"I have no time to waste," Niall said with an impatient sweep of his scarred hand. "I must deliver her to the chieftain."

"The chieftain will have Caitlin for the rest of her life," the abbess objected. "Caitlin and I will have this night."

Niall started to protest, and Caitlin was terrified he would haul her out of the abbey no matter what Reverend Mother said.

"You claim your chieftain is a just man. Then he can afford to be a merciful one. This night will mean nothing to him, or to you. It will be the most precious one of my life and gentle the parting for this girl who has harmed no one."

"I have my duty to perform." His jaw was set at a stubborn angle.

"That is true. Yet if performing your duty were all you cared about, you would merely complete whatever task was given you, then forget it. Why would you care about your name? Cleansing yourself of the stain of past deeds not even your own?" the abbess asked.

A flush spread up the cords of his neck, his eyes gleaming like sword points as they flashed to Caitlin's face, then away again. "A man is nothing without a proud name."

"No. A man is nothing without his honor. But honor and duty are not the same. Honor reaches far deeper, tests you more harshly. Demands sacrifices you believe you cannot bear." A faraway look wreathed the abbess's face. "You have been willing to bleed, to risk death for honor. Now I appeal to that honor. In twenty years of loving this girl, watching her grow, have I not earned this one night of farewell, as you will earn the right to change your name when you return to the fortress?"

Was it possible that the warrior's features softened just a little? He quickly shuttered it away, masked it with frustration.

"I beg of you." Caitlin spoke the words, certain the warrior knew just how much it cost her.

He cast her a blistering scowl, then swore under his breath. "Meet me beside the gate at dawn, then. We will make up the time we have lost by traveling at a warrior's pace, and I vow if I hear one scrap of wailing—"

Small chance of that! Caitlin thought. She would sooner be roasted over a slow fire than admit any weakness to this man! "Nay. I give you my word," she said.

The brute gave her one final, piercing look, which sent shivers skittering down Caitlin's spine. Then he spun on his heel and stalked from the room.

She shivered, suddenly cold. She should have felt relief, but as she turned back toward Reverend Mother, the pain in her breast only stabbed deeper. Betrayal. That was what she felt—an unfathomable blow from the abbess's hands. "He is a brute!" Caitlin cried. "How can you even think of forcing me to go with him?" She scrambled wildly for some reason, any reason that would turn this madness into some kind of reality she could grasp. "Did he threaten the abbey? Did he—"

"Nay."

"Then why—" Caitlin's voice broke, and she hated herself for that weakness. "You promised you would not let him take me!"

"Unless I was certain you would not be in danger. Perhaps that promise was rash of me. I can be certain of little. I know nothing but what I see in this man's eyes, and in his heart."

"He *has* no heart!" Caitlin choked out.

"Or perhaps he keeps his heart hidden away because it is too battered. Caitlin, he told me the truth. That he would take you, whether I willed it or no. You have only to look into his eyes to be certain he would make good on that promise."

"I could run away . . . hide! There must be somewhere—"

"If only it were that simple. But from the first moment you came to us, we both knew that someday you would have to return to the place where you belong. Destiny would call. You would have to go. I would have to let you."

"But I do not wish to go. Not with *him*! You do not understand! There is something about him—something that frightens me."

The abbess gave a tender chuckle.

"You find that amusing?" Caitlin demanded, wounded.

"Of course not, sweeting. I was only remembering the last time *I* was so afraid. It was the night I found you upon the druid stone and first took you in my arms. What was I to do with a babe? My own mother had died when I was born, so I had never known a mother's touch. Even more daunting, I was a nun, bride of Christ. My faith was to be my life, cloistered here with my prayers and my God. I had surrendered all hope of a babe in my care. Given it up so blithely in my innocence without ever knowing how precious . . ." Her voice drifted off, such pain, such love, such gratitude in her features, Caitlin's own eyes stung with tears.

"You terrified me when first I held you. I wanted to lay you back upon the stone, turn and flee. Slam the gates, pretend I had never found you. But in the end, I could not turn you away. I was too afraid to know what a gift God had just delivered into my hands. The chance to know the miracle of your weight against my breast as I rocked you to sleep, the warmth of your breath, the magic in your smile. I could not have loved you more if you were my own child. Though perhaps I already loved you more. You were a treasure that was never supposed to be."

Caitlin felt tears burning her cheeks. "Then do not send me away. If you love me—"

"But that is why I have to, my precious child. Perhaps there is a treasure you are supposed to find. And it does not lie within the walls of the abbey."

"I do not want it! Not if it means leaving here. Losing you!"

"You can never lose me, child. That is the miracle loving you has taught me. We will both carry each other forever in our hearts."

The abbess opened her arms to Caitlin, and Caitlin rushed in, clinging, hard, as if to keep the wings of dawn at bay.

"Not a moment of this night will we waste in tears," the abbess urged. "We shall remember everything, everything precious. Remind each other so that we will never forget."

Caitlin nodded. She curled at Reverend Mother's feet as she had so many times as a child, leaning against the abbess's knee as they both spun out tales of girlish antics, mischief, and delight. Chasing calves over the hills, the abbess teaching Caitlin to climb trees, the yearly pilgrimage to the stone to find the precious lily.

The abbess stroked a carved-wood comb through the masses of Caitlin's hair, her voice low and musical, tinged with laughter and sorrow. They had spent countless nights thus. The soothing bedtime ritual had always made Caitlin feel so safe, as if they were the only two people in the world and nothing bad could ever touch them.

But the magic gates had swung open, the world had come inside, its messenger a surly warrior with shame stitched into his very name.

Just before dawn, the abbess helped her make a small bundle of the few belongings she had gathered in her years at the abbey. Clothing, clean if threadbare, carefully patched by the other nuns this long night. A shell from the sea Caitlin could only imagine, a gift from a novice who had clung to the tiny token from her faraway home, then given it to Caitlin after final vows. The sandalwood comb with shiny imprints worn by the abbess's fingers. Then she drew Caitlin to the small chest where the bit of robe had been secreted.

"There is something I have been saving for you, knowing this day would come."

The abbess pulled a length of cloth from the chest. Caitlin gaped as she shook free the folds of the most exquisite clothing Caitlin had ever seen.

The linen glowed, rich and soft, embroidered with delicate interlacing, patterns that some ancients had carved on the druid altar, the designs intertwined with more holy ones from the abbey.

"How—however did you find this?"

"I stitched it, late at night when I wanted to cling to you too tightly. It helped me to remember that you were only mine for a little while." Infinite sadness, pride, and resignation wreathed the abbess's face. "I vowed to deliver you into the hands of the fate that brought you to me in the guise of a princess."

Caitlin's fingers drifted over the cloth, her throat so tight it ached. "It is beautiful. I—I will treasure it forever."

Gently, Reverend Mother helped her shed the coarse-spun robe, then drifted the garment down over her head. Caitlin fingered the wide sleeves, the fine edging of embroidery there, treasuring every stitch the abbess's needle had made, knowing them for what they were, a symbol of the holy woman's love for her.

"There is something more. I found it among your wrappings the first night you came to the abbey." Reverend Mother went to the chest again, withdrew an object that sparkled and shone in the light. Gold shimmered rich and strange against her hand. "It is a bracelet," the abbess said softly. "The most exquisite I have ever seen."

Caitlin touched the piece of jewelry with one finger, half afraid it would vanish. "It is so beautiful."

"Whoever sent this token with you must have loved you very much." The abbess slipped the bracelet onto Caitlin's wrist. "I know it seems you will be far away from us, my sweeting, and yet, when our special time comes at night and you look out, see the stars, know that I am watching them and thinking of you."

Caitlin's chest ached, her eyes burned. Fear clutched at her with cold fingers, dread of a world she could only imagine. "I will have courage," she promised. "I will make you proud of me, whatever fate may bring."

"I will always be proud to call you daughter." The abbess stroked her cheek. "I shall miss you, my little one."

When they could delay no longer, Caitlin and the abbess walked out into a dimly lit courtyard, the small space filled with the other nuns waiting to say farewell.

"Do not forget your prayers!" someone chided.

"God go with you, child!"

The chorus of voices, each suddenly so precious, echoed about her. Tears blinded Caitlin as she strode through the mass of sisters, giving embraces, trying to soothe them, despite the hard knot of terror in her own chest.

As she and Reverend Mother approached the gate, Caitlin could not keep from hanging back, delaying the inevitable. From her vantage point behind the abbess's flowing robes, Caitlin stared, disbelieving. The rickety portal had been shored up, made strong again. Had the sisters been so alarmed by Niall's siege of the abbey that they had labored over the gate through the night?

But it was Niall whose dark hair was dusted with curls of wood shavings, a bloody scrape healing on his forearm.

"We have you to thank for this?" the abbess asked him.

Niall shrugged, looking uncomfortable. "I could not sleep. I had to do something or run mad."

The abbess smiled. "God bless you, my son."

"I am no woman's son," he snarled, suddenly savage. Then he held out a massive hand to Caitlin. She wanted to cower away, but she remembered her promise to the abbess, to herself. Summoning up her courage, she let the brute heft her up onto his horse. He swung up behind her, his body hard and hot and overwhelming.

"Caitlin!" the abbess cried, rushing forward, clinging a moment to her hand. "Always remember, the world is as full of beauty as it is of tears. Who knows what wonders will come of this journey? Open your arms to them, my child. Embrace them as you have everything else in your life—with joy in your heart and as much delight as you can hold!"

A bitter sound of scorn came from Niall, and he spurred the beast through the gate, cursing as Caitlin strained to see behind them. Her gaze clung to the abbey until she could no longer see the abbess's face, until the stone blurred, then vanished behind the veil of trees.

"No wailing. You gave your word." Was there a wariness to the warrior's voice?

What would it matter if she cried her heart out? Caitlin thought. It would change nothing. She would still be torn away from everything she knew, everyone she loved, losing them forever.

It seemed she had already learned her first lesson in this wide, strange new world. Even if your heart was breaking, there was no use in crying. Not when there was no one who loved you nearby to dry the tears.

Chapter
3

~~~~~~~~~~~~~

EVEN THE SKY seemed to mock Caitlin, the sun arcing across the heavens like a golden ball tossed by an angel's hand. Blindingly bright, the buttery rays set velvet-green hills aglow and gilded the petals of flowers until they shimmered. Wing feathers flashed blue and red, black and silver, as birds soared against a perfect sky.

She wanted to close her eyes against the beauty of it, clutch her grief tight to her breast. She wanted to draw the cold gray veil of resentment about her, concentrate on loathing this surly stranger who had dragged her away from everyone she loved, everything she knew.

But as Niall guided the stallion deeper into the world she had never seen, Caitlin's very nature turned traitor. Eyes that should be straining to see behind her, memorizing all that she was leaving behind, were drawn forward to red deer leaping in graceful arcs and clusters of blossoms clinging precariously to tiny cracks in the rocks that strewed the ground.

In the lush countryside, tiny landholdings were tucked about rare and precious as gems. Thatch roofs gleamed in the distance, figures the size of a little girl's poppet tending cattle that seemed small enough for Caitlin to hold in the palm of her hand.

All her life, the abbess had spun stories for her about the vast world beyond the abbey's gray stone walls, but never had Caitlin imagined how it would feel—wind in her face, every glen, every hill, every blossom unexpected, new. Colors so vivid they made her chest ache, a sweep of limitless possibilities it would take a lifetime to discover. Freedom . . .

Guilt tugged at her, made her struggle to resist the pull of her own curiosity. How could she be so unfeeling? Was her love so shallow? Reverend Mother would still be grieving, would she not? Locked away with her sorrow in the tiny cell that was her world. And yet, what had the abbess said just as Niall was about to spur away from the abbey? *Open your arms to the world . . . to joy. That has always been your greatest strength.*

That was what Reverend Mother had placed her faith in. Caitlin's resilience. A resilience far more important than any lingering resentment she felt toward the man whose arms encircled her now, holding her upon the horse's back.

She closed her eyes, intrigued by a sound that seemed to roll toward her from the distance, a strange, haunting rhythm she had never heard before. God's voice, low? Echoing the abbess's words?

Opening her eyes, she strained to see in the direction of the sound, realizing that it had not been her imagination. The haunting music swelled, more insistent. In the throes of her temper hours earlier, she had vowed she would swallow her own tongue before she would speak another word to the oaf who was her guardian, but suddenly she was stunned to hear her own voice raised against the wind.

"What is that?"

"What?" He started in the saddle, as if the loaf of

bread the sisters had packed in a sack for him had suddenly gained the power of speech.

"That sound—like thunder, but not . . ."

" 'Tis the sea. It lies over that rise."

"The sea," she echoed, remembering how many times her fingers had traced the curve of a shell, as if to unravel the sea's mysteries. "I never guessed it could sing."

Dark brows lowered over piercing green eyes. "If there was a storm coming, I would wager you would not like its song."

There was enough scorn in the words to prick at her temper, as if he were questioning her courage. Her chin jutted up, stubborn. "I love storms."

He gave a grunt of disbelief.

"When I was a child, I would run out into the rain, watch the sky split, and listen to the heavens roar. It was glorious."

"You were mad."

Caitlin could not stop the tiniest smile from curving one corner of her mouth. "Nay, I was full of wondering, and I wanted to see it all. Be part of it somehow."

"You must have led the abbess a merry chase. What penance did she assign you for such a grievous sin? Hours of prayer until your knees were raw?"

The memory stirred a sweet, soft pain in her heart. "I think her only regret was that she could not come out and join me." The loss of *that* gift, someone to share with—joy and sadness, fear and discovery—suddenly seemed vast indeed. Loneliness tightened Caitlin's throat.

Was it possible the great brute of a man sensed the subtle shift within her? Or was he oblivious to the emotions warring in her breast? "The sky is clear this day, Caitlin of the Lilies. I fear I cannot summon you a storm."

She clung to those words, trying to shake free of the

melancholy, tender places in her heart too private to allow anyone, especially this enigmatic stranger, to probe. She groped for something to distract them both.

"Tell me, is your chieftain's fortress near the sea?"

"The fortress is inland. He is far too canny to build close enough to the waters for the raiders to sail in and take all he owns. If an enemy has to cross the land, there is time to raise the alarm, gather an army for defense."

Caitlin caught her lip against a wave of disappointment. "Then I suppose I will never see it. The sea. Can you tell me what it is like?"

He gave a low growl of impatience. "It is wet."

Caitlin grimaced. She had been a fool to ask him. He was nothing like the abbess, who brushed color into her stories, poetry in the pictures she painted in someone else's head. Better just to imagine the sea herself.

Falling silent, she delved into the tales she had heard—Jonah in the belly of the whale but, more delicious still, the lore of the fierce Celtic sea god, Manannan mac Lir, riding Enbharr, his wave-maned horse, across his mighty domain.

She was all but lost in her imaginings when suddenly the horse broke through a copse of trees. A cry tore from her throat as the earth fell away before its great hooves. Niall reined the beast to a halt just before they all three plunged over what seemed the edge of a cliff.

Caitlin gasped, turning toward him to clutch at his arms. "Are you crazed?" she snapped at Niall. "There is no path here!"

"Only a fool would follow one into the sea."

"The—the sea?" She peered up into his face, still saw impatience, the hardness of a warrior, his expression inscrutable. Then she turned her eyes out to a sight that stole her breath away. Never had she seen such impossible beauty, even in her own imagination.

Giant black stones descended from the lip of green turf in a steep giant's stairway twice as high as the abbey walls. At the curving base of rock, waves danced, sunshine casting glittering diamonds across a surface the mystical blue of mermaids' hair. Foam swirled, as if bits of clouds had been snagged by the hands of sea sprites to be woven in their tresses. It stretched out forever, blue and green and white and wonderful.

A tiny sound tore from Caitlin's throat.

"The horse has a stone caught in its hoof." Niall sounded almost defensive. "You might as well wander about while I dig it out. It will keep you from being underfoot."

He was still speaking, but she was too excited to hear. She slid down the horse's sweaty side, stumbling for an instant, her limbs exhausted from riding, but the aches fled as if banished by some magic elixir brewed of sea spray and sunshine.

She heard Niall's growled warnings, but nothing could have stopped her. She hastened to the edge, where the layer of turf gave way to a tangle of giant stones that formed a pathway to water so beautiful she had to touch it.

She caught the folds of her leine high above her knees and scrabbled down the stones, heedless of the scraping of rock against her tender skin. The music was calling her, the crash of waves as they impaled themselves on the stones, shattering into crystal drops of impossible loveliness before they disappeared.

She wanted to reach the lowest rock, to let the sea spray break over her. Wanted to *feel* the power of the sea, as she had the storm so long ago.

She climbed downward, breathed deep of salt air, marveled at the graceful flight of gulls as they dove toward the water. Green lace shirred the stones here and there, seaweed, picked at by tiny birds she had never seen.

She laughed aloud as the first sprinkling of sea spray dampened her cheeks, remembering tales of selkies, seals that left the water on magical nights, taking human form to find mortal lovers. It had sounded so wonderful, so romantic, when she was a child, yet now she wondered how any creature, enchanted or human, could leave a realm as beautiful as the one that danced just beyond her reach.

It all seemed so perfect, so enchanting, as she neared the lowest stone that she did not expect its surface suddenly to turn treacherous. Her foot skidded out from under her, the waves grabbing at the hem of her leine with stunningly strong fingers. She felt herself tumbling, sliding, her hands scrabbling for purchase on the rocks, failing to find it.

Plummeting into the cold water, she felt an instant of astonishing weightlessness, as if she were flying in a liquid sky. Her leine billowed out in linen wings, but suddenly the sea's mysterious beauty betrayed her.

Stones battered at her kicking legs, waves slamming against her, filling her nose, her mouth. The music of the sea turned dark, deafening, the water closing her ears to anything but the roar that filled her head.

But just as the current was about to suck her under for the last time, a violent rush of bubbles tumbled about her, something large swooping toward her as she struggled against the choking waves. A hard hand closed in the billows of her hair, strong fingers clutching at her waist, flinging her upward. Her ribs cracked hard against the rock, driving out what little breath she had left, but this time, when she breathed in, her lungs filled with blessed air that burned deep.

Niall hauled himself onto the flat surface, where

they both lay, gasping. She gazed at him through a wild tangle of wet hair, his own face gleaming with sea water, mighty, all-powerful, like Manannan mac Lir come to life. A rock had gashed the muscles of his leg, a trickle of blood vivid red against the hair-dusted skin.

"Y-you hurt yourself," she choked out.

"You all but got yourself killed!" he accused, fighting to catch his own breath. "What the devil were you doing?"

She curled on the rock, trembling now with cold beneath the sodden linen of her gown, feeling like a fool as she tried to explain the forces that had driven her toward the waves. She settled for the truth. "I never imagined anything so—so powerful, so vast. I wanted to touch it."

"Touch it?" he echoed, incredulous.

"The sea."

"Damned foolish excuse. Did you stop to consider what the chieftain's reaction would be if I presented it to him? Caitlin of the Lilies drowned trying to touch the sea! Conn would have taken my head, and I would have deserved to lose it!"

It had not occurred to her what might happen to Niall if any harm had befallen her. She had been carried away by the beauty, the power, the majesty of it all. "I did not think it would be dangerous."

"Did you not hear my warnings?" he demanded. "I nigh split the stones bellowing at you!"

Despite the chill, her cheeks burned. "I . . . rarely listen when I . . . charge out into the storm."

He looked at her sharply. "If you are to live at a chieftain's fortress, you had best learn to be more cautious. I will not be there to pull you out of whatever mischief you plunge into, and the currents can be far more dangerous than any the sea can muster."

She should have been chastened, perhaps even a little daunted at the warning. At the very least, she should have felt some guilt for the position she had nearly put him in—drowning would have been most uncivil under the circumstances. After all, Niall had been kind after a fashion. But Caitlin could not help herself, now that the danger was past. Her spirit soared, her whole body atingle with the delight of it.

She *had* touched the water, felt the power of it all around her. It had been foolhardy and terrifying, and for a moment, just a moment, it had been glorious.

Niall lifted her back onto the horse, more surly than ever. Caitlin sucked in a deep breath. "I—I want to say one thing, then I will not badger you any longer."

"You want food now? You can eat while astride the horse."

"No. I wanted to . . . ask something."

He crossed his arms over his broad chest, waiting. And for a moment, he seemed like the mate of druid magic her imagination had woven at the ancient altar.

"I just do not understand why . . ." A droplet ran from his temple down along that iron-honed jaw, stealing away all thought of what she had intended to say.

"Why?"

She glanced back into his eyes, struggled to drive away any thoughts of how that droplet was now trickling a path down the powerful cords of his neck. "Why you took me to the sea."

He sucked in a sharp breath, as if she had jammed her elbow into his midsection. The hard mask fell over his features. "The horse was growing lame. I had to—"

"There was no stone in his hoof. It sorrows me to mention it, but beneath that gruff exterior, I fear you are most kind."

"Kind? Devil if I am!" He bristled as if she had dealt

him an insult black enough to draw blood over. "I do my duty. Follow the chieftain's command."

"You need not worry." Caitlin smiled. "Your secret is safe with me."

The planes of that unspeakably handsome face reddened, his voice gruff as he scrambled to change the subject. "We will not stop again until dark. If you want food, tell me now. The nuns gave us bread and cheese."

She leaned back, turning her face to the sea winds one last time. She breathed in the fragrance of salt and distant lands she would never see, horses spun out of waves, their foaming manes feeding her imagination. "I am not hungry," she said with a sated sigh. "The sea filled me in a way mere bread never could."

With a grunt, Niall reined the horse away from the shore, still uncertain why he had come there in the first place, let her frolic about the waves. Had he been . . . kind? Or simply mad? Had he wanted this girl to have one thing beautiful before she was whirled into Conn's fortress? For once she arrived there, she would be burdened by her father's greatness as certainly as Niall was burdened by his father's treachery.

Caitlin of the Lilies—the girl-child foretold to bring disaster to the chieftain—saved from death only by Conn's great mercy, his promise to her parents that he would spare her life, find some way to outwit the curse. Was she not already a legend in Glenfluirse? Daughter of the enchanted spear caster, the most loved and honored warrior Glenfluirse had ever known?

Riding to the abbey, Niall had thought little of the woman who was to be in his charge, so consumed by his own irritation was he. Yet now he could feel something like pity for the girl. She had been transformed from a legend, a shadow figure fashioned of whispered words, into someone alive, real to him. Even so, he had never suspected how the encounter with the sea would change her.

He glanced down at Caitlin, feeling as if he had rescued no mere woman from the waves. No convent-raised girl, bred to wear coarse robes, spend her life praying in her tiny stone cage.

Had her plunge into the water turned her shape shifter? Remaking her into a creature more strange than any from otherworld lands beneath the sea?

She radiated delight, eagerness, anticipation, as if they were jeweled wings that lifted her above the drab world below to a star-spun place Niall of the Seven Betrayals would never know.

Joy. Had he ever felt it? Not in the way she did. Nor did he want to, he vowed, as long-forgotten memories of childish laughter and absolute confidence flickered in his mind.

It was dangerous to delight too much, to trust too much in anything beautiful or good. Fate had a nasty habit of snatching it away.

He remembered the abbey, the cluster of nuns, all praying fervently as he carried Caitlin away. Perhaps the prayers would protect her in the days to come. But their holy appeals seemed almost as meager a weapon as a smile sweet as sunstruck berries, and eyes that dared to shine in a world dark as sin.

He was tempted to warn Caitlin, to say something about the harsh edges of a world she was unprepared for, a world far beyond the abbey gates. But he only clenched his teeth and rode on. What the blazes ailed him? He was a warrior, not some tender-hearted bard. He had seen more terrible things than an innocent like Caitlin of the Lilies could ever imagine, things far more vile than one young woman's disillusionment.

She was not his responsibility. The instant he turned

her over to Conn, he would be quit of her forever. As for the world that awaited this Caitlin of the Lilies, she would discover its flaws soon enough.

Niall would just make certain he was not there to see it.

Flames danced, burning red and orange and blue against the night, the leaves on the towering trees whispering like unquiet spirits above Caitlin's head.

Every muscle in her body ached, her face still stinging from the scrubbing she had given it, washing away the grit from the journey with handfuls of cold water from a stream nearby. She should have been exhausted after the mad pace Niall had set. Besides, hungry though she was, Caitlin was eager to drift away into dreams filled with sea gods and horses made of waves.

But the moment Niall tossed her the coarse homespun bag containing food the sisters had sent with them from the abbey, all hope of sleep vanished. She drew out the familiar loaf, and even the glorious memory of the sea could not stave off a wave of melancholy.

Caitlin traced her finger in the slight hollows baked into the bread in the shape of the cross, the symbol that had marked every loaf she had ever eaten. Her earliest memories were of standing on a stool in the kitchen, Reverend Mother stealing away from her other duties to help Caitlin's tiny fingers make the holy shape that reminded them all where the bread and all good things had come from.

It would be the last time she would taste this bread, the flavor of home. She wished she could save it, yet the man who now sat across the fire from her was already eyeing it like a ravenous wolf.

Swallowing hard, she broke the loaf in two, then surrendered half of it to Niall. He devoured most of his portion as if this were to be his last meal, then paused long enough to glance at the bread still cradled in the lap of her leine.

"You had better eat." He wiped a crumb away from his chin. "We will have a hard day of riding tomorrow."

"You need not fear. I will not fall from the horse, I promise. I know you are in great haste to reach—" She paused, a strained laugh bubbling up. "It is so strange. I cannot even remember your chieftain's name, and yet my whole future lies in his hands."

"Conn. Conn the Ever Truthful. And the fate of every man or woman within his domain lies in his hands."

"That may be so, but I doubt he summons all his subjects to come before him. No messengers storming up on great horses demanding to carry off the daughters of every household in his lands. Perhaps this would be easier if I had some idea why."

"Why?"

Caitlin crumbled an edge of the crust. "Why *me*. Why *now*. I have been at the abbey forever. Why should I suddenly earn his notice?"

Niall took a long swallow of water from the horn cup he'd filled at the stream. "Conn's reasons are simple enough, I would imagine. You are of an age ripe to be wed. Doubtless he has picked a husband for you."

Her eyes widened. Merciful heaven, why had she not thought of that in the time since they had left St. Mary's? In the recesses of her mind, she had always expected to be married, had she not? And yet never had she imagined it in quite this way. She had thought she would have a choice, would fall in love. Even in the abbey, she had heard tales of young women shoved into wedlock against their will. What might it be like to be forever bound to and bedded by a complete stranger?

"But I . . . I cannot marry now." She stammered a protest. "I do not know anyone to . . ." She stopped, stared at him, her heart slamming against her ribs. "You do not think that you . . . and I—that the reason Conn sent you to bring me from St. Mary's was that you are to be my husband?"

Niall choked on the bread, came up sputtering. "Do not be absurd! The chieftain knows I have vowed never to wed." Yet, despite his brave words, he looked as unnerved as she felt.

He grappled with a small leather pouch tied to his waist, something that sounded like vellum crackling inside it beneath his grasp. "There is one way to know," he muttered. Suddenly, he caught sight of her questioning gaze. Reluctantly, he released whatever the pouch held.

"What is in there?" she asked.

"It is none of your concern," he snapped. "Only be as certain of this as you are that the sun will rise at dawning: No woman will ever call me husband. No woman will ever wield power over me."

Why did his vow suddenly make her sad? That this man would never have anyone to hold him, touch him, meet him on his return from battle, her eyes shining a welcome. He would have no woman to feed the hidden, hungry, tender places in his soul, no children clamoring for tales of his bravery on the field. Simple, homely offices Caitlin had dreamed of performing as a lone girl.

But Niall would only scoff if ever he guessed that she pitied him. Even in the glow of the firelight, Caitlin could see his face darken, as if he knew how ridiculously dismayed he had appeared. His chagrin was so great, it tempted her to laugh.

"Since you are so certain Conn would not force you

to marry against your will, it is possible that Conn does not intend to see me wed, either."

"And why is that so? There is an army of other men in Glenfluirse."

"Few who would accept a woman who comes to marriage with empty hands." She shrugged. "I am not so simple that I do not know the ways of the world. A wife has a duty to bring something to marriage—wealth, the honor of her family, allies to help guard her husband's borders. I can offer none of these things." She took some small comfort in the thought.

Niall dashed it as he shrugged. "Any man in the kingdom except me would rejoice to have you as wife."

"I cannot imagine why."

"You bring a bride price far more precious than land or riches to the man who weds you. His sons will carry the blood of the finest spear caster ever to go into battle."

All thought of a dreaded marriage vanished. She caught her breath. "You know of my father? My family?"

Niall picked at the bread he held, suddenly engrossed, as if the crumbs held all the answers in the world. "There is time enough for you to learn of such things when you reach the fortress."

"You cannot mean that!" Unable to contain herself, she cast her bread onto the crumpled cloth sack, then leapt to her feet, her hands trembling. "I have waited my whole life to know—know why my parents left me alone, why I had no mother, no father like other girls."

"It is not my place to tell you anything. I was not instructed to—"

"Were you instructed *not* to?" she demanded. "Is there something to hide?"

"Nay, but—damn it, woman, you are snarling everything up again."

"*I* am snarling things up? My whole life has been a tangle! You cannot imagine what it is like, always wondering, half fearing the answers, needing them anyway. But now . . . they . . . *my family* . . . perhaps they are at the fortress. I will meet them at last." She hugged herself tight, fear and delight warring inside her.

She saw Niall's eyes narrow, an odd expression crossing his features. He hesitated. "You will not find your parents at the fortress, Caitlin."

"They are someplace else, then? It does not matter. I can still find them."

He looked away. Caitlin stilled, bereft. Her voice trembled as she whispered. "They are . . ."

"Dead." He said the word so she would not have to, a gentle mercy in this man so battle-hardened.

She turned her face away from Niall to hide the glitter of tears. Silence fell. A log broke apart, raining embers. "Strange. Reverend Mother gave this to me before we left Saint Mary's." She touched the bracelet. "It must have belonged to my mother. All my life, I dreamed of my parents, wove images of them out of all my wishes. Made them beautiful and handsome, brave and noble, a mother and father who loved me so desperately—who would hold me, touch me, tell me why they abandoned me. For a moment, they were real. They were mine. And now, in an instant, they are gone forever. I never . . . never even had the chance to know them. Now I never will."

"You are wrong." She was stunned to feel the touch of his hand against her arm. "They will live in bard song for all eternity."

She looked down at him, saw the reluctance in him, yet he continued. "You are daughter of the mighty Fintan MacShane, a warrior so fine it is said he possessed fairy magic."

She brushed his hand away. "I do not want tales of

fairies and magic any longer. I spun enough of my own. I wanted someone to touch, to hold."

"It is no fantasy, what I tell you of your father. It is true."

Something in his voice made her look at Niall. "You knew him?"

"I think no one but his wife, Grainne, really knew him. He was always separated from the other warriors by his gift."

"He was a spear caster? That is what you said. Why should that set him apart?"

"Never once, in all his life, did he miss what he aimed for. An amazing enough feat in itself, but that was not the miracle of it. Fintan was blind."

"Blind? That—that is impossible! How could he even know where he pointed his weapon?"

"The bard claims that what other men saw with their eyes, Fintan saw with his heart. It is said Fintan had a rival for Grainne's love, and when she chose your father, the other man was so maddened with jealousy he blinded Fintan while he slept so he would never again see her face. Knowing what the loss would cost the proud warrior she loved, Grainne went to the fairies and offered to surrender her own sight if they would restore Fintan's to him. Her tears so moved the fairies, they took pity on the lovers and cast an enchantment upon Fintan."

"Do not." Caitlin squeezed the words through a tight throat. "Do not spin stories trying to make me feel better."

"You do not believe me? I cannot blame you. I would scarce have believed it myself, except that one of his spear casts kept an enemy from cleaving my skull in two with a battle axe. I saw the miracle of Fintan's gift with my own eyes."

"And my mother? Did you know her?"

He looked uncomfortable and more than a little defiant. "She was like you—dark-haired, blue eyes. Yet even she was not so . . ." His gaze traced Caitlin's features. He stopped. "She might have been kind to me if I allowed her. But all I could see in her beauty was the poison that killed my father."

Caitlin's lips trembled, her eyes burned. He glared at her for an instant in alarm.

"You want to know about your parents?" he asked, gruff. "I can tell you this. I once heard your father say that he had been struck blind because she was . . . all the light he would ever need."

His eyes peered into hers, sparking with something almost like hope, as if he expected something from her. Approval for the tale he had spun? Gratitude for the story he had told? Something she could not give him.

Her throat ached, and this time she did not even try to hide the tears.

"Perhaps that was why they did not need me," Caitlin said in a small voice.

She curled her arms tight about her, imagining such a great love, a love that had never been shared with her. The bracelet cut into her wrist as she wrestled with betrayal, a child's endless wondering about what terrible flaw she had that enabled them to abandon her, forget her. And now they were dead. She would never be able to ask them, make things right.

Niall rose, and she was surprised to feel the woolen folds of his cloak swirl about her shoulders. It was warm from his body, smelling of wind and earth, horse, and a faint scent that was all Niall's own.

She did not protest. She only lay down on the ground, curling herself beneath the folds of wool to hold back the pain.

Chapter

4

SHE WAS FINALLY ASLEEP. The soft shuddering of her breath as she fought to hide her tears had quieted. The fingers that had clenched on the edge of his cloak unfurled. The knowledge that the woman was resting at last should have afforded Niall some relief. But it seemed his own conscience would not.

What had Conn been thinking, sending Niall on this quest? If the chieftain had searched for a hundred years, he could not have found a task for which Niall of the Seven Betrayals was less suited.

Conn should have sent an entourage to fetch Caitlin from the abbey, a retinue manned by courtly guards skilled in easing the fears of a sheltered young woman. Perhaps Declan. Niall closed his eyes, picturing the burly flame-haired warrior who was the closest thing Niall had ever had to a friend.

Declan, the vicious scar on his face scarce visible once he uttered his hearty laugh, his merry eyes sparkling, tempting anyone nearby to see life as a grand adventure. Declan would have known exactly what to say to the woman. He would not have spilled out the news that her family was dead. He would not have let her weep silent tears alone. He would have found a way to comfort her.

Yet even if Conn *had* sent Declan, Caitlin needed a woman nearby, some female to wait upon her, soothe her during the first traumatic hours after she was torn from the only home she had ever known. Prepare her as only another woman could for her entry into court.

Even the most dull-witted man in Ireland should have guessed what a woman like Caitlin would need on this journey, and Conn, with his near-legendary wisdom, should certainly have known it would be disaster with no one except Niall to see to the girl.

Niall's gaze was unwillingly drawn yet again to Caitlin's profile, pale and perfect against the dark backdrop of cloak. One hand was tucked beneath her cheek like a child's, black ringlets and fingers of shadow tracing her lily-fair skin in patterns like the mystic writings on stone. Silky lashes curled upon the crest of her cheek, her lips slightly parted.

She might have been a fairy maid asleep in her woodland bower were it not for the dried tears tracing a path down her cheek and the way she curled her lithe body, tight, as if to guard against another painful blow.

A blow like the one he had dealt her when he had told her that her parents were dead. Niall winced. Why the devil had he opened his accursed mouth in the first place? He was supposed to guard her, not *talk* to her, by the blood of Cuchulain!

But no, he had not kept quiet. He had not let her babble on about mothers and fathers she had never seen until she tired of the subject.

He had charged into catastrophe carelessly as a moonstruck lad into an enemy's ambushing sword, and he had thrashed about until Caitlin had emerged, bloodied, not in the flesh but in a deeper place, where emotions dwelled.

He had hurt her, and yet . . . how could he have let

her ride into Conn's fortress, dreams glittering in her face for everyone to see? How could he have let her learn the truth with countless strangers looking on? The mean-spirited among them eager to see the daughter of mighty Fintan fall? It would have given any enemies she might make a terrible weapon to use against her in the days to come. And with her beauty, her grace, her lineage, exalted as the stars, there would be plenty of people at Glenfluirse ready to hate her.

Not that they would ever be honest enough to let her see—no, they would use their wit to flay her so subtly, she would not even know they had struck until she glanced down to see she was bleeding.

Why did that image even now have the power to stir something hot and poisonous in his own veins, a kind of anger he had never allowed himself to feel? He shoved it back. He had no time for such emotions. They stole a man's concentration, could distract him from his goal. And there was no way Niall could afford that.

He stared into the flames, hard, remembering every insult, every lash of scorn that had been heaped upon him. Even with Conn's kindnesses, the gaping, aching hole within Niall had remained year after year, filled with the shame and horror of his father's betrayals.

In Niall's place, most men would have ridden far away from Ireland, taken a new name to escape the shadow that clung like poison about their lineage.

Niall had stood his ground. Fought. Dedicated his life to winning back honor. Until he did, the world could hold nothing else for him. No matter how remarkable, how vulnerable, or how brave Caitlin of the Lilies was, he could not be her champion. He had not even won his own battle.

His only choice was to trust in Conn. Conn, whose

army had triumphed time and again because Fintan led the men into battle, and they believed the sea god himself could not defeat them. Conn, who had ruled wisely, justly, for thirty-five years. Conn, who had pressed two missives into Niall's hands, eyes burning, intense, as he gave out his orders.

I trust you when I would trust no other, the chieftain had said, grasping Niall by the arm. *Since your father died by my hand, I have claimed you as my son. Now you shall prove your loyalty to me. Tell me, Niall—are your enemies right or wrong? Did I trust you in vain?* And as the chieftain had pressed the sealed sheets of vellum into Niall's hand, Niall had vowed with his last drop of blood not to fail Conn. One message to read once he was outside the fortress, outlining this mission, where to find the girl. The second . . .

Niall silently cursed himself. Conn had charged him to open the second this night, as soon as Caitlin lay asleep. Heat flooded Niall's cheeks, shame that he had been so distracted by tear-bright eyes and a pretty face that he had forgotten his duty to Conn for even a moment. Thank the gods no one else would ever know.

He unfastened the leather bag that hung at his waist and carefully tugged the roll of vellum from within. The seal upon it glistened in the firelight like a fresh wound.

Niall glanced at Caitlin, remembering her innocent inquiries earlier—wondering if Conn intended Niall to be her husband. Absurd, such a thought. And yet, now that Niall considered it, the idea made alarming sense. Conn, renowned for his subtlety and his wit, knowing Niall would pay no attention to a woman unless forced to. Conn, using this last quest to chain Niall to this girl for three long days, perhaps hoping to tie the girl to his family through his foster son and finest warrior. It was a marriage that would show all at Glenfluirse the enchanted Fintan's blood still flowed among them, bringing to the kingdom his special brand of magic. For just an instant, an ember sparked in his chest—temptation?

Niall clutched the missive so tight he crushed it, astonished to find he was fearful of what it might hold. He had learned as a boy that words could be a far more devastating weapon than any sword. Had learned to mistrust them. Trust in actions instead.

Nay. He brought himself up sharply. Conn would not fail him. Conn was the one person in all the world who looked upon him with affection. Conn knew of Niall's vow. Understood his resolve better than any other man. The chieftain would not play such a grim trick on Niall. And yet what besides a proposal of marriage could be contained in Conn's carefully penned lines?

Mustering his courage, Niall cracked the seal with his thumbnail, then unrolled the vellum and held it nearer the glow of the fire. His heart slammed to his stomach, disbelief and revulsion boiling up inside him as he scanned the chieftain's words:

> *The destruction of my kingdom is written in the destiny of this woman, a doom foretold by the most powerful druid priest ever to breathe. She possesses dark power so great even her parents feared it and sent her to be locked away. The death of countless warriors, the ravages of war—such are the curses Caitlin of the Lilies will bring upon all who dwell in Glenfluirse unless you have the courage to fulfill this, the final quest I ask of you, my son. Warrior that you are, you have learned the grim necessity of death. Kill this girl as she sleeps, so that others might live. No one will know what you have done except your grateful chieftain.*

Kill her? Bile rose in Niall's throat. Nay! Conn could not mean for him to cut her down in cold blood! Everyone in Glenfluirse knew that Conn had vowed to Fintan that he would keep Caitlin safe! Grant Caitlin life as long as the spear caster entrusted his daughter to Conn's care. And Fintan had done so, followed his part of the bargain though it must have torn at his heart and at the heart of the wife he loved!

You are the only warrior I can trust . . . The chieftain's words echoed in Niall's memory, and he could almost see the dark trouble that had contorted the chieftain's features in the moments before he sent Niall on this mission. What visions of future horror would drive a just man like Conn to give such a grim decree? Break a vow of honor?

The night was suddenly deafeningly still, only the hollow hammering of Niall's heartbeat and that of the oblivious girl seeming to fill the star-scattered sky.

Death. Niall had dealt it in the way of a soldier, in battle, matching strength against strength, skill against skill, courage against courage. But to do this thing Conn asked of him—*murder*.

Sweat broke out upon Niall's brow, and he could almost hear the low purr of the chieftain's voice as he had drilled Niall in logic, in the ways of a warrior, during long winter nights at his hearth.

Who is wiser, braver, my boy? The man who marches to his death in a hopeless cause? Or the man who finds a way to stop the carnage before it begins?

Had Conn been thinking of this bitter choice even then? Preparing Niall somehow, or himself, for its bleak necessity? What was the right path to take? Break a word of honor, or keep it and risk raining destruction down on all of Glenfluirse? For a fortress without a strong chieftain would soon be annihilated. Niall shuddered.

This was the quest, the ultimate test of Niall's loyalty. This is why Conn had sent him. To stop a river of blood before it began to flow. To save an entire kingdom from destruction foretold by the druid.

In truth, Conn asked him to *save* countless lives by sacrificing just one. But did Niall have the stomach? The resolve? The faith in his chieftain to do this terrible thing?

He remembered Caitlin scrambling down the stones to the sea, wind in her hair, joy turning her incandescent, luminous, dancing amidst the salt spray. Alive—more alive than anyone Niall had ever known. He remembered the abbess, clinging to his promise—*I will keep her safe.* The vow to Fintan was not Niall's to break, but the vow to the abbess was his alone.

You are pledged first to Conn, Niall upbraided himself. *That vow must be honored above all. A warrior sworn to fulfill his chieftain's every command. Even this one, grim as it may be. The druid prediction has left Conn and me little other choice.*

Niall drew on every fragment of strength he had gained on countless battlefields, closed tighter and tighter into himself, to try to find the place where his battle fury lived—the man who was a sword arm for his chieftain, his soul no longer his own.

Slowly, Niall drew his sword, hating the weight of it in his hand for the first time, feeling as if the fingers that clenched about its hilt were not his own. Stealthily, he crossed to where Caitlin lay sleeping, the dark waves of her hair swept back, revealing the vulnerable column of her neck, white, so white in the light of the moon.

She will feel nothing—Niall attempted to take small comfort in it. *It will be over in one sweep of this sword.*

He raised the blade high, was stunned to feel his

hands shake as he took aim, readied himself to deal the blow.

In that instant, some wild thing thrashed somewhere off in the brush. Lashes fluttered on white cheeks, eyes opening, still webbed by dreams. Dreams that shifted to nightmare the instant Caitlin saw the blade gleaming hellish orange above her.

"Wh-what are you doing?"

Strike! the warrior inside Niall bellowed. *Strike, you fool, make an end to this!* "Forgive me," he ground out. "Conn's orders." He brought the sword down, stunned himself by closing his eyes at the last moment, unable to see the damage he would inflict. A scream breached Caitlin's lips. But there was no give of soft flesh, no sickening crack of bone. The blade drove hard into the turf.

Niall opened his eyes, saw her scrambling away, her eyes wild, as if he were a monster. And he was, God curse him. He was.

He lunged for her, nearly capturing one slender elbow, but she eluded his grasp, plunging through the darkness to escape him. And he hesitated, uncertain what he would do if he caught her.

Run, Caitlin, run! a voice inside him urged, hot and hard as the knot in his throat the first time he had seen Conn ride down a red deer. The image suddenly burned into his memory—the exquisite creature terrified, fleeing, desperate, while blood-drunk hunters charged after it.

Yet a deer free in the wildlands was far different from a woman, one who knew nothing of the ruthless forces that awaited hidden in the beautiful hills.

Blood of the saints, he could not let her go charging off without so much as a knife to defend herself. Nowhere to go. A much more horrible, lingering death was all she would find there. The thought of this woman, so brave, so joyful, broken and starving at the brutal mercy of the elements was more than Niall could bear.

With an oath, he gave chase. Lit by the moon, her path was easy enough to follow, marked by broken branches, trampled brush, deep-dug footprints in soft turf, and the horrible, desperate rasp of her breath as she fled for her life.

Niall charged after her, knowing only that he could not let her race off into disaster alone. But it made no sense! He had tried to kill her. Would have done so, if she had not evaded the blade.

Then, suddenly, Niall heard another sound, chilling, familiar in the darkened woods. The roar of a wild boar charging, wicked tusks dealing death.

Branches clawed at Caitlin's arms, roots catching at her feet with gnarled fingers, as she plunged through the night-dark woods, her senses still reeling with the vision of Niall standing over her, his sword blade flashing a glittering arc toward her head.

He had meant to kill her. A voice kept shrieking in her head, her imagination plunging onward, to the agony of the blade burying itself in her flesh, the horrible chill of death as her blood seeped into Niall's cloak.

The cloak he had draped about her almost tenderly before she drifted off to sleep . . .

She tripped over a stone, went down on one knee, the rough surface scraping the skin away. Blood ran down her leg, burning pain jolting through her, but she dared not let it slow her. A sob tore from her lips as she scrambled back to her feet and kept running.

He was coming. She could hear him, crashing

through the brush like a wild thing, sure-footed, determined, deadly, hunting her with the ruthless skill of one bred to be a warrior.

Nay, this cannot be happening! she thought wildly. He promised to guard her, protect her. He had sworn to Reverend Mother—was that why he had given her one glimpse of the sea? Some fragment of guilt. Knowing what was to come . . .

He had lied. She had trusted him. Not only with her life but with something far more fragile, her dreams about the mother and father she had never known. Yet if they were in the place where the dead dwelt, she might be meeting them soon.

She searched the eerie moonlit landscape for the path that would make it most difficult for him to follow her, someplace where her smaller size and lighter feet might gain her precious ground. A tangle of thorny bushes loomed to the right, and she could hear the burble of a stream. People settled near water. If she could reach it, she might find someone brave enough to help her. Or at least some weapon she could use to defend herself.

She turned into the teeth of the thorns, bit her lip as one spine gouged her leg. But as she drove deeper into the brush, she took heart. It seemed her ploy was working! Was it possible Niall's footsteps were more distant now? Or was it only her imagination? God in heaven, she did not want to die!

She pushed herself harder, faster, almost sobbed in relief when at last she plunged into a clearing. The water roared, tumbling down over a ridge of stone, a rocky cliff nearly as tall as the ones she had seen near the sea. Was it possible she could hide herself somehow among those treacherous rocks? She had to try.

She hastened toward them, suddenly froze, a bestial

roar splitting the silence. Shaking with terror and exhaustion, Caitlin stared as a massive wild boar reared its head up from where it had been rooting at the foot of a nut tree.

Lethal tusks gleamed in the moonlight, dashing any hope of escape, and Caitlin remembered tales of how the hero Diarmud had died, his body torn wide open by a fearsome creature like this one.

She glanced back over her shoulder, the sound of Niall's relentless pursuit drawing nearer, ever nearer. Swallowing hard, she faced the boar again, black bristles coating its head, small red eyes glowing where the moonlight struck them.

Death in front of her, death behind her. Only one choice: to die fighting for her freedom or to stay here, frozen, dying as a passive victim of Niall's sword.

She looked at the ground, saw a fallen branch thick enough to wield as a weapon. Scooping it up, she edged toward the boar, a desperate prayer on her lips.

The beast shook its great head, slaver coating its mouth, as if it were some hell-spawned creature jeering at her. In a thundering instant, it charged. Caitlin could not breathe, terror turning her muscles to stone. At the last instant, she leapt from the boar's path and slammed the branch down with all her strength, striking the boar between the eyes.

The branch cracked in two, a hellish sound tearing from the beast's throat, and she could see blood streaming down the side of its head. But it barely slowed the boar's charge for a heartbeat. Instinctively, she stumbled backward toward the ridge of thorny bushes, as the boar thundered toward her again, fury glowing in its pain-glazed eyes.

Caitlin clutched the short end of the branch, praying that she could somehow jam the point into the boar's throat, knowing even that would not save her life. The animal would be too close, the tusks would do their gruesome work even if the boar were in its death throes.

It seemed to stretch into eternity—the boar charging, the branch clutched in her shaking hands. She braced herself for the impact. Suddenly, something struck her from the side, hurling her from the boar's path. Caitlin screamed as she hurtled through the air, the breath driven from her body as she crashed into the stones.

She heard the boar bellow in rage, another deep voice cursing. She scrambled to her knees, swiping the hair from her eyes, stared at the man and beast locked in mortal combat.

Blood gleamed on Niall's leg where the tusk had cut. Crimson stained the sword he wielded against the massive animal. Slashes gushed blood amid the black-bristled coat as boar and warrior fought, both knowing that one of them would die.

Niall dodged and struck, his muscles shiny with sweat as he leapt out of the boar's path yet again, every movement drawing the beast closer and closer to the cliff—or was it farther and farther away from Caitlin? Nay, that was madness.

Niall could not be doing so on purpose. He wanted her dead! It made no sense! Caitlin's hand knotted into a fist, her knuckles pressed tight to her lips.

"Caitlin, run!" Niall shouted, barely evading another slash of the deadly tusks. "A tree—climb a tree!"

God in heaven, what was he doing? He wanted her dead, and now he was risking his life to help her get away?

She started to stumble backward, saw Niall glance at her for a dangerous moment, his eyes filled with something she could not name, his face hard and desperate, resolved and filled with a pain far deeper than any wound could reach.

The boar swung about.

"Niall! The boar!" she shrieked.

He braced his legs apart, his body now far too close to the edge of the rock ledge. The boar stormed toward him with the might of a hundred fiends. Caitlin saw the flash of Niall's sword, heard the horrific sound as boar and man slammed together.

Blood gushed from the boar's throat, its great head slashing about in agony. Caitlin cried out as the beast shuddered to its knees, lashing out in its death throes.

A guttural cry split the night as the boar's hindquarters slammed into Niall. Caitlin's heart froze as she watched Niall fight for balance on the edge of stone. She screamed as he fell backward into darkness.

If she lived a thousand years, Caitlin would never forget the sound of flesh striking stone, the hideous crash, the cry of pain torn from Niall's throat. Then silence. The most horrific silence she had ever heard.

She bit her knuckle, her whole body shaking as she stared at the boar, which at last lay still, Niall's sword still embedded in its body. Dear God, what should she do? If she had not awakened, that sword would have been buried in *her* body. She would be the one lying in the spreading pool of her own blood. She had seen Niall looming over her, sword in hand, hard intent in his eyes.

She had run for her life, and he had chased her, grim with determination to kill her. But why, if the chieftain had sent him to guard . . . Horror streaked through Caitlin. She feared she would retch. Only one thing could drive a man like Niall to kill. The order of his chieftain. A duty he had admitted to Reverend Mother meant more to him than heaven or hell. Certainly more than the life of one young woman he scarcely knew.

She should grab the sword, now. Take it and flee. She could lose herself in the wilderness, vanish. By the time Conn realized what had happened, no mortal living could find her.

It was simple, the decision. The only thing she could do. She crept nearer the boar, grasped the sword hilt, and, with a mighty tug, ripped the weapon free. But as she started away, a tusk caught on her leine. She bent down to untangle it, stared transfixed at the glistening white tusk, sharp as any blade. To save her, Niall had risked the horrible death it could deal. There was no other explanation. It would not matter to Conn *how* she died, as long as she was dead. Even if Niall had felt some odd shame, allowing the boar to do the bloody deed Conn had commanded him to do, it would not have mattered. Niall could have held his silence. No one would ever have known.

Tears welled up in Caitlin's eyes, burned her cheeks. "What am I to do, Reverend Mother?" she murmured, turning instinctively to that presence that had always helped her sort out the tangles of her life. "I do not know what to do!"

Leave him, and he will surely die, a voice whispered in her head.

"But why should *I* help him?" she whispered aloud. "What if he attempts to kill me again?"

Images poured through her, unwelcome but vivid as sunlight striking waves—the sea, Niall's gruff indulgence, the reluctant smile on lips she knew instinctively too seldom curled in pleasure. And another vision she would never forget, frozen in the instant before the boar crashed into Niall for the final, deadly time. Torment—not fear of death but, rather, a desolation, a reaching out of the soul.

He bled for you, Caitlin, she told herself. *He fought for you. He might even have died for you. And if you leave now, you may never really know why he tried to kill you. You will be running from it for the rest of your life.*

Swallowing hard, Caitlin edged toward the rim of the cliff, stared down its moonlit expanse. He lay on a ledge as far down as the length from the abbey tower to the ground below. A crushing distance. A deadly one. Surely, even a man such as Niall could not fall so far and live. She could say a prayer for him and then leave.

Yet she had barely made the sign of the cross when she heard it. Faint, barely carried to her in the stillness of the night. A moan.

Niall was alive.

Chapter
5

PAIN GROUND DEEP into Niall's side, black webs of unconsciousness pulling him deeper, ever deeper, toward oblivion. Gritting his teeth, he shifted his body away from the sharp edge of stone, his heart skipping a beat as he nearly rolled off the edge of whatever surface held him. A ledge? Devil alone could guess. Yet one thing was certain. Battered as he was, his body restless with pain, one slip into unconsciousness would mean he would fall to his death, alone on this rugged sweep of cliff.

He should have been furious, fighting for his life. Dying now would mean his final quest was left undone. He would be known as Niall of the Seven Betrayals forever. It was a fate he would have battled with his last breath even an hour ago. Yet now Niall lay still, uncertain which would be more vile. To die with stained honor or to kill an innocent girl to preserve it. Nay, not just any young woman. Caitlin of the Lilies, with her rare joy and courageous spirit.

He dragged one hand over his face, trying to swipe the grit from his eyes. Perhaps this agony of indecision was the reason Conn had waited so many years to order the girl's death. Aye, and the reason Conn had not wielded the sword with his own hands. Fear—fear of

the spear caster Fintan and the power of his fairy magic
even from the realm of the dead. Fear of damning himself forever in his own eyes because Caitlin's blood was
on his hands.

Bitterness welled up inside Niall, a feeling of being
used. Yet was that not a warrior's sole purpose in life?
To be used by his chieftain? Wielded like a sword to
protect his kingdom?

In all fairness, there were a score of reasons a chieftain could not chase about the countryside to cut down
one young woman. The most pressing of these was the
certainty that someone would have followed him, discovered his plan for Caitlin's death. And if any at Glenfluirse uncovered the fate he intended for Fintan's
daughter, there was no way to know what chaos it
might bring. In the years of Caitlin's absence, fear of
the curse had eased because of Glenfluirse's love for
Fintan. Conn's vow to protect the spear caster's daughter had absolved Glenfluirse from the terrible responsibility of making an impossible choice between Conn
and the only child of the hero they loved.

Even though Fintan was dead, the army's loyalty to
the spear caster was still far greater than its loyalty to
the chieftain. Fintan had bled with them, led them into
battle, become a symbol of all their triumphs and a
magic they believed in with all their hearts. Only Niall,
Conn's foster son, owed Conn a greater debt. Niall, the
one man Conn could truly trust in this impossible situation. And Niall had failed him.

A grim chuckle escaped Niall's lips. It did not matter
now—duty or failure, trust or betrayal. There was no
way to scale this cliff face. Caitlin had probably already
fled.

She possessed intelligence as well as courage. Surely,
she would have taken the horse. If she had, she could

put great distance between her and the reach of Conn's power.

Would she return to the abbey? Niall's heart throbbed, a tightness in his throat. Pray that the abbess's God would keep her safe as he had not.

He closed his eyes, fought back the image of her face when she had awakened to see his sword gleaming above her neck. He clung instead to visions of sea spray and laughter, water the color of mermaid's hair twining blue ribbons through her black curls as she slipped into the sea's embrace.

He saw again the earnest crease between her brows, the soft uncertainty in her face as she had spoken about her parents, her elation when she believed he was taking her to them.

She must hate him now, fear him, Niall thought, wincing. Why should it matter? He had been hated and feared most of his life, had always known that many in Glenfluirse thought him evil's spawn.

But somehow the knowledge that this one woman he had barely met thought ill of him was unbearable. Caitlin of the Lilies would believe forever that Niall had smiled at her, indulged her curiosity about the sea, shared bread with her and the warmth of his cloak, when all the while he intended to kill her.

Death would settle the matter, Niall thought, closing his eyes with an odd feeling of detachment. He would never have the chance to try to explain it to her, or to decide whether his blood debt to the chieftain was worth the life of Caitlin of the Lilies.

A sudden scraping sound startled Niall. He opened his eyes, half expecting the ledge to be crumbling beneath his weight. What he saw startled him so badly he nearly fell off the jagged protrusion of rock. The moon cast a silver halo about a figure peeking over the lip of earth high above. A long tangle of black hair, the pale oval of a face.

Caitlin! She should have been far away from this place by now! By the sword of Lugh, had the woman gone mad? Or was she merely making certain he could not give chase?

"Niall?" Her voice quavered. Hellfire, she *should* be afraid of him!

Should he answer? Nay, better to let her go off on her way thinking he was dead. That way, she would feel no guilt. Guilt? Why should she feel the slightest twinge of it? He had tried to murder her in her sleep. If she had pushed him from the cliff with her own hands and danced upon his grave, no sane person could blame her.

She disappeared, and he heard the thud of hooves—the horse. Thank the saints she had had the sense to go back for the animal. He swallowed hard, waiting for the sound of her riding away, was stunned at how hollow the prospect made him feel.

Strange, a man who had always been solitary, suddenly feeling utterly alone. Why? Because for one afternoon, a woman had included him in her laughter? Confided in him her most secret pain? Acted as if his father's legacy and the sullied name Niall bore did not matter?

However unwisely Caitlin had trusted him in those few precious hours, she would never trust him now. Nay! It should not matter, he thought. He would not let it matter.

Suddenly, there was a soft rasping sound, something tumbling toward him over the ledge.

He cried out as it struck him in the face, coiling upon his chest. Some night creature falling to Niall's own fate? He grasped it with battered hands. What the devil? It was a rope! Blood of Lugh, it was the rope he had all but forgotten in the bottom of the leather bag he always kept affixed to the saddle!

"Stay still," a small voice called from the ledge. "I am coming down to—to help you."

"Are . . . you mad?" he croaked, struggling to find his voice. "You cannot. Too dangerous."

"There is no other way."

"That does not matter! I . . . am not worth the . . . risk. I almost killed you!"

"It was a most unpleasant way to awaken, I admit, but—we can sort it out after you are safe on solid ground."

A rain of dirt spattered his face. Blast! She was teetering on the edge of the cliff, fully intending to attempt this insane feat.

"Get back!" he roared, his whole body screaming with pain as he levered himself up on one elbow. Demons pounded in his head. "Hellfire, you will . . . get us both killed!"

"A thousand pardons!" she cried, haughty as a queen. "Perhaps warriors are trained to sit by idly and watch people rot to death on ledges, but it is a part of our education sadly neglected at the abbey. Patience. That is what we are taught. I am climbing down to help you, no matter how much your arguing tempts me to knock you off that ledge myself."

She was trying to brace her own courage. Like a lad blustering before his first battle. Damnation, she was stubborn. Not half of Conn's army could deter her from her path.

His head was still swimming, his muscles weak from the fall, but he struggled until he was sitting upright, back against the rough stone wall, legs dangling over the perilous ledge. "The rope . . . cannot hold both your weight and mine. Let me . . . bind it about my waist. The horse can drag me up."

She hesitated. "You can never make the knots tight enough, battered as you are."

"Nay! Caitlin!" he protested. But it was too late. She was over the ledge of earth, her leine white against the black stone, the garment rippling about her as she edged down, hands clinging to the rope. Feet scrabbling for purchase on the rugged wall of stones.

Twice, a foot slipped, and she dangled, suspended for a moment between the rope and death. Niall cursed, raged at the saints the abbey so cherished, charging them to protect her. Yet the pain was closing its fist about him again, the mist swirling in his head.

He closed his eyes, willing the darkness away, fearing that if he succumbed to it now, he would carry Caitlin with him when he fell to his death. Then he felt it. The brush of her foot against his thigh as she tried to find space to stand. The touch of her hands upon his waist.

She was tying the rope around him, and there was little he could do to help her. Then she was climbing again, upward until it seemed to Niall's reeling senses she was ascending to the moon. He blinked, and in that instant she was gone.

He felt a jerk as the rope tautened, strained against his weight.

"Niall, hold yourself away from the rocks," she called down. He tried to get his feet between the cliff face and his battered body, but he was too tired, too dizzy. Almost instinctively, he curled his body away from the stone. He dangled, felt the tension in the length of hemp. He could not drive from his mind the strange litany. *I should be dead. I should be dead.*

Niall groaned as his body swung against a stone. Felt

unconsciousness clawing him down deeper into the darkness.

"Niall, you are almost safe. Give me your hand!"

He reached upward, clasped the slender warmth of Caitlin's fingers. With astonishing strength, she gave one last tug. His belly struck the turf as she collapsed, her breath rasping, her legs tangled with his.

Niall rolled to his back, forced his heavy lids open, glimpsed swirling stars, writhing trees. Caitlin, her whole body trembling, spoke low to his horse. His horse, linked to him by the life-saving rope.

With all his strength, Niall raised his head, stared at the woman whose whole body trembled, her face glowing otherworldly in the moonlight. He fought to squeeze out one word, a faint rasp as he drifted into darkness.

"Why?"

Caitlin stared down into Niall's face, stained red with the light of the rising sun. She had tended his wounds as best she could. Was all but certain he would soon awaken. Every instinct within her screamed that she should ride away as fast as she could, leaving him without a horse to give chase. She had done what she could to save him. Gotten him off the ledge. Surely, no one, not even the mother abbess, could ask more of her.

Yet she sat, arms curled tight about her bent legs, her chin resting atop her knees. What was it she had heard Sister Luca say when schooling other nuns in the healing arts? It was not the wounds on the body that were most dangerous. It was the injuries deep within, where the healer could not see.

Why should it matter to her what befell this man now? He had tried to kill her! He deserved her hatred, did he not? Because of him, she would never see the world quite the same way again. It would always be a darker, more menacing place. Yet every time she tried to leave, she heard the faint rasp of his question.

Why? . . .

How could she begin to answer? She had no reasonable explanation even for herself. She only knew she had no choice.

Caitlin started as Niall shifted, restless, a groan breaching parched lips. She took the horn cup, eased water down his throat. His lashes fluttered open, and she was stunned to see his eyes—not bleary but piercing, as if, even in unconsciousness, his spirit had grappled with questions. Demanded answers.

A shiver of fear raced down her spine, but she quelled it. Nay. He might be strong enough to open his eyes, but surely he was not strong enough to attempt to kill her. Not that he would, even if he had the strength. She had to believe that.

She hid her fear by speaking. "It seems your injuries are not so terrible after all. I think you will live."

He licked at his lips. Swallowed hard. "Because of . . . you."

She shrugged, said nothing, that green gaze piercing through her.

"Caitlin . . . you should have let me . . . die. Why did you . . . not let me . . . die? I am sworn to kill you." A choking cough racked him. "What the devil do we do . . . now?"

She stared down into that handsome face, contorted with an anguish far deeper than his wounds.

What the devil do we now? His question echoed inside her.

"I do not know," she whispered as his eyes drifted shut.

*   *   *

Rain, soft, sweet-scented. Niall could hear it pattering above him. He wanted to run into the falling drops as he had as a hurting child, imagining that it could magically wash him as it did the leaves and blossoms, making him clean and new.

But nothing in heaven or hell could ever cleanse him of what he had done. What he had failed to do. Even worse than those warring emotions was the question that had torn at him even when he had lain unconscious. What could he do now?

He opened his eyes, saw a leafy roof above his head, a makeshift shelter of cut branches keeping out the worst of the dampness. Caitlin must have fashioned it. She had even managed to cook something over a smoky fire. He had vague memories of her hand pressing the cup to his lips, something hot and a little bitter sliding down his throat. Then sleep—blessed sleep, out of the reach of the demons who kept twisting their fire-hot pincers deep in his flesh.

Blast, could any torture she devised be worse than this? Kindness when he had been ready to kill her. Had they not taught her any sense at that infernal abbey?

And now, as he awakened again, he could see her huddled under the leafy shelter, her leine soiled and torn, her eyes too innocent, her spirit too bruised. She looked like a waif, lost and alone. And in a way, she was. Trapped by the teachings of the nuns who had raised her. Stranded between Conn's sentence of death and a life running from his wrath. No family to defend her. No place she could be safe. For to return to the abbey would only bring disaster to those she loved. Even one as innocent as Caitlin must have come to that grim realization by now.

She glanced down at him, saw his eyes were opened. One soft palm pressed against his brow. "How are you faring?" she asked, then dipped the cup into whatever brew she was cooking on the smoldering fire.

Bitterness and self-loathing rolled over Niall in a suffocating wave. "Be up . . . murdering young girls before morning."

Caitlin flinched, then forced her features into a calm mask. "Drink this." She pressed the cup to his lips. "This will help you rest."

Niall raised one hand, pushed the container away. "Rescued me. Now, what are you . . . going to do with me? Planning on drugged sleep for the next . . . forty years?"

"Certainly not! I—" She stopped, saw the grim humor curling his mouth. "It would serve no purpose. I am certain your *just* chieftain will send someone to search for you—or to hunt me down." Bravado disappeared. Her voice dropped, low. Innocent she might be, but she was obviously no fool. She knew the peril she was in, the hopelessness of it all. He wished he could comfort her, smooth away the lines that marred her face. But he would not add to all the wrongs he had done her by offering her false comfort.

"Niall . . ." she said after a moment. "Why does your chieftain want me dead? I have been puzzling about it all night. Still, it makes no sense. He could have left me with the sisters forever. I was happy there. Loved." Her voice broke, the sound piercing Niall deep.

How did one explain the shadowy forces that had driven Conn to such desperate measures? Prophecies. Legends. Magic far too powerful to be ignored. He recoiled from burdening this young woman with the darkness of her destiny. And yet, did she not deserve some explanation? The truth?

"Niall, why did Conn order you to kill me? Why now? I cannot understand. I have done him no harm."

"But you will."

She stared at him, disbelieving. "That is absurd. How can one lone woman hurt a chieftain as powerful as yours?"

"It is truth. Foretold by the greatest druid ever to walk the sacred groves."

She stared at him, silent.

"I heard only bits and pieces of the story, whispered as if the court believed not speaking it aloud would keep the prediction from coming true. Conn wanted his druid to predict the future of the great Fintan's child. Cathal placed his hand upon your mother's belly, and—" Niall paused, searching for the words.

"What did he say?"

"That you would bring disaster to Conn and so to every person in his kingdom."

Color drained from already pale cheeks, leaving her ashen. "Sweet mother of God. It cannot be true. I cannot believe—" She pressed trembling fingers to her lips. "I would never willingly harm anyone!" Her eyes pleaded with him, desperate.

"I believe you would never mean to. But sometimes forces of destiny pull us into tangles we never intended." No one understood that better than Niall. His whole life's work had been battling another man's dishonor. Fighting with the ghost of his father. "I believe Conn ordered your death to stop the bloodshed he feared would come if you were left alive."

"The death of one to spare the many," Caitlin said softly.

"Aye."

"I can almost understand . . . why he would make such a choice." She shivered. "But then, why did he not have me put to the sword the instant I was born?"

"I cannot say for certain. Perhaps he could not bear

to kill an innocent child. He proved his gift for extraordinary mercy when he took me as his fosterling when everyone around him begged him to kill me."

"A mere boy? Why would anyone be so cruel?"

"In time, sons grow strong enough to avenge their fathers, Caitlin. More wars have been started over blood vengeance than any other reason. Not that I would ever—" He stopped, and she could see him push back a dark wave of bitterness, hiding it from her eyes.

"There is only one thing I know for certain," he said. "At the time you were born and for many years after, Conn needed Fintan to fight in his army. And your mother and father—they adored you. You were the only babe they would ever have. I believe that Conn spared your life because he did not have the courage to face Fintan's wrath upon your death. Conn could give you a life happy enough, tucked in the abbey, safe enough that your parents could bear it, yet keep you well guarded, cut off from the rest of the world. Buy himself time to think what to do. He could keep others in Glenfluirse from becoming attached to you, so that when he needed to kill you, no one would stop him. You would be a stranger."

The thought chafed at Niall, the chieftain he loved possessing such a flaw. And yet, had Niall not learned as a child that men are not perfect, that even those one adored could make mistakes? And this one was not nearly as vile, as unforgivable, as the one his father had made. *This* misstep was at least one Niall could understand, if not condone.

"With Cathal's prophecy ringing in his ears, Conn told your father that he would send you away from Glenfluirse, someplace where you would be raised with love. He vowed to Fintan and Grainne that when you were of an age for marriage, he would bring you back to his fortress, put you under his protection. Make certain the prophecy could never be fulfilled. You were a helpless babe. No matter how closely your parents watched over you, I am certain they understood what danger you were in, that someone might kill you out of fear of the prophecy. Fintan trusted in the promise of his chieftain. To save your life, your parents let you go. I am certain the bracelet you wear was a gift of love from them both."

Caitlin touched the circle of gold that was suddenly infinitely precious. "And when my father died and was no more use to your chieftain, Conn sent you to kill me."

Set forth in Caitlin's forthright voice, Conn's actions made Niall uncomfortable. As if he had peeked behind a mask and glimpsed some deformity he did not wish to see. Nay, Conn had no other choice, Niall told himself, but even that did not erase the ugliness of what Conn had done.

"Caitlin, I know it . . . must be difficult to hear. The reasons why—"

"I have been wondering *why* all my life. Now I know. Even before I was born, I was damned."

"Nay! It was a prophecy. Druids can be wrong."

"The sisters would say that. But what would you say, Niall? What do you believe?"

He could not meet her gaze.

"You were willing to kill me while I slept. I saw it in your face. You did not want to do it, Niall, but you would have."

He stared down at his hands—hands that would be stained with Caitlin's blood were it not for a snapped twig, such a fragile twist of fate.

She was quiet, it seemed forever, no sound breaching the silence between them but the rain. He saw her fingers tighten in the folds of her leine. "Strange. Reverend Mother always said I had a destiny to fulfill. I could tell she thought it was something wonderful, romantic. Some great gift to the world. I am certain she never imagined I would bring death and destruction to innocent people."

Awkward, rough-edged warrior that he was, Niall could not bear the desolation in those lily-fair features that should only be touched with joy. "Caitlin, life forces are like the ocean. They can change course in a heartbeat. Perhaps the doom Cathal foretold is gone."

"But what if it is not? If what the druid predicted is true . . ." She bit her lip, and Niall saw her eyes glisten, overbright. "Perhaps . . . perhaps Conn was right. The only way to be certain to stop this curse is my death."

"Caitlin, you owe these people nothing. You do not even know them!"

"But someone does. Someone loves them. They are fathers and mothers, children, sisters, brothers. Families like I have never had. If I were to die, who would mourn me?"

"The abbess!" *And I would.* The realization struck him.

"Since I have left Saint Mary's, I can never enter the cloister again. The abbess will never know what happened to me, anyway." She turned great, tragic eyes to his, the blue depths holding both terror and a courage deeper than any he had ever seen. "If you . . . fulfilled your duty—"

His gut twisted in horror. "Damnation! Have you lost your wits?"

Tears streamed from her eyes. "How can I risk being the reason for the death of so many?"

God's blood, the woman was all but giving him permission to kill her! Was arguing for her own death! Yet in all his wretched, embattled years, Niall had never known anyone who loved life more. He clenched his fists, knowing that if Caitlin died, it would be as if the light drained out of the sun. The world would be a far darker place. More like the one Niall had known before he had taken her to look at the sea.

"You cannot ask this of me!" he snapped, enraged. "I will not do it."

She glared at him, full of hurt and fear, anger and resignation. "Then what *are* we going to do?"

"Find a way to stop this prediction—foil whatever doom the druid foretold."

She gave a broken laugh. "How, Niall? Have you your own kind of magic?"

Frustration burned through him. "I do not know how we will defeat it. I only know I have to find some way." He stopped, cursed low.

"And while you are attempting to work this miracle, where do we go? What do we do? Your king wants me dead. Fears the disaster I might bring down upon his people. He will not quietly sit by, waiting at his hearth-fire for your return. As soon as he guesses something has gone awry, he will send others to hunt me."

It was true. In his mind, Niall could see the hard faces of the warriors who would ride out for their chieftain. And yet it was such a delicate matter—one misstep could cost Conn his kingdom. Surely, he would not be hasty to act. That caution alone might buy them precious time.

"We will find a place to hide you until I can think," Niall began.

"And just where would this place be? I cannot go back to the abbey. In his wrath, God alone knows what Conn might do to them. This is Conn's kingdom. His land. It would mean death to anyone who helped me. Even if there were someone brave enough, generous enough, to hide me, how could I bring such trouble down upon their heads? And you will be no better off than I am once Conn learns the truth. You will be hunted as fiercely as I am."

Every word she said was true. He had lived a lifetime in the shadow of the sword, but always knowing an army stood behind him. But this would be far different. He would be one man, alone. Only his body, his sword arm, between Caitlin and certain death.

Niall stiffened, hating the anger, the sense of futility that surged through him as he struggled to find some way to shield Caitlin. He froze, the answer piercing him swift as a well-placed arrow and thrice as painful. *Nay*, he thought, something shamefully like panic burning through him. *I cannot go back there!*

But if he did not, Caitlin would die. He would only be away for a small space in time, he told himself sharply. He would stay only long enough to gather provisions for their flight across Ireland. He would find safe haven for Fintan's daughter somewhere . . .

But even those thoughts could not keep his blood from running cold, his hand from trembling.

This was madness. He was a warrior, trained to laugh in the face of death, scorn the pain of the most lethal wounds.

His throat tightened. "There is one place in Ireland Conn would never think to search once he knows I have helped you escape. A place called Castle Daire."

"But it must belong to somebody. I cannot put them in danger."

He raised his gaze to hers. "The castle belonged to my father. It now belongs to me."

Blue eyes searched his, far too intuitive for comfort. He felt as if she were running fingers over his soul.

"Niall," she said softly. "Surely Conn would search there. It stands to reason—"

"I swore a blood oath I would never return to it."

She touched his arm, almost timidly. "But in allowing me to live, you have already broken an oath. Your oath of loyalty to your chieftain, the most important one any warrior swears in all his life. Conn will know that."

"Aye, but Conn will also know what is waiting for me at Castle Daire."

"Memories?"

Images swirled inside his head. Gray stone rearing skyward, the courtyard churning with mounted warriors. His father bound, dragged astride a horse. Shame. Horrific, suffocating shame. And the screams— his mother's screams. His sister's.

Rage surged through him, the rage of the boy he had been, disillusioned, watching his world crumble about him. Rage at the twisted cruelty of the fates that left him no choice but to return to the scene of his worst nightmares. How could he explain to this woman, so shaken, so vulnerable? How could he let anyone glimpse the dark corners of his soul?

Perhaps Christian angels did mete out judgment, Niall thought, staring out into the storm. They had condemned him to hide Caitlin in the depths of his very own hell.

Chapter
6

STARK AS A SKULL picked clean by the war goddess Morrigan, the lone crumbling tower of Castle Daire loomed against the sky. The setting sun cast a red glow across the walls until the very stones seemed to bleed. For years, the castle had haunted Niall's dreams. A bleak home to shattered illusions, ruined honor, its confines wandered by the ghosts of a past he had struggled to forget.

Niall gripped the reins of his mount tighter and stared over the crown of Caitlin's head at the stone edifice growing nearer with every strike of the horse's hooves against the debris-strewn ground. He winced inwardly, remembering those first endless nights he had spent as Conn's fosterling. Tortured with shame and loss, he had huddled beneath his cloak, bedding down at the fire like one of Conn's hounds.

Sleepless, he had stared into the fire and dreamed of possessing the might of the legendary warrior, Cuchulain. He imagined hoisting the castle onto his shoulders, flinging it so far into the vast sea even the mermaids could not find it. He had dreamed of possessing the power of the sun god, Lugh, burning the walls with his gaze until the very stones melted. A fiery blaze, wiping away every trace of the life that had once been. Obliterating it forever, as if it had never existed at all.

Yet no boy's imaginings could dash Castle Daire away. Always, in his most secret nightmares, he had known it was there, waiting. But even when the worst of his personal devils had haunted him and he had watched in frozen horror as his dream-self rode up to the stone tower, he had always been alone. He had battled a lifetime of dread with only the arrow slits of the castle to witness the sick clenching of his belly, the sweat slicking his palms.

Never had he guessed that he would face this place under the gaze of a woman who knew too much, saw too vividly, and had already probed deeper beneath his defenses than anyone he had ever known.

It made him feel naked inside, all his weapons stripped away. He hated himself for that weakness. Hated her for making him aware of it.

Caitlin shifted in the saddle, and a dull ache throbbed in Niall's leg. He welcomed the distraction, transferring both reins into one hand, kneading the swollen knot of muscle with his fingers.

"I knew your wounds were paining you," she said softly. "I told you, we should have stopped long ago. Rested for the night."

"My accursed wounds are my own affair," Niall snapped. "I need no woman to tell me when I need to get off my horse!"

She straightened. "Next time, I will say nothing. Merely watch you fall off. I wonder how proud and stubborn you will look facedown in the dirt."

He grimaced. Her words were true enough. Exhausted as he was, his bruises throbbing, it was a wonder he had been able to stay astride the beast so long.

What had possessed him to push himself so hard to

reach their destination? He should have leapt at Caitlin's suggestion to make camp on a distant hillside—delayed returning to Daire as long as he possibly could. So easy, it would have been. Not so much as a bruise to his pride. She would never know how hard he had had to fight the impulse to take her advice.

Every fiber of his being had fought like a snared wolf at the thought of returning here. And yet he had learned on the battlefield that it was best to yank a javelin from flesh swiftly, sharply. If you hesitated, the pain came alive inside you, jeering at you as it held you in its grip. Nay, delaying would only make things worse. The sooner they reached Daire, the sooner they could leave it.

"We need to reach the castle as soon as possible." He did not know why the devil he felt a need to explain to her. "Every moment on the road is a danger. If anyone saw us riding past, they might tell Conn once he begins searching."

"Niall, I much doubt they would remember me."

"With that face of yours?" he bit out more harshly than he intended. "Hellfire, any man who saw it would be burdened with its image forever!"

She stiffened in his arms, and he saw the bright gleam of tears in her eyes before she turned her face away. He cursed her. Cursed the fates that must be jeering at him even now, dragging him back to this place. Most of all, he cursed himself for the change he had caused in her.

True, Caitlin of the Lilies would always have a face so rare, so lovely, it would carve itself into the memory. But it was not the same face that had glowed with pleasure, buffed by the sea wind. Those were not the same eyes that had blazed defiance and outrage when she had struggled with him at the druid stone—a warrior queen too certain of her strength ever to fear defeat.

Now Fintan's daughter knew that the world she had raced out to meet with delight and anticipation could be cruel, ruthless. Could break her heart, if not her courage.

The horse stumbled, and Niall fought to hold Caitlin upon the animal as it scrambled to regain its footing. "Curse it! What the devil was that?" he muttered, glancing over what had once been the finest castle yard in all of Ireland. His mother's pride.

The expanse that had once been banked with flowers was strewn with refuse, the tidy paths that had been laid out most carefully now overgrown with weeds. Splintered furnishings had been scattered about, and a cart leaned crazily on one broken wheel. The blossoms his mother had tended tangled wild across the debris, reminding Niall of a shamed woman attempting to hide the disorder with her cloak.

Niall's throat tightened, and he blocked out the image of his sister toddling through the blossoms, stubbornly trying to pick handfuls of roses, no matter how many times the thorns pricked her skin.

He drew rein, slid down off his mount. Struggling to school his face into lines of carelessness, he helped Caitlin from the horse. She looked about her, and Niall could see her quiet dismay.

Not that he could blame her. The ground itself seemed to pulse with hostility, as if it would hurl the intruders from it if it could. Dark and forbidding, the walls towered above them, the stone work crumbling and sprinkled with clay-colored lichens. It seemed nature and neglect were doing what Niall could not. Obliterating Castle Daire one stone at a time.

"This will be a good place to hide," Caitlin said,

glancing about nervously. "No one could possibly live in such a place."

But at that instant, the door flew open. Caitlin cried out as a whirlwind with copper-bright hair and a rusted sword swooped toward them. Niall lunged for his one weapon, but it was too late. The point of his assailant's blade was at his throat.

"Move, and I will run you through," the grimy-faced warrior snarled with unmistakable relish, the breeze riffling through the gray rags that draped a painfully thin body. Niall could not speak, his chest afire as if the waif had plunged the blade through his very heart.

Caitlin stepped forward, compassion softening her lips. "We mean you no harm, lad. We are only seeking shelter here, as you have. We have food to share."

"I take no charity!" the waif scoffed. "This castle is mine!"

"The castle is mine, curse that it is," Niall growled, his voice harsh, unfamiliar to his own ears. "Do you not recognize me, Fiona?"

He caught a glimpse of Caitlin as she glanced up at him in astonishment that the waif before them was a girl, but it was Fiona's expression that lanced his heart. Disbelief, a tiny, unquenchable spark of joy for just an instant before it was drowned by hatred.

"Niall! You! You traitor! The chieftain's stinking cur, groveling at a murderer's feet!"

Dull crimson stained the hard planes of Niall's face. "Enough, girl." He reached up, trying to grasp the sword, but the girl dug the point deeper into the tender flesh of his neck. Blood welled up, trickled in a red path down his skin.

"Stop or die," she said fiercely, only the slightest tremor in her hand betraying her uncertainty. "There is no one in heaven or hell I would rather have die beneath my sword except Conn himself!"

Niall stared at her, trying to gauge whether she would strike. Aye, he judged grimly, if only to prove that she had the courage. Shifting only his eyes, he glanced at Caitlin's ashen face, then struggled to steady his voice as he turned back to his sister.

"Fiona—"

"Do not call me that! I am Finn now, master of Castle Daire. Quick enough with my sword to drive away the thieving bastards who used to steal from us."

The words raked through Niall, flooding him with confusion. He wished he could close his eyes, ride away, drive from his memory forever the sight of his sister and what she had become. "You were robbed?"

"Mother was helpless, and I was but a girl-child, alone, unprotected! What did you think would happen?"

"The castle was teeming with servants, and the fields—" Niall insisted, more to himself than his mutinous sister.

"Finn?"

Niall started at the sound of Caitlin's voice. Blood of Boru, could the woman not see how dangerous the girl was? Teetering between fear and fury ages old? If the sword had not been at his throat, he would have grabbed Caitlin's accursed arm. But she eased forward, hands extended palm up in the age-old gesture of peace.

"Finn?" she repeated. "Is that your name? I am Caitlin. I have earned Conn's malice as well."

"Any woman who would let such filth as Niall of the Seven Betrayals touch her deserves whatever befalls her!"

"Curse it, Fiona!" Niall snapped. "You will not insult her!"

"She can think what she wishes of me," Caitlin said. "But she needs to hear the simple truth. Conn ordered my death. Niall was supposed to kill me."

Fiona's brows lowered, her gaze suddenly flicking to Caitlin's face. "By a merciful sword thrust or by breaking your heart the way he did our father's?"

Niall's jaw clenched.

"Whatever way was most certain to end my life, I believe. Niall tried to do as Conn ordered, but in the end, he could not kill me. We are outcasts now. We need to find someplace to rest, to plan, prepare the things we need to make our escape."

Fiona bit her lip, stared a moment in silence. "And so you come here. Conn would never believe you would sully yourself with the dirt of Castle Daire, would he, Niall?"

"I would rather hide her in hell," Niall admitted.

Rage flared, hot in Fiona's eyes, almost obliterating something like hurt. "Go find the gate to the devil's lair and be damned! There is nowhere I would rather see you! Get off my land. *My* land, *brother!*"

Niall let fly an oath, but Caitlin broke in, infuriatingly calm, reasonable. "Perhaps it would be better if we found some other place to go."

Fiona's face softened a little, almost with regret. But it was obvious the harsh life at Daire had taught her to care for her own skin first. Hellfire, Niall thought grimly. Had he not taught her that himself the day he turned his back on Daire and everyone in it?

"I will do you one service, brother, out of pity for the woman. If Conn sends warriors, I will not tell them that you passed." Fiona cast a worried glance behind her. "Now, leave at once before—"

"Treasure? Have we visitors?"

Niall flinched at the voice coming from within the castle, a voice still filled with the music of the North.

"Nay, Mam, only thieves." Fiona's voice held a quiver of dread. "Stay inside! I am driving them off." Her voice dropped to a whisper. "Go now, by God, or I *will* kill you. Damn me if I will let you come back and break her heart, Niall!"

Niall wavered, wanting nothing more than to mount the horse, ride God alone knew where. It would be easier by far to face the swords of Conn's men, a swift, clean fight, even the shame and pain of execution, rather than this hideous torture. No one could ask this of him! He started to turn toward the horse. But at that moment, he saw Caitlin standing there, so bewildered, so bruised by all that had befallen her, fearful and betrayed and yet her eyes filled with compassion. For whom? Ragged, defiant Fiona? Or for Niall himself?

He turned back, allowing his sister full access to his throat. Then called out, "Mother!"

Fiona's eyes widened in fury, her face ice-white. A sob tore from her throat. He never knew if she would have killed him, for in a heartbeat, a delicate woman rushed from the castle, white hair curling about a face that still whispered of long-vanished beauty.

"Niall!" she cried out. "Oh, my boy! I knew that you would come home!"

Niall could not speak as he peered down into that face he had tried so hard to forget. What had he expected from this woman who had given him life? Anger? Sorrow? Tears streaked her face, and she looked at him as if he alone had carried the sun into her sky.

Guilt and a strange sense of irritation stirred inside him. Did the woman not blame him for her suffering and Fiona's? For the filth and the hunger? The rags and the neglect? Did she not hate him for turning his back on them? But he had not known . . . he had never suspected what they were suffering. Conn had assured him all would be well.

Tears glinted in Fiona's eyes, her face screwed up fiercely in what he knew was an effort not to cry.

"Ach, Fee!" His mother laughed. "Enough of your games! Put your sword down and welcome your brother!"

Fiona's hand trembled on the hilt, but her mother uncurled her fingers and took the blade away. She cast it aside as if it were a child's plaything made of wood.

"You know she will be giving you no peace, Niall, now that you are home. Always, she trailed after you like a wee pup."

Niall saw Fiona flinch as if her mother had struck her.

"I was naught but a babe then, Mam. I will not be troubling Niall any longer."

Except, of course, for dreaming up ways to stick a knife between his ribs, Niall thought.

His mother's gaze lit on Caitlin, and a smile wreathed her face. "And who is this? Fee, have you ever seen a face more lovely?"

"Her name is Caitlin, Mother," Niall began, "and she—"

"Niall!" Fiona snapped, a desperate plea in her eyes.

"Your son is keeping me from harm," Caitlin said. Niall frowned, but she flashed him a quelling glance. Did both women wish him to lie? Not tell his mother what danger he had brought to her threshold?

"Poor treasure!" his mother crooned. "Come, warm yourself by the fire. Fee, tell Keefe to prepare something for our Caitlin to eat."

"Keefe?" Niall echoed, astonished, remembering the

spry retainer who had trained him to snare partridges. "He is still here after all this time?"

"Take Caitlin inside, Mam," Fiona said with barely concealed scorn. "I am sure Niall would *delight* in seeing Keefe again."

Fiona grabbed him by the arm, dragging him after her into the castle. Dark, dank, the floor littered, the ceiling laced with cobwebs. Niall reeled at the ruin of the home he had abandoned. Even in his nightmares, it had remained glorious and pristine, draped in the riches he had once believed won by his father's heroism. Now he knew they had been spoils of his father's treachery.

He stumbled over something and righted himself as Fiona marched him into the buttery, grabbing half an oat cake from a barren shelf.

"What the devil is amiss here?" Niall raged. "When I left, there was plenty to care for you both!"

"Not even the servants would remain with us after Father was dead. Your precious Conn made certain of that."

Niall bristled. "Conn destroyed nothing! Any other chieftain would have sacked Castle Daire! He took not one thing belonging to our mother."

"You think Mam cared for the castle? Her pretty things, furnishings, clothing? Conn murdered her husband! Aye, and stole her son! But wait, Niall. You went willingly, did you not? You believed our father capable of the vilest betrayal. But not your precious Conn!"

"Curse it, Fiona—"

"He must have sent a dozen raiding parties back to Daire to show us his regard. They stole anything of value, broke anything they could not carry. They beat anyone foolhardy enough to remain at Daire for serving the household of a traitor."

A hard knot tightened in Niall's throat. "Nay . . . I do not believe it." He ground his teeth. Conn the Ever Truthful? Never would Niall have questioned his honesty. Yet had something not changed forever the moment Niall held Conn's order in his hand, commanding the death of an innocent girl the chieftain pretended to welcome with open arms?

Nay. Niall brought himself up sharply. Conn must have agonized for years, struggled to find some other way to overcome the prediction of doom surrounding Caitlin of the Lilies. In the end, the chieftain must have surrendered, bowed to his responsibility as a leader. Done what he thought was necessary to protect the others in his kingdom. What had it cost Conn to write that missive? Order Caitlin's death? And he had entrusted the task to Niall. Was that alone not evidence he was worthy of Niall's trust? Conn had put into the hands of his greatest enemy's son the very information that could destroy his rule as chieftain.

"Keefe was the last to go." Fiona's voice dragged Niall back to the present. "I forced him to leave Castle Daire. His loyalty had cost him a hand, and Conn's men had vowed to take the other if they found him here again!"

Niall's stomach twisted, the image of Keefe's crooked grin burning into his memory, those patient, deft hands never too busy to help an eager little boy. And yet it was unthinkable that anyone could work such acts of barbarism under the chieftain's command. "Conn could not have known what they were doing! All the kingdom knew Castle Daire was undefended. The raiders acted on their own. They came, driven by their own greed and their thirst for vengeance against a traitor they hated."

"They came under Conn's orders to make certain we

could never strike back. You do not believe me? I was here, Niall! I listened to them terrorizing the people. Saw the blade that severed Keefe's hand . . ." Her voice broke, and Niall could only imagine what that had cost her—so young, bursting with emotion, loyal to a fault.

"Fiona, you have no proof Conn gave such an order. Perhaps they *were* his men—warriors sometimes get drunk with blood lust. They do things they imagine fulfill their chieftain's wishes, *not* his orders. Or they do things that fulfill their own desires."

"Aye, make excuses for Conn, Niall. It is what you are best at. Why should you believe me when you would not believe your own father!" Her voice broke. She flushed, tightening her mouth with fury against it.

"Our father told me himself what he had done. Confessed before he met the death he deserved." Niall remembered it far too clearly, the dank cell reeking of hopelessness, his father's eyes glowing like hot embers. *I have brought this evil upon myself, my son. I have betrayed my chieftain, your mother, and you.*

"Liar!" Fiona burst out. "Nothing would ever make me believe . . ." She stopped, glared at him. "For as long as you stay at Castle Daire, you will say no more about Father!"

Silence fell between them, full of loathing and pain. After a moment, Fiona sucked in a shuddering breath. "Your own worthless hide should be safe enough here. It seems we were finally made wretched enough even to satisfy your chieftain. He has not sent anyone to Daire for the past three years." She grabbed up an oat cake, started to storm out the door. Then she stopped, turned, a single shaft of sunlight glinting on her shaggy, bright hair.

"You will say nothing to Mam about any of this. Something broke in her mind after Father was killed.

She still believes Keefe snares our meat and Fergus tends the oats and Etain mends her clothes. She does not see—no matter how terrible things are, she does not see. It is the only thing that makes life bearable here. Leave her as you found her, Niall. If you shatter her peace, I will kill you."

Niall watched his sister turn, stalk away, rigid with pride. His stomach churned. His head spun. The whole world had gone mad.

What had happened here? Conn had vowed to Niall that Daire had been left untouched. So sincere, the chieftain had seemed, so genuinely grieved that Niall's mother and sister refused the shelter he had offered them.

Niall could see the chieftain's broad brow creased with regret, his battle-scarred hand stroking his gleaming red mustache. *They are innocent, not at fault for your father's decisions. He, alone, was the betrayer. I will not see them suffer, Niall, any more than I will allow you to be punished for what he has done. Do you believe me?*

Niall had gazed up into that wonderful, strong face, believed with the faith of a lonely boy who had no one else to trust. But now . . .

Do you believe? Conn's question haunted him.

He did not know what he believed any longer. Conn had planned the murder of a sleeping woman he pretended to welcome with open arms. Yet if death were unavoidable, would not that swift, unexpected strike be a kind of mercy? Far less painful than feeling clawing terror as you listened to someone spew out useless explanations that would make no difference in your fate?

Aye, Conn had shown himself time and again to be merciful unless he had no other choice. It was unthinkable that the chieftain had ordered the ruin that lay all around Niall, condemned a women and a mere girl to near starvation because of a grudge decades old.

Whatever had happened long ago, there was only one man responsible for the destruction of Castle Daire. The man who had left it undefended for so long. The man who had let every warrior at Glenfluirse know that he did not care if the castle crumbled into dust. The man who had left the defense of his mother and land to a stubborn, angry seventeen-year-old girl while he struggled to regain his own honor.

Only one thing was certain, Niall reasoned. He could not leave Fiona and his mother in this state. He had a week at most before Conn realized he was not returning to Glenfluirse, and then the hunt would begin.

Reeling, Niall sank onto a rough-hewn bench and buried his face in his hands. What the devil was he going to do?

Chapter

7

CAITLIN SAT on the three-legged bench Niall's mother had offered her, trying not to let it topple over and spill the crumbling oat cake into the pile of ashes the woman obviously thought was a blazing fire.

Her heart ached as she peered into the once-beautiful face, the mouth too sensitive, a body so delicate it seemed the tiniest brush of a butterfly's wing would make her crumble. But it was the older woman's smile that made Caitlin's throat tighten with unshed tears. It shone, luminous with joy at welcoming her son home.

Dear God, what had happened to them? Fiona and Niall and their mother? How had things gotten so muddled? Niall, with his powerful sense of duty and the gruff kindness he fought so hard to hide—he was a man who would never stand by and let his mother and sister suffer so terribly no matter what past bitterness lay between them. And no power on heaven or earth could shake the love Caitlin had seen in his mother's eyes. A gift more precious than Niall could ever imagine.

Even Fiona's anger seemed out of place, as if the reason the girl gripped it so tightly was to shield herself from loving her brother too much. Nothing at Castle Daire made sense.

Caitlin took another bite of oat cake, casting a sur- reptitious glance over her shoulder, hoping that Niall would appear and help her navigate the unfamiliar wa- ters of his family. But he had vanished as certainly as Fiona had.

For the hundredth time since the horrific moment she had awakened to find Niall standing over her with a sword, Caitlin wished she could run to Reverend Mother, bury her face in the abbess's lap, and cry out her pain, her confusion. Ask her what to do.

How many times had she watched the abbess tend the broken souls who had found their way to the abbey's gates? Always Reverend Mother had known what to do, what to say, how to wrap the love of God about them as if it were a warm robe. But Caitlin had always been the comforted one, the cherished one, pro- tected from whatever ugliness had haunted the eyes of those the abbess ministered to.

If only she knew what to say now to this woman whose misty eyes stared out at a world only she could see. If she only knew how to reach out to Fiona with her rage and her pain, and to Niall, who now looked far more battered than when she had pulled him up from the cliff ledge.

"Is the fire warm enough, my poor child?" Niall's mother scooped the moth-eaten robe from her own shoulders and tucked it around Caitlin.

"Nay," Caitlin protested. "I cannot—"

But the older woman only patted her hand, with such innate tenderness it reminded her of the abbess. "There, now. And have you not endured enough, *mo chroi*? Warm yourself, and tell me your troubles if it would ease your poor heart."

Caitlin's eyes burned. Had it been only four days since she had left the abbey? It seemed a thousand years had passed since anyone had spoken to her so tenderly. And yet she dared not burden this poor woman with her troubles. It was obvious Niall's mother had suffered enough. Caitlin fought to steady her voice.

"I would rather not speak of it. Not yet. Only know that without Niall's help, I would be dead now."

"Jesus, Mary, and Joseph preserve us!" The older woman pressed her hand to her heart, and for an instant something *real* flickered in her eyes, a reflection of horror, helplessness, the demons that had driven her deep into a world of her own making. Then, in a heartbeat, it was gone. "You need not fear now that you are under my Niall's protection," she said with an earnest smile. "So much like his father, he is. More honor and courage I never saw in a man."

Honor? Courage? But this was the father Niall claimed had burdened Niall with his shameful name, was he not? Yet during this mad journey, the world had turned shape-shifter. Nothing had been as it seemed. Any truth she wanted she would have to unearth for herself. Whatever that truth might be, her spirit reached out to this life-battered, bewildered woman who offered her compassion with such a generous heart.

"You are Niall's mother and Fiona's, and you remind me so very much of . . . someone I love." She could not stop the tears from glittering in her eyes. Her voice faltered. "But I do not know what to call you when I thank you for your kindness to me."

"Aniera is my name, but you have no need to thank me. My husband—he would rise from his very grave if ever we turned someone in need away from Castle Daire! This is your home for as long as you wish." Aniera smiled. "It will be good for my Fiona to have another woman about. She is too much alone."

Caitlin looked into Aniera's eyes, so like her son's, and saw a fleeting sorrow there. Buried beneath the brightness, the dream world she lived in, was there some part of her that understood how much she had lost and still grieved?

On impulse, Caitlin reached out, took Aniera's hand in her own, the bones so frail it seemed they could be crushed with the merest press of her fingers. How many times had Caitlin seen the abbess do just that—touching someone, letting silence offer succor when words could not? But Caitlin was not certain whom she was trying to comfort, Aniera or herself.

At that moment, she heard the hollow echo of footsteps approaching. She knew it was Niall even before she saw the glow light Aniera's eyes. Caitlin turned and tried not to let her dismay show as she looked into the face of the man who had taken her from St. Mary's.

Even if Conn's men hunted them, Caitlin doubted they would recognize the arrogant, invincible warrior who had charged away from court to win himself an honorable name. Dark shadows stained the skin beneath eyes burning with weariness and confusion, his hair a dark tangle where he had driven his fingers through it. Despite the burnishing of the sun he had ridden in, fought in, practiced skill at arms in for so long, a gray pallor clung to his face. Bewildered and bruised, he still squared his shoulders, fought to hide his distress from his oblivious mother.

"I thought I would show Caitlin to her room," he offered. "We rode long and hard to reach the castle, and I know she must be wearied."

Aniera made a *tsk*-ing sound in obvious distress. "Listen to me babbling on, and the poor child so tired she is nigh toppling off her seat! Is this the hospitality we offer at Castle Daire? Niall, I shall take her up at once so she might rest."

"Nay," Niall said too sharply. He gritted his teeth as he saw his mother flinch, confusion clouding her face. He forced himself to gentle his tone. "I would not trouble you, Mother. Caitlin is my charge, and we need some—some time alone."

At the inquisitive tilt of his mother's head, Niall rushed on.

"We need to plan what to do, in case the people searching for her should come."

"You need not make excuses to spend time alone with such a fair young woman, Niall," Aniera teased. "It is absurd. No one in Ireland would be rash enough to attack Castle Daire. Twice your father turned an army back from these walls when there were only ten men to defend it. Aye, Caitlin, it is true. Over all of Ireland, the bards still sing praises to the courage of Niall's father."

Caitlin saw one of Niall's hands curl into a fist. What must it have been like for a boy as proud as Niall to see that hero stumble and fall? To know that the songs of praise had died, and now his father was immortalized not for his courage but rather his infamy?

But Aniera's once-lovely features glowed with love and pride, faith unwavering as she thought of the man who had been her husband. "Niall, take our Caitlin to the Sea Chamber. Of all the fine rooms in Castle Daire, it is the most enchanting."

"The Sea Chamber?" Caitlin cast a questioning glance at Niall, knew that he, too, was remembering the splash of waves, moments of laughter as the sun-struck droplets turned diamond bright.

"I was born in the North before my love carried me away. I was so young, and everything was so unfamiliar here. I grew sick with longing for the sea. Though it tore his heart, my Ronan had to leave me, to sail away with warriors to some far place. When he returned, he barred himself in the room. I wept until my eyes were raw, thinking he did not love me, regretted our marriage. And then—" Aniera touched her lips with her fingertips, as if remembering a lover's kiss.

"He gathered me in his arms and carried me up the stairs to show me the magic he had wrought. The first night we shared in that room, a babe was planted in my womb. Aye, Niall. You. I am certain of it. And later, you were born in that bed, while your father sat beside me holding tight to my hand, and I looked across the chamber into my very own sea."

"I remember something of the tale," Niall admitted, discomfort darkening his face.

"It was your favorite game to climb about that bed, pretending it was a ship sailing off to fight fierce invaders. That you were like your father—brave enough to face the perils of wave and storm." She paused, looking past them, to some vision she alone could see.

"Do you remember, Niall? How you loved it? And your father, playing sea monster, snarling and growling and trying to drag you off the bed into the imaginary waves?"

Caitlin looked at Niall, her heart aching. Had he once been that little boy? Frolicking, carefree? Brave enough to play at monster because he knew that his father would always be there to chase any real ones away?

What had that boy suffered when his world came apart? And what hell had that father endured, a warrior compassionate enough to create a sea for the woman he loved? Or were these all Aniera's imaginings? Stitching beauty and tenderness across reality to make the ugliness bearable?

Was that the reason Niall had taken her to the sea? Caitlin wondered. In honor of the mother he had all but forgotten? An innate understanding of a longing for wave and shore that reached from the time of his first flickering memories?

"Go along, then, both of you." Aniera waved them away with one frail hand, doubtless wishing to be alone with her memories. "Caitlin and I, we will speak later."

Caitlin glanced up at Niall as she followed him away from the room where his mother now sat enthroned on the rickety stool, staring into ashes.

Every muscle in Niall's body was rigid, as if he were holding himself in check, battling the need to . . . what? Bolt away from this place and the devastation he saw every time he turned his head? What had he said to Fiona? That he would rather have hidden Caitlin in hell? She would well believe it. And yet he had come here, had faced all of this because of her.

With a furious swipe, he dashed away a spider's web large enough to trap a linnet and shoved open a wooden door. A tidal wave of dust curled into the air. Caitlin stifled a cough behind her hand, her eyes watering. She rubbed at her eyelids, trying to dash away the grit. When her vision cleared, she took her first tentative look at the chamber that was to be hers as long as they were at Castle Daire.

Light filtered into a surprisingly large room, setting it aglow with an aura that was otherworldly, as if they had stumbled into a castle lost through a fairy enchantment for a thousand years.

Caitlin gasped, gazing at walls covered with what must have once been glorious tapestries. White-capped waves almost seemed to dance, a gold-thread sun gleamed above, while sea creatures spun from a wondrous imagination frolicked in the glorious blue-green swells.

Exquisite shells, polished to perfection, seemed to breathe salt air into the room.

Caitlin touched the delicate web of a fisherman's net draped over the box of the bed. "It must have been so beautiful."

"Before the wood rotted and the bed was covered in grime?"

"Nay," Caitlin protested. "I did not say that."

Niall grasped the mouse-nibbled robes upon the bed box, flung them to the floor. He stripped his cloak from his shoulders and tossed it upon the bed.

"You must have thought it. Perhaps my mother does not see that she lives in a dung heap, but I am certain *you* noticed."

His words might have wounded her if she had not felt his pain. "Niall, I am far too grateful for shelter to care about a little dust."

"A little dust?" He gave a strangled laugh. "The accursed castle is practically crumbling atop their heads! But I did not know that they were suffering." He glared at her, as if daring her to believe him. "I never knew."

"Of course you did not."

Niall stared at her. "Is it so simple for you to believe a man whose very name screams of betrayal? Then you are a fool. I thought I was burdened by that name because of my father's shame. But look around you, Caitlin." He swept his hand in an arc about the wreckage of the chamber. "*I* betrayed my mother. *I* betrayed Fiona."

"You did not know!"

"I should have! What would it have cost me to make certain they had what food and shelter they needed? I would not even have had to come to Daire myself.

There were others I could have sent. But no. I was too angry. Too bitter. Too proud. Too consumed by the seven quests that would win back my honor. Tell me, Caitlin, where is that honor now?"

She wanted to help him drive away his pain, wanted to touch him, feared he would only dash her hand away. But she reached out, laid her fingertips upon the curve of his jaw. He jerked at her touch, as if she had stung him. "I am alive because of that honor," she said.

"Are you?" His mouth curled in mockery, self-loathing. "Have you not wondered for an instant if *this* did not save your life?" He grasped her chin, turned her face up to his.

Caitlin stared into his features, so hard, so desperate, his gaze devouring her face. Her heart raced. Hunger and loathing—never had she known they could mingle in one man's eyes. "I do not understand."

"If you were not so beautiful, Caitlin, do you think I would have hesitated to kill you?"

Her breath caught. Heat shimmered along the surface of her skin, reddening her cheeks. Beautiful, he thought her beautiful, and yet something ugly lay beneath his words—the possibility that he would have completed his dark mission if she had been plain, like sweet Sister Mary with her mouse-colored hair and pockmarked skin.

She winced, loathing the possibility that all men valued were mere accidents of birth, the cast of cheeks and lips, the color of eyes and hair, not traits earned by courage and strength and kindness.

Nay, it was too painful to think Niall would have let his sword fall upon any innocent woman. "I—I believe . . . I hope that you would not have hurt me, no matter how my face looked."

"Why? Because now that I have defied Conn's orders, you see me as some sort of hero? Have you learned nothing in the days since I took you from the abbey? To be wary. Not to trust anyone, especially me." He gave a snort of disgust. "You stumble into life, blind as any babe, seeing only what you wish to see."

She lifted her chin. "I do not believe you would have hurt me, Niall."

"We will never know for certain, will we, Caitlin? Either of us. Just as we will never know if I abandoned Castle Daire and everyone in it in search of honor or because I was running away." He turned and stalked out the door.

The arrow slit glowed silver with the night, a smattering of stars twinkling in the distant sky. Caitlin pressed her face against the rough stone surrounding the opening. Worlds away in the abbey, was Reverend Mother gazing out at the same stars, thinking of her?

It seemed an eternity had passed since she had left St. Mary's. But there, everything would go on the same—murmured prayers, weeding the garden, stitching and mending and scrubbing the stone floors. And that wondrous, sweetest of all hours, before sleep, when the air was filled with serenity, and love whispered with every breath of the wind.

Caitlin's eyes stung, her throat ached. If she were home now, she would be leaning against Reverend Mother's knee, the comb stroking rhythmically through her hair as if the abbess held the power to untangle all the troubles of the day. And she had—she always had made Caitlin feel better, ready to begin again. But now there was no one to promise her everything would turn out well. Hunted, her death ordered by Conn, it was as if some dark enchantment had spilled a river between Caitlin and those she loved, one she could never get back across.

"I do not know what to do, Reverend Mother," she whispered, her throat aching. "This whole castle sorrows. And I . . . I do not belong anywhere at all."

She blinked back tears, remembering so many times the abbess had taken her hand, led her out into the garden when she could not sleep. *Look above you, Caitlin, my child. You can never be alone. The stars are angels watching over you. As I will, even when you are grown and gone away.*

The echo hurt, and yet she clung to it, picturing it all so clearly, the night-veiled garden, Reverend Mother, her face turned up to the sky, a soft smile curving her lips. And in that moment, Caitlin knew she needed to see the broad sweep of heavens, boundless as the love the holy woman had given her.

Uncertain of the direction she should take and yet determined to find the path outside if it took her the rest of the night, Caitlin made her way out of the chamber, trying to remember the path she had taken with Niall.

Three times she got lost, managed to trace her way back to her room. On the fourth attempt, she all but plunged down the narrow stone stairs. A wry laugh broke from her lips. At least one good thing would happen if she fell and broke her neck in this attempt. Niall could deliver her to Conn and could charge back into his old life as if nothing had gone awry.

Nay, she thought with sadness as she eased down one uneven riser after another. No power in heaven or earth could give Niall back the life he had known before, any more than Caitlin could reclaim her own sweet past at the abbey. He had seen the wreck of this castle, the suffering of his mother, the hatred of his sister. He had broken his oath to his chieftain.

She should have been grateful once she reached the main hall. Either Fiona or Niall had built a fire in the hearth, and it cast enough light that she could pick her way through the maze of debris without bruising herself in more than three places.

But all she could feel was grief. So much had been lost in the days since she had ridden out of the abbey gates in Niall's arms.

She pushed open the great, heavy wood door, a wave of sweet night air washing over her. Grateful, she slipped out of the shadow of the castle, wanting to see the full sweep of sky. She could stare up into the heavens, close out all earthbound things around her. Imagine until the sun rose that she was in the garden at home.

But she had barely taken ten steps when a voice rumbled, making her heart slam against her ribs.

"I would not run, Caitlin. Alone in the wildlands, you would be dead before the moon wanes."

"Niall!" She stared at the man stretched out on the ground a mere arm's length away from her, his powerful body all but lost in the shadows. "Wh-what are you doing here?"

He threw back a tattered plaide he was using to keep warm in the chill night air. "I vowed never to spend another night under the roof of Castle Daire. Considering all the other oaths I have broken the past few days, I decided I would keep this one."

He levered himself to a sitting position, his hair tousled in the starlight. "Tell me, Caitlin of the Lilies, what are you running from? Spiders the size of a cat? An army of mice mounting a charge across your bed?"

"I am not running at all," she said, a little indignant. "I only wished to see the stars."

"I find that difficult to believe." Bracing one hand

against the ground, he climbed to his feet. "The stars must have been visible from the window of your chamber, and no sane person would risk falling to her death down those stairs just to see the sky."

"Perhaps she would if she were lonely. Missing home." Her voice caught, and she turned away, regretting her admission. "Why do I even try to explain? You would never understand."

Niall shrugged one powerful shoulder. "I have never attempted to understand anything save war. The battlefield is the only home I need."

Why did his indifference tug so at her heart? "If that is true, I ache for you and for those who love you," she said softly.

She could feel the tension pouring through him, his shoulders squaring, voice hardening. "I need none of your pity. And as for this love you speak of? Tell me, did you see it in my sister's eyes? She would have gloried in using that sword against me."

"She is angry. Hurting and afraid. She needs you to help her heal. And your mother, Niall. Surely, you saw how she looked at you? As if you placed the sun in her sky."

"She did not see me," Niall sneered. "She saw a boy who does not even exist any longer. A son who died with his father's honor."

"You beat your way into life beneath her heart, Niall. She loved you long before you were born. Nothing, not time or blame, stubbornness or the mists of her dream world, can change that. You have a chance to come to know each other again. Hard as it might be to take that risk, it is a rare gift. A second chance to know your mother. One I envy you."

He cut her off with a fierce wave of his hand. "I will do what I can for my mother and Fiona. But if you are indulging in a bout of female meddling, trying to mend things among the three of us, I would advise you to save yourself the effort. I will tend to their needs because I am duty bound, but that is all."

"You cannot possibly know what it is you are throwing away. But then, do any of us understand before it is too late?" She paced a few steps away from him. Her eyes turned up to the stars.

"All my years at the abbey, I was such a fool. Always waiting for my precious destiny to claim me. So eager, so certain I would embark upon some glorious grand adventure. The older I grew, the more restless I became, impatient, so eager to begin this wondrous new life."

She gave a strained laugh. "I never realized how much I would miss the people who loved me. I never knew that the days I sometimes hated, each so much the same, were so incredibly precious. I had everything I could ever wish for there within the abbey walls."

She turned to find him standing far too close.

"You are no woman destined to be locked behind those walls. You are frightened now, but if you returned to the abbey tomorrow, I vow to you, the restlessness would begin again, and you would find yourself peering over the walls, wondering what lay beyond."

"Nay. I have lived a lifetime in the days since I left the abbey. Learned what lies beyond the walls. Treachery and hate, pain and greed. And courage," she added softly, looking up at him. "But even courage brought only disaster. It has cost you more than I can ever repay."

"You owe me nothing," he said stiffly.

Caitlin sighed, hugging her arms tight about her middle. "I wish I could return to the abbey, wipe away all the harm I have done you. Leave you as you were when I found you sleeping upon the druid stone." Had the wistfulness crept into her voice? His gentled.

"We can never return to that place, that time, Caitlin," he said, gazing down at her, the rugged planes and hollows of his face awash with mysteries ancient as the standing stones. "Even if some enchantment could carry us back, I would not go. Conn would only send another warrior. Another hand to hold the sword over your head. I still do not know if I did right when I spared your life, what my defiance might cost you, my chieftain, or the people of Glenfluirse. The one thing I am certain of is this: a cloistered life in the abbey is not the future you were born to."

"But I love the sisters, and they love me. I was safe there."

The moonlight struck his face, and Caitlin was surprised to see his lips curl in a half-smile. "You spoke of destiny," Niall said. "If you were fated for a nunnery, you would not have been given *this*." He ran his fingertips lightly over the arch of her cheek. Caitlin trembled.

"A face fair as the lily you were searching for the day I first saw you. Aye." His voice dropped low. "That is what you are. Lily fair. No man who saw you could ever let you lock yourself away from his sight."

Strange, such beautiful words coming from this hard warrior. Never would she have expected them. Longing pulsed in Caitlin for something she could not name. Alone, she felt so alone. Yet was not Niall alone, too? Needing . . . what? Someone to touch? Someone to hold?

Caitlin dared a glance up at him, stunned at the impulse to turn her face just a bit, let her lips brush against his battle-hardened palm. Scarce believing her own boldness, she whispered, "Would it trouble you, Niall? To see me go back to the abbey?"

Silence fell for a heartbeat. She heard him swallow hard as he drew his hand away. "Caitlin, you must not think of me as if I were like other men. Free to . . ." He stopped. Even by moonlight, she could see the intensity in his face. "I made a blood oath never to entangle my fate with that of a woman."

"Did some lady break your heart?" Why did the thought hurt her so? Make her hate that unnamed woman?

"It was lust for a woman that destroyed my father."

That tragedy again, that old pain stealing away so much. It was as if his whole future had shattered with his father's death. Had he lost more than his mother, his sister, this castle he must have once loved? Had he lost any hope of loving anyone ever again? The terrible waste sickened her. And yet had she not stolen from him as well? Not knowing what she had done until it was too late?

"Perhaps you are wise to be wary of me." Caitlin felt tears burn the backs of her eyes. "I have already destroyed everything you have worked for. You will never fulfill your quest because of me. The chieftain's trust will be shattered. You claim the battlefield is your home. For whom will you fight now, Niall?"

"For you. Caitlin of the Lilies. Bold Fintan's daughter. I will fight for you until you are safe, or I have given my last drop of blood."

There were men who would do all in their power to kill her, yet Niall was willing to place his body between Caitlin and their swords. His pronouncement should have comforted her, at least made her feel protected. Why, then, did it stir her anger?

"You will die for me, but you will not trust me. You will do your duty by your mother and sister, this castle, but you will not love them. Your home is the battlefield, where death is glorious. What about *life*, Niall?"

His face clouded with irritation, surprise. What had he expected? Gratitude? Some speech praising his courage, his heroism? "You talk in riddles," he growled.

"Nay. It is simple enough to understand. I see you standing here, so brave, so—so beautiful and strong, and I cannot bear the path you have chosen. Tell me. What brings you joy, Niall? What makes you laugh? Who in the world knows your secret sadness? Your faults? Those tender, painful places in your soul?"

"I need no one," he bit out savagely.

"Your heart is still beating, Niall, and yet you are already dead."

With an oath, he grabbed her by the arms, gave her a shake. "I wish I were deadened the way you claim! If I were, I would not feel what I do now!"

"Niall of the Seven Betrayals allowing himself to feel something besides bitterness and blame? I cannot believe it."

"It is your accursed fault! Every time I look at you, I want—"

Her blood raced. "You want what, Niall? You stand there, scowling at me, the way you did near the sea, not daring to come down, to touch the water, embrace the beauty of it all. Why? Because you have chosen to deny yourself anything that makes life worth having?"

Her fingers clenched, and she remembered how she had first seen him like a lord of the otherworld sleeping beneath some dark enchantment, oblivious to all around him. He had seemed like a breathing dream, all magic and possibilities. Now so much of him seemed drained of passion, of hope, imprisoned by gray walls she could not see. And she wanted to hurt him. Hurt him enough to break down that barrier, waken him from the spell he had cast upon himself.

Her chin bumped up a notch, and she looked straight

into his eyes. "It seems your name fits you far better than I had guessed," she told him. "Niall of the Seven Betrayals. You betray every gift life has offered you."

She started to pull away, to return to the castle, but his grip tightened.

"What *gifts* has life offered? Betrayal, hatred, lies—"

"Love and laughter and the beauty of the sun rising each morn. The gift of a new day, unblemished, fresh and clean, where everyone can begin again no matter what mistakes we have made. We all make mistakes, Niall. Hurt people, fail them. But when morning comes, we get the chance to decide whether to cling to the hurts or free our hearts to joy. Let the pain go."

"Is that what you are doing, Caitlin, with those accursed fairy-blue eyes of yours? Daring me to take these gifts of yours? Mayhap you are everything Conn feared, a powerful enchantress bewitching me. Wakening in me this accursed hunger, a magic spell cast so I would betray my chieftain and spare your life."

Storms raged through him. She could feel them pulse into her through the palms of his hands. For a heartbeat, she wanted to flee, afraid of the tempest she had stirred inside him. But she plunged into the center of Niall's inner storm, just as she had plunged into the sea.

"I wish I *was* a sorceress! Possessed of enough magic to make you open your eyes, see what you have become! A coward, far too afraid to feel anything but hate."

"You want to know what I *feel*, woman?" A low snarl breached Niall's lips. "I feel *this*, curse you! Aye, Caitlin, I feel this!" With an oath, he dragged her against him. His mouth closed over hers, hard and hot, more dizzying than the currents that had nearly pulled her out to sea. She reeled at the wonder of it. Melting honey, hot mead, passion sweeping an unquenchable fire through every fiber of her being.

Niall's mouth burned its contours into hers, maddened with a hunger so fierce it terrified her. Inflamed her. Knees weak, body trembling, Caitlin wound her arms around his taut waist to keep from crumpling to the ground. The soft globes of her breasts yielded against his chest and she felt the hammering of his heart like a wild stag trapped, as his hands swept over the hollow of her back, the flare of her hip, the thin cloth of her leine scarce a barrier between them.

He buried one hand in the tumbled black waves of her hair, tipping her head back to bare her throat. His mouth coursed down her cheek, nuzzling that vulnerable white skin, nipping at her neck with fierce tenderness. One large hand swept up between them to where her breasts were aching.

Nay, Caitlin thought, this was wrong. What had seemed a dare had gone too far. She should not allow this to happen. But she had not *allowed* it. She had *embraced* it. Needed so much more. She could not breathe, waiting for the shift of Niall's big hand onto her breast. She dared not turn her body into that caress, knew she should move away. But she only froze, so still, wanting . . . wanting.

A low groan reverberated from Niall's chest as his fingers edged up, brushing the outer curve of her breast, then his battle-hardened palm slid over the aching globe, enclosing it. Pleasure so intense that it stunned her pulsed through Caitlin. She moaned softly as his thumb skimmed over her nipple with exquisite tenderness. "Niall . . . ah, Niall . . . never did I even imagine . . ."

Niall froze. As suddenly as the storm had broken, it was over. He grasped her shoulders, pushing her away.

"Nay, Caitlin! We will not do this! I am sworn to protect you, not—"

His voice caught. His eyes burned black in the moonlight with rage, with wonder, with need and a denial that cut Caitlin deep. "Curse you, woman! What have you done to me?"

Caitlin met his gaze, praying her quaking legs would support her. "What have I done?" She gave a ragged laugh. "Reminded you of something, Niall. When I was—was in your arms and . . ." She stumbled on the words, her cheeks burning at the memory of the passion that had flared between them. But she raised her chin, defiant. "*That* is what it feels like to be alive."

She pulled away from him and all but ran back to the castle, scrambled up to her room, heedless of the bumps and bruises she gained on the way.

But no matter how long she tossed and turned upon Aniera's sea-spun bed, sleep eluded her. The night was filled with a mouth hot as fire, hands impossibly strong, and eyes burning with loathing for the woman who had dared to discover the greatest enemy Niall of the Seven Betrayals had ever faced.

Despair.

Chapter

8

WHAT THE DEVIL had he done? Niall watched Caitlin disappear into Castle Daire, the soft linen of her leine rippling behind her, her hair a dark tangle tumbling down her back. And he wondered, was she so innocent that she did not know? No matter how many stone walls she put between them, neither she nor Niall could ever escape what they had done. Kissed beneath Caitlin's stars as if their very souls were starving, aye, and his body . . .

Niall stalked a few steps toward the castle. Forced himself to halt. Every muscle he possessed strained toward her, demanding that he follow her, scoop her up into his arms. Carry her up to the sea bed and show his convent-bred lady just what beast she had aroused in him.

Need sharper than any sword blade that had ever bitten into his flesh. Passion so hot it burned reason away. Yet had she not stolen his reason days ago in that frozen instant when he had looked into her terror-wide eyes and known he could not kill her?

Why? Not because of honor, nobility, not even because of mercy. But because from the first moment he had seen her, she had stolen his breath away.

Beauty. He had heard bards sing about it, trailing

their fingers over their harp strings as they spun tales of ages-old lovers who had cast their lives to the fates because of passion. Yet always Niall had scorned those star-crossed lovers. Succumbing to such passion was just another excuse for weakness. A warrior should not be slave to the shape of a woman's mouth, her eyes beckoning him. Loyalty, courage, duty were the only goddesses a fighting man should worship.

And it had been enough to hold to that code of honor in the past. He had simple, carnal hungers like any man. He dealt with them as he had dealt with countless foes across a battlefield: swiftly and with finality. He had made certain any lady he dallied with understood he had nothing to give her but one night in his bed. Stripping away such needs had been simple, leaving him with nothing but vague dissatisfaction and a hard-edged amusement after the encounter was done.

But there had been no time to rally those defenses when Caitlin had glided toward him like a fairy wraith in the night. She had lanced deep into hidden places, dark, secret pain. She had dared him to *feel*.

And when they had crossed swords, there in the night, she had won, God curse her! Never in all his years had he felt such sensation, raw, overwhelming, devouring him from inside—as if all the life that pulsed and shimmered within Caitlin's lithe body had rushed into his veins, filling him, showing him exactly how empty he was.

Niall gave a bitter laugh. As if he needed anyone to show him that, here, standing in the crumbling ruins of Castle Daire, with his mother's face still haunting him and his sister's hatred digging like talons into the heart he had pretended not to have for so long.

Had Caitlin known? Had she sensed that he lay in the shadow of that tree, torn by an agony he had all but forgotten? Blessed by some fairy magic as her exalted father had been, had she bent her ear to the tiny window in the Sea Chamber and heard the voices that would give Niall no peace?

Not his mother's screams as they dragged his father away. Nay, the ghosts that had stalked him this night were far different ones. Faint images of what might have been if his father had been the hero Niall had believed him to be as a child. Echoes of his mother's laughter, sweet as summer rain. Fiona, plump-cheeked, two fingers thrust resolutely into her mouth as she toddled after him, clinging determinedly to whatever bit of his clothing she could grasp.

What kind of man might that boy have grown to be? Arrogant, so certain life would cast before him all the wonder he could hold if he only held fast to his duty, his honor, proved himself worthy to be the brave Ronan's son.

But it did not matter what might have been. Those years had merely been a sweet-tasting poison. Lies that had destroyed his mother, Fiona, aye, and the boy Niall had been.

And as if he had not been tortured enough to satisfy whatever demons were loose in the night, Caitlin had come. Floating through the moonlight like a fairy maiden, her leine shimmering about her in gossamer wings, her face soft as the dreams Niall had never had.

And for an instant, just an instant, Niall had seen the man he had imagined, the man he might have been, opening his arms to that woman of wondrous light.

Nay, she had caught him unaware, that was all. And he had tasted only lust upon her lips. Hunger of the body fed by anger, uncertainty, not something deeper. He need not concern himself. It was merely the instinct of any warrior, to conquer a creature wild and lovely, spirited and defiant.

And he had far more fortitude than many another man. He had spent every moment since he reached Conn's court hardening himself, learning that virtue his father had never mastered. Control.

The control that banished pain in a warrior cut and bleeding, allowing him to fight on. The control that guarded a man's secret weaknesses, hiding them from his enemies. The control that held a man's lust at bay when honor demanded it.

Niall's jaw set, grim. This flare of desire for Caitlin had been a moment of madness, that was all. Within days, he would have a price upon his head. Conn, renowned for his honesty, was also thorough. For any ruler who hoped to hold his lands, reprisal for one who defied him must be swift, severe.

And yet . . . Niall closed his eyes, remembering Conn's face countless times when people had dared to scorn the son of Ronan the Betrayer. Always affection had flickered in Conn's gaze when he glimpsed his foster son, and Niall could almost hear his thoughts. *Do not heed them. You are my son. You fill my heart with pride.*

A fine sheen of sweat dampened Niall's forehead, and his hands clenched into fists as he imagined approaching his liege again, kneeling before him, telling him the truth of what had happened.

What would it feel like? Witnessing Conn's shock at the conditions at Castle Daire, his willingness to do all in his power to make things right there? Niall could see the chieftain's rage and swift retribution against those bloody scavengers who had picked the castle's bones.

It would banish every shadow of Fiona's dark accusations, put to rest forever the nagging doubts that had tormented Niall, no matter how fiercely he denied they could be true.

Would it not be wiser to trust in that affection—the honor and generosity Niall knew Conn to be capable of—than to sit here waiting for his fate to overtake him?

He had enemies aplenty at Glenfluirse who would delight in killing him before he had the chance to speak before the chieftain, sway Conn to show mercy. Niall could ride alone back to Conn's fortress. He could ask for Caitlin's life, implore Conn to let him take her back to the abbey. If she swore never to leave its walls, she could not doom Conn or his domain. Surely, Conn would allow it.

Or would he? Conn must have considered leaving Caitlin at the abbey and dismissed it. What would Niall do if Conn forgave him, embraced him, yet still condemned Caitlin to death?

Caitlin's fate would no longer be in Niall's hands. A chill pricked Niall's flesh as he glanced up at the window of her chamber. For an instant, he thought he saw her there—a ripple of ebony hair, a crescent of flawless cheek, so warm, so pure, her only crime being born beneath a druid prediction of doom.

Predictions her cloistered sisters would dismiss as pagan nonsense, while Conn was willing to have her murdered to keep the prophecy from coming to pass.

Even if he dared risk his own life by returning to Conn, Niall reasoned grimly, how could he take such a gamble with Caitlin's life?

Niall flung himself back onto the ground, wrapping himself in the tattered cloak he had unearthed somewhere in the castle. Frustration jabbed at him more certainly than the twig caught beneath him. Was she mad, desiring a man like him? He grimaced. She had pulled him up from a cliff after he had tried to kill her. Of course, the woman was mad. Mad with innocence and sweet dreams. Niall stiffened, resolutely dragging his mind from ripe lips and eyes glowing with eagerness. There could be no turning back from the course they had taken. But he *could* control what happened between himself and Fintan's daughter from now on.

Never again would he touch her, kiss her, no matter how much Caitlin and the clamoring of his own body goaded him. For if he failed to protect her from Conn's decree of death, it would only make it harder watching her die.

Something akin to fear drove deep, terrifying Niall with its power. Iron bars turning a rocky cave into prison, his father's face all but unrecognizable through the grime. Niall had been too young, too innocent to know the ugly fate that awaited such a prisoner then. He was ages older now.

Nay, he would not see Caitlin suffer such a fate. Niall's teeth clenched. He had to plan, think what to do. Leave Conn's holdings? If only that would be enough. But the chieftain's power reached as far across Ireland as the color green. Any enemy whose fortress offered sanctuary to fugitives might also be willing to return them to their chieftain if the blood price were high enough. And Niall was certain Conn would cast half his wealth to the wind to capture the warrior who had betrayed him and the woman who might hold the power to topple his rule.

Niall needed time, time to think, to plan. How the devil could he win it?

Niall rolled onto his side, heard the crumple of vellum beneath his weight. Conn's missive, ordering Caitlin's death. He froze. What if he sent Conn a message of his own? Declare Caitlin dead and ask for some weeks alone to deal with the murder he had done? Conn would believe him. The certainty dampened Niall's brow with sweat. Aye, the chieftain would trust in his beloved foster son.

But to lie to the leader to whom he had sworn allegiance—more sickening still, to lie to the man who had loved him as a son . . .

He would sooner cut his own throat before he told a falsehood to Conn. Yet honor seemed a worthless thing when compared to Caitlin's execution, Fiona and his mother's deaths by slow starvation.

Stomach churning, Niall rose and entered the castle. He rummaged about until he found writing implements, scrawled a letter to Conn. He stared down at the drying ink, desperate to fling the vellum into the fire, but he could not. He would send it by the first trustworthy messenger he could find come daybreak.

Tucking the missive into his pouch, he returned to his ragged cloak and lay, staring at the sky until dreams came stalking.

The great hall of Conn's fortress glowed with a score of torches, vast tables groaning beneath the weight of a victory feast. Niall strode into the chamber, body aching from battle, his head held high.

Glorious, it was glorious, striding among the other warriors, their envious looks glancing off him as if he had been given some magic shield to deflect their jealousy, for nothing could grieve Niall as he looked to the head of the table and saw Conn standing there.

Resplendent, the chieftain's mantle flowed about him, his red mustache seeming to catch fire. Those eyes, so intelligent, so intense, glittered with pride.

"My son has made you all look like stumbling fools yet again on the field of battle," Conn bellowed so it seemed all Ireland must hear him. "I decree that the champion's portion belongs to Niall of the Seven Betrayals. The finest warrior in all of Glenfluirse."

Pleasure burned through Niall, so fierce he ignored the hostile glint hidden behind the smiles of the other warriors as they raised their tankards to salute him. He grasped Conn's approval tightly, glad to have repaid him just a little for the kindness and generosity he had shown.

Aye, it was magnificent—this surge of triumph, secure in Conn's favor, certain of loyalty, honor, the duty he must serve. All that Niall believed in.

He moved toward Conn and the haunch of meat that awaited him. But no matter how fast he strode, it seemed Conn drifted farther and farther away.

Niall fought a jab of panic and broke into a run, but smoke swirled up, stinging his eyes, blurring his vision. When he broke through the haze at last, he stumbled to a halt. Sick with horror and denial as the gray stone of Castle Daire loomed above him.

Niall woke with a start, clawing his way upright. Nay, it was but a dream—a dream, he assured himself, his skin dampened with sweat. He need only look about him, see the familiar boundaries of Conn's fortress.

Yet as Niall's desperate gaze searched about him, he froze, sick with disbelief. He glared at the stone walls of Castle Daire, enraged to find them looming over him like some gray demon. The reality of it all struck him like a javelin in his gut. His fury when he had discovered what quest Conn had sent him on. His frustration in dealing with a convent-bred girl half terrified of him. Then the missive, gleaming as he read it in the firelight. The unthinkable choice. Killing Caitlin as she slept or turning his back on everything he believed in.

A low groan escaped Niall's lips as he levered himself

to his feet. God's blood, living the beauty of that dream and awakening to this—it was like losing everything he valued yet again.

He stood, the damp penetrating to his very bones, his body aching from the bruises he had gained when he had tumbled to the ledge. He wanted nothing more than to curl back into the cloak, to dream again that nothing had changed. But that was impossible. He had to do what he could to make things right for Fiona and his mother. Aye, and to prepare for whatever retribution would come once Conn discovered what his trusted foster son had done.

Touching the pouch where he had stored the missive he had scribed to Conn last night, Niall crossed to the castle door with all the resolution and pleasure of a man walking to his own execution. He strode into the great hall, but no amount of determination could stop the wave of sick guilt and resentment washing through him.

The fire was glowing, but the chamber seemed empty enough. Relieved, Niall paced to the center of the room. Aye, this bit of time would be a mercy, time enough for him to master his emotions before his mother trailed in with her dream-misted eyes, Fiona with her loathing, and Caitlin with her stark uncertainty.

He could gather what few wits he had left, and— It was a hopeless task. His wits were still shattered by the press of soft lips in the moonlight, the bewitching scent of night wind and innocence that had rippled from Caitlin's black veil of hair.

The power of the encounter last night flooded back to him, pulsing through his veins—hot desire, the sweet invitation of Caitlin's breasts against his chest, the hardened buds of her nipples beckoning through the thin wisp of cloth that separated his body from hers. Aye, he remembered it all with painful clarity, but most torturous of all was the knowledge that not only had his body cried out for the lady in his arms, but another cry had reverberated through him in those forbidden moments—some lost, all but forgotten cry of his soul.

Niall winced. How would it be to look into those lake-blue eyes in the harsh light of morning? Excruciating . . .

Hearing a soft scraping sound somewhere above him, he paused. Determined not to let even the castle mouse see his torment, Niall hardened his features into a harsh mask. He turned his face upward just as a wave of something cold, wet, and muddy drenched him. He roared a curse, leaping aside with a warrior's instincts as a bucket clattered onto the floor a mere hand's breadth from where he had stood.

Swiping the mess from his eyes, Niall glared up to see Fiona, balanced precariously on a wooden beam high above him, a smug smile on her pixie face.

"Niall! Och, a hundred thousand pardons! I lost my balance, and—"

A flash of dark hair and soft linen dashed through the far door before she could finish. Caitlin stood, breathless, brandishing a wooden table leg as if it were a sword.

"I heard the noise. Feared that Conn might have found us. Nay, it is too soon. Perhaps thieves—" She shook back hair mussed with the restlessness of sleep, her eyes wide and misty and a little startled. Niall knew the instant she remembered the kiss. Color burned up her cheeks. She swallowed hard. "Niall . . . your face. It is full of mud."

Niall glared up at his sister, planning to strangle her the instant he figured out a way to get her down.

"What—what happened?" Caitlin asked.

Niall slashed her a blistering glare, humiliation and anger raging inside him. "The hell-born babe ambushed me!"

"I did no such thing!" Fiona swung her feet to and fro. "I was merely scrubbing things up in honor of your guest, Niall, as hospitality demands. I lost my balance and almost fell. Of course, if I had been thinking, I would have obliged you and fallen and broken my neck. One less burden you would have had to bear."

"Curse it, Fiona." Niall swiped the worst of the muck from his face. "I swear, I—"

"I told you to call me Finn."

"Niall, surely it was an accident," Caitlin intervened.

"I will believe that the instant *Finn* tells me what she was intending to clean up there. Did someone discover that mud and water act to preserve wood?"

Fiona peered at him, big-eyed with innocence. "There was a great deal of dirt up here. No one has cleaned it for . . ." She shrugged. "I can never remember anyone cleaning here at all."

She whipped her feet over the length of wood, teetering precariously for a heartbeat. Niall made a grab for Fiona, Caitlin's scream ringing out.

"Careful! You might fall—"

"I gave up being afraid of dancing on rafters long ago," Fiona said, shinnying down. "When there is never anyone to catch you, it stops mattering if you fall, does it not, Niall?"

She leapt to the floor with a grand flourish, and Niall wanted to throttle her. "You should wash your face, *brother*. You would not want your precious Conn to find you thus. Most uncivilized, being executed in such a deplorable condition."

Niall ground his teeth. As if it mattered how dirty his face was—his honor was soiled beyond repair. The ugly truth rang in his head. *I am going to betray my chieftain.*

Why he felt compelled to say any more he could scarce explain, except that Caitlin's worried expression tugged at him. "I am riding to get us something decent to eat," he growled. "I will not return for some time."

"*I* provide whatever goes upon the table at Castle Daire!" Fiona bristled. "I have kept us well enough until now!"

His anger at Fiona and at himself burst free. "You are all but starving. Thin as reeds, both you and Mother! By God, I—"

"It is none of your affair, Niall! We have taken care of ourselves these past years, and we will manage again once you are gone! You will have enough trouble of your own keeping Caitlin safe, considering the way you keep looking at her—as if you want to gobble her up."

Niall's face burned. Caitlin's fingers touched her mouth in dismay, as if she thought the evidence of their kiss had been seared upon her lips like a brand.

"Ah, so you have already stolen a sample of her charms, oh great and honorable brother of mine! The question is how greedy you became."

"Fiona," Caitlin breathed, "I pray you, do not—"

He wanted to bellow a denial, but he knew it would only make him look more foolish. Caitlin's face shone unrelentingly honest. Rage poured through Niall, fiercer than any he had felt on a field of battle.

"Fiona, damn you, girl, not another word, or I will—"

"Fiona? Niall?" A soft, worried voice came from the doorway. Aniera stood, a reed basket in her arms, creamy white clusters of elderflowers spilling over the edge.

All three turned, Caitlin fiery-cheeked and aghast, Niall fighting to master his temper and his embarrassment, Fiona with a measure of her boldness draining away. The girl glanced from her mother to Niall, a worried pucker between her brows. Curse the demon child for suddenly looking as vulnerable as a spring lamb.

"What is this about?" Aniera queried.

Your daughter is a fiend, Niall wanted to rage. Instead, he wrestled his temper into silence.

"An accident," Niall bit out. "No harm done. I will return later with meat for the fire." He started to stalk out, but his mother's hand caught him. With the edge of her sleeve, she wiped at the mud still clinging to his brow.

"Why do you not take Fiona with you? You know how she loves to trail about after you."

"Nay!" Niall snapped. "I want a moment of peace. Is that too much to ask?"

Aniera's mouth dropped open, her eyes wide. "Niall, treasure, what is amiss between you and the wee one?"

What was wrong between him and his sister? Fiona despised him. Niall was stunned by a sudden swift jab of grief. His heart had been stone-hard when he had ridden from Glenfluirse. It was Caitlin's meddling that had made him vulnerable to Fiona's barbs. Damn the woman for throwing open gates where he had held inconvenient emotion imprisoned for so long. But lashing out at his mother would only cause more pain, reveal weakness to Fiona, and allow Caitlin to see how deeply she had cut into his defenses.

Niall fought for control, grimaced. "Forgive me, Mother. I am tired from the journey."

"Aye, and worried about our Caitlin, I know. Do not fear, son. Nothing ill can befall you here. Not with your father's love all around you."

He slashed a furious glance around the hall, where the furnishings lay smashed, all former glory stripped away. *This* is what his father's *love* had bought them, Niall wanted to rage. But when he turned back to his mother, he could not say it. She was too fragile, her face still reflecting love and loyalty. Misplaced devotion to a traitor, which had caused Niall such pain to see that he had turned his back on her years ago.

But he had been a boy then, dwelling in a boy's world of right and wrong, light and dark, where heroes never stumbled, their brilliance was never tarnished.

Now he knew how easy it was to be lured from the straight hero's path onto terrain less certain. One woman's laugh, eyes that shone light into the dark corners of his soul, and he had nearly been lost.

Niall pictured his father's face the last time he had seen him, an anguished plea in his eyes, love. How Niall had hated it that the father who had betrayed him still dared to show that love. Niall bit back the bitter wave of understanding. But when his father had become obsessed with another woman's charms, he had a wife who adored him, a tiny, willful daughter, and a son.

Niall turned back to where Caitlin stood, so vulnerable, so beautiful, treacherous because of the longing she awakened inside him. The living embodiment of the one thing the bold warrior Niall of the Seven Betrayals feared. Feminine beauty, a woman's touch, a snare that entangled a man's reason, entrapped his heart. A fist of something like panic gripped his chest, and for the first time since he was a child, he felt the need to turn and *run*.

He could not let Caitlin see that with those sweetly probing eyes. Dared not let anyone guess at his shame. Yet she was worried herself. He could sense it in a way that unnerved him. Why did he feel the irresistible need to soothe what fears of hers he could for the time he would be gone? Or was he not soothing Caitlin at all? Only his own battered conscience?

"You should be safe enough for now," he snapped, unprepared for the way his heart lurched when his gaze lit upon her face. "Conn will not even suspect that I have chosen to defy his command." How could the words be so painful? As if all he had built in Conn's court was being flayed from his soul one dagger blade at a time.

"I am not afraid," she said.

It was a lie, and he knew it. She had lived all her life in that abbey, with sisters who had known her forever crowded about her. She was a stranger here, in this wretched household still writhing beneath the curse of his father. She must be alarmed, fearful, and yet Niall had no comfort to give her. He did not know the answer himself.

For an instant, he wanted to go to her, gather her in his arms. Bury his grief and uncertainty in the yielding softness of her breasts. He wondered what it would be like to hold her, to admit to someone for the first time in his life that he was afraid. But it was impossible, more fantasy than a child's makebelieve tale about the stars.

He turned, stalked out the door, heard footsteps, light, already familiar, as Caitlin followed. He felt her watching as he swung up onto his horse, was as aware of the touch of her gaze as he had been of the sweet curves of her lips the night before.

He spun his mount in a tight circle, trying to get the horse and his own white-hot imagination back under control.

With an oath, Niall galloped away from Fiona's mockery, his mother's bewilderment, and Caitlin's sweet temptation. He only wished he could keep riding until the world fell away.

Chapter
9

IF NIALL'S HORSE had carried him straight into Conn's fortress, he would not have noticed, so little attention had he given to his surroundings in the hours since he galloped away from Castle Daire. With each movement of the sun across the sky, he burned—his mind a tangle of memories, old and new, equally torturous, his heart torn by the agonizing choice he had to make between the chieftain who had loved him like a son and the innocent beauty whose life had been cast into Niall's hands.

Niall's fingers shifted again to the leather pouch at his waist, the message he had written to Conn almost like a living thing within its depths. He could not have loathed the missive more if it had been gnawing its way into his own belly. It seemed guilt—that emotion he had shrugged away with scorn for so long—had claws and teeth. Niall wondered if he would ever be free of their bite again.

If only he could rid himself of the letter, the deed would be done. His betrayal of Conn complete, no way to change it. Was it possible he could find some peace in that? No more peace than he had found in the days since he chose to let Caitlin live.

He rode over the crest of a hill, suddenly alert to the sounds of a disturbance below—a tiny croft, five boys near Fiona's age wrestling in play. But nay. Niall's eyes narrowed. This was no game—at least not to the smallest youth who sprawled in the dirt. Blood streamed from the boy's nose and cut lip as the other four lads loomed over him.

Niall's gut knotted. How many times had he been in that lone boy's place? Fighting, raging against impossible odds, driven by his own anger and shame? Even Conn's favor had not protected Niall from the fists of the other boys, especially the chieftain's six sons. It was easy enough to stalk a lone boy in the vast fortress, lie in wait to strike. Once the bloodying was over, no one had betrayed what had happened, not to the chieftain, the trainers in arms. Not to anyone.

Niall would have cut out his own tongue before he cried for help or for mercy. And he himself threatened to thrash anyone who told of the beatings he suffered.

Countless times, Niall had refused to explain the cuts and bruises on his face. In that terrible silence, Niall had bided his time, grown stronger, practiced harder, until that magnificent day he could best his tormentors himself. But during those far-off years, he had never suspected what it was like for those few who had not joined in the brawls to watch such injustice, helpless to stop it.

"Stay down, you craven cur!" A burly lad with a misshapen mouth gave the boy a vicious kick. "Admit defeat, you son of a drunken slut!"

The lad curled his scrawny body into a ball and rolled away, seeming to surrender. Then, the instant the other boy thrust out his chest and turned to his friends in victory, the small lad launched himself into the burly lad's midsection like a human javelin

Howling, the other three leapt on the boy, but he struck eight to ten solid punches before they dragged him off.

Damn fool! Niall gritted his teeth as the older boy pummeled him. He should not interfere. Nothing would have infuriated him more during the years when he had been in the boy's place. Besides, it might only make things worse once he rode away. But when three of the boys imprisoned their prey and the other began to pound him in earnest, Niall could not watch any longer.

As he urged his horse into a run, he was uncertain. Who was he riding to aid? The boy who struggled in the dirt or the lad he had once been himself?

The thunderous hoofbeats did little to quell the gang of young brutes, insolent grins curling their mouths as if they expected nothing but approval from anyone who witnessed their sport.

Niall felt as if an invisible shaft had been driven into his gut. With difficulty, he mastered the red tide of rage rising inside him. "Let him go," he said softly, a threat more terrifying than any bellow could be.

Genuine shock whitened the faces of the boy's attackers. One loosened his grip on the lad and gave Niall a sly smile.

"Beg pardon, fine sir, but you cannot understand. This coward is none but Owaine, the son of a drunken slut, his father one of any hundred men. He would not yield the road."

"So four of you fell upon him? An unfair number by any counting. Which of you are cowards now?"

The boys took a step back. One of the more daring raised his chin. "I am the son of the most powerful man in this valley. Who are you to judge me?"

For an instant, Niall thought of telling the boy his

identity was none of his affair; then he changed his mind. Considering the message he was sending to Conn, it would matter little if all Glenfluirse knew he was at Daire. What could it matter if five farmboys knew his name? Besides, the knowlege that a warrior had championed their prey might keep the boy safe from his tormentors, at least for a little while.

"I am Niall of the Seven Betrayals."

"N-Niall . . ." The other lads chorused in uneasy recognition, faces flushed, arrogance vanquished by awe.

The battered Owaine straightened, and Niall could see how much it cost him to hide his pain. "Is it really you?" Owaine asked, wonderingly. "Warrior of Glenfluirse? Champion of the chieftain Conn?"

Niall was so stunned by the adoration in the boy's eyes, he could only nod in answer. Had word of his exploits traveled so far?

"I know every one of your tales of valor! How you fought to win your seat at the head of Conn's table. The quests you set out upon to win a new name. It made me believe that perhaps I could—" He stopped, suddenly aware of the other boys. Niall could feel the exquisitely painful embarrassment that sent color rushing into Owaine's cheeks.

"You will stay with me," Niall ordered Owaine. "As for the rest of you cowards, if ever I see you tormenting Owaine again, I will teach you a lesson in courage with my own hands!"

Big-eyed with terror, the boys scattered as if they feared he would take their hearts to the throne of the fairy queen, one of the legends that had sprung up around the first quest Conn had given him.

Owaine watched the boys run away with satisfaction, a smile curving his lips despite the nasty split in the lower one. Niall knew instinctively that Owaine's was not a mouth that smiled often.

"Go home, boy. They will not torment you now."

"I am not going home. Not ever again. There is nothing for me there but shame." The boy swabbed the blood from his face with one linen sleeve. "I go to Glenfluirse, to pledge myself to Conn."

Niall raised one eyebrow, fighting to keep the corner of his mouth from tipping in a wry smile. "You might have gotten there sooner if you let those other boys pass without a fight."

"That may be so." Owaine's gaze hardened. "Except that when I decided to go to Conn's fortress, I vowed to myself that I would never stand aside again, not for any man. If you could earn respect, honor, with the point of your sword, I could. But not if I kept running away."

Niall winced. This boy, betrayed by his mother, abandoned by his father, from what the other lads had said, had chosen a poor man to make a hero in his eyes. What would Owaine think if he knew how Niall had betrayed his chieftain on this, his final quest? The thought made Niall's gut knot, and he was furious with the boy and with himself for that flash of weakness. Why should this boy's good opinion suddenly matter so damned much?

Owaine grasped Niall's dirt-encrusted sleeve, the boy nearly trembling with excitement. "Perhaps we could travel together," Owaine suggested, his eyes shining with hope. "I could tend to your horse, sharpen your sword. I would not be any trouble, I swear it! And I am used to eating scarce anything at all."

Niall looked at Owaine's bony frame, anger at whoever had so mistreated the boy, a hot lump in Niall's chest. He swallowed hard, hating to fail the boy. "I am not returning to Glenfluirse. Not for some time."

The lad's face fell. "I will find Glenfluirse on my own, then. It was what I always planned."

Niall peered into Owaine's face, that stubborn jaw, determination burning like embers in the still-child-soft face. And Niall knew a lad like Owaine had thrice the warrior's heart of any grown man he might find along this road.

"Owaine," Niall said solemnly, "I do have an important task I must charge someone with. Someone worthy of my trust."

The boy did not even have to speak. Niall knew Owaine instinctively enough to be certain he would walk through fire for him. It saddened Niall, made him shamed and proud in the same moment.

Niall untied the leather pouch, removed the missive. No fear that such a boy would be able to read it! "Owaine, will you vow to put this into the hand of Conn? Let no other man touch it."

"Aye, I swear it."

Niall drew his own dagger, the gold inlay shining in the sun. "This will be your weapon."

The lad's eyes nigh popped from his head. "Did it truly belong to the fairy queen? Did she leave it for you in exchange for an evil giant's heart?"

Niall wanted to deny it, but if the story would give the boy courage on the journey ahead, let him believe what he wished.

"If you know the tales of my quests, you must also know I am not allowed to speak of them."

"You do not need to." Owaine grinned. "All of Ireland tells the stories for you! You will live in bard song 'til the end of time." Owaine tucked the message into the front of his leine, against his heart. Niall wondered what would happen to that heart when the boy learned that his hero had given him a lie to bear to the chieftain.

But there was no help for it. No one else to send. And Niall knew enough of Conn to be certain he would never take vengeance on an innocent boy merely tossed to him by the hands of fate. Conn would see the fire in Owaine's eyes, the heat of a warrior trapped in a boy's body. Owaine would be a gift to any chieftain set on defending his holdings. A gift too precious to be squandered. Conn had always had a gift for seeing such promise in prospective warriors.

Aye, Conn was no fool. There could be no question the chieftain would see that Owaine was cared for, no matter how enraged he would be at Niall when the truth about the missive was known.

Niall watched the boy stride off, Owaine's praises echoing in his ears. *You will live in bard song*, Owaine had claimed. It was true, Niall knew. But the final verse in the tale of Niall of the Seven Betrayals would be a dark one. One cast in shame. Aye, he thought grimly. Let it be done. He turned his mount back toward Daire land.

Niall had hoped taking the longest path back across Castle Daire land would give him time to soothe nerves ragged from Fiona's plotting, Owaine's adoration, and the ever-haunting image of Caitlin's lips before he kissed her. But the forlorn countryside he traveled only fed his guilt and anger and stark confusion.

What the devil had happened? The land that dwelled in his memory was lush and fertile, impossibly green and bursting with life. Crops thrived. Cattle grew fat, their calves frolicking about their heels. Wild game abounded, delighting the little boy who had chased after it with tiny toy weapons. But the Daire of his childhood had vanished, the landscape about him bleak and forsaken as the faraway moon.

It was as if a pagan god of desolation had blown hot breath across the land, cursing it until scarce a living thing dared tread upon the grass.

Here and there, a rabbit darted, fearful. A grouse or two broke from the underbrush. But nowhere did he find sign of the wild red deer and stags that once reined over the hillsides, harbingers of plenty.

Farms that once would have provided the castle with grain and vegetables were overgrown with brambles, the huts cowering ashamed beneath sheaves of ragged thatch half rotted from the roofs. Here and there, fire-blackened ruins raised sooty skeletons toward the sky. Far too many ruins, Niall realized as he rode, to be ill luck or accident.

Whoever had wreaked this chaos upon those at Daire had taken a sick pleasure in their task. He had seen enough raiding parties and ridden past enough ruined farm huts to know the difference. Men who regretted what they must do but knew it was a necessity allowed the pathetic people enough time to gather a few supplies—pots to cook in, enough clothing to keep them warm.

Everything on Daire land had been burned, including the poor wretches who had once dwelled upon it. Niall gripped the reins tighter, his stomach turning as he saw yet another cottage, its door barred by a charred length of wood. White bone gleaming amidst the blackened household goods within. A shattered cradle, half-burned, lay beyond a window in the stone hut. A vine of wild rose had curled about the cradle, softening the ugliness of scorched and shattered wood as if even nature itself were trying to hide this evidence of someone's cruelty from its sight.

Had the child who had inhabited the cradle escaped with its life? Niall wondered. What would it be like to be barred inside your own home as the flames consumed everyone you loved? He could almost hear the parents, trapped in the building, screaming, pleading for mercy for their child. But Niall could have told them the men who had done this devilish work were not the sort to show mercy, even to the most helpless babes.

Why did this tragedy seem so suffocatingly close, so real? It had all happened long ago, when he was but a lad trying desperately to carve himself some kind of haven at Conn's court. Were it not for the chieftain's mercy, he might have met his death in such a terrible way. Aye, Fiona and his mother, too.

It was uncanny, the way destruction ringed about them, leaving them barely able to eke out enough to survive. Yet no one had taken that final step, a hellishly logical step, to punish those loyal to a hated traitor. Driving them off the land forever or putting them to the sword.

Why would anyone leave things thus? Vengeance begun but not finished? It made no sense. Anyone who hated his father enough to murder the land itself in this way would not hesitate to kill two lone women with no one to protect them.

Unless Fiona and his mother *had* had a protector of sorts, a man powerful enough to be feared, distant enough to be unaware of this kind of destruction.

Niall rubbed his aching temple. Aye, that had to be it. The only reasonable explanation for why they had been spared was that Conn had kept his promise to Niall, ordered no warrior to touch them despite the fact that Ronan of Daire had been a traitor. And these warriors had obeyed the chieftain's order with grim precision. Allowing the two helpless women to live yet destroying everything around them. Decimating land

and people, livestock and everything beautiful in Castle Daire yet not touching the two women whose murder would bring Conn's wrath down upon their heads.

When Niall found whoever had wreaked this bloody havoc, he vowed there would be a fearsome reckoning. He would see just how brave the cur was when he had to fight someone who was not helpless or weak or grief-torn.

Chilled to the marrow of his bones, Niall turned his horse toward home, all thought of hunting forgotten.

In the courtyard, he tied his horse, swung down, and stalked into the hall. He barely noticed how changed it was. Furniture polished, the floor swept clean.

"Fiona?" he called out. He was surprised to see the girl saunter out from the direction of the buttery, her face smudged, one finger bandaged.

"If any more mischief has befallen you, I am innocent," the girl said, holding up her palms as if in surrender. "I have not had three moments to plot devilment since you rode out, no matter how pleasurable it might have been. This Caitlin of yours, she might as well have a chariot whip, hard as she's been driving me."

"I do not give a damn if you have spent the afternoon plotting ways to murder me, girl. You will sit down at once. Tell me what the blazes has happened to this place!"

Fiona collapsed on a chair of carved bog oak. "I tried to tell you yesterday, but you would not believe me. Why repeat myself again?"

"The crofter's huts are burned. Father's stag and herds of red deer—I saw not so much as a flash of their tails!"

"The thieves did not content themselves with stealing what we had inside the house. They hunted down the herds, killed them, left them where they lay, just so we would have nothing to eat. As for the people, I thank God most were wise enough to leave after the first few attacks. Those who did not—you saw what happened to them. I wish to God the cowards had waited until I was grown enough to fight them."

"Fiona, they would have killed you! A mere girl, thin as a bird's leg."

His sister's eyes burned, and Niall almost thought he saw the glint of a tear. "I would rather have fought! Died! That would have been far easier than continuing to live."

Niall winced at the passion in the child's voice and the weariness she tried so hard to disguise. "Why did you not leave?" he demanded. "Go north to Mother's family? They would have welcomed you both! Why stay in this hell-cursed place?"

"I was barely four years old when Father died. Mother did not consult my wishes then."

"Blast it, Fiona, this is not a jest! It is a miracle you both survived! No servants, no one to defend you, no crops or wild game or cattle! Perhaps you had no choice when you were a babe, but even I can see that you have been tending to everything here for years. Why did you not make Mother see reason? Go where you would be safe?"

"Daire has been in our family for two hundred years!" She bristled. "Some of us consider our duty to the land and those who came before us."

"So you risked your life out of pure accursed stubbornness, then? Fiona, any girl with enough courage and resourcefulness to survive in this kind of desolation is intelligent enough to know she should have fled this place years ago."

She looked at him, eyes widening with something

like surprise at his words. Her gaze dropped to her ragged bandage. "It was . . . hell. But Mother would not leave. She insisted we had to be at Daire when you—" She hesitated, her eyes glittering, overbright, her voice hard with defiance. "She could not bear the thought that we would not be at Daire when you learned the truth about Father and came home to us."

Niall's fists knotted at the vision of his mother waiting for her son to return. A son who held her in contempt because of her devotion to a man who had destroyed her life and the lives of her children.

"By the time I was old enough to understand how bleak things were," Fiona continued, "it was already difficult enough for her to grasp what had happened. I was afraid if I forced her to leave, she would shatter completely."

"There is no reason for her to wait here any longer. I have come home now, devil take it!" Niall drove his fingers back through the wind-tangled waves of his hair, fighting for inner balance. "When the time comes for me to leave, I am taking the two of you where you will be safe. Cared for."

"Is that so?" Fiona demanded. "You think it that simple, then? Cast us upon someone else's charity, and forget us entirely? Nay, Niall. It is not so easy as that. Our mother may have been waiting for your return, but *I* was not! This is my home. Mother's home. We stay here."

"Fiona—"

"You want to ease your guilty conscience, brother? Fine. This is what you can do. Help me here, now, so that when you leave, Castle Daire is alive again. Caitlin has already begun inside. If you had only seen Mother's face when first she saw how lovely . . ."

Fiona looked away, and Niall could see her fighting

to keep her sharp little features in their accustomed rebellious lines. "Surely, such a great, bold warrior as you can manage to aid us. There are a few wild cattle in the highlands. The two of us might be able to catch them. Tame them. Bring them here. And there is a spiteful man a half day's ride from here who has boasted that he has a cow that drops twin calves whenever she is bred."

"And why would any sane man sell such a miraculous beast?"

Fiona chuckled, and Niall was stunned to realize he had already learned to dread the glint in his younger sister's eyes. "It seems he has offended the fairies, and he fears that the cow is cursed. There have been several accidents—strange happenings—that have alarmed him and anyone else who might be anxious to barter for the beast. However, I would be willing to risk the curse. How much worse can things grow here at Daire?"

"You mean that you would risk the curse because there *is* no curse. You have been tormenting the man in secret, have you not, Fiona?"

She fluttered lashes absurdly long and curly. "I could hardly expect him to sell it to me otherwise. The only difficulty came when I could not find anything he was willing to trade for it."

"You could not care for the beast even if this man did agree to the trade! How would you protect it? Tend it? You know nothing about cattle. The miserable animal would burst an udder, or someone would steal it from beneath your nose, and there would be nothing you could do to stop it!"

"I would like to see them try!" Her gaze hardened, her mouth a white line. "If I can start raising cattle, I will be able to lure a few crofters back onto the land. If I can do that, we should be able to survive. Mother and

I have simple needs. We do not want riches. We only wish to be left in peace on land we love."

She swallowed hard. "Niall, in all the years since our father died, I have made no effort to find you, ask you for anything. You, who should be guardian of all Daire, and me upon it. I am asking you this. Help me find a way to get that cow."

Why did her words send chills down his spine? All he could see was the ruin of that hut—the blackened cradle, white bones bleaching in the sun. "Do you really think whoever attacked Daire before would stand by and let you rebuild it?"

"They have not returned for three years, Niall!"

"Because there is nothing left to steal! I am not going to leave you here undefended, Fiona, whether you have managed to scare a dozen farmers out of their cows!"

"Niall, I beg you. Listen to reason," she pleaded, and for an instant, memory echoed through his mind, a sweet little lisp, a stubborn, scraped chin.

Never had he been able to resist that pleading. He could almost feel the melting sensation in his heart, the crumbling of his resolve not to let her trail along. In that long-ago time, love and frustration had mingled, fierce inside his narrow chest. In the end, he had growled that she was a pest worse than any swarm of hornets, and if she fell behind, he would leave her to the fairies. And Fiona had clung to his hand and begged him to find her a handful of the wee folk to keep beneath her bed box at home.

Pain jolted through Niall at the vividness of that memory, surprising him. Even so, this defiant girl before him was a stranger he did not know. The toddling sister of his childhood was gone. Yet damned if he would stand back and let her cast herself deeper into disaster.

"Even if I wanted to help, I have nothing to trade," he growled. "I never took my portion of plunder. All I wanted to earn was a name. But it would scarce matter if I were richer than Conn himself. All I owned would be back at the fortress. I could never claim it now."

"Niall, there must be some way!" Desperation edged her voice. "If we can only try—"

"Nay, Fiona," Niall snapped. "I will not be part of your madness. You would be wise to forget the whole matter."

"The way you forgot Daire? Mother? Me? Nay, Niall! I do not cast aside things I love as easily as you do. I will get that cow with your help or without it. And I will live and die on this land and no other."

"You will do as I tell you!"

"I will do as I please! And unless you are willing to bind me to your wrist or lock me in the highest chamber in Ireland, there is nothing you can do to stop me!" She spun away, storming off in high dudgeon.

Chapter
10

NIALL STARED after his sister, his gut clenching when he saw another figure step from beneath the arched doorway that led to the rest of the castle. Caitlin's hair was drawn back in a thick plait, tendrils curling about her face. Her hands twisted a damp cloth as if she could scrub away hurt and anger, despair and pain.

A flush burned up Niall's neck. Bloody hell, how much had she heard? Why should it matter? She had already seen the most monstrous parts of his soul. And it was no secret that his sister loathed him almost as much as he loathed Castle Daire.

"Niall, is something amiss? Fiona charged off in a rare fine fury."

"My dealings with my sister are none of your affair."

Caitlin laid the cloth upon a bog-oak table. "I am sorry. I did not mean to intrude. I just . . . I feel so responsible for all that has happened. If not for me, you would never have returned here."

"And my mother and witless fool of a sister could have starved to death conveniently out of my sight. At least, now I have a chance to see they are protected before I—" He stopped, looked away. "I thought we would stay here only long enough to provision ourselves for our escape. But now . . . I need more time. I have to decide what is right for them. Cannot make another . . ." *Mistake*. He did not say the word. He did not have to. "My mother is so fragile. Fiona would just run back here the instant she got a chance."

"We can stay as long as is necessary to make things right."

"You cannot truly believe that! It would take years to make Daire half livable! And every time the sun sets, we are taking a greater risk of discovery. Before long, Conn will realize that something is amiss. When he does, his warriors will come, and it is inevitable they will ride into Daire. When they do—" He stopped, turned away, kneading the back of his neck with one large hand.

Men he had led into battle would see him as a betrayer like his father was. In a way, he had failed them as certainly as his chieftain. He would shatter the faith they had dared to have in the betrayer's spawn. That grieved Niall more than any wound he had ever suffered, more than the loss of his future at Glenfluirse, for the battle to win their trust was the most difficult one he had ever fought.

But the battle was already lost. He had to release it, turn his face to the future. One suddenly so confused and uncertain it drove him half mad.

"This should have been over. You and I should be leaving Castle Daire by dawn tomorrow, bags stuffed with provisions, enough wealth to buy passage across the sea and build you a new life."

"We can take nothing from Daire!" Caitlin protested in alarm. "Niall, they have not enough to eat, and—"

"You think I cannot see that?" he roared, wheeling to face her. "There is scarce a living thing left upon this land! People burned from their homes, the deer vanished completely! Fiona claims they were slaughtered purposely to starve whoever remained at Castle Daire."

"Who would do such a thing to a woman and a child? They were harming no one!"

"Christ's blood, Caitlin, do you still believe that people are good and honorable and generous and kind like the sisters in your accursed abbey? Have you not opened your eyes since the night I all but killed you? Even if that incident were not enough, look about Castle Daire—see the ruin! You think whoever did this cared what befell my mother and sister? Those villains *wanted* them to suffer. *Hoped* that they would starve or leave this place altogether!"

"But who would be so cruel?"

"Fiona claims it was Conn himself who ordered this destruction. But he has shown his honor in so many ways in the past, shown nothing but generosity to me. How can I ever believe him capable of such a thing?" Lines of desperation etched deep in his face, the face of a drowning man clinging to the last shards of the ship he had loved, trying so hard still to believe it would never sink beneath the waves. She wanted to reach out to him, tell him she would never let him go down. But he was not clinging to her. It was Conn's honor he clung to, his chieftain, and all that powerful man had seemed to be to a lost, grieving, frightened little boy. Conn, someone mighty enough to pluck Niall out of a tempest, give the boy someone to believe in. The only solid thing to cling to in a world gone mad.

And yet, was it not possible that boy had been mistaken?

Caitlin sucked in a steadying breath. "I suppose a sword blow in the middle of the night would be more merciful than leaving a woman and child to starve to death," she said softly.

Niall's jaw tightened. "What the devil is that supposed to mean?"

She was treading on dangerous ground. She knew it, and yet she could not stop herself. He was tearing his soul apart out of loyalty to a man who might scarce be worthy to touch the hem of his cloak!

"Conn was willing to order my death. Why would he not be capable of ordering the ruin of Castle Daire?"

"Not another word!" Niall swore.

"I am not accusing him, only saying it is possible that he might have had something to do with the destruction you found here."

"You are wrong! You know nothing of the kind of man Conn is!"

She peered into his face, the handsome planes suddenly haggard, haunted. How fiercely he wanted to believe what he said was true!

"I know that he ordered you to kill me. And I know what kind of man you are, Niall. If you had done as he commanded, it would have haunted you the rest of your life."

"A warrior does his duty, Caitlin. You have no idea the things I have done in battle. A man who fights has to banish such things from his mind, lock them away or go mad."

"Battle is far different from what you faced in that wood. You fight for your life. Your enemy fights for his own. But you both hold swords, confront each other face-to-face. Courage and skill determine who will survive. But I was helpless, Niall. I had done no evil."

"But the prophecy—" Niall stammered, and Caitlin could see he was grappling to hold tight to all he had believed.

"If you had carried out your orders, killed me as Conn commanded, you would not have been able to forget what you had done to me, Niall. Not if you lived to be older than the druid stone where first I saw you. As for the honorable name you performed so many quests to earn, it would have been tainted by my death. Every time you heard someone speak that name, you would have seen my blood on your hands, my face just before your sword fell. The new name would give you as much pain, as much guilt, as the one you bear now. Nay, more. Because the first name came from your father's infamy. This name would remind you of your own."

Color drained from Niall's face, and Caitlin knew the truth in her words had struck deep. She wanted to shield him, hated causing him pain, and yet he had to hear what was true. She swallowed hard, continued slowly.

"Niall, if *I* know how much you would suffer, when I have only spent a few paltry days with you, should not a man who has raised you since you were a child know what obeying his order would have cost you?"

Niall took a step back, so stunned Caitlin almost wished the words back. Was he not already wrestling far too much? Guilt over the condition of his family? Loss of his position at Conn's fortress, the respect he had worked so hard for? And worse still, echoes that must fill the hall, his father's voice mingling with his own, before Niall's world had crashed down about his head.

"I will discuss no more of this with you or with my sister!" Niall snarled, starting to stalk away. He stopped, turned, casting her a glare. "Before I leave the castle for my nightly ride, I give you one last warning."

"What is that?"

"Stay out of sight until we leave here. Let no one save Fiona, Mother, and I see you. For I promise you,

Caitlin, any stranger who caught a glimpse of you would not forget your face."

"But you ride about. The great and powerful warrior. Surely, people would realize who you were long before they noticed me. What difference could it make if I—"

"I am *supposed* to be riding the hills alone on my last quest—one no one can even guess at. Even if someone should realize who I am, it would matter little, while anyone identifying you would bring disaster."

"How could anyone possibly know who I am?" Caitlin snapped. "There must be hundreds of dark-haired girls in Ireland!"

"Not with a face beautiful enough to drive any man to madness. Conn's warriors would guess your identity in a heartbeat!"

He had called her beautiful, Caitlin thought with a shiver, yet he spat out the word as if it were a curse.

"Niall, do not be absurd. I—"

"Conn must believe you are dead if you are to be safe. I have sent a message to the chieftain claiming I have carried out his orders."

He had lied to his chieftain? Caitlin knew how much such deceit must have cost him. "Niall—" She stopped, knowing nothing she could say would ease the torment he felt over what he had done. She saw something flicker in his eyes, knew he saw the pity and regret she felt for him.

"Do as I command you, Caitlin," he snapped, obviously angry that she had sensed his vulnerability. "Let no one see you, or God alone knows what hell you may bring down on all our heads. Aye, and this is another order. Do not fly about, scrubbing and sweeping and casting heather about the floors here."

No one had ever raged at her this way, ordering her about as if she had not a will of her own! Perhaps she had said things he wished she had not. Made him consider things that were painful. But she had only spoken the truth!

Her cheeks burned with irritation and hurt. "It made your mother happy. And the saints know there is nothing else for me to do while I wait to be hunted down by your precious chieftain! Why should I not clean every stone of Daire if I wish to?"

"Because it will only make things harder. As soon as I can arrange it, my mother and Fiona will be leaving Daire forever. We will have to alter the course of our escape a bit, take them to my uncle's, where they will be cared for."

Caitlin's mouth fell open in dismay. "I cannot imagine your mother ever leaving this place! It would destroy her! And as for Fiona, I think she would rather die than step a foot beyond Daire's boundaries."

"That may be so, but I will be damned before I let her get herself killed because of it! They cannot survive here alone, and there is not enough time for me to make things right so that they can stay."

"Fiona spoke of a cow. Perhaps—"

"Curse that infernal cow! Aye, and my sister with it! Can neither of you understand? There is no time! If I were to wager, knowing Conn as I do, I would bet that by the time the full moon rises again, the chieftain will realize something is amiss. He is canny, more clever than you know. I have fought my whole life to win this new name. When I do not return to Glenfluirse to claim it, Conn will grow uneasy. Conn might send the warriors out in peace to find me, or he might entrust them with the quest I was on—tell them of you, that you are supposed to be dead. Which, I cannot say. But he will send his warriors out to search. Men who have secretly hated me. Envied me for years because the chieftain showed me such favor. If a band of those warriors finds us here, Caitlin, do you know what would happen?"

Her shoulders stiffened. "I am not a complete innocent!"

"You think not? I promise you, sheltered and beloved as you were, you cannot even begin to imagine what vengeance they would take! On my stubborn curse of a sister. On my mother, even dazed as she is. Aye, Lily Fair, and on you. Especially upon you."

Ice flowed through Caitlin's veins. "Nay," she whispered, shaking her head. "I cannot believe—"

"I thought you trusted me."

She winced at the bitter edge to his voice.

"If ever once you have believed me, lady, believe me when I tell you this." Niall's eyes narrowed. "There are things far worse than the quick, clean blow of a sword. And if one of those men—just one—guessed what you have made me feel—" His mouth twisted with a pain that surprised her. He spun away, trying to hide it.

What had she made him feel for her? Compassion? Pity? Or had the passion that swept through her affected him as deeply? A tingling sensation started in her chest, terrifying and delighting her. She dared to lay her hand upon the rigid muscles of his back, felt the heat of him, smelled the wild fragrance of meadow wind and horse and a slight tang of sweat.

"Niall, I am not afraid."

"I am afraid for you!" He wheeled, his hands driving back into the curls at her temples, his eyes afire. He was close, so close his breath heated her lips, and she could taste the wondrous flavor of them, hot with barely leashed passion as they had been the night he had kissed her.

Hunger pulsed through her, and she waited, breathless with the need for Niall to close the space between them, take her mouth with his. His eyes should have burned her, they glowed so hot, his lips parting, moving ever so slightly toward hers, but at the last instant, he jerked away with a savage curse.

"Do not look at me like that! As if I could tame every dragon who ever breathed fire! Can you not see your own future now? You will be hiding from Conn forever, looking over your shoulder, wondering who might be carrying his blade to kill you!"

"As long as you are with me, no blade will ever strike."

"I cannot hold back an army, Caitlin, even if I wanted to!" His face contorted. "When Conn learns the truth of what I have done, being with me might put you, my mother, and Fiona in even greater danger!"

"What do you plan to do?" she asked.

"I will take all three of you north to Mother's people. Whatever happens next, Fiona and my mother will be far from Daire when Conn's men return here."

"Will we remain there as well?"

Niall gave a bitter laugh. "You think Conn's warriors cannot ride north? I have thought about it every night since I betrayed my chieftain. I will take you across the sea to Iona, find a place for you there, safe, well hidden. Make certain you will be cared for."

The beginnings of a smile curved her lips, so tender, so trusting, it twisted like a dagger in Niall's heart. "Conn will not find us there," she agreed, agonizingly certain he could keep her safe.

"I will not remain in Iona." Niall's hands curled into fists.

"Oh, I—I see," Caitlin said softly. Disappointment shadowed her face, and Niall felt a quick, hot terror at how much it affected him. What had the woman thought when he had kissed her? That they had sealed some sort of lovers' vow?

"I will return to Ireland, go before my chieftain," Niall bit out, wanting to drag a shield between him and this soft-eyed woman. "I will make certain he believes you are dead."

Hope sparked in those fairy-blue eyes, eyes that could still dream of happily-ever-after, no matter how much ugliness they had seen. "Then you will be able to gather up the threads of your old life. Go on as before."

"Do you think I could do that? Look every day into my chieftain's face, knowing I had lied?" How long would it take before his own conscience betrayed him? Before Conn looked into his face, realized the truth? For an instant, he imagined the bittersweetness of kneeling before Conn, confessing his betrayal, facing whatever retribution would await him. There was a cold, clean comfort in it—retribution in a warrior's realm, far from Caitlin's world of compassion and courage, from braving emotions far more dangerous than any executioner's sword.

"Niall, what will you do?" Caitlin's voice trembled.

"I will refuse the honorable name Conn offers, refuse any reward. I will leave Glenfluirse forever."

"Exile yourself? But where will you go?"

Niall squared his shoulders, looked out the arrow slit, to the world beyond he could barely see. "It does not matter. No matter how far I wander, I will never escape the truth. I am forsworn."

Words sprang to Caitlin's lips, words of comfort, words defending him for the mercy he had shown her. Words about true honor, the real meaning of courage—what it meant to be a true hero, not some imaginary perfect figure, without breath or life or flaws to be overcome, one who risked everything to save someone helpless, innocent.

Instead of speaking, she stood in his shadow, silent, her heart aching. Nothing she could say to this man would ever take away the burning wound of broken vows, of lies from lips that had only spoken truth, of betraying not only his chieftain but everything Niall had fought so hard to believe about himself.

Tears stung Caitlin's eyes. The vision of this brave, generous man wandering the world shattered and alone was more than she could bear.

He had sacrificed the only world he had ever known for her. The least she could do was make certain Niall had a life to come back to once this ordeal was over. She would breathe life into Castle Daire, bind the wounds tearing apart his family. She would leave him a gift in exchange for all he had sacrificed for her. A home, and someone to love him when this last bitter quest was done.

Chapter 11

CAITLIN THRUST a breeze-blown curl away from her cheek with the back of one dirt-smudged hand, scarce noticing the sting of the tiny cuts and blisters that had appeared after so many hours' work. Satisfaction warmed her far more than the sunshine that slanted over the rear wall of the castle to throw a yellow-gold mantle over her aching shoulders.

She had spent half the night before staring into the darkness, trying to think how she should begin to keep her vow, awaken the slumbering Castle Daire from its dark spell of hostility and neglect. The task had seemed so vast, far too hard and heavy and insurmountable for even the most determined young woman to conquer.

She had plotted and planned and prayed, discarding one strategy after another, until just on the rosy breast of a new dawn, she heard it, an answer carried upon a tender echo of Reverend Mother's voice. *A garden, Caitlin. A garden is God's promise of a future waiting to be born.*

That promise had driven her from her bed filled with purpose. The instant Niall rode out on another hunt, she had attacked the godforsaken plot of ground that had once grown food for Castle Daire, delighting in the familiar cling of rich, damp earth on her hands, savoring the memory of sweet summer days at the abbey. Hours she had spent in the gardens there, building fairy forts out of pebbles and sucking on sweet stems of herbs to learn the secrets of their healing power.

As the warmth of earth and sky penetrated Caitlin's raw heart, the misery and dread of the past week melted away, leaving in its place a fragile whisper of the contentment she had doubted she would ever feel again.

It was true, what the abbess had said, Caitlin thought, tucking rich earth around the roots of a clump of rosemary. A garden *was* life. Once Niall saw things growing, perhaps he would feel the tug of his own roots in Daire's soil and realize he could not abandon this place any more than Fiona or his mother could.

Of course, Caitlin thought with a wry grin, it was probably a good thing he was off riding somewhere at the moment. One look at the forest of weeds yet to pull, and the champion of Glenfluirse might turn and flee the other way.

Her smile died. He was doing his best to be quit of the castle as swiftly as possible. It would take a miracle to keep him at Daire, no matter what magic she managed to work in this tiny bit of ground. She struggled against a wave of sadness. In the end, it would be Niall's choice whether he turned his back on his home and family or whether he realized what a treasure he had nearly lost before it was too late. All she could do was try her best to make things right.

She strained to feel some sense of triumph as she uncovered another clump of parsnips run wild across the garden, the delicious roots all but buried by weeds. With the meat Niall had provided, there would be a savory meal tonight. But she could not help wondering if he would even notice, tormented as he was.

A long, thin shadow moved across her, and she jumped, guilty as a child caught in some mischief. She looked up to find Fiona scowling down at her, arms folded across her narrow chest. In that instant, the girl had never looked more like her difficult brother.

"You are bloodying your fingers to no purpose." The girl made a face. "That ground has grown nothing but weeds for as long as I can remember."

Caitlin felt a twinge of pain for the girl, so gruff, so uncomfortable in her own skin, stubbornly determined not to show tenderness or fear, like a babe shouting down a storm. "But you are wrong," Caitlin challenged. "Look at this." She closed her hand around the green spears of leaves, then pulled up a crisp, white root. She brushed it off with her hand. "Take a bite."

Fiona regarded the plant as if it might bite her instead.

Caitlin knew exactly how to wipe away Fiona's reluctance. "Do not be afraid," she said.

Hot color flooded the girl's face, her brow creasing with belligerence. She snatched the root, crunching it between her teeth. Her eyes widened in surprise, then pleasure. "Wh-what is this?"

"It is a leek. There are parsnips and rosemary, carrots and yarrow and heaven knows what else still growing here among the weeds. With no one to tend them, they have run a little wild, but with some work, I think we can tame them back into proper order."

Fiona munched, a troubled scowl darkening her features. "You mean to tell me that there is . . . was food to eat here all the time, but I was too stupid to know it?"

Caitlin winced at the vulnerability suddenly bowing Fiona's shoulders, as if the girl had failed some vital test.

"How would you have known what grew here?" Caitlin soothed. "The crofters and servants left. No one ever taught you."

"I thought it was all gone." Fiona choked on the words. "I stole most of what we ate."

Empathy stirred in Caitlin. All those years she had been the cherished treasure of the abbey, chasing butterflies, carefree, Fiona had been foraging like a wild animal to stay alive. No wonder the girl was rough-edged and bitter.

What would happen if Fiona suddenly had someone to take care of *her* at last? What remarkable kind of woman might she blossom into? Someone strong and rare and even more precious because of all she had triumphed over.

If Caitlin were going to stay at Daire, she would find a way to weave the softest cloth, dye it the green of a summer meadow to accent Fiona's eyes. She would stitch something lovely to surprise Fiona and delight in the girl's confusion and pleasure. For when Fiona had seen the lovely embroidery on the leine Reverend Mother had made, Caitlin sensed Fiona's secret yearnings for the pretty, the feminine, things that had been as far beyond her touch as the moon.

But Caitlin would be in faroff Iona if Niall had his way, and no one else would suspect Fiona's secret. Eyes burning with regret, Caitlin forced herself to smile.

"If I could just wander about a bit, I am certain I could bring back even more things to grow. Sister Luca used to take me with her into the woods sometimes, searching for plants in the wild. You could have a proper garden in no time."

The most fragile hope sparked in Fiona's eyes, then burst into pure eagerness. "Go now. I can root out these weeds if you just show me what to do."

Caitlin grimaced. "Niall ordered me to stay here. He fears what might happen if anyone sees me."

"Niall frets like an old woman!" Fiona scoffed. "Put yourself in my hands, and I can make certain Conn himself would not notice you even if he tripped over your nose! As for my brother, he will never have to know of your adventure, and Mother and I would have . . . we would have things to eat once you are gone. They would grow forever, would they not? Like these plants you uncovered?"

"I could give them a good start, teach you how to care for them. I am certain they would grow. But—" Caitlin shook her head. "I cannot. Niall has already risked so much for me. If I disobeyed him—"

"He is not master of Daire any longer!" Fiona pushed out her lower lip. "Niall may try to order you about, he might even think he can drag Mother and me away from Daire, but he cannot."

"Fiona, he fears for you and for your mother. He only wants to see you safe."

"Humph! He cared little enough what happened to us before. Whatever he says, I know the truth. He only wants to wash his hands of us again. He can ride away at once and never look back for all I care. *I* will stay here until I die." A canny expression curled her mouth. "Of course, if you would go search for plants for the garden, at least I would not die of starvation."

"Fiona!" Caitlin groaned, but she could not stifle a giggle. "I cannot guess which you desire most—the plants or the pleasure of getting me to defy your brother's orders."

"Both," Fiona admitted with a grin. "I would go into the hills myself if I knew what to search for, but it would be hopeless, even if you tried to describe what I should look for. Knowing Niall, he will be gone until nightfall. I beg of you, Caitlin. Do this for my mother. Do this for me."

How often had Niall's sister asked anyone for help? Caitlin stared into the girl's avid face, saw there a hint of what Fiona might have been if years of pain and disillusionment and hardship were washed away. A bundle of enthusiasm, willfulness, quick intelligence, and fierce loyalty. The loyalty she showed to her ailing mother, to the land of Daire. Loyalty she once gave to her brother.

She had had so little help in her seventeen years. Surely, it was the greater sin not to help her this once, Caitlin thought, catching her bottom lip between her teeth. She would be careful. Very careful.

"I surrender," Caitlin said at last, standing up and brushing the dirt off her hands. "You promised you could disguise me somehow. Do you really believe so?"

Fiona grasped her hand, dragging her toward the castle. "I can make you disappear until even Niall could not find you!"

An hour later, breasts bound, hair tucked beneath one of Fiona's billowy shirts, face artistically smeared with dirt, Caitlin left Castle Daire behind. But as she roamed the deserted hills, a small spade and a handful of empty cloth sacks slung over her shoulders, she found something she had not expected. Freedom, pleasure, a brief escape from the grinding tension of days past.

Fiona was right, Caitlin thought as she stared with satisfaction at her reflection in a silvery stream. She looked nothing like herself. Caitlin of the Lilies, hunted by Conn, protected by Niall of the Seven Betrayals, had vanished. In her place was a slender, grubby-cheeked boy.

She would take the unexpected gift of this sunny afternoon and be a child again, enchanted by wide blue skies, gladdened by lush green fields jeweled with rainbow-hued flowers, certain no harm could befall her.

Something was wrong.

Niall knew it the instant he rode into the castle yard and saw Fiona's face. Did another bucket full of mud await him upon some high beam? Or had she concocted some other fiendishly clever prank? At least he had returned early. She had not had the *whole* day to plot against him. And yet something in Fiona's eyes made him wish he were still somewhere far to the east of the castle with only a couple of rabbits trying to outwit him.

Nay, Niall reasoned as he stared down at his sister, no simple bucket of mud could have sparked such a brightness in her ever-present smirk. There was too much triumph in Fiona's dirt-smudged face for any trick so paltry.

"What devilment have you been about, girl?" he demanded, pretending not to notice her expression as he swung a brace of rabbits from his saddle.

"*I* have been in the garden," she informed him, regarding him with as much satisfaction as if she had managed to hurl a bolt of lightning at his head. "You would scarce believe what Caitlin found there!"

Unless it was a magic cloak that would whisk him leagues away from Castle Daire, Niall had little interest. "Mud?" he inquired with a grimace as he slung the rabbits over his shoulder, intent on readying them for the roasting fire. But Fiona sprang in front of him, blocking his path.

"Some of the plants lived! There will be more to eat!"

He stopped, the eagerness in the girl's face giving him a surprising twinge. "That is good, I suppose."

"Niall, do you not hear me? There will be food again at Daire, enough to keep Mother and me—"

So that was it. Caitlin had found a few stray vegetables, and Fiona had visions of a garden to rival those that fed Conn's whole fortress.

He ground his teeth, knowing he had little choice but to extinguish the girl's hopes as quickly as possible. It was kinder than letting her continue spinning out these impossible dreams. "I am certain the rabbits will enjoy eating the greens once you are gone."

Fiona looked as if he had slapped her, then that hard light sprang back into her eyes. "I am not going anywhere. You said you cannot leave Mother and me here because we might starve. Well, you will not have to concern yourself about us any longer! The garden will be brimming by the time Caitlin is done."

Niall swore under his breath. Caitlin. Had he not told the infernal woman to stop meddling about the castle? Now she had filled Fiona's head with more nonsense, as if the girl was not enough trouble on her own! Damnation, he would make the woman see reason this time or die in the attempt. She might think she was doing Fiona a kindness, but in reality it was the subtlest form of cruelty imaginable. It would only make things harder when he had to drag the girl away from Daire.

"Just where is Caitlin?" he growled.

Fiona sneered and gave an expansive shrug. "That I cannot tell you."

"Why the devil not?"

"She is gathering more plants for the garden. One of the nuns taught her how."

"Well, summon her immediately so I can put an end to this idiocy once and for all."

"I suppose I could try." Fiona smirked. "Of course, it

will take a while longer than you wish. But a champion warrior is schooled in the virtue of patience, is he not?"

If Niall had known he would be returning to Daire to confront a foe as formidable as his little sister, he would have paid a lot more attention to the lessons. "How far could Caitlin be?" He scoffed. "The garden is just around the corner."

"She is not in the garden. I told you, she is gathering plants for it."

Hell with patience, Niall thought. It was only prolonging this torture. "So you said!" He glared into his sister's face. "Now, where is she?"

"Wherever the plants are," Fiona insisted, looking at him as if he had lost his wits. "Somewhere out there." Fiona waved toward the distant hills.

Niall felt as if she had kicked him in the stomach. "You lie!" He grabbed her by the arm, furious. "This is no game, Fiona, no accursed prank! I ordered her to stay here!"

"You must practice giving commands if you ever hope to lead another army, brother. It seems neither I nor Caitlin care a whit what you say."

Fury welled up in Niall, disbelief mingling with sick dread. "You put her up to this, Fiona! Did you not?"

"You need not get in a rage. I dressed her as a boy and tucked her hair down inside her shirt. Her flock of nuns would scarce recognize her."

"That may not matter a damn, you little fool! Even if, by some miracle, no one sees her, Caitlin knows nothing about Daire land! She could get lost—hellfire, anything could happen to her!"

Fiona's bravado faded just a little. "She will mark her path."

"Will she? She has lived her whole life in an abbey, scarce left the grounds. Just how will she know what to do?"

Fiona swallowed hard. "She is not a fool, no matter what you might think!"

"Nay. But she is far away from home, from everything she has ever known. And you sent her out into the wilds without an accursed moment's pause just to defy me. If anything happens to her, it will be on your head!" Niall swung up on his horse. "Which way did she go?"

"That way." Fiona pointed west. She caught the horse's rein. "I will go, too. I did not—not think—"

"Go in the direction of Killian's old holdings. I will search along the stream." Niall urged his horse west, praying to a God he only half believed was real. How the devil was he going to find her?

He could not guess how long he rode, knew only that the thread of panic raveling in his gut unnerved him. Helpless. He felt so damned helpless as his narrowed eyes searched the horizon. At first, all he could do was try to guess what path she might take—the one most lush with growing things, the plants she was seeking. Aye, and the path most pleasing to the eye. She had been drawn to the beauty of the sea as if led by a silver ribbon.

Niall still felt a pang at the image that sprang to his mind, a raven-tressed water sprite racing toward the waves, her joy in the moment so vast, her delight in the beauty so complete, that she had not realized the danger that lurked there until it was too late.

This land had once been so rich and verdant it seemed to cradle one in the palm of its hand. But Niall's travels across Daire had shown the countryside now bore a far different face. Destruction. A land grown so wild it could be unforgiving.

Worse still, he did not even dare to call her name. It was far too dangerous. And the farther he rode, the more clearly he remembered that this land was full of dips and hollows, copses of trees and tiny hidden glens, a wealth of places he had hidden in as a boy. A situation made all the more difficult because Caitlin would be *trying* to keep out of sight.

If not for tracking skills learned in years of raiding, he would have had no hope of finding her at all. It seemed she moved like a fairy, leaving little sign she had passed. Even broken twigs and crushed bits of grass might have been left by some wild creature passing by.

But the footprint in the mud at the stream bank—that he was almost certain was hers. And the trail that began nearby of cloth sacks, carefully dampened and tucked in the shade, their burden of green things unwilted, gave Niall the first hope that he might actually find her.

He wiped sweat from his brow with the back of one hand as his gaze swept another green hillock. Strange. In the days he had been at Daire, had hunted and roamed the countryside of his childhood, not once had he ridden these western lands. He had stayed away on purpose, this part of the estate the most beautiful of all, ever his father's favorite.

This was the place where memories clung, thick as the spiderwebs that had spanned the Sea Chamber where Caitlin had slept. And all Niall wanted was to forget.

Yet the farther he rode, the more it seemed the land itself was mocking him, playing a cruel jest more disturbing than any even Fiona could have concocted. Caitlin was traveling the path he had taken so many times before as a child balanced astride his father's mighty ghost-gray stallion.

Nay, part of him pleaded, *do not go on*. But painful as it was, his memory plunged forward, relentless, memories dangling ripe as fruits over his head. Laughter, sunshine, the clean sweep of wind in his face. A glade so enchanted it seemed to hold magic of its own. A magic his family had reveled in. He could see it all, feel it all, taste it all, as if it had been yesterday.

Fiona, toddling about the berry bushes, insisting on picking the fruit herself. Grabbing the bright, juicy berries and crushing them tight in her little fists so they could not escape. Pleasure changing to puzzlement as she stared into her palm, trying to figure out where her treasure had gone.

Her little pink tongue licking off the streams of juice and pulp that remained. Then her fierce determination as she charged after another berry.

His mother, her eyes shining with pleasure and love, a flower crown upon her hair. The fairy queen, she was, destined to preside over the mock battle to come. But most painful and precious of all the memories was the gift his father had given him. Niall could remember how tight he had clutched it in his small, grubby hands.

The memories clutched at his chest until he wanted to shove them away, wanted to hold them forever. But he would never know which he would have chosen.

At that instant, Niall heard a rustle among the trees, glimpsed the slightest flash of movement. Caitlin. Relief surged through him, banishing all but the hollow ache of loss from moments before as he peered down at her.

Fragile flower petals of palest pink clung like pearls to the dark crown of her hair. Her body, slender and supple as a willow frond, bent and swayed at her task, a song rippling softly from her throat. Niall stilled, watching her. Fiona had been wrong when she claimed no one would recognize Caitlin in the disguise she had made. Niall would have known her anywhere. But it was not her beauty that betrayed her. Rather, it was her smile, her song, the way her face turned to the sun. No one he had ever known could glow so brightly, shine luminous as any star as she delved into such simple pleasures.

His throat tightened, his chest ached, the depth of his gladness at finding her startling him so much it terrified him.

He knew the instant she saw him. Dismay and guilt raced across her delicate features, then changed lightning swift to the resignation of one who was well used to being caught in her share of mischief.

He rode toward her, slowly, deliberately. When his mount was nigh nose-to-nose with her, he glared down and spoke. "I told you not to leave the castle."

She turned pleading eyes up to his. "I know you were worried about someone catching a glimpse of me, but I was careful, Niall. I saw no one. I swear it. And it seemed so important to—" She stopped, suddenly wary. A blush claimed her cheeks, and she retreated a step. She was protecting his hell-born sister, Niall knew with sudden certainty. As if Fiona needed it!

"I know full well that Fiona is behind this madness," he said. "You need not try to hide the truth."

The nervousness fled from Caitlin, her leaf-spattered shoulders squared. "If you choose to blame anyone for this, Niall, blame me. I make my own choices."

"Aye. And brilliant ones they are, lady. Hauling me up that cliff after I had tried to kill you—"

"It sorted out well enough in the end, did it not? You did not hurt me."

"But I could have! I *should* have, considering the orders I had been given." Niall sighed, taking in the stubborn jut of her chin. He might as well be talking to Fiona.

"Niall, Fiona did want me to gather plants, but that was not the only reason I went wandering. I am not used to being locked away inside all the time. I was restless. I did not mean to wander so far. Intended to be back long before—before you returned."

"That much I believe."

"Not to deceive you, but so you would not worry. You carry so much on your shoulders now." She peered up at him with such tenderness his breath caught in his throat. "I have no excuse to offer except that the day was so beautiful it was hard to resist. And this place, Niall! It must be the loveliest place in all the world! And it only grew more lovely the farther I came."

Niall understood the lure far too well. As a boy, this land had always seemed like an enchanted road, leading him onward, toward something so magical he could not even imagine it. But he had never guessed what he would find here as a man—a fairy maid, the embodiment of every dream he had never allowed himself to have.

He wanted to grab Caitlin, lash his horse into a run. Ride far away from this place that made him burn and ache like the rawest yet surprisingly most precious of wounds. But he was stunned to realize that for the first time since he had ridden up to the crumbling castle, confronted the ruin, not only of his future but his past, he felt as if he could *breathe*. Why? Because at last he had faced not only the grim memories but those other, bright-spun moments of the past, ones he had feared, avoided for so long.

Aye, this would be the most painful place he could ever return to, he thought resolutely. Once he had seen it again, the worst would be over. It could not haunt him anymore. He swung down from his horse.

"I have one question for you, madam," he said, leveling her a hard stare. "Exactly how were you planning to haul all these heavy sacks back to the castle?" He pointed to yet another dampened, dirt-stained, over-stuffed bag bristling with green things.

Caitlin gulped. "In a way, Niall, I—I am most glad to see you. You see, I fear I grew a trifle—er—greedy."

At his reluctant chuckle, she dared flash him a smile. "Niall, this is such a wondrous place! Treasures every-where! It is just like a fairy bower! How could you bear to leave it?" She stopped, aghast. "Forgive me. I did not mean—"

He hated the way her face fell, the banishment of joy. Oddly, it troubled him more than the pain of his own past. The past was a mere shadow, already gone. Caitlin was here. Now. Living, not dead like this part of his life.

"My father said this was the heart of Daire land," Niall said, wanting to comfort her. "We owed it to the land to leave this place untouched, for this heart was the power that gave the rest of the estate its bounty."

"How beautiful," she breathed. "If land can have a heart—aye, and a soul—I am certain your father was right."

"He claimed it belonged to the fairies, but I think he just loved it for its beauty. He had found something so rare he wanted to leave it as he found it. Perfect. Un-touched." Why was his gaze drawn irresistibly to Caitlin's face when he said it?

She flushed pink. "The plants, then, I should not have disturbed them."

"Nay. Even the fairies would hold it an honor that Caitlin of the Lilies had found their growing things worthy to gather." A petal clung to her cheek. He brushed it away with his thumb.

Surprise widened her eyes, and a shy pleasure that

made him want to share more, feel some sort of bond with this woman who embraced the world in all its joy and sorrow.

"We came here the day before my father was taken prisoner," he said. "All four of us. Mother and Fiona on one horse. Father and I on another. He had been away nearly two months. There had been trouble. Mother wept and made us pray for the man who was Father's dearest friend. He had died, but I could not fathom why she was crying. He was a warrior. He had died fighting."

It was the death Niall had wanted for himself for so many years. Why did it suddenly seem such a waste as he stood here, watching the sun chase blue-black shimmers through Caitlin's hair?

"I cannot say how, but I sensed that something was different. Something amiss. Father told my mother everything had been made right. But perhaps somewhere deep inside, he already knew he had but a little time left. I was not afraid. My father could fend off sea monsters, dragons, whole armies of wicked warriors. He was Ronan of Daire, a hero bards sang praises of. What could ever defeat such a man?"

"It must have been such a gift, feeling so safe."

"I did not know it then. Took for granted he would always be there, constant as the sun and moon. Such certainty only made it even more painful when he was gone." Niall's voice dropped, low. "That last day, Father did give me a gift. A wooden sword. He presented it to me as if I were a warrior grown. Commanded me to guard my mother and sister. My chest nearly burst with pride." Niall winced. "I made poor work of the mission he gave me, did I not?"

"You did the best you could. You were a boy, hurting, confused. Your father would have understood."

"I am a man now. The excuse sounds hollow." He did not know what force drove him to act—regret, guilt, or the power of all the love he had once believed was his? Niall only knew he suddenly needed to see that place again. Needed to show Caitlin.

He took her hand, led her up the hill. Their own special kingdom it had been—his mother's and Fiona's, his father's. His own. As a boy, Niall had believed if they stayed there forever, they would be immortal, like the warrior Oisin who had traveled to the Land of the Ever Young.

"There is a standing stone above the rise," he explained, "with carvings like those near the abbey." But as they crested the hill, it was not the ancient stone that held him transfixed. It was something else, something that altered the place forever.

A cairn of piled stones lay beneath the tree where they had eaten a feast that long-ago day, the last time they would break bread together as a family. Niall's throat closed as he stared at the large mound of heavy stones.

A grave. It could only be his father's.

He glanced at Caitlin for an instant, saw understanding fill her eyes.

"Your father," she breathed.

He nodded, turned back to the cairn. No weeds sprouted up around its base, no vines trailed across it. It was clean-swept, tended as if someone came to it often. Fiona, Niall thought, his heart twisting. Such unexpected tenderness from a neglected child. A girl fighting to survive yet still taking precious time to remember . . . berries on a summer's day, games of sea monster and dragon fire. Fiona trying to remember what it felt like to be loved, to be cared for, to be safe.

A bunch of fading flowers marked the top of the

stones. Caitlin bent to touch them, her face soft with sorrow.

But as some of the wilted blossoms fell away, Niall froze, staring at what lay half-hidden beneath them. A small wooden sword.

"Oh, Niall," Caitlin whispered, her eyes overbright.

Niall swallowed hard. He dropped to one knee, his fingers tracing the exquisitely carved wood of their own volition. "I fell asleep, forgot the sword here the day before my father was taken," he said hoarsely. "He promised we would come back, get it the next day."

"Where did your father get such a wondrous thing?" Caitlin asked in awe.

"He carved it himself. I remember watching him in the firelight, the shavings falling in long gold curls. Fiona kept trying to hang them upon the hound's ears."

"Whatever his mistakes, your father must have loved you very much. He would not have taken such time and care to make a child's toy if he did not."

It was true, what she said. Niall remembered the pride shining in his father's eyes whenever he had looked upon his son. The way that big hand had tousled his hair, the way his father's strong arms would swing Niall high, carrying him everywhere astride broad shoulders.

A wistful softness curved Caitlin's lips, her fingertips touching the gold of her bracelet. "It must have been wonderful, being together. Sharing everything—laughter and tears. Being so certain your parents loved you, wanted you. All the years at the abbey, I wondered why my parents abandoned me. I was lucky. The abbess loved me with all her heart. But it was not the same as having a real family. A mother and father, sisters or brothers, who were mine and mine alone. She belonged first to God, then to the abbey, then to me. Does that sound selfish of me? Ungrateful?"

"You are the most unselfish person I have ever known. And grateful? You welcome everything with joy."

"But I could never welcome my father, Niall, or fling my arms around my mother. I cannot remember feeling her heartbeat beneath my cheek or her hand upon my hair."

Her fingers traced the bracelet as if she could somehow stroke life, breath into the mellow gold curves.

"I would trade this bracelet in an instant if just once I could have felt the touch of my father's hand."

Niall's throat ached with helplessness, sadness. All the quests he had conquered, all the battles he had won seemed useless since he was unable to grant Caitlin this one impossible wish. He squeezed her hand, silent. Nothing he could say could restore what had been stolen from her.

After a moment, she turned shimmering blue eyes up to his.

"Sometimes the hardest lesson of all is to learn to forgive, Niall," she murmured. "Perhaps if you could forgive your father, remember what was good, you might start to forgive yourself."

Niall flinched inwardly. "Nay. You do not understand. After what I have done to Mother, to Fiona, how could I ever—"

"When I was a little girl, I got in so much mischief. I had such a hard time obeying rules, being good. But every time I forgot and ran in the chapel or shouted in the abbey, Reverend Mother would gather me in her arms and tell me this: It is never too late to begin again."

"Caitlin—"

She turned to him, clasping both his hands in the warmth of her own. "Listen, Niall. Truly listen to Fiona. Open your eyes, see the love in your mother's face. Do not turn away."

"I will only fail them again. In the end, I have no choice but to make them do something that will shatter their hearts. I will force them to go north, to leave Daire. They cannot stay."

"Then what little time you have left is even more precious. Fiona is not clinging to stone and earth but memories—memories of love, of being safe, of the family she has lost."

"But it is gone. Gone forever."

"Your mother only wants to love you. Let her, Niall. I swear, you will not regret it! I know it seems as though you have lost so much since you left Conn's fortress. And you have. But maybe, just maybe, you can regain something here that is even more precious. Do not think about tomorrow and worry what will happen then. Just grasp today in both hands."

"Is that your secret, Lily Fair?"

He wondered if Oisin had been lured from the world of the mortal by a fairy maid such as she. He could not take his eyes off her, the earnest beauty, the soft plea in a face as velvety soft with hope as the first flower of spring.

"But I have made so many mistakes, betrayed everything I believed . . ."

"I believe in you, Niall. Perhaps protecting your family and healing their wounds is your real quest, the one your father gave you so many years ago." She took up the wooden sword, laid it in his hands.

Chapter
12

❧

THROUGHOUT GLENFLUIRSE, the whispering had begun. The chieftain who had spent his reign surrounded by a retinue of warriors or bedding the most beautiful women now spent his nights alone, far from the eyes and ears of those who watched his every breath, his every shift of expression.

Strange? Aye, it was. The gossip spread, and yet each morning the chieftain returned to the great hall as if nothing had changed. If his face was a bit pale, his laughter was hearty. A secret lover? All of Glenfluirse wondered. But no new woman came forward. Would not any lady he so honored boast about being taken to the chieftain's bed?

Others pondered whether he was ill. That was enough to strike dread into the hearts of his most loyal followers. For who had the power to heal the chieftain?

The old druid he had trusted for so many years was fading, his powers melting away as if he had angered the spirit world he served—some claimed since the very day the druid had pronounced the destiny and doom of the great Fintan's baby daughter.

Nay, that was not it, those who knew Conn best scoffed. The chieftain was merely missing his favorite, his champion, the foster son so many resented—Niall of the Seven Betrayals, missing since the full of the moon.

But in the end, all their puzzling did not matter. No one really knew what transpired during the nights Conn barred himself in the tower room, no one except the chieftain himself.

Dreams.

Dreams that had stalked him from the day Niall had left Glenfluirse. Dreams so real they sickened the great chieftain, left him cold with terror.

In the isolated chamber, Conn fought the most grueling battle of his life, driving off sleep until it would not be denied and it grasped him in claws of blood-black velvet.

Conn writhed among his bed robes, biting the insides of his lips until they bled as he felt his enemy overwhelm him once again.

Someone had draped the dais in blood, sheets of red-stained linen gleaming upon the platform from which he had ruled nearly thirty years, the floor slowly fading as insubstantial as mist beneath his feet. Conn fought for balance, struggled to pretend nothing was amiss, as his warriors stared up at him the way they had for thirty years; yet despite his efforts, a low murmur rippled through the crowd.

Sweat ran down his spine. Could they see what he saw? The spectral figure of the spear caster looming over him, his weapon clutched in one skeletal hand. And those eyes . . . eyes blinded in life and death spitting hatred and condemnation, flaying Conn to the very bone.

My daughter . . . Fintan's voice pierced Conn deep as the spear in the dead man's hand. *I guard her even from my grave.*

Conn dared not answer the spirit, dared not say a word lest the warriors suspect . . .

Suspect what, Conn? That you are a coward? A liar? The chieftain's throat closed as another ghostly figure stepped from Fintan's shadow the way it had every night before. Ronan of Daire, forever young, vital as he had been the day he died. A man with a warrior's body, his dark hair gleaming, his face so like his son's it turned Conn's blood to ice.

Before your sword fell on me, I warned you. The dead man sneered. *The day of your reckoning will come. Your lies will be torn away like a hideous scar, and all will see the treachery beneath.*

"Nay," Conn grated under his breath, hating Ronan even in death. "It will be over soon, and your son will bury my secret with the lifeless body of Fintan's daughter."

The specter laughed. Laughed. *I know my son in ways a man like you never could. Fintan knows the truth about you. Soon my son will. Then all of Ireland. The blood price you owe so many will be paid at last.*

"Your son! You know nothing of your son! Niall hates you. I have seen to that. Aye, and made certain of this as well. Before the midsummer feasts are over, your son will be dead, and the truth will die with him!"

Ronan should have been angry, enraged, twisted with fear that he was helpless to aid his child. But Ronan only laughed . . . laughed the way he had in the cold of the dungeon, a strange triumph shining in his eyes, even when the sword blade cleaved his head.

Conn woke with a start, his body sweat-soaked and shaking, every sinew thrumming with echoes of terror. By the blood of Lugh, when would it end? Fintan stalking him through his dreams every night since Niall had slipped through the secret gate and ridden away from

Glenfluirse, not knowing he held the death warrant of Caitlin of the Lilies in his hand. Ronan, mocking him, triumphant . . .

But the victory had been his own, Conn assured himself. Ronan lay dead, the truth about his "betrayal" buried with him. And Niall, the traitor's son, was nothing more than a weapon in Conn's hand.

Conn rose from the tangle of bed robes to splash water from a bowl onto his face. He crossed to the arrow slit and peered out into the darkness. Let his enemies own his dreams. The world of daylight was his.

It would all be over soon. The plan he had perfected years ago. The instant he got some word from Niall, the power Ronan and Fintan held over him would be broken forever. And the dangerous whisperings of those at Glenfluirse would be silenced.

Aye, Conn reasoned, pacing the chamber. Niall would not fail him. He would ride through the secret gate, his sword warm from the girl's blood, his loyalty still like a sickness in his face. And then it would begin . . . Niall's destruction.

The deed Niall had done would eat him alive from the inside out. After all, Conn thought with a weak smile, Niall was the honorable Ronan's son.

When he could no longer bear to live, he would strike a quick stroke with his own sword, and Niall of the Seven Betrayals would be dead by his own hand. If the betrayer's son proved too strong to do this, Conn would merely stage his death, make others believe Niall had taken his own life.

The plan was brilliant, Conn assured himself. It could not fail.

Wrapping himself in fresh clothes, Conn schooled his features into a careless expression, then left the room that still echoed with the voices of the dead. But he had barely stepped beyond its confines when Magnus, his eldest, strode into the hall.

Brawny and shrewd, ruthless and cunning, he was a son any chieftain could take pride in, Conn thought as he watched the heir for whom he had fashioned a kingdom approach him.

Not that Magnus suspected his father's ambitions for his future. Nay, as a boy, he had been fed on praises of Niall's battle skills, his sense of honor, until Magnus and all of Glenfluirse had seethed with the suspicion that the son of a traitor, a boy who should have been killed years ago, would someday stand as chieftain above them all.

The illusion had served its purpose well, hardening Magnus, teaching him to play political games, win allies and keep them, if not through loyalty, then through fear. Lessons that would serve Magnus well in the years to come.

Of course, there had been one unforeseen difficulty, Conn had long admitted to himself. There were those at Glenfluirse whose bitterness toward Niall had turned to respect, men now eager to have Niall as their overlord despite the stain of his past. It had taken great subtlety to remind them just how unfit he was to rule. Fortunately he had had an ally in that quest: Niall himself, who would forever feel unworthy.

Conn kept any hint of affection carefully out of his expression as he faced his sullen son.

"Can a chieftain not be given a few moments' peace upon arising?" he growled.

Magnus stiffened. "A scrawny whelp of a boy insists upon seeing you—one Owaine come in from the wilds west of Glenfluirse."

Conn yawned. "Let me make a guess about his purpose. He wishes to become a warrior."

"Aye, though a well-aimed sneeze would likely blast him all the way to the Irish Sea."

Conn grimaced. He had little patience for the grandiose dreams of stripling boys at present.

"But that is not all the boy said." Discontent simmered in Magnus's eyes. "He claims he carries word for you from one of your warriors."

There was only one warrior Conn wished news from at present, and that man would send no messenger. He would feel honor bound to ride in alone, deliver his news himself. But it would be reckless to stir the curiosity of anyone in Glenfluirse. If they suspected Conn only had one matter on his mind, they might begin to probe for answers. He must still rule his lands whether Niall made haste back to Glenfluirse or no.

"Bring the message to me, and send the boy on his way."

Magnus glowered. "He will give the message to no one, the insolent wretch. Not even the chieftain's son! He says he promised to put it into your hand."

"And did this difficult whelp say who sent the message?" Edgy from his restless night, Conn's voice dropped to that low, dangerous tone that made even the hulking Magnus pale a trifle.

"The message is from Niall." Magnus all but spat the name. For an instant, Conn thought he had misheard him. Then he stared in disbelief. Relief warred with confusion and a wild eagerness he fought to hide. Pray the gods nothing had gone awry, Conn thought. If anyone discovered that he had planned the girl's murder, it could mean disaster.

"Send this *Owaine* to me."

"You would see this insolent pup who has insulted me? Why? Because he comes from Niall?"

"I would see the devil himself if Niall sent him.

Now, go. Has anyone else in the fortress seen this messenger?"

"Most were still sleeping. As for the others, do you think I would let any man in the fortress see him treating me with scorn while spouting Niall's name as if he were lord of the sea?"

"You were wise, Magnus, to guard your dignity so carefully. You have so little of it left."

Rage mingled with humiliation shimmered in the young man's eyes, but he stormed away without another word.

Aye, Conn thought. Let Magnus's wounds fester only a little while longer, then he would be tempered like a blade in fire. "Soon you will be hardened enough to do whatever you must do to rule, my son," Conn murmured.

It seemed mere moments before Magnus returned, the boy in tow. He did not even reach Conn's chin and looked as if he had not eaten in weeks, but his eyes burned with that inner fire no mere training with sword and spear could match. Pity he had become embroiled in this matter, Conn thought. A boy of his kind could prove quite useful.

"So this is the messenger chosen by the mightiest warrior of Glenfluirse." Conn let a smile spread across his face. "The choice calls into question my foster son's judgment, I am afraid. Tell me, boy. Just how did Niall choose you?"

"I was on my way here when he found me thrashing four knaves twice my size." The boy thrust out his narrow chest. "I come to offer my services as a warrior."

"You? A warrior?" Magnus gave a snort of laughter. "Niall must have lost his wits!" Laughter burst from Magnus.

Color burned into the lad's cheeks. "I will match my skills against yours whenever you are ready!"

"There will be time aplenty for you to thrash Magnus after you give me your message." Conn could not stifle a smirk. "Magnus, you had best grab your sword and make ready to go to the practice field. Leave us," Conn ordered his son. "I am always eager to hear what Niall has to say. And awake the bard. Perhaps there is yet another quest to be immortalized in song."

Magnus slunk off with a parting glare that boded ill for the boy. After all, Conn thought, if one could not take his anger out upon Niall himself . . .

When he was alone with young Owaine, Conn planted his hands upon his hips. "Now, tell me, boy, what is this message you carry? Speak up!"

"I cannot tell you. It is written, and I would not shame myself by prying into what is meant for your eyes alone."

"Ah, a good boy. An honorable one. Niall always did have a gift for finding such traits in others."

The boy reached into his grimy shirtfront, extracting a sheet of vellum sweaty and stinking, much battered from the journey.

Conn grimaced, then turned his back on the boy and read. Triumph surged through him, delight purer and more exhilarating than the moment when he had struck off Ronan's head.

It is done! he rejoiced. Better still, his plan had worked even beyond his own imaginings. Niall was already so devastated by the act he had performed that he could not face his chieftain, could not face the other warriors. Before long, the most honorable warrior Conn had ever known would not even be able to face himself. What poetic justice that would be, everyone in

Glenfluirse believing Ronan's only son had died by his own sword, drowning in shame.

Conn thrust the missive into the fire that burned in the hearth, watching the flames devour it. At last, he turned to Owaine.

"Curiosity is a powerful force. You are certain you did not read what Niall wrote?" he asked again.

Outraged at the insult but trying to conceal it, Owaine peered up at him, guileless as a calf at slaughter time. "Even if I were such a deceitful cur, I could not betray the greatest warrior of Glenfluirse. I cannot read."

Conn smiled. "You are a fine lad. A brave one. One deserving of a reward. You say you wish to be a warrior. Every warrior needs a weapon."

Conn drew the dagger from his waist, the jeweled hilt shimmering. "Come here, boy. Close. I will honor you with the dagger of a chieftain." *Aye*, a voice in Conn's head jeered, *and a death far above the station of a beggar the likes of you.*

But Owaine took a step backward. He could not possibly suspect Conn was about to kill him?

"I wish to keep the dagger I have," the lad asserted stubbornly.

Conn gaped, stunned. "What weapon could be finer than the dagger of a chieftain?"

"The dagger of a hero who will live forever." Owaine's eyes filled with awe, with worship, as he drew the familiar, shimmering weapon from beneath the folds of his dirt-encrusted clothes. "The magical blade Niall of the Seven Betrayals won in his quest."

Irritation bit deep. Why should it annoy him so? Conn wondered. It was nothing but the rejection of a fool boy, too stupid to be canny, blinded by hero worship and the tales men whispered of valor in battle and hintings of Niall's mysterious quests.

Conn grimaced. It had seemed so wise years ago when he had forbidden Niall to speak of his quests. Conn had thought silence would keep Niall from growing too powerful, too famed among the people. Niall had kept that oath, but in the end, Ronan's son had turned that sword against him as well. There were others who discovered fragments of stories regarding Niall's feats of courage, men who filled long, dark hours of night with tales that grew grander, more magical, with each telling. Strange that in all his plotting, Conn had never guessed that mysterious scraps of tales would only make the people ravenous for more, the bits of tales they could glean about Niall's heroics far more intriguing than full-blown stories could ever be.

In the end, those tales would have made Niall immortal while Conn faded into the mists of time, until no man living knew his name. But the death of Caitlin of the Lilies would change all that. Once all Ireland knew Glenfluirse's great warrior had cut her down in cold blood, Niall of the Seven Betrayals would live in infamy until the end of time.

Murderous rage ripped through Conn, rage he had so seldom allowed himself to feel. Even now it was a mistake.

He saw something flash into the boy's eyes—the wariness of a wild thing that has had to fight its whole life to survive. With an oath, Conn lunged for Owaine, the dagger blade aimed at the boy's throat. But Owaine flung up his arm, Niall's dagger blocking Conn's blow with a strength and skill impossible for a boy so small.

Thrown off balance, Conn stumbled, fell, striking his midsection on the hard edge of a table as Owaine darted past him. Conn could not speak, could not breathe, his chest a burning pit of pain as the boy raced from the room.

Conn gasped, staggered after Owaine, but the boy was gone. "Magnus!" Conn struggled to cry out, certain his son would have the sense to grab the runaway boy. But Magnus was busy taking out his own anger upon one of the castle hounds.

Conn kicked over a bench to get his attention. Magnus wheeled, eyes widening in shock as he saw Conn doubled over. "The boy," Conn croaked. "Catch the boy!"

An hour later, Magnus returned, failure and dread etched in his face. "It is as if he vanished by some druid spell!" he defended himself, rubbing his sweaty brow in bemusement.

Conn's hands knotted into fists. "Gather a score of the warriors you trust most. Send them in search of this Owaine."

Magnus stared in astonishment. "The . . . warriors that I—"

"Aye, you fool! Are you deaf? Those loyal only to you." *And those who hate Niall*, Conn left unspoken, for that core of loyalty Niall had won in some warriors was as unyielding as iron. "Did the boy say where he came from?"

"The west."

"Aye. That is where he will flee, to try to warn his hero, to tell Niall—" Conn stopped, glared at his son. "Begin your search in that direction. Tear the countryside to shreds if you need to. Whoever shelters the boy must be killed. And whoever finds the boy will be rewarded beyond his wildest hopes, as long as he speaks not a word to the lad, aye, nor to anyone except you. This is what you will tell your men."

Magnus beamed.

"I offer you a chance to prove yourself," Conn said.

"I will bring the boy to you, and the warrior as well," Magnus vowed.

"Nay." Conn fingered the blade of his own dagger. "You will kill them both."

Magnus blanched. "But—but if the warrior is loyal, why must he be killed?"

"There are times a chieftain cannot risk even the most loyal men knowing his secrets. Friends can become enemies in a heartbeat, then take revenge by telling all the world what you would have no man know." Conn staggered to the arrow slit, glaring out into the countryside beyond. "It is time you learned to rule. Do not return to me without blood on your hands."

Chapter 13

IT WAS MORE THAN A WEEK later when Fiona stormed into the neat little garden, a fresh-carved spear in one hand, her brow drawn in its perpetual glower. Caitlin glanced up and wondered if the girl's face would freeze that way one day. She stifled a sigh and struggled to muster a smile for Niall's sister.

"I have finally unraveled what all this—this madness is about." Fiona waved the spear in the air. "My brother cannot fool me with all these dripping acts of concern. The vile knave is trying to poison me!"

Caitlin could not help but laugh as she brushed the dirt from her hands. "Fiona, I am certain that he is not—"

"And to make doubly certain he is plagued by me no longer, he has devised another plan in case the poison fails. An unfortunate hunting accident when he is teaching me to throw this woman-sized spear!" She cast the beautifully formed weapon into the pile of half-wilted weeds Caitlin had spent the morning uprooting.

Caitlin winced, touching the fallen spear with an odd twinge, knowing it was as close as she would ever get to touching the soul of the man who had been her father. "Fiona, Niall would never hurt you. Whatever could have given you such a crazed idea?"

"This is the third morning in a row I have come down to find a basket full of berries sitting at my place at the table. I have pondered it long and hard, and there can be only one reason Niall put them there. He has doubtless poured some potion over them to drug me insensible so he can bend me to his will!"

Caitlin laughed, shaking out the skirts of her leine as she stood. "For the love of the saints, Fiona—"

"And as if that is not villainous enough, there is the despicable way he is behaving toward our mother!" Fiona shuddered in pure outrage. "Do you have any idea what he has done to her?"

"I cannot begin to imagine."

"He has taken her to gather flowers!"

"An innocent enough pastime, I would think."

"He intends to place them upon our father's grave!" If the girl had accused Niall of tossing babies about on spear points, she could have seemed no more horrified.

A surge of sympathy squeezed Caitlin's chest—sympathy for this confused, angry girl, her bewildered, life-battered mother, and the man who was taking his first stumbling steps across the chasm of hurt and betrayal that had kept him separated from them for so long.

"Perhaps it is time they both mourned," Caitlin suggested softly.

"Mourn? Niall hates our father. He has made no secret of it. This is just a trick to put us off our guard. Niall is Conn's son now! I should have guessed that it was only a matter of time before he resorted to the chieftain's ways. Aye, lure your enemy in with a show of false kindness when he is most desperate, offer forgiveness like some sweet goblet of silver when he is dying of thirst, then the instant he starts to take a drink, yank the snare tight about his throat until he cannot breathe!"

Caitlin stared at her. "Do you truly believe Niall is capable of such treachery toward anyone? He is the most honorable man I have ever known."

"He is the *only* man you have ever known!" Fiona scoffed. "Growing up in an abbey did not furnish you with many examples, I would imagine. *I* have seen what men can do! The best—men like our old servant Keefe, who gave his hand, would have given his life to protect us. Aye, and my father, with his courage and honor. And I have seen the worst in the men who raided Daire." Fiona paced across a cluster of tiny parsnip shoots, so distraught she trampled several of her precious new plants. She caught sight of the bedraggled little stems and cursed under her breath.

Wheeling, she glared at Caitlin in blatant accusation. "I knew how to treat Niall before. But now——" Something vulnerable stole into her eyes for a heartbeat before she shuttered it away.

"Now you are afraid?" Caitlin suggested. "For it would hurt you too terribly if the change in him was not real?"

Fiona bristled with denial. "I am not afraid! Niall is nothing to me anymore."

"If that is true, I am sorry for you both. I know you mean a great deal to him."

"Bah!" Fiona spat on the ground. "You are mad."

"The day I wandered off gathering plants, he——"

"Doubtless raged at you for daring to defy him."

"A little, at first," Caitlin admitted, surprised at the tender throb she felt in her breast at the memory. "He had been searching for me a long time, had feared for me. He takes too much responsibility upon himself."

"Tell me nothing about my brother's sense of *responsibility*, Caitlin! We have all but starved on it here at Daire."

The hard accusation was true, Caitlin knew, and yet it was far too simple to lay blame at Niall's feet. What had happened between Fiona and Niall and the land that was their birthright was far more complex than either of them could admit. The web of pain and hurt, torn loyalties and betrayal and reluctant love, was spun between them in a tangle that Caitlin had puzzled over through countless restless nights. A tangle that still left her bewildered and aching for them all.

"I can only imagine what it was like for you, losing your father and brother, being left alone here to struggle to take care of your mother. But I do know this—after Niall found me wandering the hills, he told me about the last day you all spent together as a family here, your mother's joy, your father's laughter. He described the way you darted about the bushes like a fairy child, gathering fistfuls of berries, remembered you could not eat enough of them. When he spoke of you, I saw how vivid the memory was to him, how painful, how precious. He recalled just how much you loved the berries so long ago. Is it not possible that his gifts are telling you things he cannot say?"

Fiona fretted her bottom lip. "The only thing Niall can do for me now is to ride away from Daire, leave Mother and me as he found us! I want nothing from him."

"If that were true, you would have thrown his wooden sword into the fire, not kept it, safe, tucked away upon your father's cairn so many years."

Fiona gaped, her cheeks flaming as if she had been caught in some shameful act. "How—how did you know?"

"Niall and I found the sword together. It is a beautiful place where your father sleeps, Fiona. So peaceful, well tended, filled with the love and memories you tried so hard to keep alive. After what I saw there, you will never make me believe that you had forgotten your brother."

"Nay!" Fiona said in a hard little voice. "I *buried* him there, in my heart, with my father. It was easier to pretend he was dead than admit that he left me behind on purpose and never even glanced back. The brother I knew is dead."

"He is alive, Fiona. And devoured by his guilt. He was only a boy when Conn came to Daire, a helpless child just like you were, caught up in things he could not control. He lost his father the same terrible way you did, but you still had your mother and Daire, fragments of their love all around you. He was swept away from everything and everyone he had ever known."

"You cannot expect me to give him sympathy?"

"He is not asking for your sympathy. Not even your forgiveness. All he is asking you to give him, Fiona, is a chance."

"A chance for what? To play at fairies and dragons again? A chance to bandage scraped knees and soothe my hurts? A chance to be part of the family he cast to the devil? It is not so simple to forget all that happened. You cannot begin to understand!"

"That is true. I never knew my family, and now I never will. They are dead. It is too late for me. But not for you. Niall meant to kill me in the woods that first night after we left the abbey. I could still hate him for that. But I have not regretted for a moment offering him another chance. He has shown me anger, aye, and impatience, but also great tenderness, a questing spirit, a desperate desire to do what is right. He is a man with flaws like anyone, but he is a man who tries, Fiona."

The girl stared at her, almost pouting, obviously torn. "But what if . . ."

"If he fails you again? Then you will be as you were when we found you—alone. But if you can mend things with Niall, heal this wound between you and your brother . . . think, Fiona. Neither of you will ever be alone again."

The girl swallowed hard, and, despite Fiona's best efforts to disguise it, Caitlin saw a flicker of hope in her face. "Is this how your nuns argue people out of lives of sin?"

Caitlin smiled. "I do not believe anyone could persuade you to do anything you did not want to do deep inside, Fiona. But if you sift through what I have said, if it feels right to you, then why not take this chance?"

Muttering imprecations on nuns, brothers, and perfectly good rages ruined, Fiona turned and walked away. Caitlin sighed, noting that Fiona strode determinedly in the opposite direction from the path Niall and his mother had taken earlier.

Stubborn and brave, bruised and still hurting, the girl tugged at Caitlin's heart almost as much as the stalwart man who was Fiona's brother, a man who had finally opened his heart to the most fragile sense of hope.

Twilight ran fingers of rose and gold across the green hills of Daire, setting their crests aglow with impossible beauty. Niall paused for a moment at his task. A rusted knife he had unearthed amidst the rubble of the castle mews days earlier was dulled with scraps of wood shavings as he gazed up at the countryside that had once been his home. As the adored son of Ronan, he had been too busy about his mischief to take in the magic of this place. And as Conn's fosterling, he had been too bitter to remember Daire with anything save shame. But now, he saw the land as his father must have an eternity ago, with an unbidden welling of pride, an unwelcome ache at the rich gift of belonging to such a place.

But nay, Niall thought with a twinge of sadness. He could never truly belong to Daire. Soon Conn would grow impatient with the absence of his strongest warrior and the foster son he had affection for. The longer Niall was absent, the more suspicions would be aroused that something was amiss. It would not be long before Conn would send men searching. Niall would have to ride away, leave Daire behind. Strange that a place he had hated, land he had despised for years, should suddenly steal into his heart.

The knife skidded off a knot in the wood, and he cursed as it nicked one finger. Niall stared down at the drops of blood soaking into the turf at his feet. Aye, his blood, the blood of his father, his father's father, all had flowed from this land, made it almost . . . sacred somehow. What a terrible time to realize such a truth, just as he was losing Daire again forever.

But he would take memories with him, and so would his sister. Precious things no chieftain or cruel twist of fate could ever steal. He turned back to the object he had labored on for nearly three days, uncertainty and pride warring inside him. It was nearly finished. Perhaps somehow it would help Fiona understand.

A crunching of footsteps on the stone-scattered turf startled him. He leapt to his feet with a warrior's instinct. His cheeks burned when he saw Fiona smirking down at his cut finger.

"Did Conn's warriors fail to teach you how to handle sharp edges, brother?" she asked, shaking her head in mock dismay.

A stinging retort sprang to his lips, but he swallowed it, forcing himself to look past Fiona's nasty expression to the softness all but hidden in eyes so like his own.

But her gaze had already fallen on his carving—a box just big enough for her to carry, its wooden surface gold and new and sweet-smelling from the stroke of his knife. "I could understand you spending your time carving the spear. It is a weapon, after all, even though I cast it in the dirt. But Niall of the Seven Betrayals, Conn's mightiest warrior, taking up the task of a mere underling?" She pressed her hand against her breast in mock dismay. "What could be so important you would lower yourself to such depths?"

"This is." Niall straightened, stunned at the flutter of excitement and unease in the pit of his stomach, wanting so much to please her. "It is a—a chest."

"I can see that." She pulled a face. "What is it for? The heads of your enemies? The blood gold you should have gotten for Caitlin's murder?"

He would not let her burning words anger him. "I made it for you."

Fiona's eyes widened, something sweet and fearful and precious curving her lips. Surprise. Disbelief. Hope.

Niall sucked in a deep breath. "I hoped that you could put your treasures in it, all the things you wish to remember. That way, you can keep a part of Daire with you even after we must leave it."

The tentative softness in the girl's face ripped away, leaving her eyes hollow with a pain and disappointment so great it stunned him. "I fear you did not make it big enough," she said. "It cannot hold my father's cairn. Do you think I would leave him behind? Abandon him as you did?"

The accusation cut deeper than any blade, a surge of grief and loss crippling Niall as he stared into the hate-filled face of his sister. He could not bear to suffer her loathing another moment without trying to explain—

explain what? Impossible things, things he could never alter, regrets he would carry forever. Perhaps he might even make her understand.

"I did not abandon him!" Niall said. "I left him because he told me to do it!"

Fiona wheeled on him, snarling. "What are you saying?"

"Perhaps it is time you heard the truth. You think you know what I did so long ago, Fiona? Why I did it?"

"Why should I care—"

"I do not know, damn it to hell! But you are going to hear it. The day Conn took Father prisoner, I went with the riders because—because I believed I could save him somehow. It sounds absurd now. I know it. A mere boy pitted against Conn's whole army. But my head was bursting with hero tales, the tales Father told us around the fire on long winter nights. Cuchulain, the greatest hero Ireland has ever known, was just a boy when he performed some of his greatest feats. And when we held mock battles, Father had always claimed I was strong as Cuchulain himself."

"Aye," Fiona whispered. "I remember."

"When Conn scooped me up onto his horse, I remember thinking that if only I had not forgotten my wooden sword, I could have dashed him to the ground. But I knew I would have to find some way to help Father without it." Niall's hands tightened into fists as he remembered his anger, his confusion, his childhood terror that somehow he would not be strong enough, brave enough, cunning enough for what lay ahead. That he would fail the father he adored.

"When we reached Glenfluirse, Father was dragged away, and I was taken to Conn's own rooms, thrown in among his sons and the warrior training them. I begged Conn to let me see Father every time the chieftain came near. I even got down on my knees. I knew Father would hate it that I had, but I just wanted to see him so much. If I could just see Father, he would laugh and make me believe this was just some grand adventure like the legends we loved. In the end, everything would be well." Niall's voice broke. He turned away from his sister's gaze.

"The warriors and Conn's sons said terrible things about Father. They claimed he had murdered his best friend, raped his wife. And when Conn rode to stop him, they claimed Father killed the woman so no one would bear witness to his treachery, leaving her fortress burning and her babes in a pool of blood."

"I heard it all, too, Niall," Fiona cried, "spat out by Conn's men when they destroyed Daire. I still do not believe it!"

"Do you think I wanted to, Fiona? Believe that our father was capable of such treachery? That he could sweep me up on his horse, ride and laugh in the sunshine, play at swords with me and make flower crowns for our mother, when he had done such hideous things?"

"How could you even think it for a moment?"

"Because Father confessed the truth to me, Fiona! I heard it from his own lips!" Niall shuddered inwardly, the ball of fire in his gut alive again as if, even now, he stared through the barred window of his father's dungeon.

"Late one night, I managed to sneak away from the warrior guarding me. I had plotted and planned for weeks, discovering where the dungeon was, learning how to slip through the fortress without alerting the guards. I had even managed to steal the key from Conn's own room. I was going to release Father, Fiona, so that both of us could ride back to you. But when I reached him, he sent me away. Father told me to leave him to his fate. He was the one at fault. He said that the truth would always be stripped bare in the end."

Tears streaked Fiona's cheeks. "Nay," she whimpered, sounding so much a child. "He loved our mother. Loved *us!* He would never—"

"Then why did he tell me he had done such terrible things?" Niall demanded, his own voice tearing. "He was going to die the next day, Fiona. I was his son, the only one on earth who could have—*would have*—defended his honor with the last drop of my blood. I wanted to believe he was innocent, honorable, all the things I had always believed he was! No one wanted to believe in our father more than I did!"

"He was Ronan of Daire!" Fiona shrilled. "The bards sang of his honor, his honesty!"

"Do you not see, Fiona?" Niall asked in stark despair. "That is why I had to believe him when he told me. I never heard him tell a lie, did you?"

Fiona choked on a sob. "There must—must be some reason—"

"Why? Why would he make me believe such terrible things about him if it were not true?"

"Because Conn threatened to kill you if he did not—"

"Conn did not even know I was there. He never knew, Fiona. I was alone with Father that night. Why would he lie?"

"I do not know!" Fiona cried, shaking. "I only know I will not believe—"

"You do not have to." Niall reached out, gently touching his sister's tear-wet cheek. "But believe this, Fiona. Our father would not want you clinging to this land, alone, half-starving in his name. I know Father loved you too much to want to see you destroy yourself this way. Staying at Daire is not being loyal to him,

Fiona. It is the greatest sin you could commit against his memory."

There was a longing, a grief, so fierce in Fiona that it made his chest ache. In that instant, she was his tiny sister again, with her shining hair and bright eyes, clinging to his hand as if he could slay dragons.

"This chest I made is to hold things you remember, Fiona. It is time for all of us to let go of old pain, to take what is good and treasure it."

Fiona stared at him, and he could see battles being waged in her eyes. After an inner struggle so fierce it seemed she might shatter, she backed away. "Nay, Niall. I will not listen to you! Even if Father . . ."

Even now, she could not bring herself to say it. "You left me behind! Alone! I always believed you would come for me, as you always had before. I remember crying for you, watching for you until my eyes ached, but you never came!"

Her bitter laugh tore at him. "Aye, that is, until you were an outlaw, knowing soon half of Conn's army would be pursuing you. Niall, the legendary champion, my great, heroic brother! Finally trapped in a corner so desperate you were willing to endanger our lives to save your own!"

The words scalded him in their agonizing honesty.

"Give me one reason why I should trust you!" Fiona demanded. "For years, as I wandered the hills, I have heard stories of your mysterious quests from those journeying through—what little could be spoken aloud. Tales of encounters with the Queen of the Fairies, turning back the charge of a full army with only your sword, crossing the sea to pluck the harp of the Tuatha de Danaan out of enemies' hands—the tales reached us even here."

"Fiona, most of it is nonsense. Stories other people

made up to entertain wee ones about the fire. Surely, you must have known that. I am forbidden by oath to speak of the quests."

"And were the other stories I heard *nonsense* as well? Tales of the feasts held in your honor while Mother and I went hungry? You cared nothing for either of us then. You came to Daire only because you found a reason to use us."

Shame darkened Niall's cheeks. "I will never forget what I have cost you," he said. "But what is past is past. I can never change it. I will not lie. I came here because I had no other choice. I hated this place. Everything about it. It was too raw, Fiona, too painful. But now, I do not regret riding into Daire any longer. When I did, I found you."

He looked into her face, so strong yet suddenly so fragile. Pain too great. Betrayal too deep. Aye, Niall thought with a sick jolt. He had begged forgiveness too late. She was afraid, too terrified to trust him, because he had failed her so terribly before.

"We were strangers before you came here," Fiona said in a cold, hard voice. "That is how we will part." She turned her back to him, walked away, and it was as if he had lost her again for the very first time.

Niall stared down at the box, closed the lid he had carved with such rare hope. Good things he had asked Fiona to store away inside it, but all his sister had left was pain.

Stars scattered the heavens like cascades of glittering blue blossoms cast by a fairy child's hand. The new moon beamed silvery approval down on the earth below, ground bursting with the power of life renewing itself. It seemed all of Daire was heavy with the weight of that mystic spell—green things flourishing at impossible speed, wild creatures who had fled the bedraggled lands once again daring to creep about the old castle, trailed by their enchanting wee babes.

The sight had lifted Caitlin's spirits as little else could have, each soft-eared baby rabbit or gangly, tottering fawn giving her a sense of hope, something she had desperately needed in the days since Fiona had cast the newly carved spear at her feet.

Caitlin stroked the wooden shaft she so often carried with her of late, taking comfort in the feel of the weapon in her hand. The balance and suppleness of the wood, the promise of flight that emanated from the spear, in a way, so like herself. For no matter how carefully fashioned the spear might be, it would never soar through the air as it was meant to, just as she would never soar into the life of freedom and love and joy she had dreamed of for so long. Both of them were earthbound, hidden away. Imprisoned without bars to hold them.

But she was not the only one suffering loss, she thought with a sigh. Despite all her hopes and all her entreaties, things had gone awry between Niall and his sister again.

She leaned her cheek against the smooth length of wood and closed her eyes. It was painfully evident her pleas that Fiona try to forgive her brother had fallen on deaf ears. The girl's resentment boiled beneath the surface like the distant thunder of a summer storm, while Niall's silent pain etched even darker circles beneath haunted glen-green eyes.

Yet he had stoically soldiered on with heartbreaking determination. He kept watch over his mother with an attentiveness that made Aniera seem to grow younger with each day, and he still attempted to reach out to his bitter young sister no matter how many times she pushed him away.

Caitlin prayed she had not made things worse for Niall by her interference, making him hope for things that could never be.

But this was the season for miracles and hopes, and she could feel the awakening of Daire all around her. Why should she not hope and pray for the healing of hearts as well?

A loud quack startled Caitlin from her musings, and she could not help but smile at the droll sight of a mother duck settling her fluffy yellow babies for the night in their nest among the reeds.

It had taken a deal of persuading to keep Fiona from scavenging the eggs the morning they had found the duck's nest, Caitlin remembered. But in the end, they had broken their fast with greens from the garden and berries Niall had found, and left the nest alone.

It was good to have a bit of company, especially tonight, Caitlin thought, even if the ducklings could not talk back to her. For this was not a night to be alone.

It was Imbolc. A time of festival for all who dwelled west of the Slieve Mish mountains. Fiona had babbled on about it for a week. Bonfires and feasting, dancing and singing, a celebration so sweeping it was even open to the destitute outcast women of Castle Daire.

Fiona had tantalized Caitlin with descriptions of the revels for days, entreating her to come along. After all, Fiona had badgered her, what life had she seen in a convent? It was past time Caitlin opened her eyes and gazed at the world around her.

In the hours before Niall had ridden off hunting that morning, he had only seemed all the more weary at Fiona's assault against the rules he had set for their safety, but his quiet fear for her had unsettled Caitlin far more than his imperious commands of weeks before.

So, even though she was sorely tempted, Caitlin had remained behind at the deserted castle while Aniera and Fiona had gone off without her, cascades of flowers woven in their hair.

It was better this way, Caitlin assured herself. She was beginning to love Daire, and no mere festival was worth putting her newfound friends at risk. Even more surprising was the fact that every day that passed made it harder to think of leaving the castle and the family she had found there.

It was as if their lives, their loss, their love, were winding about her like a silken thread until she wanted to believe their hopes and dreams and fears were her own.

Her eyes burned at the memory of Aniera, mere moments before she and Fiona had left, the older woman stroking Caitlin's hair with the same innate tenderness the abbess had. Aniera's voice had grown soft, filled with affection more precious to Caitlin than she could say.

I remember how Ronan and I danced upon this night so many years ago. Always we dreamed of the day our son would swirl his love about the fires. Then, one day, Ronan was gone. Niall was gone. And I stopped hoping, until the first time I saw Niall with you. Do not despair, child. The fires of Imbolc will burn for you yet.

The words had left Caitlin puzzled, encouraged. How much did Aniera truly see? How much did she remember? Such a sensitive heart lay in Niall's mother's breast, and it had seen such tragedy. Yet there was love and hope in her as well. A heart so like her son's.

What would it be like if all these troubles could be banished? If Daire could truly come alive again and Niall could lead her to the bonfires, letting the golden light illuminate both their faces without fear? How marvelous would it be to listen to music she had never heard, to have such a man teach her the steps of dancing she had never seen before?

But she could not even imagine the festival Aniera and Fiona were enjoying, Caitlin thought sadly. Her mind did not know what kind of image to paint.

She sighed, her eyes straining toward the faint glow atop a hill she could barely see. If only Niall would come back so she could explain to him how much she wished to catch a glimpse of the celebration, just a peep that would harm no one. But there was no way of guessing when Niall would return, if he would ride in too late to grant her wish.

And he would if he were able, Caitlin knew. He had been gentler with her since the secrets they had shared near his father's cairn, more understanding. Surely, if she kept herself hidden, took only the shortest peek at the revelers, he would not mind so very much.

But how to let him know where she had gone? She glimpsed the flowers left over from the crowns Fiona had woven earlier that day. Niall must have memories of the festival from his childhood. With Fiona's anticipation still echoing in his ear, surely he would remember and guess Caitlin had gone to the celebration, too.

Gathering the discarded blossoms tenderly, Caitlin left them upon the scarred wood table, where he would see them the moment he entered the hall. Just as she started to turn away, she paused, taking up one sweet white bloom to tuck in her hair. Inhaling its rich perfume, she stole away into the gathering darkness, following the path she had watched Fiona and Aniera take hours earlier. After a while, she caught the faint sound of music, glimpsed the glow of flame high on a hilltop, the light guiding her on her way.

The sky was blue-black by the time she neared the edge of the celebration, the faint music reaching out to tease her with its unnamed beauty. Like the jewels on the abbey's chalice, the bonfire glowed against the soft cup of night's hand. And rich, unfamiliar scents that made Caitlin's mouth water drifted from where the feast spread out beyond her sight.

Yet as she crept nearer, it was the swaying bodies of the people that held her in thrall. Laughter rippled in crystal waves, jests rang out between the couples feeding an intensity hotter than any fire that ever burned. Even in her innocence, she sensed there was not mere lust between those who swirled in the dance but, rather, passion for life primitive and unfettered, fierce and consuming.

Her heart pounded at the sight of it as she crouched behind a stone, the pulsing rhythm of the music seeming to beat in tune with her own racing heart. Never had she dreamed of anything like this. Never had she heard sounds like those echoing from the instruments she had never seen. The pounding of a drum, the allure of strings and pipes, voices mingling in song and laughter.

This was life distilled to its very essence. Magic, enchantment, the wild refrain of the Irish hills that had called to her even long ago behind the abbey walls. She was desperate to be a part of that whirling, beautiful force, but she dared only to peek at it through the shadows, still hidden away from the world, as she had been her whole life.

Nor would that ever change, Caitlin thought with a sting of sorrow. Any sight of her would be dangerous in the years to come; anyone who showed her kindness would be placed in danger of Conn's vengeance should he discover that she lived. After all Niall and his family had sacrificed by helping her, she could never risk putting anyone else in the same kind of peril. She would forever live in the shadows, watching the brilliant colors and tastes and scents of life swirl past without her, as useless and untested as the spear that would never fly.

But she swallowed the unbidden tears that rose in her throat, determined that she would not waste one moment of this night in grieving for what she could not have. She drew into the darkest haven of shadows, closing her eyes, letting her feet move as they would to music so wondrous it made her throat ache. She imagined Niall smiling up at her, sweeping her skyward in arms so strong he could sail her to the moon itself.

She could almost hear the rare, precious gift of his laughter as he caught her again, feel his mouth on hers, hungry, eager, despite the crowd all around them, unafraid of the pulsing of life itself in their bodies, unashamed as they celebrated the lush gift of fertile ground and greening fields.

It is ready, all the world seemed to sing. The womb of earth and doe and woman swelling with the mystery of the yet-to-be-born. And Caitlin's own body stirred with a hunger and a grief she had never known she would feel.

She opened her eyes, saw a broad-shouldered youth drag his laughing partner off into a copse of trees, as if both were unable to bear the torture of their separate bodies another moment. Caitlin flushed, knowing instinctively they were stealing off alone to celebrate the desire that shone in their faces.

How would such a celebration begin? She was not certain. She only knew she had felt the same desire singing in her own veins. She wished Niall would teach her.

But that would never happen, she knew. Indescribable loss swept through her, leaving her barren. She looked away from the bonfire, knowing it would be too painful to stay any longer.

But as she turned to leave, she stifled a cry behind her hand. Standing against a veil of moonlight was Niall, his broad shoulders silvered by moonglow, his dark hair a tangle around a face hard with wanting, burning with need . . . for *her*? Caitlin thought in wonder. But the instant he saw her gazing at his face, he covered those raw emotions as if they somehow shamed him.

She swallowed hard, waiting for him to reprove her for the danger she had put herself in, but he only stepped nearer.

"I returned to Daire as soon as I was able," he said in a strange, thick voice. "I looked for you there."

"I know I should not be here."

He stunned her, a melting-honey smile spreading across his face. "You are mistaken, Caitlin of the Lilies. I returned so that I could bring you here myself."

Caitlin's breath caught. "You? You were going to—to bring me—"

"I thought you should see a little of this land, listen to the music, the laughter, hear the tales your father and mother heard, before you leave Ireland forever."

Stunned at the depth of Niall's understanding, Caitlin instinctively touched her heart. "I never imagined anything like this," she said, waving toward the oblivious revelers. "It is as if life boiled up from the very ground, swallowing up doubt and fear, leaving everyone naked in their souls, new."

"Aye," Niall rasped, low. "There are those who would claim this is a sin," he said. "Such unbridled pleasure is wrong between a man and a woman."

"I cannot believe it," Caitlin said. "If there is love between them—" She looked away, suddenly shy, suddenly shaken. "I imagine what they feel is the closest we can come to touching heaven. I am sorry that I will miss it." The ache knotted in her throat again. She would not let him see it.

"Miss what, Lily Fair?"

A shiver of pleasure rippled through her at the tender name he used again, an endearment all her own.

"You think me innocent, and I am, I know. Grown up in the abbey, tasting so little of life. But I do understand what it will be like for me, Niall, once I flee Ireland. There will be no wandering about, dancing around bonfires. I will be an exile in hiding, forever clinging to the shadows as certainly as I am now."

She could not keep the wistfulness from her voice. "I do not mean to sound ungrateful to you for saving my life. It is just that I wish my life could be like everyone else's, even for just one night."

"It can be."

So calmly he said it, so certainly. She raised her eyes to his, saw the quiet burning in those dark green depths.

"Dance with me, Caitlin."

Her cheeks flamed, and she stumbled back a step, thrusting her hands behind her like a child caught reaching fingers toward something hot and sweet just come from the fire. "But—but someone might see us," she objected weakly.

"Every man here has eyes for his lady alone this night. They are drunk on poteen and moonlight. In the darkness here, what will they see? The shapes of just one more man with a woman? Not even the moon knows who we are."

Caitlin raised her eyes to his. "I do not know what to do. I have never even seen such dancing until tonight." He reached out his hand, took her fingers in his own.

"Trust me," he urged her as the music swelled, seeming to dare the very stars to dance in time to it.

Caitlin's whole body tingled with something silvery and warm, her hand trembling in Niall's strong grasp. Sword-callused and hard, a warrior's hand, yet it was so warm, so inexpressibly gentle.

Trust me, he had asked her. How could she not? She loved him. The realization was almost more than she could hold. It welled up inside her, sweet and magical and utterly impossible.

She had taken so much from this man already. She could not ask him—so strong, so vital, so brave—to share her shadow-world, forever cringing in the shadows, forever fearing discovery. She loved him too much, understood him too well to condemn him to such an existence. He would have to be free of her, build a life of his own. A new life far away from Fintan's cursed daughter, if he was ever to have a chance to feel the sun on his face.

That truth hurt her more than she could bear, and yet she turned her face into the moonlight, letting the breeze brush away sorrow and loss. Should she not be grateful for this gift the fates had let her taste even so briefly? Some women lived their whole lives and never loved a man so completely.

In this one night, aye, and what little time remained, she could fill herself up with this secret, precious love, gather memories she could keep forever.

Even as she turned to smile up into the rugged planes of Niall's face, Caitlin knew there was one thing she could never do.

She could love Niall in silence, but never could she tell him.

Chapter
14

No STAR HAD EVER SHONE as bright as Caitlin's eyes when he touched her. Niall lost himself in the dark-lashed depths, swimming in their rare blue light more certainly than he swam in the sea the day he had pulled her from the waves.

She had never danced before, this exquisite woman, and yet as her willowy body swayed and dipped, her graceful feet flashing, scarce brushing the ground, it seemed as if the ancient ones were alive in her, matching her every movement to the pounding beat of his own heart.

Her hair rippled in fairy-kissed waves about the glowing oval of her face, her soft white brow creased in earnest concentration, and her lips, pink and delicate as new roses, parted in a smile so sweet he longed to taste it.

Never as a youth and seldom as a man had Niall joined such festivities—first because he had guarded his dignity so fiercely, those surrounding him all too ready to jeer at the awkward fumblings of the infamous Ronan's son. Later, he had scorned the dance because he saw nothing in its movements but danger, the seductive allure of that most perilous of temptations—

the wiles of a woman's body that had fired his father's obsession, driven him to an act so terrible it sickened Niall. Made mockery of his father's honor and shattered Niall's family forever.

Aye, he would do better to drink poison than need a woman, Niall had often reasoned. The draught was far more honest about the destruction it would leave in its wake, and it killed only the one who drank it. It did not drag any innocents along its path into hell.

Yet this night with Caitlin was as she had said—like touching heaven. Not that solemn place filled with sober-faced angels priests told about, but a mingling of the joy and magic of Tir naN Og and the wondrous imagination of the One who had created, not merely dry duty and saintly toil, but life in all its chaos and brilliant colors, its beauty all the more precious because it was fleeting, changing swiftly and certainly as the face of the very sky.

Because in this wondrous place, one day a man's soul could be parched, abandoned, filled with futility, and the next day a fairy maid could awaken him to a world so green, so lush, so enchanted, he scarce dared to believe it was real.

But this *was* real. Niall clung tight to the knowledge, the hard shell that had caged his heart for so long splitting, allowing breath and life and light to touch it after so long.

For just one night, Caitlin of the Lilies, bold Fintan's daughter, belonged to him.

The music swelled, soaring toward its climax, the power of it bursting in a shattering release of strings and drums and wailing of pipes. Niall caught Caitlin in his arms and flung her skyward, her laughter replenishing his soul as certainly as spring rain after endless winter.

He drank in the vibrant waters of her spirit as he caught her midair, but he could not set her on her feet as the dance demanded.

He pressed her lithe, warm body against his so tight he could feel every supple, feminine curve, every secret hollow melding to the battle-hardened landscape of his own much larger frame. Shuddering bursts of warmth brushed his cheek as she struggled to catch her breath, her heartbeat racing like a wild thing, caught in his arms—a fairy maid plucked from her bower by a mortal too enchanted with her beauty to let her vanish into mist.

Aye, Niall thought, he was stealing this moment with her as certainly as if he had taken her from the realm of fairies. He had no right to do it, and yet, never had anything in his whole worthless life felt so true.

The music began again, soft at first, a plaintive strain as if the wind itself were weeping. A gangly boy with a voice clear as a secret stream sang of the greatest love Ireland had ever known. Heroes and maidens shivered to life in his song, suffered impossible passion and excruciating loss, the blessing and curse of the bleak destiny that had driven its cruel blade between the two lovers.

Suddenly chilled, Niall lowered Caitlin to the ground. So light was she, her feet made scarce a sound, but in that instant, he could hear the sky crashing down around them.

He had heard the love legend a hundred times in all its beauty and tragedy, but never had the tale of Dierdre and Naisi touched him until this night. Ill-fated lovers racing across Ireland, hunted by a king, only the night sky and the standing stones to shield them. But in the end, they had died, their hearts broken by fate.

The tale moved Caitlin as well. He could feel it as

she pressed one cheek against his heart, her arms twining about his waist. Holding her, both unmoving in the moonlight, Niall listened, ached. And as the boy's haunting voice mourned the tragic lovers' deaths, Niall felt Caitlin's hot tears soak through the wool of his garments, seeming to pierce his very soul.

His arms gathered her even closer, some irrational part of himself thinking that if he could only hold on tight enough, nothing could ever make this precious woman cry again. His warrior's body, which had endured the bite of countless sword blades, the stab of spears in battle, could finally suffer wounds that mattered, wounds gained in shielding this miracle he held in his arms.

It seemed he held her forever. Forever was too short a time. And in those moments, he knew what Naisi felt, the desperation, the terror, as his love was ripped from his arms.

He groaned a protest as Caitlin pushed herself away from him, but he released her, knowing it was a fleeting privilege she had allowed him when she had melted into his arms seeking comfort.

She raised her tear-streaked face to his and rubbed at the damp spot she had left on his chest. "Forgive me. I could not help but weep." She bit her lip as if to steady herself. "The tale was so beautiful, so sad."

Niall wiped away the droplets that still clung to her cheeks. "I wished only joy for you this night. I would I could spare you tears."

"You cannot, Niall, no matter how much you might wish it." Her face grew pensive, earnest, heartbreakingly resolute. "There could be no joy without sorrow, just as there could be no day without the dark of night. When I was at the abbey, I never wept. Everything there was so quiet, so safe. Even death was nothing to mourn. It was a gentle journey from the trials of earth to heavenly bliss."

Niall could not imagine such a serene existence, a peace his questing spirit had never known. To him, death had always glistened blood-bright on the blade of a sword, a gateway to the glory of legends or to the anonymity of an unmourned grave.

"And as for our days," Caitlin continued, "each one was so much alike, I could scarce tell one from another."

"You loved it there." Why did that make him feel somehow bereft?

"Saint Mary's was the most gentle of dreams, Niall. But I was asleep behind its walls. There were so many things I never felt until I rode through the gate in your arms."

Niall touched her hair, guilt clenching him tight in its fist. "I taught you well in the days since I took you from the abbey, did I not, Lily Fair? Taught you about treachery and betrayal, hatred and fear. Unveiled all the ugly dark corners of men's souls. If I could, I would take all those shadows back again, so you could be free and happy, as you were before I charged into your life."

"Nay!" Her gaze flashed to his, almost alarmed. "I would not turn back to that quiet dream for something so fleeting as safety. I would run to meet whatever fortune offered, the way Dierdre did in the boy's song. Joy, adventure, and a love so great no sword blade ever forged could sever it—they would be worth any forfeit destiny could demand. If I could not have forever, I would drink in whatever the fates allowed me, and I would be grateful."

A flush spread over her cheeks, visible even in the uncertain light of the moon. She looked away, silent.

Niall could not allow her to hide herself away. He cupped her chin in his hand, turned her face up to his. "You would be grateful for what is good, is that not what you believe?" It was an echo of what he had said to Fiona days before.

Caitlin shrugged. "I would rather embrace life than hide from it. But there is no help for that in the days to come. Conn's power is far-reaching. Word travels between clans. I cannot place anyone else in danger as I have done to you."

"Caitlin—" He started to object.

"Nay, Niall. We both know it is true. I will have no choice but to secret myself away. I only wish . . ." Her lips trembled.

"Wish what?" Niall asked, vowing to capture the moon if it would make her smile.

"I wish that before I leave the world of the living again, I could know what it feels like to . . . to be loved by a man as Dierdre was. Feel passion and life and magic just once before I have to hide away, alone."

Niall peered down at her, so innocent, so beautiful. Aye, it was a tragedy. Caitlin, so full of love never to be bestowed on any man, never to be lavished on a bevy of blue-eyed babes with thick black curls like her own.

Caitlin, who embraced life with such passion, never to know what it felt like to share her body as well as her valiant spirit. From the first moment he had seen her in the druid glen, he had known she was more of earth than heaven, more fairy than angel. A woman destined to revel in the sweet bounty of her body's pleasure, and that of a man with the courage to match her, gift for gift.

Regret burned through Niall, the impossible wish that he could somehow transform himself into the kind of man Caitlin needed, the kind of lover she deserved.

But that piercing-sweet longing was as futile as the yearning he had felt at his father's cairn, when he had wished he could turn back the tide of the moon until he could see his father again as the bold, noble hero he had once believed in with all his boyish heart.

He started to look away, the music saddened, the dancing dimmed, the pleasure he had sought in Caitlin's company seeming only a taunting dream. Then he saw the plea dove-soft in her eyes.

She wanted him. The knowledge reverberated through every fiber of his being.

With eyes guileless as the first woman desiring the first man in the magical innocence of the beginning of time, Caitlin was asking him to take her away. To lay her back in the soft, sweet grass and strip away the layers of cloth between them. She was asking him to make love to her for the first time, perhaps the only time. The only chance this bright, loving woman might ever have to feel a man's touch.

And he wanted to give her everything she desired. God help him, he did. "Caitlin." He fought to keep his voice steady. "It would be madness to make love to you. Too dangerous."

"Dangerous?" She gave a sad little laugh that twisted his heart. "I could be dead tomorrow, Niall."

The very thought lanced through him. "Nay!"

"You know it is true. If Conn should find me alive—"

"I will die before I let him take you!"

She smiled, such a fragile, heartbreaking curve of her lips. "But that would be the most tragic loss of all. For then our chance to share this one night would be gone forever."

Something tore deep inside Niall. The grief, the futility, the hate and the anger that had seethed inside him forever suddenly seemed a hideous waste when a woman like Caitlin had the courage to open her arms to him. But did he dare risk what he had feared for so long? The terrible need for someone else? Someone who could fail you, destroy you, vanish from your life, and leave your heart bleeding?

Did his fear show in his eyes? He was the champion of Glenfluirse, renowned for his courage, and suddenly his hands trembled like a frightened babe's. He wanted to look away, shamed, but he could not. Caitlin's smile grew too tender.

"I have decided not to waste time being afraid any longer," she said earnestly. "Whatever comes will come, whether I fear it or not. But I have now. This moment to cherish. It is all any of us can be certain of."

He swallowed hard, fear a knot in his gut. It was true what she said. How many men had he seen—brave warriors, strong ones—struck down between one heartbeat and the next?

Sucking in a deep breath, Niall took the most terrifying chance of his life. He cast aside the betrayals that had branded him with his hated name. He banished fear and doubt.

Sweeping Caitlin off her feet, he carried her in his arms, away from the music, away from the dancing, toward a haven where they could tend fires of their own making.

She curled herself against him with a trust that terrified him. Trust that he would not hurt her, faith that he would know what to do. But his couplings in the past had been hasty matings driven by nothing more than mutual lust—coarse appetites that turned to cold ash the instant he spilled his seed. Caitlin would be different.

Far from the festivities, he found a hidden glen, gilded with moonlight, as secluded and untouched as the place where the first man and woman made love.

Niall swept off the folds of wool wrapped about his body, until only a thigh-length shirt of billowing linen covered his nakedness. With the greatest of care, he spread the soft piece of wool on the ground to make his lady a bed. Then he took Caitlin's hand, guided her down upon it.

He could scarce breathe as he looked at her, a fairy vision, ebony hair rippling like furled wings about her shoulders, her face pure as the lily she was named for.

Since he was a boy, he had been ridiculed, loathed, scorned because of the legacy his father had left him. Even as a champion, he had seen only lust, coarse curiosity, in the faces of women who desired him—as if they were ashamed, afraid his touch would somehow taint them despite the deeds of courage, the quests he had performed. But the blue pools of Caitlin's eyes shone with something more precious than anything he had ever known—trust.

For her sake, he asked once more. "You are sure you want this? Want . . . me?" He only half believed this magic could be happening between them. For a moment, she was so quiet a cold fear gripped his heart, fear that she would change her mind, turn him away. Never had he opened himself to such a crushing rejection. Yet despite the clamoring of his loins, he knew she had but to say the word, and he would take her hand, lead her back to Daire and her own virginal bed.

But Caitlin dashed away his doubts. Threading her fingers through the dark hair at his nape, she drew his lips down to meet her kiss.

Warm and soft and seeking, she explored his mouth with the earthy innocence of a queen of the fairies, bestowing upon her love the kiss of immortality. And Niall drank in the healing magic of her touch, a trait as instinctive to her as the warrior's blow of death was to him.

He had built his entire existence around taking life, battle and violence and destruction disguised under the deceitful name of valor. But never had he imagined what he had stolen from the men who had felt the heedless blows of his sword.

This wild, hot wonder, this tenderness and hunger that melted the jagged edges of a man's war-torn spirits and spilled light into the most consuming darkness. The chance to touch, just for this one night, redemption.

Niall opened his mouth against hers, deepening the kiss, drinking her in as if she were drenched in a fairy nectar that could make him forget—forget pain and betrayal and a lifetime of being alone. She moaned, her own lips parting as his tongue traced her mouth, dipped inside.

She tasted of honey and half-forgotten magic, realms of lost legends and dreams Niall had not dared to believe in for so long. And he wondered if he could ever taste enough of her, ever feel enough of her to sate the cravings she aroused not only in his body but in his soul.

Heart pounding with an eagerness he had never felt before, Niall lowered his body atop hers, his warrior's frame hard and hot and ready, wild with impatience. He was nigh mad with the need to thrust into her generous warmth, afraid that the fates who had played so many bitter jests upon him would snatch Caitlin away.

Even so, he fought back his own needs, grappled for control. But it was nigh impossible to hold himself in check as he unlaced the tight bodice binding her breasts, then slipped the billowing folds of her leine over her head. Moonlight spilled over the lush curves of her body, adoring it like a lover.

Niall could not breathe as he gazed in soul-searing hunger at the gentle hills of her coral-tipped breasts, the tender hollow of her navel, the dark, dewy curls peeking shyly from their haven between her thighs.

Naked in spirit as well as in flesh, she peered up at him, an unspoken question old as time in her eyes. *Do you think me beautiful?* Was it possible this enchantress could doubt it?

It was all he could do not to grab her in his arms, pound into her body with all the fierceness of the warrior he was. But he delved deep inside himself, trying to find tenderness for her.

"I am a man of weapons, not of words," he ground out. "But I wish I were a bard this night. I would weave a song that would make your beauty live until the end of time."

A smile brighter than morning sun dawned upon her face. She ran her fingertips across the swell of his bottom lip. "And I would sing of how much I . . ." She hesitated, her voice breaking, just a whisper. "How magical it is to lie here in your arms."

It was not what she meant to say. He sensed it. But he was too dazzled to question her. The huskiness in her voice inflamed him, unnerved him, made him crave so much more than just this one joining. But with fierce resignation, Niall resolved he would take what chance had given him, make this night as perfect as he could for her.

Slowly, he cautioned himself, he must not frighten her. And he moved with the tenderest of care as he stroked the hollow of her throat, the delicate wing of her shoulder, the dainty, pale place where her breast began to swell. Smooth as new cream she was, and when she shivered in need, he could no longer resist tasting her. Trailing his lips across new places, secret places, Niall let his tongue discover dips and hollows and swells no other man had ever explored.

Caitlin whimpered with pleasure, clutching restlessly at handfuls of his leine as he let his mouth open over the rosy temptation of her nipple. He drew her deep into dark heat, suckling her with a tender fervor that set her atremble.

Had any woman ever responded this way in another man's arms? He could not believe it. This was as miraculous and new as the first mating, the lovemaking that had created all life to come.

A low cry tore from her lips, and she writhed against him, in wild innocence, the little mewling sounds deep in her throat only driving him to be more tender, more selfless in his onslaught against her senses.

He cupped her other breast in his hand, circling his palm against the hardened bud of her nipple as he suckled its match. Then, slowly, he trailed his fingers down the fragile cage of her ribs, the faint, impossibly soft swell of her belly, to where her body wept with need for him.

She gasped, arched instinctively into his touch, but he stilled at the pleading cry she uttered.

"N-Niall." She choked out his name, half prayer, half sob.

It took more strength than he had ever spent to draw his hand away. "What is it, *alannah?*" he murmured.

She was trembling, so lovely, long skeins of her hair like ebony rivers against the flawless shores of her skin. "I want to—to touch you. Your skin, your body, the way you touch mine, with nothing between us."

Niall growled low in his throat and levered himself to his knees, yanking the billowy linen garment that covered his chest free with a force that tore the stitches. The crisp night air bathed his sweat-sheened body, but it could do nothing to cool the ardor clamoring inside him as he saw the astonishment, the curiosity, the admiration that wreathed Caitlin's face as she gazed at his nakedness.

He held himself still, let her learn the scarred, stone-hard landscape of his body, first by sight, then with the most tender of touches. Sensitive, feminine fingers reached out, a little wary as they touched his mouth, his chin. Then, catching her bottom lip between pearly teeth, she let her fingers journey downward, splaying over the dark hair that feathered across the expanse of his chest.

Niall bit back a groan at the torture of it as she traced ridges of muscle, pale white scars, the flat discs of nipples so sensitive it all but unmanned him when she circled her fingertips upon their hardened points.

"I dreamed about this so many nights," she admitted, her cheeks rose-pink. "But never—never did I imagine you would feel this way," she breathed. For an instant, Niall felt shame—shame in the twisted, ugly scars he had once worn with pride, shame in the heavy muscles that seemed so crude somehow next to the impossible delicacy of his lady.

"I am a warrior," he muttered. "Rough and coarse and—"

"You are like the cliffs you showed me beside the sea, rugged and powerful and so very beautiful. I want to plunge into you, the way I did the waves that first day. I want you to surround me, enclose me, until I cannot guess where I end and you begin." She flattened her hands on his chest, her eyes wide, her breath ragged.

"That is what I want as well, Lily Fair. More than you will ever know." He lay down beside her, and she draped herself over his body. He cradled her full length against his nakedness, his blood roaring hot through his veins at the dizzying pleasure of her softness yielding to his hardness. Her breasts flattened against his chest, her slender legs tangling with his sinewy ones, the soft, slight swell of her belly cradling the rigid length of his shaft.

She moved, restless against him, running her hands over his shoulders, his ribs, his hips, pressing her lips to whatever bare skin she could reach.

The throbbing low in Niall's loins grew deafening before he dared continue his own quest. Laying her back, gaining a slight, precious distance between their bodies, he eased his big hand down the curve of her belly once more, to where soft curls clung to his fingers.

Delicate, so delicate, so perfect and fragile was she, the petals of her femininity like a flower he might crush in his clumsiness. But even such fears could not keep him from slipping his fingers lower, until Caitlin arched, writhed, guiding his touch to her hot, damp center.

Niall clenched his teeth with agonizing pleasure as he slipped one finger inside her untried opening. She was ready to receive him, eager and melting in her very core.

But this was her first time, Niall reminded himself ruthlessly. There would be pain when he entered her, dashing away the glorious pleasure that now set her face aglow.

With grim determination, he found the pearl beneath those delicate rose-hued folds, awakened it to sensation with the most gentle of strokes. She gasped in surprise and a hint of fear.

"N-Niall, what—what is . . ."

"Do not be afraid, *mo chroi*," he murmured against the sweet cream of her breast. "It is all the magic that lies between us. Close your eyes, let yourself feel . . . feel how much I want you."

Her lashes fluttered, then drooped to her cheeks. She lay there, trembling as he eased her thighs apart with his hand.

With exquisite care, Niall teased her, pleasured her, until she could no longer hold back her cries. He could feel the crest rising within her, irresistible as the tide. He felt her racing toward it with that wild, sweet abandon only Caitlin could know.

He wanted to be with her when she shattered, wanted to feel her sheath clutch his shaft in perfect pleasure, but he feared if he pierced her maidenhead, she would not know the rapture he craved for her far more fiercely than the mere fulfillment of his own desires.

He kissed a fervent path down her body, then pressed his mouth to her core in passion, adoration. She shattered, screamed, her head tossing as the waves of pleasure consumed her. Triumph surged through Niall at the knowledge that he had given her joy.

Yet it seemed his lady wanted more. She tugged at his shoulders, and he rose above her, gazing down into a face transformed by his loving.

Eyes still wide with wonder, mouth swollen and ripe from his kisses, she stunned him, reaching down between their bodies to cradle his shaft in the cup of her palm. Exquisite pleasure drove through Niall.

"I do not know what—what to do," she whispered. "I only know I want you to feel what I felt when you touched me that way." She stroked him, trying to imitate his movements from moments before.

He captured her hand in his, thrust once against her soft palm. "Take me inside you, Caitlin," he groaned. "I need to be inside you."

She lay back, opening her thighs to him, opening her arms to draw him close. Niall felt the blunt tip of his sex nudge her fragile opening, his hard hands clasping her hips. He wanted to be gentle, tender, wanted not to hurt her. But he was too big, too hard. He knew before he moved that a painless entry into her body was too much to hope for.

But already Caitlin was restless beneath him, shifting against his body with a sensuality as maddening as it was innocent.

With a groan, Niall surrendered. He drove his hips forward, piercing her with one swift, clean thrust.

She cried out in surprise, her pliant body stiffening as her maidenhead tore. And Niall wished with all his being he could have endured that pain in her place.

He kissed her cheeks, her brow, his hips agonizingly still, letting her grow accustomed to the feel of his shaft embedded deep inside her. It was the most exquisite of tortures, the most wondrous of miracles, when at last he felt her rigid muscles ease under the tender stroking of his hands. He whispered against her bare skin, praises he had never thought to utter.

And she answered him with her body, moving against him, sighing with building pleasure. When she moaned softly, eagerly, Niall knew it was time.

Unable to hold himself back another moment, he drew his hips back, then thrust ever so gently into the sweet sheath of her body. Caitlin gasped, her arms twining around him, her long legs shifting restlessly against his. He guided her legs about his lean hips, taught her how to draw him deeper, ever deeper. He pressed hot kisses against her cheeks, her breasts, suckling her as he drove himself again and again into her body.

She was sobbing now, pleading for the release they

both craved, and Niall reached for it, strove for it, with every sinew in his body. When he felt himself careening toward release, he slipped his hand between their bodies, and finding her tender nub one more time, he stroked it once, twice, as he moved hard within her.

Caitlin buried a scream against his shoulder just as his own climax crashed over him, spilling his seed at the mouth of her womb.

An animal groan tore from Niall as he collapsed atop her, struggling to right himself as the world spun away. He clung to her, his chest heaving, his heart pounding. After a moment, he shifted his body until she lay alongside him. Silent, shaken, he cradled her in his arms, half afraid he had broken her somehow, this woman of dreams and light and fierce generosity.

She lay there, so quiet against him he could not bear it. He raised his head, looked into her face. Tears streaked her cheeks, her lips quivering.

"Did I hurt you?" he rasped, wiping away the moisture with the tips of his fingers.

"Nay."

"Then why do you weep?"

"I cannot bear to think what I almost lost. I might never have known what it felt like to be loved by you. But now—now I will always remember how tight your arms held me, how you kissed me and suckled me and—" She stopped, her voice unsteady. "Now, even when I am alone, I will always remember."

Niall peered down at the quiet resolve in her face, his own chest aching. *When I am alone.* Her words echoed through him, impossible, unthinkable.

How could he let her go after what they had shared? How could he walk away? He wondered, stroking the silky curve of her shoulder in silence.

But he had managed to walk away before, had he

not? From Daire, from Fiona and his mother and the memory of his father. Could it be so much harder to leave Caitlin behind?

The desolation that swept through him nearly drew a cry of protest from his lips. He had been blinded by his own pain when he had abandoned his family years ago. But now he had seen what his selfishness had cost them. Was he coward enough to cast Caitlin to the winds of fate as well?

But what choice did he have? Conn would be satisfied by the letter Niall had sent for only a brief while. Soon the chieftain would expect his champion to present himself at the fortress, to take up arms again in his name.

What would Conn do if Niall refused to fight any longer? If Niall left the fortress for the seclusion of Daire? Would Conn suspect . . . what? That Caitlin lived? That Niall had betrayed his trust?

Nay, Niall reasoned with a twinge of guilt. Conn believed in his foster son. He would never imagine the boy he had cared for would deceive him. It was a dark deceit to pin a future upon. And yet Niall could not help but feel a stirring of hope.

Was it possible he and Caitlin could stay at Daire? That she could be safe here? No man on earth or angel in heaven could guard her as well as he could.

If she were careful, if he were vigilant, was it possible that they could build a life together, here on this secluded patch of land with its memories and its strange fascination, its irresistible spell of enchantment?

He gazed down at Caitlin, her eyes closed now in sleep, and he imagined forever waking with her in his arms, the tenderness in her eyes driving back any memory of mockery and scorn and shame.

Niall drew the folds of wool around her, warming

her in his arms. She made him believe that anything was possible, if he had the courage to trust in her, in himself.

For an instant, he almost confided in her, told her of the secrets he now held in his heart. But he did not dare. For if he failed . . .

He shoved the thought away, unable to bear it. Nay, he would not risk hurting her so deeply. He would work in secret, use all his skills, his strength, to find some way to make things right.

He would do his best to believe enough for both of them—in a future he had never imagined, in love he had never believed existed, in roots dug so deep into Irish earth he could never think of leaving the land behind.

Aye, Niall resolved with a terrifying surge of hope, this would be a new beginning for all of them. Surely, this time, the fates would not deny him this chance for joy—a chance to rebuild the trust of Fiona, to know the love of his mother, and, most miraculous of all, to make Caitlin his wife.

Chapter 15

KNEE-DEEP RIVERS of heather meandered in purple waves across the green meadow. Billows of glossy petaled kingcups lifted buttery faces to the sky. Never had there been such a glorious day, Caitlin thought as she emptied another armful of fragrant flowers into the overflowing basket at her feet.

She turned to cast a loving glance toward Niall's mother perched upon a mossy stone half a hillside away. The woman who had spent years dozing amidst dust and spider's webs and ashes of dreams now delighted in the sunshine, her once-empty days filled with chatter as bright and cheery as the blossoms she plaited into her soft hair.

Reverend Mother had often said such days were a gift, God's warm hand upon the shoulders of those who suffered. Yet living behind the abbey walls, Caitlin had never foreseen that there were other gifts she would find far more precious.

Hidden treasures Niall had unearthed in her body and her soul. He had all but dragged her through the abbey gates into a world bursting with glorious emotions too great to hold. A splendor Caitlin could never have dreamed of behind the cloistered walls.

The restlessness that had made her body ache and her blood boil for so long had a name now. The willful voice that urged her to such wild abandon had finally revealed that mysterious *something* she was so desperate to run to.

Niall. The earthy miracle of his hard male body and the astonishing secrets he had unveiled in the tender hills and valleys of her own naked form.

Caitlin shivered with delight. Six nights had passed since she and Niall had danced under the moonlight and her world had been changed forever. Nay, it had changed the instant he had roared into her life, snarling beside the druid altar.

He had introduced her to laughter and anger and passion. He had brought her to Daire, offered her the chance to experience the sweet affection of his mother. He had shared the reluctant amusement and frustration Fiona's antics produced in everyone around her.

Without intending, he had granted Caitlin's dearest wish, showing her the joy and hurt, the sadness and strength that came from being part of a family.

Her eyes burned with unshed tears. Aye, he had changed her so much she barely recognized herself any longer.

Abandoning the basket full of heather for a moment, she drew near the rippling surface of the stream that burbled nearby and smiled at her reflection for the third time that morning.

Madness, it was. Sister Luca would call it vanity. But Caitlin could not resist. She was entranced by the woman who stared back at her. Blue eyes that had never shone so bright brimmed with anticipation. Rays of morning sun warmed cheeks glowing as they never had before, while her lips were soft and eager with longing for nightfall to come again.

Darkness sang its siren song, enticed her into pagan worlds where the pull of her own passion grew more powerful than any spell a sorcerer could conjure. Her heart soared, danced to those primal rhythms, awakening earthy cravings the abbey had tried to shut out with its high walls.

But no barriers made of stone or of innocence could curb the magic her body was fashioned to feel or rob her of sensations so exquisite she seethed with impatience for the darkness that would bring Niall to her bed.

Throughout the day, he would ride afield, as if he could not bear to be near her without touching her, kissing her. At dusk, he would return, fighting to conceal the fever in his blood, devoting himself to pleasing his mother and trying with small success to mend things with Fiona.

When at last everyone retired to their chambers, he would pace beneath Caitlin's window until he was certain the rest of the castle slept. Then, when she was wild with impatience, he would steal up the stairs to the Sea Chamber with all its beauty and imagination.

Niall's hot hands would strip away the layers of cloth that draped her body, while she tore at his own garments until they paused, breathless, their naked bodies gleaming in the flickering rushlight. And as Caitlin traversed the deliciously familiar cliffs and ledges of Niall's body, she would rejoice in the wonder of his response to her: his strong hands trembling, his heart thundering beneath her palms, his ragged gasp of pleasure when at last her slender fingers cradled the hard length of his shaft.

Beguiled, she would marvel at the pleasure she had almost missed, her fascination with Niall's naked body matched only by her amazement at the unexpected wonders she discovered in her own.

And as day faded into night again and again and again, she lived for the time when he would steal to her chamber like a shadow lover, a shape-shifter. When he would take her in his arms and make silent, desperate love to her.

Nay, Caitlin thought with a soul-deep throb of sadness. It was not love Niall brought to her bed, only a craving for her body and the magic they could make together. The mere fact that this proud, wounded man succumbed to any emotional need at all was a miracle, she knew. That Niall should risk admitting to love was too great a bounty to hope for.

Yet she yearned for it, dreamed of it in the hateful brink of dawn, when he stole away to preserve their secret for yet another day.

The reflection that peered back at her from the stream suddenly grew pensive, touched with sorrow. Caitlin shoved the emotion away. She would have the rest of her life to grieve over the fact that Niall could not love her. She would not waste one moment of this precious idyll.

Yet she knew that if she had a lifetime in Niall's arms, she would never get her fill of him—his gruff tenderness, his fierce honor, his desperate striving to please her, to drive her to higher, wilder peaks of bliss. She would never stop hungering for the haunting beauty in his rugged face when the crest was past and he lay beside her, stroking her hair until she slept.

It broke her heart, that nameless longing she sensed in him, the quiet terror, his astonishment that she could want him again and again. It made her wish she had forever to help this battered warrior see himself through her eyes. A man of honor who admitted his mistakes and tried to right them. A man of courage who risked his life to defend those weaker than himself.

A man of such generous spirit he had championed a woman who was all but a stranger and surrendered his future to save hers.

A rustling in the heather made Caitlin look up to see Aniera walking toward her, her newest flower crown perched on her soft hair. A bunch of small white blossoms was clutched in her hands.

Caitlin smiled. "I have another basket full of heather to sweeten the fresh rushes on the castle floor," she said, struggling to banish memories of nighttime and Niall. "I thought I would start back. Will you come?"

Aniera shook her head, casting a glance at the hollow from which she had come. Her vague eyes shone as if a lover awaited her in the lush grasses. "I will stay awhile with Ronan. We often lingered by this stream."

"Very well," Caitlin agreed. "But you must not tire yourself, lest Niall grow angry with me."

Aniera's laugh, light as fairy bells, tinkled out, rare and sweet. Caitlin wished she could hear so much more of it.

"As if my boy could ever be truly angry with you, *cailin*." Aniera's whole face sparkled with a teasing light. "You both play at fooling me. You think I am too old to see the way his eyes follow you at every moment."

Caitlin's cheeks burned. It was absurd, her sudden dread that the older woman might sense the illicit pleasures Caitlin and Niall had shared. Caitlin laughed in an effort to make light of it. "How can his eyes follow me every moment when he is gone from dawn to dusk?"

"I am old now. And . . ." Aniera looked down at the flowers, a shadow of sadness crossing her delicate features. "And my Ronan awaits me in Tir naN Og. But I remember love's face."

Caitlin lay her hand upon Aniera's arm, grieving

with the woman for a loss still so fresh, a love still so precious. "Of course, you remember Ronan's face," she said gently.

"Aye, I do. I see him each time I look into Niall's eyes. But that is not what I meant. You love my son."

Alarm jolted through Caitlin, mingling with the sweetest pain. "You must not speak of such things to Niall. He—he . . . has been hurt."

Sweet Lord, Caitlin thought, a flutter of panic in her breast. How could she possibly explain this to Aniera, who eased her own pain and loss in the mist where she had sought refuge since Ronan's death? Being forced to face any scrap of reality might hurt the fragile woman more than Caitlin could guess.

"Aye. He has a hurt, my Niall. But you make his eyes shine, child, the way Ronan's did when he gazed at me."

But when you and Ronan fell in love, he had not suffered as Niall has, Caitlin wanted to argue. He had not withstood the betrayal of the father he adored or suffered the scorn that left such hideous scars on Niall's fierce pride. He had not been tormented by the dark suspicion and self-doubt that made it impossible for Niall to trust anyone—be it his lover or himself.

And as for you, Aniera, Caitlin thought with gloom, *you were not condemned by prophecies of disaster, hunted by a chieftain who wished you dead.*

But Aniera sensed none of her turmoil. "Before Ronan was taken away, he told me the babes would be safe," she said softly. "He would see to it, no matter what else befell him. They were strong, he said, born of a love stronger even than death." Aniera raised her gaze to Caitlin's, her face so tender. "I am shamed to admit I had begun to doubt him, until I saw Niall look at you. Then I knew it."

"Knew what?" Caitlin asked, her voice trembling with yearning.

"That my Niall is safe from harm at last."

"Nay." Caitlin's voice quavered. "You do not understand. Because of me . . ." She stopped, unable to continue. How could she tell this woman the impending doom she had brought down on Niall's head, the destruction of all his dreams? How could she admit that because Niall saved her, he would never be safe again?

A lark's song broke the quiet of morning, somehow lonely in its solitary flight. Aniera gazed up at the sky. "I know why you came to us, *alannah*. Ronan whispered it to me in the night. You have come to teach our son a precious lesson. How it feels not to be alone."

Aniera tucked the white flowers into Caitlin's hair, then turned with a smile and strolled away. Caitlin stared after her, her heart aching. *Ronan whispered it to me in the night.* The brief flicker of clarity had been no more than an illusion, leaving the older woman more lost than ever in her dream world.

And yet perhaps Caitlin could give one gift to this man who had sacrificed so much for her.

She would show this solitary man what it felt like to have someone waiting with joy and eagerness for his return. That would grant Aniera's wish, would it not? Niall would learn not to be alone.

More satisfied than exhausted, Caitlin plucked bits of heather from the rush basket she held against one hip and flung the sweet-scented purple flowers upon the fresh rushes covering the floor, bringing inside the scent of the meadow in which she and Niall had first made love.

She had left Aniera dreaming among the flowers, a

rare peace in the older woman's eyes, Niall's mother as distracted by the beauty of the blossoms as any winsome child.

The only real hope Caitlin had had for help with the daunting task of cleaning out the flooring of the great hall was Fiona, but the girl had made herself scarcer than her enigmatic brother of late, wandering the hills far into the night, until Caitlin feared for her safety.

Not that any word of caution was appreciated by the girl. Fiona had scoffed at any warning, claimed she had been wandering the estate alone since she was a babe and was not about to change her habits now.

Fiona's reasoning was sound, Caitlin admitted, and yet there was something in the girl's pointed features that unnerved her more than ever, raking against her ragged nerves. Resolute chin cocked at a reckless angle, the girl pulsed with a raw energy more intense than ever before. Trouble was afoot.

At dawn that very morning, after Niall had left her room, Caitlin had gone in to wake Fiona and discovered the girl's bed had not been slept in. Caitlin had wavered in an agony of indecision until Niall rode out for his day's wandering. Twice she had almost told Niall what mischief the girl had been up to. And yet any mention of Fiona's antics would only drive Niall to distraction with worry while the inevitable scolding that would follow would drive yet another wedge between Niall and his sister.

Unable to bear the thought of making things worse between them, Caitlin had swallowed her unease and condemned herself to an interminable day spent wondering what mischief the child might be embroiled in.

Reaching into the basket on her arm, Caitlin flung yet another handful of heather upon the rush-strewn floor. True, Fiona *had* returned at long last, but her arrival had done little to ease the knot of tension at the base of Caitlin's neck. The girl was more skittish than a scalded cat.

And as for helping her mother prepare for the journey the four of them were to make as Niall had asked, Fiona had ignored that task, as she had so many others.

Yet the cost would be high if someone did not speak to the bewildered woman soon. Their flight from Daire was still inevitable despite Niall's efforts toward his family. Necessity could drive them from the castle at any moment. What in the name of all that was holy would happen to Aniera once the poor woman discovered that she was losing the home her husband had loved?

Caitlin winced, imagining the gentle woman's confusion and grief with a vividness that tore at her. For the time spent with Aniera gathering rushes and flowers had made Caitlin understand that leaving this place would break what little had remained whole in Niall's mother's battered heart.

Color now blushed Aniera's once ashen cheeks. A twinkle glinted in her eye. Most wondrous of all, Caitlin could sense a reaching out in the woman, as if Aniera were trying to grope her way through the hazy barrier between the real world and her own to take her first stumbling steps across the void.

Yet part of Caitlin wanted to warn the gentle woman to turn back into the mist that had protected her for so long. What would Aniera find when she awakened from her dreams? Her husband's betrayal and dishonorable death? Her rebellious daughter grown up wild and hardened and hating the brother who had deserted them both? And worst of all, to any mother's heart, would she find the real Niall and finally realize what he had suffered?

Caitlin swiped a strand of hair from her sweat-damp forehead and scattered the last of the heather in the farthest corner, wondering if she was making things worse with her efforts to make the castle seem more like a home.

The door crashed in with a deafening bang, and Caitlin dropped her basket as Fiona came bolting into the castle, her cheeks flushed, her eyes overbright.

"Caitlin, there is a man not far behind me!" she cried, breathless, as she slammed the door shut behind her. "You must not tell him I was gone last night."

Caitlin straightened and cast a nervous glance at the door. "I cannot tell him anything at all. Niall insisted I keep myself hidden away, lest someone tell Conn's men they have seen me."

A fist hammered so loudly at the portal it seemed the very stones trembled. "Open this door, you little thief!" a hoarse masculine voice roared. Caitlin glanced at Fiona, and a chill ran down her spine.

"Fiona, what have you done?"

The girl tossed red curls. "It is no one's affair but my own!"

The fist slammed on the door again. "Do not make me kick this in, girl! What the devil have you done with my cow?"

Caitlin could have shaken Fiona until her teeth chattered when the girl flashed her a weak smile.

"Fiona . . ." Caitlin breathed. "Mother of God, tell me you did not steal—"

"Aye. And I would do it again in a heartbeat! You need not worry. I will be rid of this pest in an instant."

Pausing to scoop up a few sprigs of heather, Fiona stuck them strategically in her hair. She grabbed the empty basket, then sauntered to the door. Heart pounding, Caitlin dodged into a shadowy corner, hiding behind the great mass of a wooden chest.

"Is that you making me deaf, Gormley?" Fiona demanded as she opened the heavy wood panel.

A coarse-looking man stood framed in the doorway, filthy and crude, with eyes as deep-set as the boar Caitlin had run afoul of. Bristly straw-colored hair crinkled all over his forehead. His eyebrows ran together in one thick line.

"Deaf? Girl, I will see you lose your hand for thievery. My cow! The one that bears only twin calves. It has disappeared!"

Caitlin's stomach lurched at the accusation, but Fiona merely slid the basket to the floor, wiping the back of her hand across her brow as if she had been slaving in the hall for an eternity. "I heard tales that the beast was fairy-cursed. Perhaps the Tuatha de Danaan finally decided to spirit the beast back to the Land of the Ever Young."

Gormley's face screwed up even tighter. "And did the fairies leave footprints in the muck just the size o' yours? And did me own wife not see you wandering about just before the animal disappeared?"

Caitlin shivered at the brutality in the man's face, the arrogance of someone larger and stronger confronting an unprotected woman, certain he would win any battle.

"Do you think these rushes cut and scattered themselves, old man?" Fiona demanded, betraying not so much as a flicker of unease. "Your wife's eyes must be failing her. Of course, if I had to look at that sour face of yours every day, I might think the loss of sight was a blessing."

"Do not dare mock me, girl! There are plenty hereabouts who remember your father and what he did.

They would be happy to see such vile bloodlines ended forever."

Caitlin glimpsed the slightest tightening at the corner of Fiona's lips, prayed Gormley could not see it and realize what a raw place his words had struck.

"There may be those who hate my family," Fiona said with a toss of her red curls, "but you would have to prove me guilty of a crime, Gormley, and that you will never do."

Caitlin could see the girl's narrow shoulders square, and she wondered how many times in the past the child had faced down people more powerful and more ruthless than she was, armed with nothing but her wits.

Empathy and admiration formed a lump in Caitlin's throat as she imagined a succession of Fionas, from childhood to now, marching out to do battle, to preserve her mother and Castle Daire by whatever means came into her small hands.

At the moment, it was her flair for the dramatic she drew upon, a most worthy weapon. The girl sounded so innocent that even Caitlin might have been deceived into believing her if, at that unfortunate moment, the mournful lowing of a cow had not drifted from deep inside the castle.

Horror jolted through Caitlin.

"There!" Gormley howled. "That noise . . . 'tis my Boann! I would recognize her if she were clear at the bottom o' the sea! I will see you pay for the trouble you have caused me!"

Fiona made a desperate attempt to block his path, but Gormley shoved his way into the hall, charging in the direction of the sound. Caitlin knew she should stay hidden, but she could not abandon Fiona to such a vile man. Keeping silent in the shadows, she crept after them as they withdrew deeper into the castle.

In the farthest reaches of the crumbling building, a place so hidden and disreputable Caitlin had not even known it existed, lay a shaggy brown cow.

Caitlin's heart wrenched when she saw a flower crown dangling from its crumpled horn. She could envision Fiona, trying to banish her fear of being caught by dancing about in triumph, draping the wreath of blossoms over Boann's horn. Fiona, who had known a brutal existence for so many years, must know that if she were caught stealing a cow, the life's blood of Ireland, she would face disaster.

Gormley stumped over to the beast, ripping the flowers from Boann's head. The cow lowed, backed away, fear darting into her eyes at the sight of her master—a man with a capacity for cruelty Caitlin was certain the forlorn beast knew all too well.

"By the feast of Saint Columcille, how did she get in here?" Fiona feigned shock, struggling to find some way, any way, out of this tangle. "Perhaps a fairy hoax."

"The fairies be damned! 'Twas your trickery from the beginning, trying to make me believe the beast was cursed because you wanted to cheat me out of what is rightfully mine!" Rage of a man who loathed being made to look the fool ignited in Gormley's sunken eyes.

One meaty fist grasped a handful of Fiona's hair, twisting the bright curls in a brutal grasp. Caitlin winced as she saw Fiona sink her teeth into her lower lip to keep from crying out.

"You are coming with me," Gormley snarled. "I have waited a long time to find some excuse to see you dead, girl. Rid the land o' vermin, I will. Hoped the warriors would save me the trouble, but now, I vow, I will see to your end myself."

Caitlin saw the flicker of fear in Fiona's defiant face. For years, Fiona must have done as countless other small creatures—darted away when enemies drew close, outwitted them, outmaneuvered her foes by relying on speed and intelligence to escape. But as with those other creatures, once a predator sank its massive claws into her flesh, the game was over.

Caitlin swallowed hard, knowing it might mean disaster if she stepped into Gormley's sight, but what else could she do? Saints alone knew when Niall would return. Even if he went to fetch his sister the instant he rode into Castle Daire, the girl might be dead by the time he reached her.

Caitlin searched desperately around her for something, anything, to use as a weapon, but she found nothing. Like Fiona, she would have to rely on her wits. Sucking in a deep breath, she stepped out to block their path. Gormley nearly slammed Fiona into her, nose first. The girl gaped at her in disbelief and alarm.

"What the—who—" Gormley's jaw went slack. Caitlin shivered, down deep in her soul, at the filthy expression in those glowing pig-eyes. "Aye, and who is this, Fiona? Is it the fairy queen herself you have stolen away like my cow? You need not fear, my ripe little beauty, Turloch Gormley will take care o' you now."

Drawing herself up as though she were mistress of Daire, Caitlin leveled a glare at him. "You will release Fiona at once," she commanded.

"Nay, not even for you, my pretty dove." Gormley gave a coarse chuckle. "She is a thief and a liar, a wee rat scrabbling about decent folks. Been trying to catch her in her wickedness for years, find proof of her ill deeds, and now, at last 'tis time for Ronan's daughter to face the devil."

"She says she does not know how the cow got in here!" Caitlin argued with little hope. "Perhaps it wandered in when I—we were gathering the rushes."

Gormley's mouth puckered like a bag whose string was drawn too tight. "Do you take me for a fool? She stole that cow, and now she has to pay for it."

Pay—the word rang through Caitlin's mind. The bracelet of gold seemed to grow warm upon her wrist, her one link with her mother and father, the token of love they had tucked amongst her wrappings when she had been taken from their arms forever. It had been dangerous enough to let Gormley see her face, but once she revealed something so rich, so exquisite, it was certain the pig-eyed lout would never forget her.

Aye, a voice grieved deep inside her, and if she surrendered the bracelet, she would never again be able to cradle it against her heart as she lay in her bed, knowing her mother's and her father's hands had touched it. Those parents who had loved her but she had never seen.

Caitlin swallowed hard, raising her chin with defiance she did not feel. "If Fiona could pay for the cow, you would let her go, Gormley?"

"I did not steal his infernal cow!" Fiona protested, so absurdly Caitlin wanted to shake the girl herself.

"You must be newly come to this place!" Gormley said with a nasty chuckle. "There has been nothing at Daire worth spitting at for years. But if you could pull a bag o' gold from the air, fairy queen, I might be convinced to forgo the pleasure o' making this scrap o' vermin squeal."

Caitlin fought to steady her voice. She dared not let this man know how terrified she was. Beasts like Gormley thrived on fear. "I have something I might be willing to trade for Boann. You call me the fairy queen, and everyone who has met you of late has heard you complaining that this cow is cursed. You have had little but ill luck since you got her."

"I tell you, this miscreant girl is the cause of all that!" Gormley blustered.

"Aye," Fiona said hoarsely, "blame it on the fairies, on me, on anyone but yourself! You look at her, see the scars on her! Scars from you beating her—"

"Damned if I will let such as you accuse me!" Gormley sputtered.

"It is true!" Fiona raged. "I cannot even guess how many times I have seen you, drunken and mean, lashing at any creature who stumbled into your path. Your cows, your wife, your sons! Aye, and then they beat whatever poor wretch they can lay hands upon!"

God above, Caitlin marveled in terror, was it possible the girl did not know what kind of wrath she was about to bring down on her head?

"Fiona, do not—"

"And as for stealing your accursed cow, what about all you stole from Daire when I was still too much a child to stop you?"

"Girl, close your mouth, or I vow I will close it forever!" Gormley's face washed red. "I will not be accused by the likes of you!"

"Anyone with eyes can see through the window—chairs with my parents' initials intertwined. A bridal bench my father carved with his own hands during the winter they were first wed."

Caitlin saw the guilt flash for a moment in Gormley's face, not out of remorse but because he had been caught. Then he sneered, puffed up with the knowledge Fiona was helpless to do anything about his crimes.

"The cow should be mine! Payment for what *you* stole, old man!"

"Then why do you not summon your famous brother to do battle over the wrongs done you, little rat? You always claimed he would when you were a stripling girl! Remember how you would howl threats at us? *Niall is coming soon! My brother will flay you—*"

"Be quiet, old man, or I swear I will see you dead!" Fiona's voice broke, her face ashen, and Caitlin's heart bled for her.

Gormley gave a cruel laugh. " 'Twas most amusing all those years past. But now you know what we knew even then, do you not, Fiona of Daire! Your brother, the bold champion of Glenfluirse does not care if you starve and rot here any more than I do!"

"That is not true! Niall is even now—" Caitlin could not keep from protesting, then almost bit her tongue. Had she not already made enough of a mess of things? Gormley must not know Niall was here! But it was too late. Gormley's eyes glowed. "The great champion has come to take the scrapings of Daire's pot at last, has he? He will not tarry long here. All Ireland knows he hates this place, despises every stone—aye, and cares not if you and your mother starve as well, eh, Fiona?"

Caitlin wanted to argue, wanted to fling angry words back at him, but it would only make matters worse if this cur realized just how much Niall now cared.

"No one cares what happens to Daire scum, and you should know that above anyone, Fiona!" He sneered. "All Ireland knows you deserved what befell you, after what Ronan did."

Fiona's eyes burned with murder, and Caitlin made a last, desperate attempt to deflect that rage before any hope of striking a bargain was gone.

"You said that if we paid for the cow, you would let Fiona go," she reminded him levelly.

"Perhaps so, but after what she has been saying, it

would take a king's ransom to equal the pleasure I would get from making her pay."

Caitlin reached for the bracelet, felt the gold warm her skin one last time. "Would this be enough?" she asked, slipping the exquisite circlet from her wrist. She held it out to him, the gold mellow and infinitely precious in the dim light.

The man's eyes nearly popped from his head. "That is a finer piece than ever I saw in my life, girl. Wh-where did you get such a thing?"

"It does not matter." Caitlin swallowed hard. "Will you accept this as payment for Boann?"

"Caitlin—" Fiona gasped.

Gormley licked his lips, greed extinguishing his rage. "Have you lost your wits? You could buy a herd o' beasts for such a price. Yet you are willing to trade it for just one?"

"Aye." Caitlin squeezed the word through a throat tight with unshed tears. She could scarce bear the feel of his hungry gaze upon the circle of gold, wanted to wrap her fingers tight about the bracelet, hide it away from this slavering pig. But he snatched the bracelet away from her, smudging the gold, running his fingers over the magnificent craftsmanship with sickening avarice.

Gormley spit, nearly striking the tip of Fiona's toes. "The little rat can live for all I care." He polished the bracelet against his grimy sleeve. "A thousand thanks, fairy queen," he said with a nod toward Caitlin. "You can be certain I will not be forgetting you if I live longer than the sun itself." He chuckled. "When your brother comes back to Daire, Fiona, be sure to send him to this lady's fairy lair. Is that not the kind of quests Niall of the Seven Betrayals is said to perform? Slaying fairy kings and giants while he lets his sister rot alone?"

"You have what you came for," Caitlin snapped, unable to bear the torment on Fiona's face. "Leave before I decide to take the bracelet back."

Gormley chuckled. "As if you could take this from me!"

But then, as if thinking twice about losing his treasure, he flung Fiona to the floor and disappeared into the hall. The girl sprawled across the floor, the rough stone raking her left cheek. Blood welled in the wake of a nasty scrape. Caitlin tried to help her up, intending to dab the blood away, but the girl jerked her arm free.

"What did you do that for?" Fiona demanded, scrambling to her feet. "I owed that fat wretch nothing after all he stole from Daire!"

"That may be, but he did not agree with you. He would have seen you dead, Fiona. God knows what he would have done to you!"

"The day I cannot outwit a knave like Gormley is the day I will cast myself from the castle roof. What were you thinking, plunging in like a witling? Now look what you have done!"

"I know I should not have let him see me, but—"

"See you? You might as well have had heralds announce your presence to half of Ireland when you gave him that bracelet. No one hereabouts has anything half so fine since Castle Daire fell into ruin. And for someone *here* to be casting such a treasure into someone else's hands—thunder and fire, the whole countryside will be talking about nothing else soon, what with Gormley, braggart that he is, thrusting the thing under everyone's nose!"

Fiona might even have seemed furious, if her voice had not cracked just a little bit. "Caitlin, do you know what you have done?"

Sick with a sense of doom, Caitlin swallowed hard. "I could not let him take you away."

"You might as well have done. When Niall discovers what happened today, he will kill me himself. That is, after he has ground your bones to dust between his accursed teeth!"

"He will be angry, but once he hears the tale, he will know there was nothing else to do."

"Aye, there was. Plenty." Fiona regarded her with a suddenly solemn face. "You could have kept yourself hidden, waited for Niall to return, or see if there was some way to get me out of Gormley's clutches without putting yourself in danger. It is what I would have done."

"Fiona, you know you would have helped me."

The girl nibbled at her lip, a sad self-reckoning darkening her downcast eyes. "I have not stayed alive this long by hurling myself into danger on behalf of a near stranger, Caitlin. I learned early that I could barely hope to take care of Mother and myself.".

Caitlin's chest ached as she saw the desolation in the girl's face, knew what Fiona said was true. Regret softened Fiona's features with self-blame. Caitlin cupped the girl's wind-chapped cheeks in her palms, saw Fiona gaze up at her, still amazed by what she had sacrificed moments before. "I am sorry that you have been so long alone," Caitlin said softly.

Fiona's throat worked convulsively, and Caitlin knew there were tears in her eyes for just a heartbeat before the girl willed them away. "I like to be alone," Fiona said, her chin jutting out in a pale copy of her usual defiance.

"I might as well take poor Boann out to the pasture now," the girl said with a shrug. "I thought if you heard the lowing in the night, I could say it was a ghost, but it was going to be bloody hell dragging armfuls of grass all the way back here without you or Niall growing suspicious."

With that, the girl went to the cow, leading her out by the crooked horn. Caitlin listened to the sound of hooves upon the stone, felt them echo, hollow in her heart.

Eyes stinging, she pushed back the sleeve of her leine and stared down at her naked wrist. Strange, she had had the bracelet for such a short time, yet it had become a part of her, the one tangible link to the parents she would never know.

A life for a life, she thought. Niall had bought her life with everything he owned, with his past and his future. He had initiated her into a world of passion she had never hoped to know, compelled her to love him. Surely, a simple bracelet was not too much for her to give in return when his sister was in peril.

And yet . . . she shivered with sadness and loss and resignation. God help Fiona and Caitlin herself when Niall learned what they had done.

Chapter
16

Druid stones held secrets. From the first long-ago morning his father had lifted him up to touch the ancient carvings with grubby child-fingers, Niall had felt it, sensed it. Enigmas captured not only in the ancient writings scribed upon the rocky faces but deeper, more mystic enigmas hoarded within the stones' hearts.

Even now, as he stood braced, defiant in the first rays of moonlight, Niall knew what treasures lay there. Wisdom lost from the beginning of time, echoes of ages past when the veil between worlds of flesh and spirit were thin as mist, and a man had only to step across that airy divide into a realm beyond imagining. Voices so strong, so sage, even death could not silence them.

Niall's chest tightened as a memory shivered to life in the darkest reaches of his mind. A child's joyous chatter, a father's indulgent smile, a day so magical Niall could still feel the gritty scrape of rock against his skin, feel the sun bake his nose.

Is this the gate to Tir naN Og? his eager voice queried. *Show me where it is, I beg you!*

And let you steal off to the land of the fairies without me? Nay, anam cara. *You will have to be patient awhile longer.*

*Grow tall and strong and brave. But know this. When you
do pass through those gates, I will be waiting for you.*

Even now, Niall could remember the prickling of
foreboding, unsettling enough that he spoke despite his
jealously guarded dignity, trying and failing to hide his
fear from the man he adored. *But if you were in Tir naN
Og, Fiona would be lonely for you.*

His father tousled Niall's hair, smiled down, tall as a
mountain, stronger than the fairy king. *Do you not know,
my little man? No fairy magic could keep me from watching
over those I love. Even when you can no longer see my face,
I will always walk by your side.* He had grinned, Ronan of
Daire, mindful of Niall's boyish pride. *You tell Fiona that
for me, if ever she is afraid.*

Apprehension quelled, Niall had dashed off with a
shout, chasing a rabbit that darted through the grass.
Yet he had carried his father's promise with him, as
confident that his father would watch over him as he
was that the sun would rise at dawn.

He had believed until angry warriors dragged his father away from Daire, until those dark, hopeless nights
at the mercy of Conn's strapping sons, when Niall had
strained with all his being into the dark night sky, desperate despite his anger, his betrayal, his fear, to feel his
father's presence beside him.

Niall raked his hand through his wind-tossed hair,
that lost boy's anguish fresh inside him. Was that the
moment he had begun to truly hate Ronan of Daire?
The moment he realized that he was alone?

Niall shook his head, scattering the images to the
wind, half tempted to mount his horse again, to ride
away from the glen and his father's cairn and the druid
stone with its secrets.

But he was seeking an answer only the stone could
give, desperate for some sign that he had not run mad.

Yet as Niall summoned his courage and pressed callused palms to the rugged gray stone, the ancient carvings only mocked him, hoarding their secrets despite his silent plea.

His cheeks burned despite the bite of the wind. Why was the accursed stone silent? Had the Tuatha de Danaan who ruled from the earth's secret depths judged him undeserving? Ancient wisdom was for heroes, champions, not liars the like of Niall who had betrayed their chieftain.

And yet, even if Niall himself did not merit an answer, surely Caitlin would. He could only hope that mighty Fintan would care more about his imperiled daughter than Niall's dishonor.

Closing his eyes tight, Niall reached out with all his will. "Give me a sign, you dwellers of the hills. Fintan, I am blinded, like you. I know not what to do. Should I keep Caitlin here, at Daire, or carry her away to Iona, leave her . . . ?" He could not finish, his throat cinched so tight. Bleak, unthinkable, the possibility he would have to leave his lady behind.

"I will do it, curse you all!" Niall roared aloud. "Turn my back on her on some far-flung isle. Walk away. But only if you give me some sign she will be safe. Speak to me, curse you! Fintan! Father!"

Was it desperation? Fury? A conjuring of his imagination? Stone burned, alive in an instant, pulsing beneath his hands. Niall's eyes flew open, but he did not draw away.

"Answer for *her*, Fintan, if not for me. If ever you loved your daughter—"

Thunder cracked, shattering a cloudless sky. Jaw clenching, Niall only ground his palms tighter against the rough surface. A cry of anguish, denial, ripped from Niall's throat. The pulse in the stone grew fainter, the surface suddenly, painfully cold. Dead.

Sick with despair, Niall let his hands fall to his sides. He staggered a few steps away, sagged down onto the ground, and buried his face in his hands.

They had answered, the old ones, without words. The future he had dared to dream of in Caitlin's arms would never be. But had he not known from that dream's first stirring it was madness? How could a hero like Fintan give his daughter to a traitor and a liar? A man forsworn?

Niall's gut burned with unspeakable loss. But despite his anguish, there was one thing he could be grateful for. He had not been reckless enough to let Caitlin guess the pretty illusions his heart had been painting. Despite the nights they had shared their bodies, she would never suspect he had hoped they might share a future. Fill Castle Daire with their loving, their laughter, a flock of babes with his eyes and Caitlin's valiant spirit.

A low moan tore from Niall at the image he had cherished throughout those beautiful nights—Caitlin's body swelling with the sweet fruit of their loving, Caitlin drowsing in the crook of his arm, while their dark-curled babe suckled at her breast. A family for Niall and his lady. A precious place where they could both belong. But those babes would live only in Niall's imagination now.

His throat knotted, his chest burned, and for a moment he could envy his mother, wandering in the shadow world where dreams were real, the dead walked beside one, and love could work miracles even beyond the grave. But no such sweet escape waited for him. He had to think clearly enough to spirit Caitlin off to safety. He had to be strong enough to let her go.

Wearily, Niall dragged himself to his feet and trudged toward the hollow where his horse stood, grazing. He grabbed the reins, readying himself to swing up onto the horse's broad back. Suddenly, he froze, stunned, awed, his heart taking flight.

A sign. He had asked for a sign! But never had he guessed what it would be. He laughed, staring into the shadows, in wonder, knowing what he would do.

He would carry his offering back to the castle, kneel before Caitlin, before Fiona and his mother. He would tell them of the miracle the old ones had granted and offer them one of his own: the magic of new beginnings.

For six nights, twilight had been a greening time, promising fresh rapture with each new banner of rose or gold that unfurled across the horizon. Darkness became an ally who would bring Niall to her side.

But as Caitlin peered out the open doorway into the arch of landscape beyond, the world appeared suddenly dreary, even the faint flickering of the stars no longer offering her comfort.

The sharp yearning she had suffered weeks before, when she had struggled to maintain a link with the abbess, had dulled. Tonight, as the moon's silver light brimmed over the lip of its emerald chalice of fields, she felt a far more powerful tug deep in her chest. Caitlin glanced over toward the hearth, where Fiona perched near her mother, every muscle in the girl's body twitching with barely leashed energy, like a frightened bird poised for flight. Her eyes glinted, feverish bright, her gestures a little more reckless, her laughter high-pitched and wild. Aniera had not noticed any difference in her daughter, but ever since Gormley had left the castle, Fiona had fairly sizzled with restlessness, trying with all her might to hide any hint of self-blame. But the girl was eaten alive with it, no matter how often Caitlin had tried to soothe her.

Caitlin's heart squeezed in empathy. If only she could find some way to make Fiona believe the truth! Frightening as the confrontation with Gormley had been, angry as Caitlin was at how heedlessly Fiona had cast herself into such danger, and much as Caitlin was dreading Niall's reaction when he learned what had happened, she could only thank God she had been there, able to help Fiona out of trouble when the girl's plans went awry.

Aye, Caitlin thought, chagrined. There was a reason she no longer wished for the abbey, for the sights and scents that were so familiar. Somehow, during these past, precious days, she had discovered something as astonishing as it was wondrous and unnerving.

Daire was home.

The first real home she had ever known.

Caitlin winced. What was she thinking, growing to love this place so much? The crumbling castle, more hospitable to spiders and mice than people. The gentle old woman who wandered a fairy world. A rebellious girl who would rather leap from castle roof than admit she needed anyone. And a man so battered, so betrayed, he might never be able to love anyone, especially when he loathed himself.

They were nothing like what she had imagined as a girl dreaming in the convent, and yet, when Caitlin had least expected it, the three of them had become the family she had longed for all her life.

But they were *not* hers, had never been hers, Caitlin reminded herself grimly. So why did she feel so bereft at the thought of what she must do?

She shuddered, moving through the dreaded paces in

her imagination as she had all that endless afternoon. She had dreamed of running into Niall's arms when he returned, laughing and loving and welcoming him home as she had vowed to. Show her beloved warrior he was not alone. But now that homecoming would hold the chill of a nightmare. She would meet Niall at the doorway, tell him what had transpired with that vile cur Gormley. And in so doing, she would put an end to any hopes or dreams she might have, impossible as they had been.

For there was little doubt in Caitlin's mind what Niall would do once he learned what had happened. He would sweep them all away from Daire like a hound snatching his flock from beneath the jaws of a wolf pack. He would carry her far away, leave her behind.

Unless . . . unless she kept her secret, swore Fiona to silence. Unless she told him she had lost the bracelet somewhere in her wanderings and with that lie placed all of Daire in horrible danger because of her own selfish needs.

Caitlin's chest ached. She blinked back tears. Nay. Better to be honest. From the beginning, Niall had intended to leave her behind, had he not? On that enchanted night he had first kissed her, he had agreed to attempt to mend his relationship with his sister, not reclaim his family. He had promised to give his mother some happiness, not take his place again as her son. And he had come to Caitlin's bed to share indescribable ecstasy with her, not to give the love she so craved.

She was the one who had longed for more, clung to false hopes like a greedy child, stubbornly refusing to imagine what it would be like when the game was done and she was left alone.

Shivering, she paced toward the open door, the wind brushing wisps of curls across cheeks wet with unbidden tears. She dashed them away, then wrapped her arms about her middle, pretending it was Niall who held her. She imagined that time could stand still, everything remain as it was, improbable, imperfect, joy more rare and precious than she had ever known.

But it seemed the fates were jealous of even this short, stolen time. Hoofbeats drummed nearer, the familiar if curiously slow approach of Niall's horse.

Swallowing hard, she stood and watched him shape-shift from sound to shadow to man. His breeze-tossed mane whisked about the hard square of his jaw. One strong hand gripped the reins, the other cradled something against him, a bulky object draped gently across the horse's withers.

But it was his face that struck Caitlin to the heart. Even in the twilight, it glowed with a luminescence brighter than any sun. His smile shone, wide and white and wonderful, with a boyish joy she had never seen in him before. And his eyes—his eyes sought her greedily, gratefully, quickened with emotions so deep they stunned her.

"Caitlin!" he shouted out, eager as any youth come home to his heart's desire. "Call Fiona and Mother! See what I have brought you!"

But before she could force her leaden feet to move, his cry brought Aniera hastening out to greet him, Fiona trailing in her wake, eyes glittering hard with defiance.

Fiona grimaced. "Ah, so the great hunter has brought us something to eat before we starve to death. All hail Conn's mighty champion!"

"I bring you something far better than mere food, little sister," Niall called out. He dismounted, gathering the mantle-wrapped bundle carefully in his arms. "I bring you everything you have wished for."

"What I wish should be simple enough to grant, even for you," Fiona muttered. "Merely show me your backside as you leave Daire forever."

Niall laughed, undaunted. "What I bring is for all of us. For you, Fiona. Aye, and you, Mother. And for Caitlin and me as well. Something I have dreamed of but was too afraid to confess."

Caitlin sucked in a deep breath, hating herself for having to speak, to dash the exuberance from Niall's face. "I have something to tell you as well," she began. *And I wish to God the telling was over with*.

"Whatever it is, it can wait," Niall said, tenderness and passion vibrating in his deep voice. Caitlin's soul wrenched at the beauty of it. "Nothing can be more important than this, *mo chroi*." *Mo chroi*, he had said, *my heart*, the endearment so beautiful it made Caitlin ache.

"Today I rode to the standing stone, seeking answers from the old ones. Do you remember, Mother? How Father taught me?"

Aniera smiled. "Aye. He loved the stone, my Ronan. The power of it, the mystery. It was the stone who blessed our love, your father's and mine. Promised great happiness and great woe." Her voice hushed, her eyes clear for an instant. "The happiness was worth every bit of pain."

"I promise you happiness again, here at Daire, if the three of you will help me to build it," Niall vowed. "A home you can take pride in, Fiona. A son who will strive to be worthy of you, my mother."

"Och, my treasure," Aniera crooned, cupping his cheek in her hand. "Sure, and you have ever been the finest boy in all of Eire."

Niall turned to Caitlin, and her heart lurched at what she saw in his face. His voice roughened, trembled. "And for you, Lily Fair, I offer myself as a husband, if you will have me. Babes to fill your arms if you will let me give them to you."

Every dream she had ever had, more love than she had ever imagined, a lifetime in the arms of the man she adored. The vision shimmered before her, so exquisite she could not bear it. A future born the instant before a cruel twist of fate snatched it away.

In that instant, she wanted to hate Fiona for the recklessness, the defiance that had cost Caitlin so much. But she could not. She had only to glance into Fiona's sharp features, remember all she had suffered, and know that when the girl had first stolen the cow, Fiona had never guessed what a high price fate would demand for her crime.

"Niall," Caitlin choked out, her heart breaking into tiny pieces. "You do not understand—"

Almost reverently, he laid the bundle down on the shadowy turf, then straightened and turned to face her. "You think I have not seen the dreams in your eyes when I hold you in my arms? You think I have not wished I had the power to grant you everything your heart longs for?" Niall's voice broke, and Caitlin was humbled at the honesty in him, the courage of this valiant warrior daring to lay open the bruised reaches of his heart.

"But—but it is too dangerous," Caitlin stammered. "You said—"

"Ah, but do you not know, Caitlin?" Fiona mocked. "My brother is the boldest warrior of Glenfluirse. He laughs in the face of danger."

"I may have to strangle you yet if you do not hold your tongue, wee one. For a moment, only. I do not expect miracles." Niall chuckled with an affection that once would have filled Caitlin with the sweetest gratitude. Now, it burned like a fresh wound.

He turned the full force of his gaze upon Caitlin. "I

have sworn to guard you with my life. How better to do that than to keep you at my side? We will take care, lady. You will be safe."

"Nay!" Caitlin moaned, warring inside herself, some dark, selfish beast inside her struggling to break free. To keep the dreadful secret of Gormley and the fact that the heinous man had seen her. She wanted this future so badly, loved Niall so much. Too much to keep a secret that might put him in danger. She whispered, "I cannot let you sacrifice—"

He stopped her words with his fingertips, then glided his thumb in an awed path across her cheek. "Do you not know by now?" he rasped. "Loving you is the purest thing I have ever done."

Loving? Caitlin's heart shattered; even Fiona was suddenly struck dumb. Slowly, Niall sank down onto one knee.

"It is true, lady. From the first moment I awakened to find you at the druid altar, I felt this pull of destiny, fiercer than I had ever known before. I ignored it, denied it, fought it, until . . ." His gaze flashed up to hers, eyes greener than a forest primeval filling with emotion more intense than any she had imagined.

"Let me show you what the old ones sent as a blessing on our union, Caitlin. A gift from your father, mighty Fintan. And from my father as well." Niall shifted the bundle until it lay at her feet, illuminated in the shaft of light spilling from the doorway.

Fiona gasped, pointing at the bundle. "It moved!"

"Aye, Fiona. It lives, and it breathes, and it will grow, just as I hope your trust in me will one day."

Ever so gently, Niall folded back his mantle, revealing what had lain wrapped inside it. Wide brown eyes peered wonderingly at the world from a russet face, the newborn calf giving a plaintive *moo*.

So stricken she could not speak, Caitlin stared at the tiny animal, Fiona standing, frozen as well. Only Aniera bent down with a mother's instinct, stroking its silky head.

"Poor wee mite. Have you no mother to tend you?" she soothed.

"We will have to nurse her by hand with a rag soaked in milk. But we can raise her." Niall glanced from Caitlin's stricken face to Fiona's reddening one. Confusion creased his brow. "You need not fear. Someone will surely be willing to spare a bit of milk."

Fiona broke first, her wail more child than woman. "How could you do this to me, Niall? Have you not caused me enough grief?"

Niall climbed to his feet. His smile vanished. "What the devil is ailing you? Fiona, can you not see? This is the beginning of Daire's new herd. The herd you dreamed of starting. We will work together, you and I, and between us we will make Daire mightier than ever before."

"Why could you not have brought the calf yesterday?" Fiona cried. "Or a week ago? Now it is too late!" A sob broke from the girl's lips, and she fled into the darkness.

Niall took a step after her. Stopping, he turned to where Caitlin stood, her face white and strained in the light of the newborn moon.

"Aniera."

Niall stiffened. Caitlin's voice did not sound like her own.

"Could you take the calf inside, warm it near the fire? Perhaps soak a bit of oat cake in water and try to feed it?"

Only a little bemused by her daughter's strange reaction, Aniera gathered up the orphan. " 'Twas joy made

Fiona weep." Aniera tried to comfort her son. "She will tell you herself when she returns." Then, cuddling the calf close, she disappeared into the castle, singing an off-key lullaby.

Niall's blood chilled with foreboding in the dreadful silence left behind. Nay, it had not been joy that sent his sister running into the night sobbing.

"I do not understand," he said, unable to bear the clutching stillness at last. "I was sure the calf would please Fiona, and you . . . you would be satisfied to stay here at Daire with me."

"I want it more than life," Caitlin confessed so raggedly Niall dared to feel a faint reawakening of hope.

"Then why do you look at me thus, as if your heart were bleeding?"

She turned her face to the shadows, and Niall knew a moment of panic, as if she were somehow melting into the hills, bleeding into the land itself like the Tuatha de Danaan. "There is something you must know," she began slowly. "Something happened today that changes things."

"Fiona up to some sort of mischief? Nothing we cannot sort out together, I am certain."

"I wish . . . hope that somehow we may."

"What is it, *alannah?*" Niall chuckled to fight off his unease. "Has she pierced the water skins with that spear I made for her? Has she dumped ashes on some poor wayfarer's head? Tonight I feel as if I could mend anything."

"This you cannot. And yet, if only there could be a way to—to make things right."

"What is it, my love? Tell me. Trust me." He cupped her cheeks in his rough warrior's hands, feeling as if she were as fleeting and insubstantial as moonlight and as impossible to hold.

"The cow Fiona wanted . . ." Caitlin began.

"Aye, she was worse than a demon, tormenting me about it, and now she has one. A bit small, I admit, but give it time, and it will grow."

"Niall, she—she took it."

"She what?"

"She thought it was her right. Gormley had stolen so much from Daire. Fiona only thought she was taking back a piece of what was hers."

Niall felt a flare of heat in his belly, that creeping sensation of disaster about to fall down on his head. A sensation he would forevermore associate with his sister. "Tell me Fiona did not steal that cow!" he demanded, as if his own temper could keep it from being so. "Does the little fool have any idea what would happen to her if anyone discovered what she had done? Where the devil is the beast? I will drive it back across Daire's borders before anyone realizes—"

"It is too late. This—this loathsome man, Gormley, he came to Daire, ready to drag her off. God only knew what he planned to do to her."

Niall mustered a wan smile. "But the girl got away from him. Aye, Fiona would find a way to wriggle out of catastrophe. Thank the sea god she is as resourceful as she is infuriating. I will go to Gormley tomorrow, make amends so the girl is out of trouble."

He chuckled, but there was little mirth in him. He shuddered to think what Fiona might have brought down on Daire. "Tell me, Lily Fair, what do you think it will cost me to pull one small sister out of the flames?"

"A gold bracelet."

Niall jerked around to stare into Caitlin's face. His blood turned to ice. "What the devil do you mean by that?"

Was it possible for Caitlin's face to grow whiter still? "Fiona hid the cow in one of the abandoned rooms in the back of the castle. Gormley found it." She turned away. "I traded my bracelet for Fiona's freedom."

"Tell me he did not see you," Niall pleaded, knowing it was impossible.

Caitlin nodded.

"Nay!" Low, anguished, a cry of denial ripped from Niall's chest. "I warned you to keep out of sight!"

"I feared that he would kill her. What choice did I have? Even if it costs me everything I have ever dreamed of . . . a life with you. Your love . . . even then, I cannot regret what I did. *You* cannot regret it."

"Aye, I can!" Niall raged. "I can curse the little thief to hell for it! Why could she not have waited? Just one day more—"

"She was afraid. Afraid of losing Daire. Afraid of trusting you."

"And now you—you are defending her?" Niall cried in disbelief. "Can you not see, Caitlin? Your bracelet is gone, the only treasure you had from your parents. But we have lost more than that. We cannot stay here now. If Conn should ever see that bracelet, hear Gormley's story, he'll know the truth. Daire is lost to us."

She reached out, touched his face, her fingers trembling against his skin. "But we still have each other. Fiona will get over losing Daire in time. And your mother will be comforted by her love for you. I meant what I said. I will follow you wherever you lead. Aye, to hell itself, as long as you are at my side."

Niall bellowed a black oath. "You think I would condemn you to such a fate, loving you the way I do? Hunted? Afraid? Chased through the night like a beleaguered doe?"

"But I would not be afraid. I would be with you."

"Nay." Niall drew back, his mind spinning with improbable plans, thick panic roiling in his gut. "There is only one thing to do. I must get you as far from me as possible."

"Nay! I will not—" Caitlin protested, but he scarce heard her.

"Soon as someone sees Fintan's bracelet and hears Gormley's boasting, the tale will travel back to Conn. Conn will know I have lied to him," Niall reasoned. "He will guess I would guard you, defend you. He will still want your death, but he will hunt more fiercely than he has ever hunted any man before to silence me. Keep me from betraying the truth—that he ordered me to murder you, Fintan's daughter. That he broke his vow to your father. When he finds me, and he *will*, Caitlin, by your God, he will—"

"Nay! Niall—"

He could feel her shattering inside, whatever remained of the dreams in her eyes turning into sharp fragments, piercing her soul.

Out of love, he did what he swore he would never do. He lied to her, his voice gentling. "Perhaps he will not find me. But I cannot let that matter. I will do what I have to do. Take Mother and Fiona north as planned. Settle you in Iona. And then I will do all in my power to lead Conn and his dogs away from you. Leave a false trail to madden them. Then—" He stopped, trying to spare her.

"Then what, Niall?" she quavered.

I will let them run me to ground in some far-off land where they can never find you, Niall thought bleakly.

She clutched at his arm. "Niall, let me come with you! I beg of you. I would wander Ireland with no other shelter but your mantle and count myself the most fortunate woman on earth."

"Caitlin—"

"I would rather have whatever time God gives us together, no matter how brief, than live to be old without you."

For an instant, a wild, desperate madness took hold of Niall's heart. He wanted to snatch Caitlin up onto his horse, to ride away into the night wind. He wanted to seize the impossibly precious gift of whatever time they had left.

It took more strength than he had ever expended to shove that last chance away. He turned his back on her, unable to bear her suffering.

"It is finished, Caitlin," he rasped. "This is why I never dared to dream. No matter how beautiful, in the end, you have to awaken."

And it had been a dream, more wondrous sweet than anything he had ever hoped to know. Now it was ended. Niall squared his shoulders, resolute.

"You do not know what you are asking of me!" Caitlin cried. "To be left behind by you—to lose you— there could be no pain worse."

"It is over, Caitlin."

She must have heard it, the conviction in his voice, hard and unyielding as the blade of his sword. She turned, fled, as Fiona had, into the darkness. Niall sagged against the castle wall, her words still echoing through him.

To be left behind by you . . . there could be no pain worse.

He closed his eyes, hearing his mother's agonized screams ring in his ears, seeing the hideous torture contorting his father's face as he was dragged from her arms.

If only you knew, Lily Fair, Niall thought, anguished. *When you love as fiercely as we do, there is pain far deeper than loneliness. I will not let you see me die.*

Chapter

17

❦

CONN PACED the breadth of the great hall, the massive brace of wolfhounds that guarded Glenfluirse cowering whenever he drew near. Beasts who had torn the throat from massive stags and slain packs of marauding wolves without ruffling a hair of their shaggy gray coats eyed Conn with the wariness of wild things. Their great bodies quivered in terror at white-hot rage they sensed but no one saw.

The curs were wise to fear him at present, Conn thought. But there were others whose fear should cut far deeper: those incompetent warriors who were still blundering around the countryside.

The task he had set for them should have been simple enough. Capture one scrawny, friendless youth possessed of more bluster than brains. Cut the boy's throat to silence him forever, preferably with the blade of the *enchanted dagger* Niall had given to the lad so he could protect himself. Conn's lip curled in a sneer that sent the dogs scrambling from the room, leaving their booty of marrowbones behind.

Curse Magnus and the pack of incompetent fools who followed him! Rank failures, the lot of them. Conn swore. Would the chieftain of Glenfluirse have to hunt the boy down himself?

Every hour the lad continued to elude them, there was a greater chance Owaine would tell someone what had happened at the fortress. More perilous still, the lad might find Niall himself. And if Niall ever discovered that the boy he had sent as an emissary had almost been killed for his efforts, hell would not be dark enough for Conn to hide in.

Conn shuddered, suddenly cold. Aye, if Niall learned the truth, that would be peril indeed. For from the night Conn had first thrown Ronan's son into the pack of his own, expecting him to quail before the much older boys, Niall had shown a maddening iron-hard core of courage. Loyal to his chieftain and foster father he might be, but Niall of the Seven Betrayals also had too much honor by half and possessed an oft-inconvenient determination to protect those weaker than he.

Not that the trait should surprise Conn. Blood will out. Niall was the son of Ronan of Daire, in spirit as well as flesh, while Conn's own heirs were sly, clumsy-witted fools who would cheerfully cut their brothers' throats to gain the title of chieftain. But not their father's throat, Conn thought with the smallest stirring of satisfaction. Nay, he had made certain they were too afraid of him to dare.

Conn grimaced. It was a pity he could not have had Magnus send the warriors loyal to Niall out to search. Doubtless *they* would have had the skills, the tenacity, and the cunning to flush Owaine out of the underbrush.

Ever since Fintan's death, Conn had watched those who had been loyal to the blind warrior begin to turn to Niall. Conn had seen the spark of devotion fire in their eyes, and he had hated the knowledge that Niall possessed that elusive quality his own sons did not: the ability to lead men. The same gift that had driven armies to charge into battle behind Fintan and win despite impossible odds.

But Conn did not dare muster Niall's followers. They might be nearly as dangerous as Niall himself if Owaine betrayed the truth—that Conn had attempted to murder Niall's messenger. Suspicion bred suspicion, and once doubt was planted in the warriors' minds, it was but a small step to discovering what Conn dreaded most of all. That he had ordered the murder of Fintan's daughter—

"Hellfire," he muttered savagely. "Can no man in Glenfluirse follow a simple command? Will I be forced to do anything of importance with my own hands from this day forward?"

Aye, a voice inside him whispered, stirring up an odd twinge of regret. *For once this intrigue is finished, the only warrior you can trust completely will be dead by his own hand or by yours.*

A servant girl too small to shake a cat scurried in, bobbing up and down with such nervous abandon he was tempted to step on her feet to hold her still. "I watched the road the way you ordered me to," she cried, breathless. "Riders are coming at last. Looks t'be Magnus an' a crowd o' his men."

Conn fought not to betray his emotions in his face—anticipation, unease, relief. *It must be good news they bring*, he reasoned. Surely, Magnus would not be fool enough to return to Glenfluirse without the boy's blood on his hands.

"Inform my eldest son that I will see him in my chamber at once. Alone." Conn turned and strode through the maze of gray stone rooms, until he reached his most private chamber.

It seemed an eternity before he heard his son's boots tromping toward him. An odd, rather strange shuffling sound echoing in his wake.

Alarm bit deep. Surely, even Magnus in all his arrogance would not be foolhardy enough to drag Owaine back to Glenfluirse. If he had, Conn vowed he would take his son's head himself!

But before Magnus entered the room, he shoved his companion onto a wooden stool.

Conn drew himself up to his full height, the rage of the past weeks thundering inside him as Magnus strode through the arched doorway.

Conn's eyes narrowed, disliking the expression on his son's face. "You have accomplished the task I set for you?"

"The boy is dead."

Relief. "You sent him to his grave?" Seeking reassurance he would never have needed from Niall.

Magnus shrugged. "I did not have to. A weakling boy the like of this Owaine could not survive the wildlands for long. We searched night and day, but it was as if he had vanished from the face of the earth. Last eventide, we discovered what had become of him about half a day's ride from Daire."

"Pray enlighten me."

"He was devoured by wolves. All we found were the bloody rags he wore, a few bones, and—"

Fury burst free at the fates who dared mock him. Now he would never know for certain whether or not he was rid of the boy. "How the devil can you be certain it was Owaine?" Conn raged. "It could have been anyone! Damnation, if the boy were clever, it could have been a ruse!"

"It was no ruse. I found *this* buried in the wolf carcass that lay nearby." Magnus extended his hand. Conn

peered down at the exquisite contours of the dagger
Niall had given the boy, Owaine's greatest treasure.

Triumph surged through Conn as he took the dagger
in his hand. "You are right," Conn murmured. "The
boy is dead. He would never surrender this dagger
while he yet lived."

Magnus thrust out his chest. "So I have proven myself worthy to you. I have completed the task you set
for me."

Conn gave a snort of disgust. "The wolves are the
ones I should reward. They killed the boy. You stumbled into the midst of their victory by accident."

Magnus's face reddened, his gaze sullen. "I knew
that you would say that. But you will not discount me
so easily when you see what else I have brought you. I
stumbled across this thief soon after leaving the
wolves' kill. He was gloating over his treasure, too
much a fool to hide it from us or read what was scribed
on it."

Conn chuckled with scorn. "Nothing a witling like
you could discover would interest me."

Magnus's eyes grew hard, a reminder that cubs could
turn to wolves, and one might not realize it until teeth
pierced throat. "If you have no interest, perhaps I shall
take the glory for this myself," Magnus boasted. "I trow
there will be glory aplenty for the man who snatched
this treasure from a thief's hand."

Magnus rummaged in the front of his leine, drawing
an object from the travel-grimed folds of linen. He
thrust the object into a shaft of sunlight. Gold shimmered, rich, lustrous, exquisite.

Conn had treasures aplenty of his own, but he could
not restrain himself from reaching toward the circlet of
gold.

"Nay, Father." Magnus snatched it from his grasp.

"You claimed you had no interest in it. So this bracelet, carved with Fintan's name, is mine forevermore."

"Fintan?" Aye, that was why the bracelet was so familiar, Conn thought, thunderstruck. He remembered seeing it on the wrist of the spear caster's wife long ago.

Conn feigned indifference. "It is no great marvel that someone snatched this trinket from beneath the spear caster's nose. Fintan was gifted at aiming a javelin, but the man was still blind. To steal from him would have been easy enough."

"Even so, the people revere him. The warrior who brings to justice the thief who dared rob such a great hero would gain much honor, would he not, Father?"

"Aye." Conn twisted his fiery mustache, brows lowered in contemplation. "You would gain more warriors as allies. Solidify your claim as future chieftain."

"Now you will have to name me as *tainist*. Your heir. For *I* will be the man people whisper of in awe. The rescue of this bracelet will be more than a match for Niall and his accursed quests!"

How many times had Conn heard his sons grumbling thus? How many times had he warned them that in using Niall's feats as their measure, they admitted his superiority over them? Conn turned away, suddenly weary.

"Judging by his heroics, Niall will be difficult to surpass in the eyes of the people," he cautioned. "Yet men of his kind are reckless. Misfortunes befall them every day." Conn felt an unexpected stab of loss. Irritated, he brushed it aside. "Now, let me see this thief you have snared. We will make his execution a spectacle Glenfluirse will remember forever."

That was the course he must take, Conn thought as Magnus strode out to reclaim his prisoner. Conn would play the outraged chieftain, demand justice for the mighty Fintan, even though the spear caster lay dead. Even Conn's aspirations of being known as the Undefeated One had been lost in the shadow of Fintan's greatness. But if he used this thief to the best advantage, surely he would be worthy of a bard song then. The more conspicuously he could figure in Fintan's legend, the better chance Conn would be remembered.

It was a bitter draught to swallow, knowing his only claim to legend was as vassal to another man—not in rank but rather in valor. But he had repaid Fintan for the slight in a way no one else would ever know. Despite all Fintan's courage and fairy magic, the legendary spear caster was dead. He had not had the power to save his daughter's life from beyond the grave. Caitlin of the Lilies lay moldering in the dirt, dead at Conn's command.

Grim satisfaction filled the chieftain as he heard Magnus reenter the chamber. Conn turned, catching his first glimpse of the thief.

Filthy hair clung to the squat dome of his skull. Thick-fingered hands twisted in the folds of wool covering a coarse body. His features, repulsive enough, were made ridiculous by bristly eyebrows that crawled like a fat caterpillar from ear to ear, stretching in an unbroken line. Most disgusting of all, he was blubbering, so terrified Conn feared the wretch would soil himself at any moment.

If only Fintan could see this disgrace of a man who had outwitted him. It was a pity Conn could not reward the thief rather than execute him, but then, this man was such a pathetic figure, perhaps execution would be the greatest mercy Conn could show to him.

"So," Conn intoned ominously. "*You* are the thief who dared steal from the greatest warrior Glenfluirse has ever known."

"N-nay, oh great one! I am an honest man!" The wretch cringed. "I swear on the Stone of Fal that I stole nothing!"

"A brave man or a foolish one, since the Stone will blast a liar into eternity." A liar, Conn thought with a twinge, or a false chieftain. "If you did not steal this bracelet, then where did you come by it, my fine fool? In a fairy bower?"

"It was traded for a cow I owned. A most wondrous cow, bewitched, she was, and—"

"Bewitched?" Magnus chortled. "Liquid gold would have to pour from the beast's teats to be worth such a price! Father, this fool keeps babbling nonsense. But no one with half a wit would make such a trade!"

"It was not only for the cow," the man amended. "It was payment to keep someone's head from beneath the blade of a sword. She stole the cow from me, she did! I admit to looking forward to seeing the little witch get her due—er, at seeing justice done. But life is hard. I—"

Conn glared at the groveling mess before him, out of patience with the whole affair. "From whom did you get this bracelet? The truth, man. And no more blubbering, lest I am tempted to sever a finger for each unnecessary word you utter."

The man's doughy face went gray, and he stuffed his fists behind his back. "I do not know who gave me the—I mean, I had never—"

"Magnus." Conn coldly held out his hand. "Give me that dagger."

"Nay! Oh, mighty one! I tell you what I know! The witch who stole my cow is called Fiona, the betrayer Ronan's spawn. Wicked as her father, is she, and—"

"The daughter of Ronan of Daire? Thieving cows?"

The man nodded so hard it seemed his head would pop off.

Conn waved away the dagger Magnus offered, the chieftain pausing to allow himself a chill smile. Fintan and Ronan might hold thrones with the Ever Young, but when the two warriors who had been his nemeses gazed beyond the enchanted walls of Tir naN Og, they would finally know how powerless they were against him. He had killed Fintan's only child and turned proud Ronan's daughter into a starveling thief.

Conn turned away, stroking his mustache. "There might be truth in what you say. Fintan's wife was a tender-hearted creature. Fintan and Ronan comrades in arms. Grainne could have sent the bracelet to Ronan's widow in secret. Aniera of Daire would have kept such a treasure."

"The bracelet would not have lasted a fortnight at Castle Daire!" Gormley exclaimed. "I would have taken it when I—" The man choked the words off as if he had swallowed a nest of bees. "I mean to say, the women have all but starved since Ronan's death. Fiona would have traded the trinket long before her brother returned."

"Her brother?" Magnus scoffed. "You see, Father? Proof this wretch is lying! Niall would sooner have his skin flayed from his body a sword stroke at a time than return to Daire!"

Nay, Conn thought with a smile, it made perfect sense. Where else would a man like Niall go with innocent blood on his hands? He would hurl himself into hell. But despite its lack of fire and brimstone, Daire was an appropriate replacement.

"So my champion has returned home at last," Conn said, savoring the image of Niall's reaction to what he must have found there. Destruction, poverty, all at Conn's command. He had intended it as his final sword stroke against Ronan—reducing the proud warrior's wife and daughter to nigh beggary. Now, their plight would prove useful in a way he had not anticipated. There were rumors Niall's sister was half wolf cub by now, feral and angry and raw with hatred. Nothing would be more likely than that additional burden of guilt to give Niall the tiny push he needed to fall on his own sword or make it seem logical he had done so to anyone who might question the death Conn planned to deal him should Niall prove uncooperative.

Was it possible the noble champion had stooped so low as to steal booty from the corpse of the wench he murdered? Was the bracelet to be proof to Conn that the deed was done? Or was it a cross to tie about Niall's neck? Either was a pleasant thought.

"I will ask you one more time, Gormley. Where did the bracelet come from? Did Niall trade it for the girl's life?"

Gormley's mouth fell open like that of a dead fish. "Nay! I would not have dared . . . if Niall of the Seven Betrayals—" He shook himself. "The wench gave it to me. The wench hiding behind the chest. Never laid eyes on her before that day, though by God and the saints, I will never forget that face now."

Conn's nape prickled. "There was another woman at Castle Daire?"

"Aye. A rare beauty she was. I would have traded the cow for just one ride between her legs."

"Her name," Conn snarled. "What was her name?"

Gormley swallowed hard. "Fiona called her Caitlin."

Caitlin. Conn's blood froze. His hand knotted on the bracelet. "What did she look like?"

"Hair black as night. Eyes blue. Like pools. And a face—never had I seen such a face. Beauty the fairies would envy."

Poetry from this swine of a man. A bracelet of gold

bearing Fintan's name. And honor—the girl had traded it for the life of someone she scarce knew. Conn closed his eyes, the face of Grainne, Fintan's wife, swimming before him in the darkness.

Fintan's wife was fairer than any flower in Ireland. "Was this Caitlin lily fair?"

Gormley raised his eyes heavenward. "She would make Cuchulain himself forget he was a hero born."

Or seduce Niall of the Seven Betrayals to abandon his quest, his chieftain, the honor he had fought to win, Conn thought. The chieftain's hand clenched on the bracelet until it nearly cut his palm.

Ronan's son had betrayed him! Aye, and had been clever enough to hide the girl away. Niall would try to spirit her off again, to a faraway place where Conn could never find her, and, by God's blood, if any man could protect the girl from the chieftain's wrath, it would be Ronan's son!

Conn paced to the arrow slit, his skin icy despite the warmth of the sun. As long as Niall lived, as long as the girl lived, his hold as chieftain of Glenfluirse would be in peril. He should have seen to the girl's death himself instead of plotting and planning. His schemes had trapped him now!

"Magnus, you will take your prisoner to the great hall. Feed him. Then let him go."

"Then I—I am free?" Gormley all but wept in relief.

"You have done me a great service. I will repay you as you deserve."

"Father!" Magnus objected.

Conn turned hard eyes on his son. "You will do as I command you. Once our friend Gormley is breaking his fast, you will return to me here."

Scowling, Magnus did as he was ordered.

The moment the chamber was empty, Conn braced

himself against the rough stone wall and battled back sick waves of panic.

He was undone.

The woman foretold to destroy him was alive, and under the protection of the only living warrior in Glenfluirse whose abilities Conn held in awe. Not awe, he realized with a start. Not anymore. It was fear he could taste on his tongue, thick as the stench of death and sickly sweet.

"This riot of fear in your head will not save you!" Conn muttered fiercely under his breath. "Calm yourself! *Think.*"

Always before when his rule had been threatened, he had found a way to avert disaster. Why? Because he was willing to sacrifice anything, anyone, to rule—but no man in Ireland had ever discovered that fact and lived to tell.

What weapons had he chosen? Not the clumsy, unpredictable blades his warriors brandished. His weapons were his wits, his secret ruthlessness, and his mastery in keeping his own emotions hidden so that his quarry never suspected they were about to be destroyed until it was too late. He had begun to believe he could never fail.

But this time, the contest of wits had gone awry. The prey now scented the hunter at his heels, and Conn's greatest allies, deception and surprise, were lost. The chieftain knew Niall far too well not to dread the enemy he had roused. Running his champion to ground would be the most demanding challenge Conn had ever faced. He knew Niall well enough to be certain of that. Or did he truly know Niall at all?

He had sent Niall on this quest, so certain of what his champion would do. But Niall stunned him. The warrior who carried his honor like a fever in his blood had

forsworn himself. And for what? To spare the life of a
woman who was all but a stranger to him.

Aye, Caitlin of the Lilies was a stranger to Niall,
Conn thought in disgust, but Conn the Ever Truthful
was not. For years, Niall had been loyal to him, grateful to him, trusted him. Was there any way to use that
to advantage?

Niall knew of the prophecy dooming Caitlin. He was
warrior enough to understand why even an honorable
ruler might choose the death of one woman over chaos
in his lands, and that was all Niall knew of this abysmal
affair. He had no suspicions of how dark and tangled
Conn's plotting had grown—that Conn desired not
only the girl's death but Niall's own as well.

Niall believed Conn had sent him on a final quest to
test his worthiness as a warrior. Considering all Niall
felt he owed Conn, the warrior would be eaten alive
with guilt because he had failed the quest. Or had he?
The question snaked into Conn's consciousness. He
froze.

What if this quest had been the most clever test of
all? What if the only way Niall could triumph over this
quest was to disobey Conn's order? Place the life of an
innocent above his own desires, even above his own
chance at redemption?

Conn straightened, fear fading, confidence welling
inside him like a dark, secret spring. He smiled as Magnus stalked back into the room, more sullen than ever.

"You feel I have robbed you of your pleasure with
that wretch Gormley, my son?"

Magnus shot him a surly glance. "*You* are the chieftain. I do as you command."

"Then I command you to do this. Follow Gormley
when he leaves the fortress. Kill him. But let no one
suspect who felled the cur."

Magnus's eyes gleamed.

"I have pleased you," Conn said. "That is well. I wish my next decree might also delight your heart."

Had he betrayed himself somehow? Conn wondered. Magnus eyed him with suspicion.

"What do you mean by that?"

"All in good time, my son." Conn sighed. "I begin to despair you will ever learn patience. Send a servant to garb me in my finest raiment. Then summon every man who can ride. They will await me in the bailey."

Before two hours had flown, Conn stood before them, resplendent in robes striped in brilliant colors, his hair blazing like fire in the sun. Conn pointed one long finger toward the bard, who stood, his clarsagh slung over one shoulder, his poet eyes ever watchful, capturing men and moments for the generations to come.

"Awaken the strings of your harp, bard," Conn proclaimed, his voice ageless as the mountains. "A legend is born this day! Niall of the Seven Betrayals, my beloved foster son, has earned his place among the heroes who dwell in Tir naN Og!"

Shouts of praise and surprise rose from the crowd.

"Warriors of Glenfluirse, heed your chieftain's command. You will spread my decree to every corner of the land, carry it to the people, and raise them in wild celebration. Niall of the Seven Betrayals has triumphed over his final and most formidable quest."

A roar of approval echoed in the bright air, its sound mingled with groans of outrage.

"It is easy to take what one wants and call it honor," Conn continued. "But only the greatest of heroes would sacrifice the reward he has worked toward for so many years so that he could protect a helpless stranger."

Disgust rose in Conn as he saw a half-measure of the crowd nodding in agreement. *You are as foolhardy as Niall himself is*, Conn thought in scorn. *To rule, you must take what you want, no matter who blocks your path.* But Conn took care to let only jubilation show in his face.

"Because Niall has turned death into life, he will be granted the reward he sought with such courage and bravery. A new name."

Conn glimpsed a small boy dancing in glee, and a sliver of dread pierced through him. Always Niall had gained the loyalty of such little wastelings. And if one in particular—that wee demon Owaine—managed to reach his hero, even this plan might fail. Conn cut off the swell of cheers with a wave of his hand.

"There is more to rejoice in." His eyes narrowed. "Niall will be given the rank of *tainist.*"

"A murderer's son! Future chieftain?" Magnus exploded in a black oath. "You promised it to me! You cannot—"

"I name Niall of the Seven Betrayals heir to all I command." Conn's voice boomed over his son's protests. "All the fortress of Glenfluirse will prepare to give him glorious welcome. *Now, ride.* Search every hill and glen near Castle Daire."

Conn raised high the exquisite circlet of gold scribed with Fintan's name. "This bracelet—a treasure greater than any you have ever seen—will reward the man who brings Niall of the Seven Betrayals back to this proud father's embrace."

Chapter

18

‹❦❧›

FIONA WAS CRYING, fierce, silent tears so terrible they tore at Niall's heart. She would have been horrified to realize he knew her guilty secret, detected her weeping despite the cold rain that dampened her cheeks, aye, and knew as well that she clutched in her hand a fistful of Daire's black earth as if to cling to a piece of the land she loved forever.

Even as a boy, he had always known when she cried, no matter how hard she tried to hide it. He had sensed it like a cold fist in his gut, been willing to attempt anything from wild jests to dangerous feats of daring to playing at fairy king in his efforts to cajole her from her sadness.

But as the bedraggled, rain-soaked band of travelers trudged away from Castle Daire forever, there was no comfort Niall could offer.

He was taking his sister and bewildered mother away from the place they called home. He was forcing Caitlin to trudge farther and farther from the dreams they had both shared. He was marching them all toward a future none of them could imagine.

Niall glanced up to the two figures who sat upon his horse, Fiona's young arms keeping their mother balanced astride it as Aniera's eyes strained backward in confusion, a wilting flower crown on her rain-soaked hair. Did she really understand that she would never be able to return to the castle where Ronan had made her his bride? Did she guess how terribly Niall regretted it?

Aye, *regretted it*, Niall thought in aching surprise. In a few short weeks, the castle that had haunted his nightmares had been transformed into the cradle of his dreams. Dreams so precious, so new, they still left him awestruck. He wanted to tell Fiona that he forgave her now for her desperate bid to keep the only home she had ever known. He understood why she had stolen the cow. Fought so hard. For Niall remembered at last— not just the one, terrible day of agony that had cleaved their family but treasured moments without number: pulling silvery salmon from the streams, building fortresses behind fallen trees, the forays they had made into the woods fairy hunting, using Fiona's fresh-picked berries as bait.

He had wished for a lifetime at Daire to remember it all. Had imagined sharing those adventures with a brood of his own babes. Sisters and brothers he prayed would share the fierce loyalty, the gruff affection, he and Fiona had known before it was stolen away from them.

I would have slain every dragon in Ireland to please you, my wee sister, Niall thought, a lump in his throat. *I would slay the dragon that threatens you now, if I could. Find some other way, any other way, to keep you safe.*

He would have given his sword arm for the strength to say those words aloud. But what difference would it make? How could he expect Fiona to believe he had rediscovered his love of Daire when he scarce believed it himself?

Maybe one day he would tell her, but for now, Fiona

had no room in her heart for anyone's pain but her own. Defeated in her lifelong struggle to hold on to Daire, she had still not surrendered the land she so loved. Her fingers clenched tight around a clump of soil she had scraped from the garden she and Caitlin had sown with such high hopes.

Niall swallowed hard, his own eyes burning. Perhaps his mother's misty confusion was a blessing this day, for she was never truly alone. Aniera carried with her the shadow figure of her husband, always young and strong and invincible beside her.

The rest of them traveled this road alone. Oceans stretched between them, leaving them solitary even though they had only to reach out their hands to touch one another.

Only Caitlin had had the courage to try to bridge that impossible chasm. She walked close by his side, and twice she had tried to take his hand. He had avoided her touch, busying himself with checking the horse's girth or the reins he used to lead it. He did not want to be comforted now.

He deserved to feel the anger and loss, the guilt and futility. *He* had created this disaster. Deserted his mother and sister because he had not had the courage to face his own pain, then intended to use Daire as a haven when he was in peril. He had brought the threat of Conn's vengeance to their door.

Aye, they had been scarce scraping along, in poverty that had alarmed him—or had it jabbed at his pride? The sister of the champion of Glenfluirse scrabbling for food like a wild dog?

Yet Fiona had felt rich enough. Niall understood that now, when it was too late. She had been rich in the land and the secrets it kept. Her treasure the bones it cradled and the stories the white wind told. She was unique and rare, a creation carved from Daire's soil by the fingers of wind and rain. Her soul drew strength from the castle walls her ancestors had raised, her remarkable courage pulsing into her spirit from Daire's green turf, life force pounding inside her in the ancient, earthy rhythm of the *bodhran*.

In that instant, he envied his sister. No honor won in battle, no quest he had triumphed over, no feat of daring or courage he ever performed had given him the wealth Fiona possessed. She belonged to Daire the way sea cliffs belonged to waves. She understood what the old ones and the land expected of her. And she had fought for them more valiantly than any warrior Niall had ever battled beside.

Would Daire have granted such a gift to *him* if he had possessed the courage to return to it? Or was it possible that he had not squandered that inheritance after all? In spite of his determination to turn his back upon Daire and everything it stood for, had that primitive bond to the land only been sleeping inside him, waiting patiently to awaken? Daring him to risk, to prove himself worthy . . .

It is too late, he charged the voices in his head. *Can you not see that?*

Too late for him. Too late for Fiona and his mother. Too late for the woman who walked beside him, sorrow and resignation in her soulful blue eyes.

Fingertips drifted onto Niall's arm, and he stiffened, unhappy that he had been too distracted to avoid Caitlin's touch. He angled a glance at her, his eyes filled with anger and loss, the tempests he was feeling. She winced, and he cursed himself for letting her see.

"Niall," she said softly. "Someone is coming."

Every battle-honed nerve sizzled to awareness. With a muttered oath, he swung to face the horse, reining the animal to a halt. "Fiona, you and Caitlin take Mother, hide in the underbrush. Make haste!"

He knew Fiona would not have cared if Conn's whole army were descending upon them at that moment. Only her devotion to their mother made her swing down, then reach up to help Aniera slide from the animal's back to the muddy earth.

Aniera stumbled just a little, and Niall knew she was already weary and numb from the hours spent riding. How would she ever withstand this grueling journey?

Caitlin pulled at his sleeve. "Niall, the footprints in the mud are there for anyone to see. And they end here. Would it not make whoever is approaching more suspicious if they found you alone?"

"By the blood of Lugh, aye, curse it! You are right," Niall admitted. By instinct, he maneuvered Fiona and his mother behind him, intending to shield them from whoever was coming. Stalking to Caitlin, he yanked her hood closer about her damp cheeks. She would all but suffocate in the clinging wet folds, but at least no one would see that unforgettable face which could prove the ruin of them all.

"Say nothing," Niall warned the three women. "If anyone asks, we are traveling to a wedding feast. Your sister is to be wed," he said, jerking his head at Caitlin. He scowled as she fidgeted with the hood, doubtless trying to gain a bit more space to breathe. "And for the love of your blasted God, woman, keep your face out of sight this time, or—"

"—who knows what disaster will befall us?" She finished the sentence for him, pain cutting so deep in her voice Niall winced. "It may be your chieftain was right when he called me a curse," she said, meeting his gaze. "I have been one to you. To your family."

"Do not ever say that!" Niall berated her, savage. "It is not true."

"Is it not?" she demanded in quiet misery. "Castle Daire is lost because of me. Your sense of honor will never let you return to your chieftain, even if he believes I am dead. And if he discovers I am alive, you will be hunted, maybe even killed, for your kindness to me."

He wanted to rage at her, shake her until he drove such damning thoughts from her mind. But there was no time for another word. A lone rider bore down on them like a denizen from the otherworld, half concealed by billows of mist and the cold, gray veil of rain.

Niall's gut clenched as the figure neared, and he fingered the hilt of his sword. He would do whatever he had to in order to protect his family.

His family.

Caitlin, with the healing fire in her eyes, defiant Fiona, so young, so impossibly valiant, and the gentle, dazed mother he had tried to forget.

Wild panic churned in his gut, shaking his confidence in the sword arm and battle skill that had served him so well. Was this how his father had felt the day Conn's men had ridden into the castle yard? This fearsome vulnerability, this earth-shattering love, this ice-cold terror far greater than his own paltry death could ever hold?

Niall's hands clenched until his nails dug deep into his palms, awareness jolting through him, lightning clear, illuminating everything. Suddenly, he knew why he had spent his life running—into battle, into danger. He had not been chasing honor or glory or a name made eternal by bard song.

He had been running away from anyone he could love. Because if you loved no one, not even yourself, you had nothing to lose. But it was too late to run again now. He loved these three women with every fiber of his body and soul.

He reached out, squeezed Caitlin's hand, nodded to Fiona with a look that told her more than he had ever dared to say. *Do not fear, little sister. I will take care of you.*

The grief in Fiona's face was beaten back for just an instant before she turned away.

Niall squared his shoulders, bracing himself to meet the rider. But as man and horse emerged from the mist, Niall's jaw dropped in astonishment. Declan MacHurley towered above him like a benevolent giant, the grizzled warrior's broad, honest face still twisted by an enemy sword cut, his grin wide and open as a summer sky. Even through the rain, the warrior's whole body seemed to shout welcome.

Of all the fighting men at Glenfluirse, Declan had been the first who had offered Niall the hand of friendship. Niall had not wanted friends then. Thought he scorned them. Now he knew he had feared them.

Some men might have hated Niall for that rejection. But Declan had shrugged it off, no more rebuffed than a yearling pup. The scar-faced warrior with the merry eyes had simply guarded Niall's back in countless battles, eased the outcast lad's path in so many quiet, subtle ways Niall had been hard-pressed to subdue the grudging sense of trust Declan fostered inside him.

But what duty could drive Declan from his fireside to scramble around the countryside alone? His task was to guard the fortress or ride with Conn's army when it marched against an enemy. And nothing else would have the power to force the man away from his own hearth.

Not that Niall could blame Declan. The man had one of the warmest-hearted wives in Glenfluirse and a pack of children any warrior would envy. Declan would not leave his lady's side unless—

Fear's cold blade trailed down Niall's spine. Had Conn already learned the truth? Sent men searching?

Declan reined in his dun-brown mount in a spray of mud, water, and enthusiasm, then swung down into the muck with a roar of greeting. " 'Tis my life you have saved by letting me find you, Niall! So it is!"

Niall stiffened, sensed the throb of fear in the women behind him. "Find me?" he echoed.

"Aye, with every warrior from Glenfluirse who can ride out searching!"

Niall forced his features into their accustomed reckless lines. "Why would anyone search for me?"

" 'Tis just that Conn has offered the greatest reward ever seen in Glenfluirse to the man who delivers the mighty Niall of the Seven Betrayals back to the fortress."

Caitlin stifled a tiny cry, and Niall could sense the tremor of fear rippling through Fiona. His mother's wide, bewildered eyes tore at him.

Disaster, he thought, fear cold as a stone in his belly. This summons was the catastrophe they all had feared.

And yet such misfortune made no sense when brought by the hand of Declan. Plenty of men in the fortress would delight in the prospect of dragging Niall to his death, but Declan? Never!

Still, Niall had to be careful. One misstep, and he could betray them all. "And why is the chieftain so eager for my presence?" he queried with a shrug. "Is there a battle in the offing? A contest to be settled with another chieftain's champion?"

"Nay, man! No merry wars to be fighting, more the pity, but the masses in the fortress will not perish of boredom because of the lack of some contest of arms.

Not when all Glenfluirse is waiting to welcome you!"
Declan clapped one beefy hand on Niall's shoulder, the
warrior's voice cracking with gruff affection. "You triumphed as I ever knew you would."

"Triumphed?" Niall repeated, perplexed. "Nay, Declan, I—" He choked into silence. Fool! He had almost
betrayed himself. And yet how could he lie to this good
and honest man?

"Och, you are thinking you have failed, are you not,
my fine lad?" Declan raked back a lock of rain-soaked
hair from his forehead. " 'Tis a grave thing to defy a
chieftain."

Niall reeled, stunned, trying to reconcile Declan's grin,
his open welcome, with the shame Niall was branded
with—that of a warrior forsworn. "You know what I did?"

"Every man, woman, and babe in Glenfluirse knows.
You surrendered everything you have worked for,
dreamed of, fought for, sacrificed it all to save an innocent stranger's life."

Niall squared his shoulders. "Then I am to be executed for my crime against Conn?"

The big man cursed in exasperation. "Blood and
thunder, Niall! Can you not hear me?" Declan shouted,
flinging his arms wide. "All you have ever wished for—
it is yours! The name you earned through your brave
deeds. Aye, and rewards greater still. Your questing is
over. You are to receive a welcome that would make
Cuchulain himself burst with pride!"

Declan cast a glance at the cluster of women, a laugh
rumbling from his chest. "Perhaps one of you ladies
can help me make this thick-brained fool understand
the honor he has won! Which of you is the dove he
championed? I want to see with me own eyes the
woman who made Niall of the Seven Betrayals for-
swear his chieftain."

Declan stepped before Aniera, something almost tender in his eyes as he peered into her once-lovely countenance. "This is a face that could launch a man into war."

Aniera smiled, her cheeks dimpling, her eyes soft. "My Ronan fought a dozen suitors to win my hand in marriage. He always swore he would have battled all of Ireland for just one night in my arms."

No loss clouded her face, the memory more real to her than the steady drumming of the rain. Compassion darkened Declan's eyes with the sorrow Niall's mother had forgotten for so many years.

"Methinks I would have fought for you myself," Declan said softly. "But Ronan of Daire would have defeated me. And yet Niall is an even more skilled warrior than his father was."

Aniera's eyes shone. She reached up, patting Declan's scarred cheek as if he were a dewy-faced boy instead of a man of war. "My son is a good boy, is he not?"

Compassion softened the warrior's eyes, then he flashed Niall a mischievous grin. "Aye, madam. The finest of *boys*."

"You look weary of riding. I shall gather some wild herbs I saw just beyond the path. They will soothe the pain in your scar." Aniera gently ran her fingertips over the nasty cut. Niall stared, astonished as Declan. Niall and perhaps Declan's beautiful Eva were the only two who guessed what pain the old wound still caused him when he rode for too long.

Yet Niall could only feel grateful to see his mother wandering toward a bank of bedraggled flowers, beyond the reach of these words that could disturb her peace.

Declan, cheeks crimson, more than a little daunted by the revelation of what he saw as a weakness, turned back toward the two remaining women with feigned heartiness. Pointing to Fiona, he laughed. "You cannot be Niall's damsel in distress. You look as if you would flay alive any man fool enough to try to rescue you."

"Aye!" Fiona snapped. "Do not tempt me to sharpen my blade upon you!"

Abandoning Fiona, Declan reached toward Caitlin's hood. Moved by instinct more feral than he had ever known, Niall knocked the warrior's arm away.

"Do not touch her!" he snapped, grasping his sword hilt.

Declan's eyes rounded, wide as a babe's. "You cannot think I mean to hurt her, Niall!"

The fear seemed absurd as he glared into Declan's face, but was it? "Conn ordered me to kill her," Niall ground out. "Why should I trust you will not?"

The tension in Declan melted away. He chuckled, then grasped Niall's arm, the decency, the goodness, the honor in this man seeming to ripple out from his palm. "Your lady is safe. I swear it on the life of my own beloved. I am but a crude warrior, awkward when it comes to words. I fear I have made such a muddle of this, my sweet Eva will scold me until my ears are blistered when she hears of it. Let me begin again, my friend."

Declan sucked in a steadying breath. "This quest Conn arranged for you was the most difficult and the most clever test of all, Niall. No man in Glenfluirse could deny that you have always had courage in abundance. Aye, and a wealth of honor despite your tainted name. But it takes a great man to open his heart enough to sacrifice for a stranger—to surrender all you fought for, all you held dear, in order to do not what duty demanded but, rather, *what was right*. Aye, lad, that is the virtue that makes you a hero."

Niall stared into Declan's face, a countenance as

scarred as Niall's own heart. Was it possible what Declan said was true? Was self-sacrifice the lesson Conn was hoping to teach him in this last quest?

Niall scowled, anger at the chieftain welling up, churning in an uncomfortable mixture with astonishment and relief. If this ordeal *had* all been one of the chieftain's cunning schemes, it had been an accursed dangerous gamble to take. One that had nearly cost Caitlin her life.

He shuddered at the memory that would haunt his nightmares forever—that harrowing moment when his sword had loomed over her slender neck, a heartbeat away from cleaving away her life, robbing the world of her incandescent light until the end of time. He had come so close to killing her that night, losing not only his own soul but the perfect love the fates had fashioned to save him.

But she was alive, his valiant lady. And safe. By some miracle, *safe!*

"You must come with me, all of you, back to Glenfluirse," Declan urged, stretching out his arms as if to embrace life itself. "Come, my pretties, are you not eager to see Niall's triumph? A name he can take pride in. Aye, and an honor greater still, to be named *tainist*, he who will rule when Conn is in his grave."

Niall staggered back a step, breath driven from his lungs. *"Tainist?"* Niall echoed, incredulous. "Conn cannot mean to make me his heir! He has a quiver full of his own sons to choose from!"

"It is not blood alone that makes an Irish chieftain. You know that, Niall. The chieftain is chosen for the good of the people. The man who inherits must be the most fit to rule, the strongest, the wisest. A leader chosen by his deeds, not merely at the whim of chance because of the man who sired him."

Dazed, still unable to grasp what Declan had said, Niall turned to the three women clustered behind him. It seemed impossible, this deliverance, a burst of brilliant sunshine after it seemed the sky was crashing down upon their heads.

Niall glanced at his mother, the vulnerable curve of her back, as she added another wet blossom to those clutched in her hand. He searched each face with his gaze. Fiona's sharp features shaken from the grief that had lain over them earlier. Declan's broad, honest grin. Caitlin's face still obscured by the folds of her hood, but he could sense in her the desperate longing to believe in miracles, the same need racing in his own blood.

"What think you?" Niall asked. "I can scarce believe it is true. Caitlin, you are free, free to embrace life, live unafraid in the sunshine, as you were always meant to do. Fiona, Daire is yours again. Now and forever."

"Nay!" Fiona cried, stricken. "You cannot mean to tell me you trust Conn. Niall, it is a trick. I know it!"

Niall's throat tightened at the emotion in his sister's voice, a terror, a fear, that betrayed the truth. Somehow, during these past weeks, when he had despaired of ever making her care about him again, she had forgiven him. She had just been too proud to show it. Inexpressible tenderness welled up in Niall, making his eyes burn.

Urged by memories ages old, he reached out to tug a lock of hair into her eyes, the gesture that had been his only option as a teasing, gruff boy moved to show his sister affection. Recognition lit Fiona's eyes, and she sniffed audibly.

"Whist, you hellborn babe," Niall said gently. "Why would Conn proclaim me *tainist* before all Glenfluirse if he meant me harm?"

"I do not know! How could anyone guess what

plottings go on in his twisted mind? But I promise you, there is always poison mixed into the honey he offers."

The panicked look in her face was unbearably precious. Niall wished he could embrace her, comfort her, despite Declan standing there like a benevolent giant. But such a public display of affection was one transgression Fiona would never forgive. Niall would have to comfort her using reason.

"Even if Conn is cunning, ruthless, as you say, he is no fool. He has built his name upon being Ever Truthful. He craves nothing more than the favor of the bards. They would vilify him for eternity if he betrayed me now. He will keep his word."

"Pah! You think he is honorable because *you* are! But Conn twists and writhes like a shape-shifter, taking on one form, then another, to work his treachery. Smiling and praising all the while he is plotting destruction. You saw what he did to Daire when he told you all was well there. And to Caitlin—promising her father her life, then, once he lay dead, luring her out of the abbey, inciting you to murder her in her sleep! Tell me, you great ox-headed fool, did your precious Conn keep his word to Fintan MacShane?"

"Fintan?" Declan echoed, looking as if the spear caster had struck him with a lightning bolt from Tir naN Og. "You cannot mean . . . Niall, this woman you spared was Fintan's daughter?"

Caitlin stepped forward, her delicate fingers drawing the hood back from her night-black hair. No rain or gray sky could dull her beauty. Despite everything she had endured, she shone with the unexpected brilliance of a jewel against a beggar's palm.

For a long moment, Declan gaped at her. At last, he stammered out, "I cannot—cannot believe 'tis you. Caitlin of the Lilies." Declan fell to one knee before her, heedless of his garments dragging in the mud.

"Nay," Caitlin objected, and Niall could sense her discomfort. "Pray, do not—"

But Declan stayed as he was, paying her homage. "I would not be alive today but for your father's magic. Aye, nor half of the other men in Conn's army. Now I understand why Niall was spurred to show mercy. It is little wonder he spared the life of the daughter of noble Fintan."

Fiona thrust herself between them, all but spitting fury. "It would not have mattered to my brother if she were the lowliest servant girl in Ireland, you mud-sucking ox!" Fiona's eyes burned with such fierce loyalty, Niall swallowed hard to keep his voice from breaking.

"Whist, now," he soothed. "Do not be carving up poor Declan before my eyes. He did not mean to insult me. He is a good man, Fiona, and true."

"You cannot think Conn would hesitate at having a good man lead you to disaster. Look at the way he tried to use you to kill Caitlin!"

Declan rose, managing to look as disheartened as a scolded puppy despite his hulking girth and gruesome scar. "I would cut off my own hand before I would do your brother harm, lady," he vowed.

Fiona's brow crinkled. "Perhaps it is true you would not willingly harm Niall. But if Conn wishes Niall destruction, he will find some way to see it done."

"Why would Conn wish your brother harm? He has treated Niall as a son. No man values your brother more than our chieftain does. I would stake my life upon it."

Fiona gave a scornful snort. "It is not *your* life you gamble with—at least, not yet—and I prefer not to take such a risk. I just got my brother back, and I will not lose him!"

Declan thumped his fist against his heart. "By my sword, lady, you risk nothing. Conn is the most honorable of rulers."

"He is the most conniving, the most cunning, the most ruthless villain ever to defile Ireland! One day, both you and my brother will discover it." Very real fear flared in the girl's eyes. "I only pray by the time you do, it will not be too late to save yourselves from disaster!"

Fiona shoved past Niall, appealing to Caitlin. "Caitlin, talk to Niall! Make him see reason. We cannot let him fall into this snare."

Caitlin dared what Niall had not, capturing Fiona's trembling hand in her own. She looked as regal as a queen as she turned to Declan. "You have given us much to think about, Declan. If we might have a moment alone to speak of it?"

The warrior swept her a bow full of reverence. "I will go aid the lady Aniera. It seems she plans to brew a vat of her philters large enough for ten warriors." He nodded toward where Niall's mother stooped, bedraggled blossoms already overflowing her slender arms.

The moment Declan ambled away, Caitlin turned to peer up at Niall, her eyes filled with hope and dread.

"Niall, I want to believe all Declan says is true as much as you do, but I cannot help mistrusting Conn. What kind of a chieftain would order an honorable man to kill an innocent woman as some sort of perverse test of honor?"

Niall closed his eyes, remembering countless times he had caught Conn watching him with hooded eyes, the weight of the chieftain's hand cupping Niall's shoulder as he praised the outcast murderer's son when others scorned him. Always, Conn had seemed to recognize in Niall some merit no one else saw. And even as a boy, Niall had sensed the chieftain treasured that elusive "something" hidden inside him.

"What kind of man would test me in such a way?" Niall echoed, warmth flooding through him. "A man who knew me better than I know myself. He must have guessed I would not hurt you."

"Guessed?" Caitlin exclaimed. "If he had lost the wager, he would have paid with *my* blood. This was no game, Niall, no diversion to while away a boring day. Lives were in peril. Yours as well as my own. If you *had* done as Conn commanded, it would have destroyed you."

Unease curled in Niall's belly, but he shoved it back. "I did *not* kill you. Nothing was lost."

"Nothing?" Caitlin exclaimed, her eyes glistening with unshed tears. "You spent the past weeks devoured by guilt, in a torment of uncertainty! I know. I saw. I will never forget it."

"Do you think I care about that now? Look at what I gained in return! A love I never dared hope for. I found my mother and sister again. Aye, and my father, in spirit. Whatever Conn's motives were, whether he was wrong or right, does not matter. We can build a life together, all of us, at Daire. It is what you wanted, Caitlin. And you, Fiona."

Fiona's voice cracked. "I do not care about Daire. Look!" she cried, casting her clump of dirt to the ground. "I have emptied my hands of it forever."

"But you will never empty your heart of it," Niall said, touching her cheek. "And neither will I. I have to take this chance to make things right, Fiona. Can you not understand? If I do not return to Glenfluirse, present myself to Conn, we will never know for certain if we are safe."

"Niall, do not ask me to watch you go back to that—that devil's lair! It will swallow you up the way it did before. And I . . . I will be alone."

Curse the girl's dignity! Niall swept her up in a fierce hug. "I have only just found you again, wee one," he murmured against her hair. "You will never be alone."

It was the same promise his father had made to him so long ago, Niall realized with a start. The only vow to him Ronan the Brave had ever broken.

"Fine, then, you—you stubborn, ox-headed fool!" Fiona's fingers dug fiercely into his waist as she clung to him. "We will all go to Glenfluirse together."

His gut clenched. Why did he suddenly feel such dread if he was nigh certain all was well? There was a simple reason, Niall acknowledged grimly. He had a difficult knot to untangle with Conn when first he arrived at the fortress.

Even if all Declan said was true, even if Conn did welcome Niall with the open arms of a father, it would not change one thing. Niall had lied to Caitlin, to Fiona, and to himself moments before.

He could forget the pain he had felt the past weeks, but he could not so easily forgive the torment Conn's game had put Caitlin through. The terror, the disillusionment, the despair. Only her rare courage had enabled her to survive, but brave as she was, she would never regain her total faith in the world. Some would call that loss of innocence fate, unavoidable. A tragic necessity for anyone living.

Yet, knowing she had suffered that loss not through chance but rather by design or selfish carelessness, in a game . . . that was a transgression he could not so easily forgive.

"You are not going to Glenfluirse, *cara*," Niall said, stroking his sister's cheek. "With your unguarded tongue, you would land yourself in trouble the instant you entered the gates. Besides, someone must tend the gardens and watch over the start of our new herd, or we will be gnawing withered parsnips again when winter comes."

"I do not care!" she cried, thumping her small fist against his chest.

"Aye, you do care, Fiona. About the earth and growing things, the cows and the castle. You will tend to it all while I am away, and when I return in triumph, I will be amazed by all you have done."

"Nay!" Fiona cried. "Do not leave me again!"

Niall winced at the memory of the day Conn's warriors had ridden away from Daire—Niall clutching the waist of Conn himself, while Ronan, bound and bleeding from a gash on his head, had struggled to cast a smile back at his tiny daughter. Had their father known even then he would never see that winsome, wee face again?

Fiona had chased after the horses as they thundered out of the castle yard, shrieking Niall's name. *My bruvver . . . give him back!* The last thing Niall had seen was Fiona sprawling in the dirt, sobbing.

He cradled her close, stroking her fiery, damp hair, comforting her as he had not been able to so long ago. "I will only be gone for a little while, Fiona."

"Nay! I will not let you go!" Fiona cried out, pulled away, turning her back to him.

Niall swallowed hard, feeling her pain, the old pain and the new. "I know when I left last time, Mother was lost in the mists of her grief. You felt alone. This time, you will not be. Caitlin will stay with you at Daire."

Caitlin's eyes flashed panic. "Nay. I go with you, Niall. We face whatever the fates decree together."

"When all is settled and the time is right, you will be

welcomed into Glenfluirse with the glory befitting Fintan's daughter."

"I want only to be your wife."

Tenderness crushed Niall's heart. He cradled her cheek in his hand. "Do you not know, Lily Fair? No mere words can make you dearer to my heart than you already are. In my soul, you are wife already. The most precious gift any man was ever given. I want to share a lifetime with you, *alannah*. That is why I ask you to stay behind."

She pressed her fingertips to her brow. "I do not understand."

"If, by some strange twist of fate, anything is amiss, I will be able to escape more quickly without you." He struggled to fix a teasing smile on his face, banish her fear. "Unless, of course, you possess some of your father's magic that you have not told me about."

"If I did, I would have used it to turn you into a toad the first night you took me from the abbey!" she cried, temper flaring.

Niall chuckled. "I suspected as much. Though a bit of Fintan's sorcery might be most welcome if you could banish this miserable rain."

"This is not a jest, Niall! We love you. Fiona and I and your mother! Nothing—not even Daire—is worth the risk of losing you!"

"There is something worth any risk to me, Lily Fair. My babes are even now dancing in your eyes. They need a home, *mo chroi*, and so do you."

He cupped her face in his hands, kissed her brow. "The next time I see your face, you will be watching as I take my place as *tainist*."

Tears brimmed over the thick fan of her lashes. "I wish you to be my husband, nothing more."

He smiled, memorizing her face, rain-damp and lovely. "Do not be afraid," he bade her.

Why was he? Fear struck him like a fist in his gut, stone cold, undeniable. Nay, he was mad. Every rash dream he had dared in the past weeks suddenly lay just within his reach. Caitlin would be his wife. He could give Fiona her cherished Daire in exchange for the far more precious gift she had just given him—her love returned. In time, dark-curled babes would toddle about, so winsome they would lure his mother back from her world of mist.

Was not such abundance worth any risk? Even the life he had regained in Caitlin's arms?

"Trust me, *mo chroí,*" he murmured, taking Caitlin's hand. He turned, grasping Fiona's grubby, rigid fingers with his other. "Trust me, my wee sister."

Fiona flung herself against him with a sob. Caitlin did not move. Only her eyes pierced him, to his heart, to his soul. She swallowed hard, and Niall knew how much it cost her not to weep. "I will take care of them for you," she vowed. "Your mother will be my mother. Fiona the sister I always dreamed of."

"D-dream?" Fiona choked out. "I am a n-nightmare. Just ask N-Niall."

Niall gathered them both in his arms, looked over Caitlin's shoulder to where his mother was wandering toward them, her face so fragile, so earnest, as she clung to one of Declan's flower-filled arms.

"I will not fail you," Niall vowed, so fiercely the foundation of Tir naN Og trembled at the force of it.

Castle Daire stood waiting, its wise stone face almost alive, its arrow-slit eyes beaming welcome, as if it had known from the beginning of time that Niall would return a third time. Destiny, that irresistible force that had stolen Caitlin from her mother's arms, then brought her, like a miracle, into Niall's heart—Niall could hear it, whispering to him upon the wind.

He listened as he built a roaring fire in the hearth. He strained to understand as he settled his small family before the blaze to dry their rain-drenched clothes. But the wind's voice was as indecipherable as the writings on the standing stone beside his father's cairn.

I cannot fail them, Niall thought fiercely, embracing each beloved one in turn as he prepared to leave them. *Fintan, father of this woman I love, help them understand. My own father, protect them in death as you could not in life.*

He kissed his mother's cheek. Fiona's brow. He tasted Caitlin's lips, memorizing the taste of them, the sweet miracle of her love.

Niall's own eyes burned as he left them, going out to where Declan waited with the brace of horses.

Once a lance had grazed Niall's chest, leaving a searing gash in its wake. This pain was far deeper. Niall of the Seven Betrayals, the warrior men whispered had no heart, now knew that he did. He was leaving it here, at Castle Daire, in the keeping of the three women who had dared to love him whether he deserved it or not.

"The storm, 'tis growing worse," Declan called out, handing Niall his reins.

"It does not matter," Niall answered. Thunder rumbled a warning, dark clouds racing along the horizon. Niall's eyes narrowed as he tracked their flight. Some men claimed the wind and the storms were messengers from Tir naN Og. If only he could understand what they were telling him. He had been open to the voice of the standing stone, but he could not decipher the wind's song now.

Or had he closed his ears to the voices on purpose, knowing even enchanted warnings could not shake him from this course? He had to learn the truth from Conn himself. Had to take this risk if Fiona and his mother were to have a home, if Caitlin and he were to win love forever after, without fear, without hiding from the sun.

"We will not stop until we reach the gates of Glen-fluirse, no matter how harsh the storm blows," Niall called to his friend.

"See who reaches those gates first!" Declan challenged, spurring his mount to a gallop.

Resolute, Niall swung up onto his own mount, spun it in a circle as he settled himself upon its back. But before he could urge the beast into a run, he heard the patter of running footsteps from the castle. He winced. Had he not begged Caitlin and Fiona to stay by the fire? The last thing he wanted was to carry with him the memory of them standing forlorn in the rain.

As he turned to face the figure who was approaching, his eyes widened in surprise. His mother, her hair tangled about her desperate face. His horse shied, and Niall battled to rein the beast in. His mother raced toward him, heedless of the danger.

"This is yours," she cried breathlessly, extending the long rag-wrapped bundle she held in her arms. "He said you would need it."

"Who said?" Niall's brow furrowed in confusion, his gaze flicking to where his friend's back was quick disappearing. "Declan?"

"Nay! Your father."

"Go back inside, and warm yourself by the fire," Niall said gently. "The wind bites deeper and deeper."

"Niall, you must listen to me!" she cried so fiercely her voice broke, her eyes afire with pleading. "Do not dismiss me as if I am mad."

Was that not what he had labeled her so many times these past weeks? First in guilt and frustration, later with quiet grief, that he could not reach beyond the mists that separated her from all around her.

Stunned at the desperate sanity in her words, Niall swung off the horse. He reached out, taking what his mother offered. Niall's hands trembled as he unwrapped the most exquisite sword he had ever seen.

He stared in awe at the gleaming weapon, remembered clutching the sword as a boy, scarce able to get his grubby fingers around the hilt. He could hear his father laughing as Niall struggled to lift the heavy weapon from the floor.

You will grow to fit it soon enough, my little son, Ronan's deep voice echoed in his ears. *And then no man in all Ireland will ever defeat you!*

Grief washed over Niall in suffocating waves, soul-wrenching mourning for all the years that reckless boy and his invincible father had lost.

He started at the feel of his mother's hand curving upon his wrist. He looked up into her face, stared at her, his breath snagging in his throat. Her eyes! They shone piercingly clear, filled with love and faith and grief.

"*It is a sword fit for a chieftain,*" she murmured, stroking the hilt as if it were the contours of her lost love's face. " 'Twas the last thing your father said before they took him away from me."

Chapter

19

CAITLIN HAD LIVED almost her whole life in a world without men. The rhythms of a household made up of only women should, at the very least, have felt familiar. But even the stones seemed to strain to hear Niall's heavy tread, the three women rattling around, restless, edgy, leaping at the slightest sound, as if ghosts had come ahaunting Castle Daire.

And they had. So many ghosts. Ghosts of doubt, suspicion, regret. Long, chill shadows cast by the past clouded the tenuous future.

No one spoke of the strain they were under. Nay, it was as if they just kept busy enough with mindless tasks so that they could outrun disaster. As if the mere act of not speaking of their fears would keep them from coming true. And, maddening as the situation was, not even Caitlin dared break the silence, lest some black curse descend upon them all. The curse that had loomed over Caitlin even before she was born.

She shivered, chilled despite the afternoon sun warming her shoulders. How could she bear it if *she* had brought this danger down upon the heads of those she loved?

With a flick of her wrist, she finished draping the last

of the clothing upon a bush to air, then stepped back, wondering what else she could find to take up the interminable minutes, hours, days, weeks, until Niall returned to her.

If he ever does.

Unbidden, the words slid down her spine like the cold kiss of a blade. Terror plunged like a stone into her stomach, her hands suddenly trembling. She thrust them into the folds of her leine in an effort to still them.

"You cannot think such things," she told herself fiercely. "If you do, you will go mad! Niall is the finest warrior in Glenfluirse, in all Ireland! If he survived in Conn's fortress as a hated, friendless little boy, he can surely survive as the chieftain's champion, a hero lauded throughout the land. *Tainist.* The chosen one."

Yet when one man was chosen, others were not. How many might hate him, secretly or openly? Even if Conn had summoned Niall in good faith, how many other warriors at Glenfluirse might wish to destroy him? So many things could go wrong, so many private dangers might lurk beneath public smiles.

She closed her burning eyes, tried to banish the sudden tightening in her throat as her mind filled with the image of Niall, so tall, so strong, so honorable, riding into the gates of the fortress she could only imagine, a warrior like those in the legends the abbess had told her what seemed a lifetime ago.

Always, the hero had won honor, immortality, yet sometimes at the cost of his life. She did not want to spend her life, her body cold, her womb aching with emptiness, listening to bards string golden phrases into a hero crown for her beloved to wear. She wanted Niall in her arms, in her bed, wanted his laughter and his anger, his tenderness and his uncertainty, not praises of his courage charging into danger alone.

But he was not alone. Declan rode at his side, trustworthy, brave, believing that Niall would regain his inheritance—a name he need not be ashamed of. The castle he dreamed of rising up from ruins. The life he had been destined to live before his father had given violent rein to his dark obsession for another woman. Before tragedy had flooded every corner of the land he loved. Before his family had been shattered, his sister turning wild with rebellion, his mother embracing a gentle madness.

Aye, it was a grand quest he had set out upon, Caitlin knew. The one hope they all had—Fiona and Aniera, Niall and Caitlin herself—of building a home, creating the kind of life most people took for granted. Simple joys. Simple pleasures.

If only she could bear the nights! They stretched to forever without him. Caitlin rubbed her palms against her opposite arms, trying to chafe out some of the wildness that pulsed through her veins. Her whole body burned with feverish need, her very soul so restless it was driving her mad. The uncertainty, that was the worst torture. Yet Niall had vowed he would not fail them, had he not? He swore he would ride back into Daire's castle yard, safe, triumphant.

But she did not care about triumph or glory. She only wanted to be with him. Banish the emptiness that left her aching.

Strangest of all, she did not care if he were being greeted even now as Declan predicted, with a welcome Cuchulain would envy. She wished she could snatch him away from Glenfluirse. Out of the grasp of his chieftain, the lavishness of his old home, the lure of his old life.

Jealousy? Was that what she was feeling? She had no doubt other women had seen Niall's handsomeness, and now that he was named *tainist*, power and strength and honor would be an elixir few could resist.

Yet in spite of all the temptations that must have been dangled before him, all the women eager to bed the champion of Glenfluirse, Niall had never cared for a woman before her. He had told her that, not only with his lips, which never lied, but with his body—their lovemaking something as new as the dawn of time.

Why then this gnawing dread? Did she fear that once he returned to Glenfluirse, he would change his mind about returning to Daire, wish to remain at the fortress where he had earned such honor? The lauded hero, *tainist*, it was a temptation to power few could resist. Or was her fear more simple even than an assassin's knife, a deadly betrayal? If Niall became *tainist*, their dreams of Daire as home could not come to be. The heir to Conn's lands would face heavy responsibilities. Niall would have to remain at the chieftain's disposal . . .

The chieftain. Caitlin shuddered. The man who had ordered her death, whether in a wager or no. The man who had put her and Niall through torture unimaginable these past weeks.

She winced at the memory of Niall when Declan had found them along the rain-drenched road. Niall had looked so earnest, wanting desperately to believe in the man who had been like a father to him.

He had sought desperately for some way to excuse the chieftain for what he had done, and even now, days later, Niall's description of Conn still haunted her: *A man who knew me better than I knew myself. Knew you were never in danger.*

Caitlin shivered. Could the answer be so simple? So many things in this whole situation did not make sense. The destruction of Daire, Fiona so fiercely honest, claiming Conn's men raided here. It was possible Fiona's imagination had been fired by her hatred of the man she blamed for her father's death and the destruction of her family.

It was also possible that Niall had been right as well when he claimed the warriors could have struck without Conn's knowledge, disguising their perfidy from the chieftain, Niall's own indifference to his former home the shield they could hide their vile acts behind.

But whatever the truth about that might prove to be, there was one question Caitlin could not answer. How could she ever trust this chieftain?

Conn had announced to all of Glenfluirse that Niall was a hero. He had rained honors down on his foster son's head. Such a public display made it impossible for the chieftain to betray Niall yet again, did it not? So why did she feel this creeping sense of disaster? Nights tossed on the sharp blades of terrifying dreams, days racked with confusion, desperate bargaining with the fates?

Unable to bear being alone any longer, she abandoned her task and walked out to the garden. Aniera knelt among the growing things as she had so often in the time since Niall rode away. But his mother no longer aimlessly gathered flowers. Rather, she worked with a will, purpose in her hands, a fresh clarity to her eyes.

Caitlin grimaced, suddenly aware that anything she confided would only worry Niall's mother as well. Resigning herself to more pointless prattle, she knelt down beside the older woman, aiding her in thinning some of the tiny sprouts. Not that her heroic efforts mattered.

After a few moments passed, Aniera leveled her with a probing, tender glance. "And so it begins for you, my poor treasure," Aniera said, casting her a sympathetic smile. "I pity you. Aye, and envy you with all my heart."

"I do not understand. Because of what?"

"The waiting. 'Tis the lot of any woman who dares to love a warrior. Off they dash into battle, so eager, so determined to do brave deeds, they scarce glance back no matter how much they love you. A kiss, a vow of devotion, and we are left to battle something far more treacherous than a sword or a spear. Uncertainty. Loneliness. Helplessness."

Aniera sighed, peering out into the empty blue of the sky. "We watch them die a thousand times in our dreams. They scream our names as they wade through rivers of blood, but we cannot reach them. Then we awaken to the deafening silence, rise from our solitary beds, and tend the babes, work in the garden, stitch by the fire, never letting anyone guess we are dying inside without them."

Tears sprang to Caitlin's eyes, the hard lump that never seemed to leave her throat choking her. "I cannot bear it, not knowing what could befall him. He is such an honorable man, he cannot fathom dishonor in anyone else."

"He is his father's son."

"His father is dead!" Caitlin cried, all the fear, all the frustration and fury, bursting free so suddenly it stunned her. "I do not want Niall to follow in his path!" She stopped in horror, pressing her hand to her lips. "Aniera, forgive me. I did not mean to—" To what? Be cruel, brutal, ripping at wounds that had never healed?

Niall's mother rolled back onto her heels, her hands gripping the feathery small shoot she had just plucked from the ground. She stared down at the delicate stem, broken as she had been for so long. Her eyes flooded with pain.

"You think I do not know that my Ronan is dead?" she asked after a long moment. "My bed is empty. My body still aches for him, even after so many years."

"But you—" Caitlin hesitated, too appalled at blunders she had already made to risk another one.

"Act as if he is still with me?" Aniera finished for her. "I wander the hills with him, talk to him, sometimes laugh or cry with him, it is true. Not in imaginings, Caitlin, but because we were so much a part of each other. My Ronan does not revel with the other heroes in the realm of Tir naN Og. He lives now in my heart."

How could a man inspire such devotion when he had shattered his wife's heart? "You loved him very much."

"Perhaps *too* much." Shame colored Aniera's faintly lined cheeks. "Ronan is dead, but his son and his daughter are alive. What have I done for my poor babes?"

"Loved them," Caitlin affirmed, wistful, trying to imagine her own mother's face, arms that must have held her with such desperate love before the beautiful Grainne surrendered her tiny daughter forever. "I never had a mother."

"And you think my babes did?" Aniera gave a brittle laugh. "I abandoned my son to the man who murdered his father. And as for my daughter, I cast my responsibilities onto her shoulders when she was so very small. I closed my eyes and my heart to anything save holding tight to Ronan, yet he was already gone. It was only when Niall returned, when you blew into the castle like the sweetest breath of spring, that I started to awaken."

She smiled, soft, sad. "Sometimes I wish I never had," Aniera said. "Then I would not have been forced to see what I have done."

"But Fiona loves you with all her heart," Caitlin protested. "Niall as well—"

"That is the miracle of children. They love you whether you deserve it or no."

"Aniera, they do not blame you."

"They do not have to. I blame myself."

Caitlin winced, remembering Niall's confession, his shame and pain at his father's violent obsession with another woman. What must that have done to Aniera? The mere thought of Niall in another woman's arms shattered Caitlin's very soul. "It was your husband's sin, not yours." The words escaped before she could stop them. "If he had not gone mad over that other woman—"

"Aye. The other woman. Has Niall told you of her? What little my poor boy knew, that is. What he heard in the fortress of Glenfluirse. Seven Betrayals. They tried to bury my husband beneath their weight, then my son. But I was the one they crushed."

"It would have destroyed any woman to hear that the man she loved lusted after another woman so much he was willing to kill his closest friend to take her by force," Caitlin protested.

"To hear it was painful, aye. Yet why was it so easy for me to believe Ronan could desire her? Perhaps I had always expected Ronan's gaze to wander to other women. What I could never understand was why his favor had fallen on me to begin with. I was ever quiet, so shy my father despaired of me, wanted to protect me, see me settled somewhere safe." Aniera wrinkled her small nose. "Safe to him meant close by, so that he could keep his fragile hatchling under his wing." It was far too easy for Caitlin to understand the urge to guard Aniera closely. Had not Fiona done it all her young life? And Niall and Caitlin as well from the moment they had entered the door of Castle Daire? Aniera *was* like the small, winged creature she described, her feathers lovely but so very fragile.

"There were warriors enough who asked for my hand in marriage, hoped to bind themselves to my family, make powerful allies, and perhaps some who wanted me for myself. Yet when Ronan dashed into my life, so strong, with his face so glorious and his smile that broke any woman's heart, I could hardly believe he loved me." She chuckled. "No one could. My sister stalked off to pout, my father was astounded, my mother in dread that he would break my heart. It was their doubt that seeped into my heart."

"How could Ronan fail to love you?" Caitlin asked. Aniera rose, took Caitlin's hand, and crossed to where a tree cast a delicate interlacing of shade across the turf. Aniera lowered herself to the grass, curling her legs beneath her, agile as a young girl. Caitlin followed her to the ground, scarce wondering what Ronan had found so delightful about his young wife.

Her beauty, aye, but there was a restfulness about her despite her fragility, a peace and gentle rejoicing about the miracle of the smallest blade of grass or the shyest of all-but-forgotten flowers. It must have quieted Ronan's restless soul, soothed battle-fevered blood. Taught him to dream.

"I went with him before ten days had passed, knowing I would never see my family again. Knowing they were afraid for me. *What do you know about him?* My mother tried to reason with me through the night. *He is a stranger.* But even then, Ronan and I had known each other's heart before time began."

"Then how . . ." Caitlin hesitated. "If he loved you, how could he even have looked at another woman, let alone murder someone to try to force his way into her bed?"

"It was said every man in Ireland wished to master her in their bed. Scota, her name was, a warrior maiden from Iona, trained in all the arts of battle by her father, a champion who lacked a son. Ireland, too, bred women the like of Scota, but they have grown rarer and rarer over the years. And never has legend captured one as beautiful as Scota of Iona."

"But you were beautiful—*are* beautiful!" Caitlin objected loyally. "Anyone who gazes into your face can see it."

"I was pretty enough, in my way. Quiet, soft, like a wildflower half hidden beneath a stone. But Scota's was a wild, rare beauty." Aniera closed her eyes, a flicker of pain still shadowing her features after so many years. "A face like the earth goddess, passion for life wild as the sea waves. Her hair shone with the luster of hammered gold, her eyes blue fire that challenged any man to tame her on the field of battle. Even Ronan spoke of her with a special kind of awe."

Caitlin swallowed hard, envisioning all too clearly the woman Aniera described, strength and courage, fire and passion. What man would fail to be dazzled by such a woman? Even Niall would have to be tempted. The thought wrenched at her heart.

"Lorcan, my Ronan's foster brother, won her in marriage. Every woman in Ireland rejoiced. I did, too, in secret, stilling the whispers of doubt in my heart." Aniera pleated a fold in her gown. "If I had only had courage, Caitlin, just the tiniest measure of my Fiona's valor or Niall's, I could have stopped the madness that destroyed my family. But I was weak. Too afraid—"

"You did all that you could. I am certain of it."

"Nay. I had been so foolish. Feared . . . love is such a strange thing. So strong yet so fragile, like a thread that can be snapped. When Ronan declared his love for me, I could scarce believe such a bold, handsome warrior could desire me for his wife. He could have chosen any woman he wished . . . just as Scota could have chosen any man."

"But he chose you. Loved you so much he carried the sea into your bedchamber."

A pained smile curved Aniera's lips. "Strange that I did not remember that when we traveled to Glenfluirse to the festival. The Sea Chamber and our loving there seemed so far away.

"I remember standing near the practice yard watching Scota show her skill, the men baiting her, each dare more outrageous than the last. She crowed with delight as she overcame opponent after opponent, leaping about, lithe and wild-hearted as a doe, so lovely no man could take his eyes from her."

Aniera cast her gaze down to the turf, her thick lashes still unable to veil the echoes of old pain. "I was awkward, heavy, more than a little sick. I knew all the signs I had suffered before with Fiona and with Niall. I carried a new babe. I planned to tell Ronan at the festival, add to his joy."

What would it be like to hold such a joyous secret close to her heart? Caitlin wondered. To wait for the perfect time to tell your beloved one that a child would be born out of the miracle of your passion? She ached for such a moment, yearned for it with all her heart.

"Fiona was three," Aniera continued, "all smiles and delight on the journey. But once she reached Glenfluirse, it was as if the very air vexed her. A rash spread across her stomach. I remember my poor babe crying, fighting, restless even then, determined not to be comforted. Night after night, I battled the mysterious *thing* that was making the wee one so miserable. Ronan, he did what little he could to aid me, but he had duties elsewhere. Time after time, he charged off to practice feats of arms with the other men."

"I remember the young novices whispering; they said men were insufferable that way, forever eager to show they surpassed any other warrior in their skills."

"I fear the novices spoke true. At this festival, the men were fighting for their position in Conn's army, and no man at the festival had been challenged as many times as Ronan of Daire. Your father, he was always untouchable as Conn's champion, an honor Ronan never begrudged him. I remember Ronan telling me he was certain that Fintan would trade all his wondrous fairy-kissed power to see his wife's face for just the rising of one sun. And Ronan vowed he would sooner lose his sword arm than ever sacrifice the joy of watching me frolic with one of our babes. Fintan would never even hear his little daughter's laughter, Ronan mourned. *Your* laughter."

Aniera hugged her slender waist, as if remembering that precious time. "Ronan had his duty to fulfill at Glenfluirse. I knew it was true. I tried to hold on to that. Counted the days until we could leave the brash gaiety and return to the warm embrace of Castle Daire. Then one night, while I struggled to calm Fiona, Niall escaped me, bold wanderer that he was. Ever a warrior's son, he disappeared and, unknown to me, found his way into the armory. I was crazed with worry, searching everywhere for him. Just when I was certain I would run mad, Conn himself came to find me. He returned Niall. The boy I feared would be dead bloomed rosy and laughing, playing with a toy sword belonging to one of the chieftain's sons."

It was all too easy to imagine Niall, intrepid, determined, stubbornly finding his way to where all those delicious swords gleamed. A dark-curled, resolute-chinned outlaw, already issuing challenges to anyone who dared try to deter him.

"Conn was most . . . kind," Aniera continued, a troubled crease between her brow. "But his eyes—they snapped with a strange anger. The kind my father and brother had displayed when anyone had treated me carelessly. Conn said . . ." Even after so many years, she seemed to stumble over the words.

"He said Ronan should be carving a wooden blade for his own son and keeping watch over his own wife instead of wasting every moment trying to best Lorcan's bride on the practice field." Aniera sucked in a shaky breath.

"Was that where Ronan had been rushing off to all this time? To another woman's side? Another woman's smile? I cannot tell you how the question raked at my soul. I did not want to believe it was true, but the seed had been planted. The tiniest flicker of Ronan's eyes toward Scota at the banquet table in the nights that followed became torture. His smiles at her, his jests, were like blades in my heart."

Caitlin slipped her hand over Aniera's cold one in comfort, imagining all too vividly how this gentle woman must have suffered. How Caitlin herself would have suffered—after she flayed Niall alive! But to admit such vulnerability, to ask your beloved if he had been bewitched by another woman, how could any woman dare that? Just giving it voice might make it real. And if it *were* real . . . Caitlin's heart wrenched.

Aniera laced her fingers with Caitlin's, her eyes glistening with gratitude. How long had she suffered in silence? Bearing the pain alone?

"It was agony whenever they were together," she went on, "and they were always together. It seemed Conn contrived a myriad of ways to keep them near him. A kindness? I still wonder. He was a gallant man, a subtle one. In so many ways, he hinted to me that he was trying to keep the two of them occupied with him so they could not steal off and betray all of us—Niall and Fiona, Lorcan and me, Conn, Ronan's own honor and Scota's virtue. Seven betrayals . . ."

She could not continue. She seemed to grope for words, at last settled on some she could bear. "I suppose Conn was trying to protect me, aye, and shield Lorcan's pride. Lorcan was fired of the same mettle as my Ronan, fiercely proud, brimming with honor and a fiery temper aimed at any who dared challenge it."

A mist veiled her eyes. "That was what terrified me, what was most damning of all—the fury in Lorcan's eyes, building and building. A rage too fierce for anyone to control. It burst free at last as I feared it would. Late one night, Ronan returned to our chamber, his eye bruised, his lip split. The next morning, Lorcan and Scota were gone, away to Dunsearcha, Lorcan's distant land to the south."

"You must have thanked God," Caitlin said, knowing she would have, most heartily.

Aniera's mouth twisted, bitter. "Aye, I was thankful. Overjoyed they were gone. But a shadow fell over the festival from that morning, a thunderous, seething tension. When night fell, Conn cautioned Ronan before the whole banquet table that no woman was worth severing loyalties between foster brothers."

Caitlin winced. If Niall was indeed like his father, she could imagine the effect such an announcement must have had upon proud Ronan of Daire. To have his honor questioned would be hideous enough, but to be scolded like a wayward lad by his chieftain in front of all the other warriors—to be humiliated thus—would rake his soul raw.

"Ronan was furious," Aniera said. "I remember his rage, aye, and his hurt. He saw the doubt in my eyes.

All the warriors of Glenfluirse saw it, too. He scarce spoke during the days he took me and the babes back to Daire, then he rode away. By the new moon, I heard what had happened after Ronan left me. Lorcan was dead. Whoever had killed him had tried to claim Scota. Scota was dead, the dagger that never left her side buried in her breast. No one knew for certain how she died, but I always believed she had killed herself rather than surrender to her husband's murderer. Only one man could be guilty, it was rumored through all of Ireland. Ronan of Daire."

Bile rose in Caitlin's throat. "How—how could you bear it?"

"You do not understand, child. That accusation was my salvation. Perhaps I did not believe in the strength of Ronan's love for me, but Lorcan and Ronan had grown up together—*anam cara*,—soul friends—from the time they were boys. No mere lust of the flesh would make Ronan draw his sword against his brother."

"But if Lorcan struck first—"

"That is what happened the night Ronan's eye was bruised. Lorcan struck, and Ronan would not fight against him. More certain even than that truth was another I knew about my husband. Ronan of Daire would sever his own hand before he forced himself on any woman."

As his son would, Caitlin realized with stark certainty. Nay, not an angel himself could make her believe Niall capable of such a hideous act.

"When Ronan returned to Daire, I was shamed by the joy I felt. I rejoiced in the chance to tell him I believed in him. I doubted no longer."

"But even though you believed in him, all Ireland judged Ronan guilty. Were you not afraid?"

"Ronan swore there was nothing to fear. We were in no danger. Soon after Ronan arrived at Lorcan's fortress, a hunting party from Glenfluirse arrived, seeking shelter. Conn was among them. They found Ronan there, devastated amidst the carnage. Conn ordered Ronan to return to me, to his children. Vowed that he would discover whoever was guilty of such a treacherous act. When he did, they would be punished."

More mercy from this chieftain Fiona hated, Caitlin feared. To send a man all but condemned home to his family, promising to search out the truth rather than rushing in with brutal judgment, that was an act of wisdom and kindness, was it not?

"I can scarce believe Ronan did not stay at Dunsearcha—lend his own sword to the chase."

"Conn insisted Ronan's presence there would only make things more difficult to unravel. Besides, he claimed the children and I had suffered enough. Ronan owed it to us to come to Daire, ease our fears. The chieftain vowed he knew Ronan was incapable of such cowardice and betrayal. He would find proof of who had done this heinous thing. And Ronan himself could name the punishment.

"Ronan named it, then: death to whoever had murdered his foster brother. Eternal shame cast down upon anyone who carried the blood of the betrayer, so no one would ever forget . . ."

Caitlin winced, sick inside. "Then it was Niall's own father who condemned him to carry that awful name? One whose shame he never earned?"

Aniera nodded. "When Ronan returned, we both grieved for Lorcan and Scota, but our own love, happiness, our own future, had come so close to being snatched away that we were determined not to waste another moment in misery. We would celebrate Lorcan's boldness in our son, aye, and tell of Scota's courage to our tiny daughter one day. We delighted in every moment we had together, drank it in like honeyed mead, as if we could not get enough. Ronan carved the wooden sword Niall had longed for, and in the darkness, he forgave me so generously for ever doubting him, and at last I forgave myself."

"But did you not fear what might happen? Everyone who had been at the festival suspected Ronan of the evil deed. Why did you not flee?"

"Because we believed, Ronan and I. Heroes do not die in shame. He was innocent. We both knew it. We believed our chieftain knew it as well. Justice was ours for the taking."

"Then how . . . why did Conn's warriors come to Daire?"

Pain raked lines deep into Aniera's face, her eyes bewildered. "Witnesses who had seen Lorcan's murderer came forward. More damning still, they found a message Scota had scribed in her own blood before she died. *Ronan*, it said, then farther along the wall, *kill*."

"Merciful God!"

"Is God merciful, Caitlin?" Aniera asked, tears flowing down her cheeks. "Where was He that day? They dragged Ronan away from me. They took my son. Fiona . . . I can still hear her screaming. All I could do was cling to Ronan, crying that I believed . . . believed in him."

She fell silent for a moment, the pain of that tearing apart somehow new.

"I left Fiona with servants, took Keefe, Daire's most trusted man, and tried to follow Ronan to Glenfluirse, but the new babe in my womb made it difficult. I had just told Ronan about the babe that day by the standing stone. His joy had been so fierce. We would name it

Lorcan if a boy. Scota if a girl. I agreed. Jealousy banished, I mourned them both as much as he did."

She swallowed hard. "That wee life fought me every step of the journey. What little food I ate I could not keep down. The constant jostling on the horse bruised me, battered the babe inside me. I miscarried the little one a day's ride from Glenfluirse. A little boy."

Grief washed over Aniera's features in dark waves. Caitlin grieved with her, tears dampening her own cheeks.

After a moment, Aniera went on. "I buried him beneath a bank of elderflowers, healing flowers that could bloom as my babe never would. By the time Keefe and I crawled into Glenfluirse, it was over. Ronan was dead."

Too late—were there any more tragic words? And yet someone else had been waiting at the fortress, too, grieving and confused and helpless.

"What of Niall?"

"I begged a word with Conn. Asked for my son. Aye, and to take the body of my husband back to the land he loved."

Caitlin's heart broke at the image of Aniera begging mercy from the man who had executed her beloved.

"Conn was . . . kind." The word seemed to choke her. "He had me bathed, gave me a new robe. Fed Keefe and me. Then he sent for me. He grieved over Ronan's death as I did. But there was no doubt Ronan had killed Lorcan. Conn was a chieftain. Sometimes chieftains were forced to make terrible choices. Justice was a brutal master. Because of the love he once bore Ronan, he asked me to let him protect us from those angry enough to take vengeance on all of Ronan's blood. He asked for my son."

"Your son?" Caitlin cried. "How could you let him—" She hated herself for the cruel accusation.

Aniera shrugged, hopeless. "What could I do? A lone woman in a land of strangers? I had no family nearby, strong enough to help me claim my child. I had no proof Ronan was innocent, except for the certainty in my heart. All Glenfluirse was lauding Conn's great mercy in making Niall his foster son. I asked to see my son one last time, waited for him, but Niall never came. Conn said I was part of his old life. A shame to him. The boy had suffered much, Conn insisted. I was dead to Niall because of his shame."

"I do not believe it!" Caitlin protested. "If only Niall had come to you—"

"But he did not. I carried back to Glenfluirse my husband's body, my empty womb, and the knowledge that my son despised me. That was when the madness came, filling those empty places where Ronan, Niall, and the new babe had been, brewing visions and voices. They lured me toward the cliff edges and high arrow slits, urging me to fling myself off, join Ronan and wee Lorcan wherever their spirits wandered, but I could not bear to leave Fiona. So I stayed with her, the only way I could, with half a heart and pretty dreams to hold the madness at bay."

"I am so . . . so sorry," Caitlin grieved, knowing mere words were not enough.

"If I could wish you one thing, *asthore*, it would not be happiness, though I hope it will be yours. Nay, not even love, glad as I am that you hold my son's battered heart. I would wish you no regrets."

Caitlin opened her arms to the older woman, and Aniera leaned against her breast. Sobs ages old poured from a well deep inside Aniera, a flood of healing tears raining forth.

Regrets? Caitlin had only one. She had let her beloved, her bold warrior, ride into danger without her.

She had scarce dried the last of Aniera's tears when she heard odd, dragging footsteps. Fiona burst from the underbrush, her shoulder wedged beneath the arm of a scrawny, dirt-encrusted youth. Vicious scratches scored his face, and a hunted light flickered in eyes all but obscured by a ragged fall of straw-colored hair.

Caitlin sprang to her feet, Aniera scarce a heartbeat behind. "Who is this? What is wrong? Fiona?"

"Found him under a blackberry hedge, hiding like a wounded deer. Mad with some kind of fever." Fiona raised fear-glazed eyes to Caitlin's. "He keeps calling Niall's name."

"You brought him here? In spite of fever, in spite of danger?" Caitlin asked.

Fiona's voice broke on a sob. "I would have dragged the devil himself to Daire if he could help my brother!"

Caitlin nodded, her own eyes filling with tears. She hastened over to help Fiona with her charge. It seemed forever before the three women got the lad into a bed. Caitlin smoothed a cool cloth scented with wild rose over the boy's badly scratched face. She looked up at Fiona. "He looks like a beast run to ground. What could have happened to him?"

"I know precious little. He carried a message for Niall. Was trying to find him."

Caitlin bent over the lad, stroking back a lock of his hair. "You are safe now. I pray you, tell us your name."

The lad looked up at her with helpless, fear-filled eyes. "O . . . waine."

"You were searching for Niall. I . . . am his lady. You may trust me. I love him more than life."

The boy grasped at her leine with shaking fingers. "Tell him . . ."

Caitlin leaned forward, straining, desperate.

"What, Owaine? Tell him what?"

"In . . . danger . . ."

Caitlin gripped the boy's hand fiercely. "Who is in danger? You or Niall? What kind of danger? I beg of you, you must tell me."

The lad fought valiantly, his ashen lips struggling to form words, his throat convulsing as he battled to force out sounds. But exhaustion, pain, and exposure proved to be too much for him. His eyes fluttered shut. Caitlin cried out in denial, rushed about the bed in a flurry of cool cloths, desperate urgings, and pleading shakes, but nothing would wake him.

Seeing her efforts futile, Caitlin surrendered at last. Sinking down on a bench, she raised her eyes to where Aniera and Fiona stood across the bed box, terror stark on their faces.

"Is he . . . dead?" Fiona queried, ice pale.

"Not yet."

"Do you think he will . . ." Fiona shuddered, then burst in outrage. "After I dragged him halfway across Ireland, he does *this?* Who knows what illness he might carry! He might be a thief, a murderer—"

"But he was searching for Niall," Aniera reminded her. "Why? What do you think . . ."

"We will not know until he awakens. All we can be certain of is this: Niall must be in danger."

"Because of what? Who?" Aniera asked. "The boy said nothing—"

"Do not be fools!" Fiona cried. "It has to be Conn, the traitorous cur! I tried to warn Niall, but would he listen? Nay! Not one of you would!"

Aniera's face crumpled with terror ages old, unspeakable fears, Caitlin sensed. For if it was true, that evil lurked where she had seen compassion, how could she forgive herself for her blindness?

"You cannot know it is Conn for certain," Aniera

cried. "We cannot even begin to guess what this poor boy is trying to tell us. We will just have to wait—"

"Wait?" Caitlin cried. "How can I wait here, helpless, while Niall is threatened? Nay. I have to reach Glenfluirse with all haste. Warn him that something is wrong."

"How do you mean to do that? By traveling on foot?" Fiona scoffed. "By the time you reached Glenfluirse, this boy would have sprouted a beard. And whatever he is trying to warn of will already have happened."

Aniera plucked at the coverlet. "What if the boy awakens? If he can speak at last and tell us whatever is locked away inside him now? You will already be gone!"

"I have seen others sick in this way, brought to the healing sisters at the abbey. They can linger thus for weeks." Caitlin's voice dropped low. "Some never awaken at all. I cannot risk waiting a moment more."

Aniera fretted her lower lip. "But if he tells us why he was searching for Niall, if he gives some sort of warning—"

"Then Fiona will come after me, carry the message to Glenfluirse," Caitlin cut in, certain the girl would get through even if hell itself barred the way.

"I swear I will," Fiona vowed, her eyes glowing fierce as her warrior brother's.

Caitlin clung to that strength, the will that had kept Daire alive when things were most bleak, the instinct for survival that flowed through Fiona's blood as intensely as Niall's own.

"Then I have only one more favor to ask of you, my sister. A skill sadly neglected in my lessons at the abbey. One you have already proved apt at."

Caitlin clutched Fiona's hands tight, bracing herself with the strength, the feral protectiveness, that made her love this intrepid girl. "Teach me to steal a horse."

Chapter
20

Glenfluirse.

Niall squinted his eyes against the sun's glare and stared at Conn's magnificent fortress crowning a towering hill. Even as a boy, Niall believed it had seemed to shimmer with greatness, power as old as the Irish hills.

A place where legends could be born, soaring in fiery arcs to immortality. Fintan MacShane with his enchanted spear, his tale had been sung by the bards from the time Niall was a boy, the glorious story of the blind spear caster urging an outcast lad to strive harder, fight more fiercely . . . dream of great deeds he would do one day. Glenfluirse—the bloodless battlefield upon which Niall of the Seven Betrayals would win redemption.

Yet now, as he rode toward those familiar gates, the magic seemed to fade, Glenfluirse reverting to plain stone and wood, like any other fortress Niall had seen. It was little wonder, he thought, his lips curving in a grin.

What claim to glory could any walls on earth hold when they did not enclose the laughter and passion of his Caitlin, when Fiona's fiery valor did not warm even the coldest gray stones, and his mother's gentle, undeserved love did not brighten the shadowy corners?

Before his eyes, the fortress shape-shifted to Daire's familiar stone face, etched with ancient wisdom, whispering of a future yet to come. Castle Daire. Wonder welled up in his heart, a pure, sweet spring, watering the barren reaches of his soul. *Home.*

Niall lifted his gaze to the sweep of blue sky, wishing he could be transformed into a hawk, soar away from this place, sail waves of wind to Caitlin's welcoming arms. Nay, Niall thought, he would not trade Castle Daire for a hundred fortresses like Glenfluirse.

And yet, if what Declan claimed was true, Glenfluirse would be his one day. Niall's smile sobered, the thought dulling his joy of moments before. The man named *tainist* would be duty bound to rule his vast lands from this place, the center of trade, the seat of justice, the people's bastion in time of war. How could he tell Conn, tell the people of this fortress, the truth? That Niall of the Seven Betrayals, the champion of Glenfluirse, the warrior who had battled so long in an effort to find honor in their eyes, no longer cared about being captured in bard song, no longer dreamed of his sword one day gleaming in a place of reverence beside Fintan's spear upon the great hall's stone wall. Niall of the Seven Betrayals did not want to rule over anything save the heart of his Lily Fair.

His fingers trailed to the hilt of the magnificent sword, his father's weapon, bound to his waist where his own fine weapon had hung for so long. Strange, in the days since he and Declan had ridden away from Castle Daire, the sword seemed to possess its own brew of magic—a silent clamoring that had raked at his nerves until he surrendered this very morning, strapping the sword about his lean waist. Like a talisman, a charm, a thing enchanted. Nonsense, of course. If the blade held any magic, it was this: its weight reminded him of his father's mistakes.

What madness had his mother been prattling about? His mother's desperate, vulnerable face, so soul-battered by tragedy, swam before his eyes. His brow furrowed. Aye, she had claimed that Ronan of Daire told her to give the sword to him, said it would make a fine weapon for a chieftain.

Strange last words for a man to speak to his wife when he was riding off to die. What had his father been thinking at that dire moment? A son who would rise up to avenge him? Yet what good could come of drawing blood over an execution Ronan had earned by deeds so black they still tortured Niall's dreams?

Declan gave a shout, yanking Niall roughly from his musings. Niall's whole body jerked, so startled he nearly fell off his horse. He swore under his breath as he tried to right himself. A fine beginning this would make for even the most reluctant of *tainists*—plunging face first into the muck and botching his grand entrance into the fortress!

Cheeks firing hot, Niall struggled to regain some semblance of dignity as several people on the outskirts of the fortress paused in their labors, shielding their eyes to peer at the riders approaching. Suddenly, a roar of cries erupted.

" 'Tis *him!* Our champion!" a plump old man bellowed. "Niall of the Seven Betrayals has returned!"

The boy beside him capered about in a wild little dance. He dashed into the fortress, every fiber in his wiry body bursting with delight at being the one to carry such momentous news.

The child's cries brought a trickle of figures beyond the castle walls, the trickle swelling to a sea of people cascading from the gates, cries of welcome, of celebration, welling up around Niall.

Joy.

He could see its glow in so many of the faces as they clustered about him. Boys reaching up to touch the travel-stained edges of his garments as if some of the champion's courage might rub off upon their fingers. How many times had Niall done so himself? Straining to reach Fintan MacShane's elbow or the smooth wood length of the fairy-kissed spear?

But Niall felt hardly worthy of such adulation. He was still the betrayer's son. No honor, no title, not even any new name he won, would ever change the fact that Ronan of Daire's blood flowed in his veins.

But as Declan's wife and children swarmed in delight about their husband, their father, the scarred warrior obscured by their elated embraces, Niall suddenly realized he would no longer change the fact that he was Ronan's son even if it were in his power. For to relinquish the blood of the betrayer who died, he would also have to lose the bold, laughing father who had given him the wooden sword, the father who had played at monster in the chamber that captured the sea Niall's mother loved, the father Fiona still defended with all the passion in her loyal heart. Even for a name that was clean and new, irreproachable in other men's eyes, he would not surrender those treasures, tarnished as they might be in the eyes of the world.

A ripple of awareness seemed to go through the crowd, a sudden hush falling over them as they drew aside, forming a path down their center. Only one inhabitant of Glenfluirse could command such a tribute.

Niall's heart lurched at his first glimpse of the man striding toward him, resplendent in robes that glowed with green and red, gold and silver, his hair and mustache burnished bright as copper.

Conn the Ever Truthful, the man Niall had called father for so long, the chieftain whose armies he had led into battle, the one ally who had held Niall's trust.

How many times had Niall dreamed of entering Glenfluirse in such honor, the people's acclaim and his chieftain's pleasure washing away the taint of shame? How many nights, alone in his bed, had Niall imagined this moment, resolved to make it come real if it cost him his last drop of blood?

Yet now it was as if strange music played a warning within him, dulling his pleasure, drawing him back from all he had once desired. Had Fiona awakened this sense of caution inside him? Or was it the wind flowing past his father's sword that sang in such unsettling tones?

More likely it was the cluster of surly-faced men in Conn's wake, the redhaired, haughty sons the chieftain had sired. Sons who had no choice but to bow to their father's will and watch one they despised and hated from childhood seize their place at his side.

Niall reined in his mount, then swung from his horse, ignoring the jarring pain of his feet striking the ground after three days of riding. Raking wind-tousled hair back from his travel-grimed face, he paced toward Conn.

He knew he should sink to one knee in tribute, had done so often enough. Why did his body suddenly turn rebel?

Niall caught the questioning flicker in Conn's shrewd eyes at his omission, heard the rumble of outrage from his sons. But after a moment, the chieftain's mouth stretched wide in a grin. Conn opened his arms wide.

"I command you to welcome my son, all you who dwell in Glenfluirse!" Conn shouted as if to awaken the very stars. "This is the man upon whom I shall bestow all my lands, my wealth, as well as the champion's portion of a father's pride."

A roar rose from the crowd, joyful cries mingling with grumbles of disapproval, the faces of Conn's sons strained with suppressed rage.

Knowing what was expected of him, Niall stepped into his foster father's embrace. It was not the first time Niall had been so honored with this gesture that none of the chieftain's sons had ever won from their father. A gruff show of affection Niall had ever cherished.

Yet as Conn's hands pounded hearty greeting against Niall's back, all he could think was that these were the hands that had signed the missives condemning Caitlin to death. This was the man who had ordered his father's execution. This was the chieftain Fiona swore had given the command to reduce Daire to rubble.

A sense of loss shot through Niall, sobering him with the knowledge that whatever happened in the time to come, he would never again be able to come into his foster father's embrace without this darkening of suspicion inside him, the maddening scratch of uncertainty against his nerves.

His whole body stiffened, awkward, and he drew away before Conn made a move to release him. The chieftain's eyes narrowed just a whisper, but his smile remained fixed on his face. He peered past Niall's shoulder, as if seeking something.

"I can see that Declan has won the prize I offered for returning you to me, but tell me, where is this woman you risked so much for?" Conn inquired. "I have waited half my life to give proper greeting to the daughter of Fintan MacShane."

Niall stiffened, uncertain why Conn's words unsettled him so. "Caitlin of the Lilies has endured much in the past weeks. I would not ask her to endure the hardship of yet another journey."

How could Conn fail to miss the edge of accusation in Niall's voice? The chieftain's eyes widened.

"Your . . . gallantry increases, I see. And toward a woman!" Conn turned his face toward the crowd. "There are those within these walls who remember well a vow you took, that you would never be so moved by one of the fairer sex. Surely, all of Glenfluirse is as astonished as your chieftain. Two vows broken by the warrior who swore only honor would ever hold claim to his heart!"

"You summoned only me, or so Declan said."

"Aye, and so I did. If I wished for the lady's presence, I should have commanded it. And, of course, as my champion, my foster son, the man I named *tainist*, you would have obeyed your chieftain's order." Conn's brow arched. He expected a reply.

But Niall would not lie. He said nothing, certain only that no power on earth could have made him bring Caitlin here if there was even the slightest chance of danger. The silence seemed to stretch out forever, but at last, Conn chuckled, clapping Niall on the shoulder.

"You have journeyed far, and even the boldest champion grows weary. I command you to take a well-deserved rest, my son. Is that not an order you can obey?"

Niall sensed a jagged edge to Conn's words, could scarce blame him for his displeasure. Or was it hurt he saw, buried like an ember deep in the chieftain's eyes?

Guilt tugged hard. What must it be like for a man who had extended such generosity, risked so much in loving an outcast child, to see suspicion in that same foster son's face? Especially after the chieftain had heaped such honors upon Niall's head?

Niall cursed silently, torn between Conn's familiar, much-beloved face and the dragging weight of his father's sword—two loyalties, so vastly divided it seemed as if one man could not contain them both. Two paths that could never cross. Two separate destinies.

Yet, despite Niall's confusion, the chieftain deserved better treatment from his foster son, if only in payment for the kindnesses Conn had shown that lonely young boy.

Shoving his doubts aside, Niall stepped away from his foster father and bowed, paying him homage. Conn himself urged Niall to straighten, the smile beneath the red mustache warm now, almost like the one Niall knew so well. The smile Niall had fought to win time and again as a youth.

"You are my son. My heir," Conn proclaimed, his voice resonating, deep and clear. "No man in all Ireland is more valued by your chieftain than Niall of the Seven Betrayals. When the moon rises seven times from now, I shall grant you the reward you have won, a name of your choosing, cleansed of all blame."

Shouts rose from the crowd. "So long? Why delay?" Niall heard someone cry. "Give him his name at once!"

Conn cast a glance across the mass of his subjects, quieting them. "It will take seven days to bring another guest of honor to our celebration. Fintan's daughter!"

Cheers all but deafened Niall, adoration of the hero all Glenfluirse had loved.

"Aye, Niall," Conn repeated. "Summon Fintan's daughter to me. Caitlin of the Lilies has helped you earn your reward. Let her have her rightful share in your glory."

Niall started to protest, said nothing. He would reason with Conn about Caitlin once they entered his private chambers.

"Does the wench look fertile? I hear she is even more beautiful than her mother, Grainne, was, and Grainne was said to be the most exquisite beauty in all Ireland. Though there was another who could have challenged her for that title in some men's eyes. Scota—so beautiful she bewitched even your father."

Niall stared hard into Conn's face. It was bland, smooth as new cream. Why, then, did Niall feel as if an invisible rope were tightening around his chest?

Conn grinned beneath the impressive mustache, guileless, honest. "I have a motive I have confessed to no one save you," he murmured under his breath. "I am considering easing my eldest son's jealousy by offering him the lady's hand. What think you, Niall? Is that not wise?"

That cur cannot have her! She is mine!

Protest welled up inside him, but Niall crushed it into silence with a warrior's instinct as he felt the intensity of Conn's gaze. *Nay*, Niall resolved, *show no weakness, reveal no vulnerability that could be used against you . . . or, more terrifying by far, against Caitlin.*

"Aye," Conn answered himself in a voice Niall alone could hear. "It seems only fair in view of what my blood heir has lost—the position of chieftain traded for the honor of mingling Fintan's bloodline with my own. What think you, Niall? Shall Magnus take a bride?"

Nay! Niall screamed in silence. *Give him Glenfluirse and all its power and riches! Let Ireland itself sink into the sea, as long as Caitlin of the Lilies can be my wife.*

"I have no right to answer for Fintan's daughter," Niall evaded.

"Why should she object as long as her heart has not been given to some other man?" Conn chuckled. "And there can be little fear of that. Convent-bred from the time she was a suckling babe. I wager you are the first man she has ever seen, save some groveling, toothless priest. Unless the lady has fallen in love with you?" Conn gave a hearty laugh. "Has she, Niall?"

With all his strength of will, Niall shrugged. "What woman would be so unwise as to love the man who almost murdered her?"

Conn roared with laughter, but his gaze probed Niall's face, searching, seeking. Niall turned away, terrified he would see that Niall's reckless beloved had dared to give her heart into his keeping and that Fintan's daughter had pierced through all the anger, all the pain, every dark vow Niall had ever made, and had brought him back into the land of the living, reborn.

"No woman in Ireland can be bound without her consent," Niall said, as much to ease his own gut full of fear as in answer to Conn's questions. *And Caitlin would never consent to marry any man save me*, he finished in silence. *She is wife already, mated to my soul.*

But could that not be the most dangerous truth of all?

"Do we not owe the woman some small courtesy, at least? Let her stay where she is. Give her time to forget that you wrote an order condemning her to die."

He shifted his gaze away from Conn's probing one, and his heart slammed against his ribs. In the mass of faces, one stood out, the hatred etched in those features virulent, seething. Deadly.

Magnus, Conn's oldest son.

From the time they were boys, Magnus had loathed him, despised him for his tainted blood, hoarded up every defeat, every humiliation Niall had dealt him on the practice field. Always, Niall had known Conn's true-born son was counting the moments until he could make Niall pay for stealing his father's favor, smug in the certainty that that day would come. Magnus had cheated, schemed, stooped to any secret dishonor to try to bring Niall pain. The man's hatred must be fired hotter than ever now, humiliated as he was before all Ireland.

Niall's blood ran cold. He was right to keep Caitlin hidden at Castle Daire. Right to conceal his love for her. And at Castle Daire his lady would remain, safe from the intrigue that seethed in Glenfluirse. Aye, he would find a way to protect her from this threat, through reason or with his blood.

The heavens would fall before he allowed Magnus to use Caitlin as a weapon in his game of revenge. Besides, Niall reasoned, there was nothing to fear, was there? There would be time enough to reason with his foster father in the days to come. Conn had shown himself willing to grant him a kingdom. Surely, once Conn understood, the chieftain would give Niall the one thing he desired: Caitlin of the Lilies as his wife.

Conn tugged at the fringe of his mustache, his eyes fixed on the crowd that still reveled far beneath him, their spirits rising faster than the ascent of the moon. Disturbing. Nearly half of Glenfluirse embraced Niall as *tainist*, that position Conn's own blood son should hold.

How had Conn underestimated the allies Niall had won? Such divided loyalties could be dangerous even to a reigning chieftain if some unpopular secret were discovered and held against him. Worst of all—Conn grimaced—he had flung wide the door to this danger with his own hand.

Yet it was an error in judgment that would be righted soon enough. He would mark these men whose loyalty belonged to Ronan's son, and they would pay in good time. Not by Conn's sword but by a more subtle blade—cunning, ruthlessness, the genius that belonged to Conn alone.

They worshiped valor? Conn scoffed. His measure was no greater than most men's. Strength? His body was satisfactory enough. But his mind . . . aye, his mind surpassed any weapon these bumbling warriors hoarded in their armories. He would emerge the victor this time, as he always had before, because of one irrefutable truth: there was *nothing* he would not sacrifice to gain what he desired.

He glanced one more time at the sky, then smiled. Magnus should be drunk enough by now, wallowing in rage at the reception Niall had received. It was time to visit his son.

Servants scattered, even Magnus's friends fleeing like frightened deer, as the chieftain strode into his son's chambers. Conn grimaced in disgust as he saw evidence of Magnus's rage—shattered benches, torn cloths, every stick of furniture shattered or upended. An inexcusable rage. A witless display. And yet one a wise man could turn to his advantage.

With a wave of his hand, Conn dismissed the few who had been brave enough to linger. They rushed from the room with all haste.

Magnus cast a bleary glare at his father. He raised high his leather flagon. "Hail, the conquering hero returns! Tell me, Father, are you pleased with what you have done? I vow, if Fintan himself had risen from the grave and marched into your fortress, Glenfluirse could not have given him a more joyous welcome."

Jaw clenched with disgust, Conn stalked over to his son, knocking the flagon from Magnus's grasp with a knotted fist. "You think all this matters?" he demanded, gesturing to the slit in the stone through which the sounds of the revels rang. "Did I not promise you that if you had half the courage of Ronan's son, all of Glenfluirse would be yours?"

"And how could I hold it? Did you see them, the accursed fools? Flocking about him? They would not suffer me to be *tainist* now."

"That may be." Conn sneered. "Aye, and who could blame them, looking at you now, you drunken fool? Yet, even though you deserve none of my help, I will give it to you. You are my son—my son—though the gods know I can scarce believe anything so useless could spring from my loins."

Magnus swore, drew back his fist, but even in his drunken haze, he did not have the courage to swing at his tormentor. Conn smirked. "You would make a pitiful chieftain, it is true. But the people would forgive almost any weakness to have the blood of Fintan rule over them."

"Fintan? The spear caster is dead, may he rot!"

"But his daughter lives. The most beautiful woman in Ireland, some say. Bind the wench to you as your wife, and no man would dare speak against your rule."

Magnus's eyes cleared just a little, and Conn could almost feel his son scrambling to gather what few wits he had not drowned in mead. "That may be so . . . but that cur Niall—"

"Will be dead. You, my son, will kill him."

Magnus caught his breath, a dart of fear in his eyes. "You are mad! No man in Glenfluirse could defeat Niall!"

"You think I expect you to challenge him face-to-face like a man?" Conn laughed. "Do not be absurd. We are not bound by his code of honor, you and I. I had planned another death for my foster son, hoped to make it look as if Niall had fallen on his own sword."

Magnus snorted. "Why would he do such a thing? All of Glenfluirse grovels at his feet."

"Exactly. Which is why we must manage things another way. This is how it will be done. A philter slipped into Niall's cup while he is celebrating."

"Poison?" Magnus asked hopefully. "Aye! 'Tis a masterful plan!"

"It is not so easy as you believe, my son. All of Ireland would suspect treachery if Niall of the Seven Betrayals, my champion, dropped dead at the banquet table. We shall have to be more subtle. You must prove yourself worthy to be my heir."

"But how—"

"We will use something that takes its effect slowly, weighing him down like the onset of a sickness. When Niall feels the exaustion begin to overtake him, he will retire to his chamber. You will slip from the great hall, steal in, and kill him. But you must do so before the evidence of the poison is written across his face."

Magnus's eyes widened in fear. "But he is most skilled. What if—"

"He will be weak as a newborn babe. I will make certain the potion is strong enough so that even you can kill him."

Magnus flinched as if Conn had lashed him across the face.

"Come, my son, tell me, how many times have you imagined this in your dreams? Your sword piercing Niall's flesh, his eyes round as he sees his death in your eyes, his blood gushing hot over your hand. Finally, finally, the cur who should have scrabbled for scraps at your table but stole the prize portion instead will pay for his insolence. We will make him pay, you and I."

"But would not every eye turn to me if Niall is cut down? All Glenfluirse knows how I hate him."

Conn smiled as his son regarded him with the special dread accorded a sorcerer or the devil himself, wavering, wavering. "Do you believe your own father would put you in danger? You kill Niall. Trust me to arrange the rest. No one else in Glenfluirse will ever know that it was you who dealt Niall death."

"But how? I do not understand."

"You will make it look as if it were an accident. After all, a man everyone believes is in his cups often slips, falls. It is possible he could injure himself with his own sword, is it not? No man could prove Niall was murdered after you drive Niall's own sword through the wound you have made in his body. Only you and I . . . we will know the truth, will we not, my son?"

It was a lure a far stronger man would have been helpless to resist, the soft, secretive purr in Conn's voice, the slyness of his smile. Magnus wavered. Surrendered. He rose to his feet, bracing himself upright with the edge of a shattered bench.

"I will do it," Magnus vowed as Conn always knew he would. "Let the betrayer's son die."

Conn peered into the face of his firstborn, a twinge of guilt in his gut. "This is one grim truth any chieftain must accept," Conn said, his voice edged with regret. "Death is often necessary to safeguard his rule."

Sometimes even the death of the chieftain's own son . . .

Chapter
21

❧

THE BANQUET HALL shone bright as a new-polished sword, tables groaning beneath the weight of the finest foods Glenfluirse could provide. Yet no delicacy Conn's cooks could prepare could hope to match the flavor of excitement every person beneath the timbered roof now savored.

Weaned from their mothers' breasts to be nourished by the hero tales of Ireland, they gloried in the promise of witnessing the birth of a legend. They moved through the days of celebration as people in a dream, burning with the awareness that their children's children would sit before roaring fires generations from now, listening to bards not yet born spin out the tale of Niall of the Seven Betrayals.

Garbed in their finest, they relished the fact that they were here during this magical time. Torcs and bracelets coursed gold rivers about white throats and wrists, bodies adorned with rich billows of cloth ornamented with threads of madder and saffron and green. Warriors boasted of their own feats of valor, while wives and daughters clustered about them. But no man in Glenfluirse this night could compete with the guest the banquet honored, the champion Conn had claimed as his own.

Niall leaned against the table, reminding himself that the bard accorded him a rare honor. The harp, that most exquisite of weapons, waited a mere arm's length from where he sat, the bard, with his ageless eyes and his voice rich with the essence of time, had promised all present a rare treat—a new epic, written for this occasion, to capture for all time Niall's courage and his quests. Merely two moons ago, Niall would have rejoiced in all of it—the feast and the praise, the honor and the triumph.

But despite the haunch of the finest meat—the champion's portion—which steamed before Niall, despite the mad gaiety of a people who loved their revels nearly as much as their merry wars, Niall could scarce wait until the night was over and he could find respite in his own solitary bed. For even the halls of Conn's fortress were haunted now by shades from Castle Daire.

From the moment the feasting began, all he could think of were the women he had left behind. How Fiona's eyes would have widened at such a repast, how amazed she would be at countless delicacies she had never tasted. How Caitlin's beauty and courage would have glittered in this setting, a jewel so rare she would outshine any woman in the chamber.

Only his mother was impossible to imagine in this hall. Too many ghosts still lingered to overwhelm her fragile spirit. The faces might have aged in the years since she left Glenfluirse for the last time, but scattered among the crowd were some of the same men who had condemned her husband to die.

Why had he never considered that? Niall mused, picking at a splinter in the wood of the table. He had lived at this fortress most of his life, knew almost all who dwelled within these walls, but never had he searched the faces, wondered who among them had taken pleasure in Ronan of Daire's execution and who might have felt regret.

He scanned the crowd, seeking out the grizzled beards, the lined faces, the hair threaded through with silver, wondering. After a moment, he shook himself inwardly. What was he attempting to do? Make this endless night an even worse form of torture? He should at least *seem* to be enjoying himself.

Resolutely, Niall tore a chunk of rich meat from the haunch with his teeth, but the venison tasted as dull as dried leaves. Even so, he could not bear to waste it. Fortunately, there was one at Glenfluirse who would devour the haunch in a twinkling, Niall thought. He grinned as Owaine's grimy face rose in his memory.

The boy he had charged to bring his message to Conn had obviously carried out his task in good faith. The vast remains of the champion's portion should put some meat on his scrawny bones so he would at least have a fighting chance on the practice field he had yearned after for so long.

Aye, Niall thought, an hour in Owaine's company would dull the worst of this tearing yearning to be home. Excusing himself to the bard, Niall made his way to where Conn sat in his place of honor among his six sons. Ignoring glares that once would have pierced like lances, Niall bowed before Conn.

"Ah," Conn said, his smile touched with censure. "He comes to his chieftain at last, this son I honor above all others."

A discontented rumble sounded from Conn's flame-haired offspring.

"I feared you had abandoned me forever for the company of the bard. Of course, *he* will carve your name in the standing stones of time. What feat can even the wisest chieftain perform that can compare to that?"

"In truth, I come to you with a request." Niall chuckled, thinking tenderly of the grimy, fury-spitting scrap of humanity he had hauled out of the dust of the road.

A hard light sparked somewhere deep in Conn's eyes. "I thought I had already granted you one, withdrawing my . . . invitation to the woman—Fintan's daughter— to join us at Glenfluirse. Not that I had much choice. Your reasoning was sound. It would do me little good to have the people see the marks of strain on the girl's face. It might rouse their sympathies where they are not needed. Make them question—"

"Yours was an act of great kindness and understanding, after all she has suffered."

"At my hands, my foster son? Or at yours?"

"I would say neither of us is blameless, would you not agree?"

Conn chuckled. "You never were able to flatter your chieftain as every other warrior manages to. Nay, painfully honest you are, when it is needed. So tell me, what is this request you bring to me?"

"I was appalled to realize there is someone I should have given thanks to long since. I would remedy that omission."

The chieftain's eyes glittered, overbright. "You need not be so harsh with yourself, my son. I am certain you have thanked me aplenty."

"You?" Niall shifted, uncomfortable, as if the hearth flames suddenly licked beneath his feet. "You know that you have always had my gratitude."

"And once your unquestioning loyalty. But that, it seems, is altered."

Was something hidden beneath those words? A sharp stone beneath a deceiving blanket of moss? Nay.

The strain of the past weeks was telling at last, causing his imagination to run wild. The chieftain's grin stretched so wide his teeth shone beneath his mustache.

Niall returned Conn's smile with his own. "Rebuke me all you wish, but I know the truth. Even before I rode through the fortress gates that first day with your missives in my hand, you knew I would never harm the woman."

"There are few men either brave enough or foolhardy enough to profess to understand the workings of my mind." Conn's lashes drooped, concealing what Niall was certain was a conspiratorial twinkle. "However, I suppose you might possess special powers of understanding. You *are* the chosen one of fate, he who is about to step into immortality."

Niall snorted in dismissal. "You know as well as I do that I am not the hero they think I am. They see what they wish to see. A creature of imagination."

"Wise words, those. And surprising ones. I remember other revels in your honor when we celebrated your triumph over other quests. Then you believed as they do—that your feats could carry you to a plane far above the rest of us mortals. You cannot deny it."

Niall grimaced. "I was an arrogant fool, thinking all the mysteries of the world were unveiled to me when I understood nothing at all. Some would say I was scarce even alive."

Some, he thought, his heart squeezing. *One* vulnerable woman had dared to tell him that truth, shake him from his cold existence of duty into a world of bright color and joy and the only immortality that could ever hold real meaning—that of being cherished forever in his Lily Fair's heart.

"Ah, so *now* the mysteries of the world are truly unveiled to you, is that what you are saying? I would be most intrigued to know how you were so enlightened in the brief time you were parted from me. Perhaps you will share your secret, if I share a treasure with you."

The chieftain reached for his jeweled cup, drained it, then gave it to the son standing closest behind him. Magnus, his eyes glittering with a frantic gaiety, his face flushed from drink.

"You will fill this for your *tainist*," Conn commanded with a careless wave of his hand. "For soon the cup of leadership shall belong to him."

Niall expected anger, resentment, a show of the poisonous hatred seething inside Magnus for so many years because Niall held Conn's favor. But the warrior merely bowed, carrying the goblet away as if he were a servant instead of a chieftain's son.

Little that had happened in this season full of surprises astonished Niall as much as the manner of Magnus's departure did now. Niall peered after him. Was it possible that the most ambitious of Conn's sons could become so quickly reconciled to losing his place as Conn's heir? Impossible. From the time they were both boys, Magnus had brooded endlessly over the most insignificant slight Niall had dealt him and exacted revenge for it in some way. Niall would have to be careful, watchful and wary.

Conn's voice roused him from his dark musings. "Now, tell me again, why have you come to me?" Conn inquired. "You bring me a request, was that not what you said? You wished to thank someone you are grateful to?"

Niall's unease faded as he remembered his purpose in coming to Conn. Owaine. Despite his concern regarding Magnus, Niall could not keep his lips from curving into a half-smile at the memory of Owaine's feral determination, the abundance of anger and humiliation, pain and courage waring in that small, battered face. Emotions Niall understood far too well, pain he remembered far too clearly from the days when he first drew his sword on the practice field of Glenfluirse, believing he could slice away the aching in his heart if only he were brave enough.

"I wish to thank the boy who carried my words back to Glenfluirse," Niall said. "Young Owaine who would become a warrior."

"Owaine?" Conn's brows knitted in confusion, then awareness seemed to dawn, and he laughed. "Ah, *Owaine*. A most determined lad."

Niall himself had chuckled over the boy more than once. Why, then, did Conn's amusement regarding Owaine chafe? "The boy will make you a fine warrior if you give him the chance," Niall attested. "I would stake my life on it."

Conn's lip curled in an odd expression.

"Owaine is fired of a rare, fine mettle," Niall insisted.

"The same mettle as you were," Conn said. "Is that not what you are trying to say? Fired in the flames of hardship, rejection, shame?"

Niall's face burned, but his jaw set hard. "A boy who has endured such trials will fight and die for any man who shows him kindness instead of cruelty, honors him instead of scorning him. Whatever welcome you give the boy will be repaid you a hundredfold."

"I fear you are mistaken, since he nearly gave me a bleeding nose when first we met."

Niall frowned. "I do not understand."

Conn laughed. "He was most, er, exuberant when he arrived. Ready to slay dragons, storm fortresses, decimate enemy hordes single-handed."

Niall's frown melted, gruff affection for the boy tugging hard at his heart. "And you with no dragons nearby." He shook his head in mock regret. " 'Tis a terrible misfortune, I vow."

"You have been around to dispatch all the impossible quests at Glenfluirse for so long that I fear there is a shortage of bold adventures at present. Not knowing what else to do in this predicament, I sent the boy off on a mad chase with the understandable hope that he might wear off a bit of his enthusiasm before he hurt himself or goaded someone else into quelling his exuberance for him. He seems to me a lad who will create trouble when he cannot find it, imagine danger where there is none."

Niall's chest ached. Conn might as well be describing the boy Niall had been. "I am sorry to miss the chance to speak to him again."

Conn shrugged. "I have no doubt he will return far too soon for anyone else's peace of mind. Unlike my son, who has carried out his task at a dragging pace." Conn cast Magnus a reproving glance as the burly warrior returned with the chieftain's cup.

"I am not accustomed to tending a servant's task," Magnus observed with unsettling mildness, wiping at a dark, damp stain down his front.

"You had best become accustomed to serving Niall," Conn growled. "Tending his needs will be your lot in life from this day forward, aye, and the lot of your brothers." The chieftain all but yanked the goblet from his son's grasp. The liquid splashed over its rim, the gold vessel shimmering between Conn's long fingers. He held the goblet to his lips, tipped it back, his throat convulsing. Wiping his wet mustache with the back of his sleeve, Conn handed the goblet to Niall and smiled.

"Sample this, and tell me, my foster son, does the drink of a *tainist* taste different from the fare of a simple warrior?"

At the moment, Niall thirsted for nothing but a scrap of peace, and yet, even with all that had changed inside him before he returned to Glenfluirse, it seemed he could still be provoked by the taunting of Conn's haughty sons. Surrounded by their muttered insults, he returned their scorn in the most effective means in his power: he raised the chieftain's goblet to his lips and drained it.

Conn's eyes burned with intensity. What had he done to so please his chieftain? Niall wondered. Was the blaze in Conn's eyes approval at Niall's act of defiance in the face of Conn's sons?

"You have given me much pleasure in the years since you first came to me," Conn said. "I take in you a father's pride. That is why it grieves me to disappoint you on this night, filled with tales of your victories. Tell me, Niall, is there no other boon I can grant you?"

Niall searched the familiar landscape of Conn's face, the shrewd eyes half-hooded beneath coppery brows, the bold blade of nose, the drooping mustache that veiled his mouth. And the smile, that smile that seemed to draw a magic circle around just the two of them, as if he and Niall shared a secret bond no one else would ever understand.

Niall felt a stab of sadness at the trust he and his foster father had both lost somewhere in this final quest. There had been another time in his life when he had fought against the lure of that smile—as a boy, trusting no one, especially not himself. And yet, in the end, wariness had always softened in the light of that smile. Now a strange, slow warmth spread through Niall— from the mead he had drunk or the glow of Conn's approval, he was not certain.

He was astonished to hear the sound of his own voice. "There is one reward only I would ask." Had he run mad? Niall felt a sudden sting of alarm as he struggled not to let anyone see how dismayed he was that the words had escaped him. He had nearly confessed the truth about his love for Caitlin!

Yet would it not be wisest to tell the truth about the love they shared before Conn's boasting fool of a son announced his betrothal from the fortress gates? Magnus had been humiliated once already by the foster brother he scorned. He would not suffer another such slight without taking grim revenge.

Conn clapped him on the shoulder, and Niall fought to steady himself in an agony of indecision, a sheen of sweat dampening his body.

"The untarnished name you have fought for so long is yours," Conn proclaimed, "one fit for a hero who will someday dwell in Tir naN Og."

Niall kneaded his temple with his fingers, trying to clear his head, sort things through, the exhaustion and strain of these days at Glenfluirse taking a toll at last, tangling his thoughts. But he was determined to be honest in this much at least.

"I no longer wish to change my name," Niall confessed.

Conn stared. "How can that be? You have fought for this one boon your whole life, to rid yourself of your traitor father forever."

Niall's cheeks fired even warmer. He glanced down at the sword hilt glittering at his waist, and a knot tightened in his gut. Little wonder he felt so strange. Somewhere, buried deep inside him, he had been dreading this moment of truth with Conn and with himself, knowing it would come. And that when it did, he would somehow injure this man who had been his staunchest defender.

He leveled his gaze at Conn, certain the chieftain

would never understand, no matter how hard Niall tried to explain. "No mere words have the power to change the fact that I am the son of Ronan of Daire," Niall said slowly. "His blood runs in my veins. His face will forever be my own, just as your sons bear your mark in their features, the reflection of your spirit in their eyes."

"It is not the same!" Conn's mouth crumpled in denial. "You carry a vile murderer's name. It is a burden I would rid you of."

"Many years have passed. It is my name. Mine alone." The name Caitlin had first known him by, loved him in spite of. How could mere words hold any sting when she spoke them with such love in her voice?

"A *tainist* bearing a name carved in shame?" Conn snarled in disbelief. "A chieftain whose name echoes with betrayal? Who would follow such a man?"

Fintan's brave, generous-hearted daughter; Fiona with her rebelliousness and her fearsome loyalty; Niall's mother, whose love for him had never faltered. Who would follow such a man? The only people who mattered.

Niall wiped the sweat from his brow, fighting an odd lightness in his head. He squared his shoulders, wishing he could explain the truth to Conn, knowing this man, above all others, deserved honesty from one he had raised as a son. He confessed as much as he dared. "I want no man to follow me. I never wished to be chieftain."

Conn jerked back as if Niall had slapped him. Niall winced, regretting the confusion on Conn's face, the barest hint of alarm in the chieftain's eyes.

"Every man wishes to be chieftain!" Conn insisted. "Every man craves power to rule over others."

Niall wanted to rule over nothing save the calves

Boann would bear, the mischief his sister would cause, his mother's visits to the fairy folk, and the love in Caitlin's heart. And yet, did he dare confess that truth to anyone here at Glenfluirse until he was certain all was well? Would it not put Caitlin in danger?

Was she not already in jeopardy, which would only grow more grave given time? Had not Conn suggested giving her in marriage to appease Magnus? What would the warrior do when he found himself robbed not only of his inheritance but of the honor of taking Fintan's daughter as wife?

He started as Conn gripped his arm. "What place would I hold in your tales when they are sung if I did not choose you as my heir?" Conn demanded. "Seven quests performed for a chieftain who offered you nothing in return? I would be shamed for all time! *Tainist* I proclaimed you, and *tainist* you will remain!"

Niall's gaze locked with his chieftain's, Conn's eyes suddenly burning with an anger Niall had never seen before. He could sense how much it cost Conn to extinguish it, the chieftain ever so slowly unclenching his fists.

"You have endured much since you left on the quest I set you. You look weary this night. Go to your rooms. We will speak of this tomorrow when you are rested."

"The bard—" Niall objected. "I would not dishonor him or shame you . . ."

"It is not every man who is lucky enough to watch himself become immortal."

Was there a touch of envy in the chieftain's voice?

"The honored one should be able to enjoy his epic the first time he hears it, should he not? The bard will forgive you as I do. All this will keep until the morrow. Go to your chamber and sleep. Your chieftain—nay, your *father*—commands you."

Head aching, body sweating, more exhausted than he could ever remember being in his life, Niall acceded. With a bow, he wove through the crowd toward the door.

Twice he nearly stumbled, so tired had he become. He scarce saw their confused faces and did not so much as glimpse the hard glance that passed between Conn the Ever Truthful and his hot-eyed eldest son. Nor did he suspect that the instant the crowd turned again to its revels, Magnus grasped the hilt of his dagger and followed him from the room.

Chapter

22

NIALL'S FOOTFALLS echoed on the stone floor, torches casting weird patterns on the walls, as he made his way toward his chamber. The instant his body struck the bed, he knew he would sleep, as deadened to all around him as a corpse within its grave.

The prospect should have been a relief after eight endless strained nights, lying awake until dawn, aching for Caitlin cuddled close beside him, fearing for his valiant lady despite the welcome he had received in the fortress. Dreading that he would stumble somehow, make a mistake, lose the future more precious to him than any bard song ever composed.

Aye, he should have been grateful for the waves of exhaustion weighing him down more insistently with each step he took. He *would* have been, if not for warrior's instincts that could not be set aside even within his own chieftain's fortress, the knowledge that sleep rendered one completely vulnerable, as grimly evidenced in the memory that tormented him—Caitlin, the night he had taken her from the abbey, so innocent, so beautiful, so helpless, curled up beneath his robe, her throat gleaming white in the moonlight just a heartbeat from the cut of his blade.

Niall's stomach lurched at the memory, so hideously vivid. He cursed under his breath, pausing for a moment to brace one hand against the cold stone wall, his feet unsteady. Would he ever be able to banish that terrible, frozen moment from his mind? Why did he still feel as if he were trying to wrest that blade away from his lady's throat when all at the fortress seemed well? Even his last, lingering fear should have eased when Conn acceded to his wishes, withdrawing his command that the lady join them at Glenfluirse.

His head throbbed, as if someone had heaved a battle axe at his brow. He ground his fingertips against the ache. It was good that Conn had excused him from the banquet, he thought grimly. It would be best to sleep this pain away. Besides, each night that passed brought him closer to the day he and Caitlin could be reunited.

A draft of cool air wafted over his sweat-sheened face, and he turned to see an arrow slit an arm's length from where he stood. Squinting his eyes in an effort to focus them, he caught the glimmer of a lone star in the slice of night sky.

Stars . . . Caitlin's stars. He smiled weakly despite the mist swirling in his head. Had she not claimed they were a mystic link between those who loved? Surely, if the heavens could bind Caitlin to the abbess who had raised her, the stars would carry a love as strong as his back to Castle Daire, where his lady waited.

Yearning crushed his chest. Instead of stumbling up the stairs as he had intended, Niall turned around, retracing his steps to the doorway. Fumbling to open it, he slipped out into the night, the sword at his waist clattering against the stones rimming the doorway's edge.

Blessedly cool, the wind bathed his face, the chill driving back the strange swirling in his head a bit. He raked the tangle of hair back from his sweating brow.

Even here, alone in the castle yard, he could hear the sounds of celebration, feel the press of countless people who filled the fortress. The sounds and commotion of Glenfluirse had always marked his life. Why was it that suddenly he could scarce endure them? He would give anything to be standing under the solitary oak at Castle Daire, listening to the stillness with Caitlin in his arms.

Away from the intrigues of Conn's fortress, away from men who condemned innocent boys for their fathers' crimes, who mocked and scorned them, then groveled when that boy grew to be a fierce warrior. Flattered though they still despised you. And now, since that outcast boy had been named Conn's heir, both their mock fawning and their very real hatred would run deeper still.

By the ancient stones, he wished he could stride out through the fortress gates and never return, but it was obvious Conn was not willing to let Niall escape the ruling he had handed down. Niall was condemned to be *tainist*.

If only Conn's sons could know how he hated the very word! But they would never believe a man so ambitious, so fiercely determined to bring honor to his name, would refuse the highest honor in the land. He would not have thought it possible himself until Caitlin shook the very foundations of all he believed in.

He had spent a lifetime craving another name, so he could pretend he was no longer the son of Ronan of Daire. He had never guessed it was possible to shed all that hatred, doubt, loathing—to step through some fairy-spun veil and become another man. One who could remember his father with some tenderness. One who could love a woman more than honor or power. In the end, it did not matter if Magnus and the others believed—Niall knew the truth. His lady had changed

him utterly. He would spend the rest of his life thank-
ing her for that gift.

Another wave of dizziness engulfed him, and he almost lost his balance. He crossed to where a leather
otter skin hung against a wall, surprised at how long it
took him to reach it. He poured water from it into his
hands, splashed the chill moisture onto his face. He
hoped it would clear his head, but it seemed to drive
him madder still.

The night seemed alive with echoes of Caitlin. He
could *feel* her pulling against his heart, as if she were
gathering in a mystic thread that linked them together.
He could *sense* her as if she *were* one with the stars, as if
that special magic she had told him of could carry her
to him in a chariot built of longing, across a shimmering bridge of moonshine.

Could a man make love to moonshine? He felt an
unreasonable urge to reach out his arms in an attempt
to gather her close.

Impossible.

He smiled. Yet was anything impossible in the light
of the love Caitlin bore him? Had any other man ever
felt this craving? This sweet madness that made the
most resolute warrior in Glenfluirse want to reach out
to fairy-spun dreams? Believe he could conjure his
lover from silvery light and longing?

He turned toward the fortress gate, knowing she
would not be there. Knowing with his mind she needed
to stay far away in Daire, safe, regardless of the rebellion taking hold in his heart.

Yet it seemed even the fairies were amused by the
fact that stone-hearted Niall of the Seven Betrayals
writhed with love pangs, the mischievous Tuatha de
Danaan conjuring up mystical visions before him.
Something pale glided toward him, wavering like living

mist from the castle gates—a figure so like a woman's it made his heart stop.

Yet what woman would be out at this time? Every woman in Glenfluirse celebrated in the great hall, and no living, breathing female would dare cross the wildlands to reach Glenfluirse in the darkness. No reasoning man would believe it possible for a moment.

Still, if this was madness, Niall knew he never wanted to be sane again. His gaze devoured the ethereal figure, white linen rippling about her, the soft oval of her face a bright smudge on the darkness. A shapeshifter, gliding toward him, a dream lover reaching for him from the conjurings of his own mind.

Caitlin . . .

"Behind you!"

Her warning split the night, her voice impossibly real. He swung around just as something hurtled from the shadows. Pain seared his ribs as blade bit flesh. He flung himself to one side, barely in time to keep his attacker from burying a gleaming dagger in his heart.

But he had escaped for only a moment, he realized dimly. The swirling haze sucked him deeper, pulling him under thick, dark waves.

What was wrong with him? Niall wondered with stark panic. His body had turned traitor! Arms trained for years in battle grew awkward, all but useless, his instincts terrifyingly dulled.

He staggered toward his attacker, a hulking figure woven of torchlight and nightmare charging him, savage as the boar that had tried to rip his body open on the cliff.

But this was no stalker born of night terror. Torchlight gleamed on Magnus's bared teeth, filled the bowls of Magnus's hate-filled eyes with flame. His clothing reeked, the stain from where he had spilled the cup still wet and stinking of ale.

Magnus, the man who had been waiting all his life to kill Niall.

Realization shattered into fear as he glimpsed the figure from the gate running toward him, the vision taking on shape and substance, her face filled with terror, her hair a black tangle in the wind.

Caitlin!

Nay! a voice screamed inside him. She could not be real! Or had he summoned her somehow from the sky? He wondered in the whirling confusion of his addled senses. Had he brought her here through some mystic link beyond time, beyond magic? Carried her into danger? His gut froze with the coldest of terrors.

Desperate, Niall shoved back his sick dizziness, summoned his last strength to meet his attacker. Praying to a God he half believed in, Niall dove for Magnus. A roar of fury erupted from Magnus as the burly warrior tried to slash the blade down to cleave Niall's flesh. Somehow, Niall twisted from its path as Magnus tried to slam the dagger home.

Grabbing the warrior's wrist, Niall drove the weapon down, felt the sickening sensation of the blade piercing Magnus's belly. Magnus's hellish scream split the night, but Niall barely heard it or the sounds of people spilling from the castle's door.

He crashed to the ground, his gaze fastening on Magnus's face. The dying warrior's hand clamped on his arm.

"Cannot . . . end this way," Magnus groaned, writhing. "You . . . defeating me again. Glenfluirse . . . was mine by right."

Niall fought off the dizziness, clamping his arm tight against his own side, wet and hot with fresh blood. "Conn give Glenfluirse to a coward? To a man who would stab another in the back? Did you really believe . . ."

"Should have been so easy." Magnus's eyes rolled wildly. "Saw you staggering out of the hall. Stumbling from drink just like . . . said you would."

Awareness pierced Niall despite the waves of dizziness that assailed him. "The drink? The cup you offered me . . ."

"Poison." Magnus's lips twisted in a grotesque smile.

"But your father—he tasted it—"

"Said . . . if you drank it . . . even I should be able to . . . kill you."

Rage spread hot through Niall's veins, and he struggled with all his will to cling to his wits despite the dragging haze. "You gave the cup to your own father! He could have died—"

"Promised . . . he promised . . ." Magnus whimpered like a child, tears running down his cheeks. "All would be well if . . . just did as he . . . said."

"Who?" Niall roared. "Curse you, who plotted this? Who put that knife in your hand?"

Magnus's agonized gaze pierced Niall's. "Father."

"Nay! Impossible!" Niall recoiled, remembering the shimmering gold between Conn's fingers, the burning intensity in the chieftain's eyes. "He drank from the cup before he offered it to me."

"Pretended. Lull any suspicion later."

Niall's stomach churned with realization as Magnus's mouth curled with triumph even in death.

"*My* . . . father. He was . . . *mine*," Magnus cried fiercely. "N-never yours." The warrior convulsed, cried out. His body went still.

Niall struggled to his feet, fought for balance. There were people spilling out of the fortress, their faces weaving dizzily around him, weapons ready. Had they heard the sounds of battle? Believed it an attack by an enemy? A few of the faces shone stark with shock. Disbelief. Horror as if they had heard . . .

He glimpsed Caitlin, held back by a pair of spear casters, an intruder, a stranger who might be responsible for whatever had just happened. Her beloved features contorted in terror, anguish. Real. She was heartbreakingly real and in the grimmest of danger.

For if Conn had plotted Niall's death, the chieftain must thirst for Caitlin's as well. Desperation screamed through Niall's veins. How much time did he have left before the poison finished its work? He had to save Caitlin! And there was only one sure way: his sword buried in Conn's lying throat.

"Conn!" Niall bellowed, staggering around the ring of people, searching for the chieftain's face. "Murdering coward! Come forward! Face me like a man!"

A murmur of discomfort, disbelief, rippled through the crowd. Suddenly, Niall glimpsed the chieftain, standing apart upon a raised dais, his red hair gleaming in the torchlight, his robes seeming to writhe like flame.

"I am here, betrayer's son," Conn said. "Come forth if you dare. The rest of you, stay back! This matter is between me and this foster son of mine."

"Nay!" Caitlin cried out, struggling against her captors. "Niall, do not!"

But there was only one way he could free his lady now. Niall staggered toward Conn, determined to face the chieftain, kill him, before the poison ended his own life. But the wound in his side was draining what little strength he had left, his head threatening to explode. Niall stumbled to the dais, the sword in his hand so heavy he could scarce hold it. He dragged himself up the stairs to the floor which seemed to heave beneath him like waves in a sea storm.

Conn shimmered, swam in the orange glow, like a

dragon in a hero tale, deadly and terrifying. Invincible. "The sword is too heavy, Niall," Conn murmured with peculiar gentleness. "I know you cannot lift it."

Niall tried to prove his nemesis wrong, but it was as if the chieftain's words had cast a spell upon him, robbing him of the last of his strength. "You . . ." Niall struggled to force the words from his throat. "You wanted to kill me. Why . . . not do it with your own hand?"

Conn's eyes widened with something like hurt. "I had an affection for you."

"Yet you used your own son?"

"Some men value sons far more than others. I view them as expendable—regrettably expendable, but expendable nonetheless. Perhaps because I had so many of them. Your father, however . . ." Conn tugged at his mustache meditatively.

"My father . . ." Niall echoed.

"Perhaps it is safe for you to learn the truth at last. An eternity of guilt will be a fitting blood price for killing my son. All these years, you have hated Ronan of Daire. Loved me. Were loyal to me. All this time."

"Nothing you can say will change anything. I know the truth. Father . . . told me himself. Love him . . . in spite of it."

"How generous of you. You love your father in spite of the fact that he lied to you."

"Never . . . lied."

"Everything he told you from his prison was a lie. He killed your love for him with those lies so that you might live."

"K-killed?"

"I gave Ronan a choice. Condemn himself to you and to all of Glenfluirse, declare to all Ireland he was a traitor who murdered his closest friend for the lust of a woman. Make everyone believe *he* was responsible for the blood that was on *my* hands, and I would let his son live."

Niall staggered back, horror all but buckling his knees. Horror and the certain knowledge that Conn told the truth. "You?"

"Scota was a most intriguing woman. Sons sired on her body would have been magnificent. A fitting legacy to my rule. Not like the puling lot I got on my wife. It was simple enough to smear your father with guilt in the minds of everyone in Ireland. Merely dipping Scota's finger in blood, writing Ronan's name. I could not believe my good fortune when the lout rode up to Lorcan's fortress scarce an hour after I had killed her. I made certain many people saw him. Then I appeared, shocked and grieving at the carnage I found. Only my most trusted men knew what had really happened. I missed them very much when accidents befell them."

"You monster . . ."

"Can you think of no better name to call me? Your father did, I assure you. Especially when he was wrestling with the terrible choice I gave him—to live forever in infamy and shame and let his son be raised by the man who destroyed him or to watch you die. I expected to have to kill you as well. Imagine my astonishment when I discovered that Ronan loved you more than his honor, more than life, more than truth."

Conn sneered. "I wonder what your father felt when he saw your love for him change to hate. When you ran away from his cell, I was watching from the shadows. The great Ronan of Daire wept there, all alone. It might have comforted him a little—how loyal his wife and daughter remained to him after his death. No fire or storm I could rain down upon them would shake their faith in him, make them hate him as I desired."

"You laid waste to Daire. Just as . . ." *Nay!* a voice

screamed in his head. *Cannot remind him of Fiona, leave her vulnerable in case I fail—nay, but I will not fail.*

"So much loyalty to someone a chieftain has executed can be most dangerous after all. I *had* vowed to let them live as well, but I hoped fending off starvation would keep them too busy to think about revenge."

"Curse you . . ."

"I hope Ronan saw their sufferings from the halls of Tir naN Og, but more than that, I hope your father saw every quest you fought to rid yourself of his name. I fed your hatred of him, so certain you would sacrifice anything to free yourself of the taint of his supposed treachery. I staked my lands on it, my title of chieftain. But you surprised me. You did not carry out the quest I planned for you from the day I brought you to Glenfluirse. You refused to kill Fintan's daughter."

"You . . . you planned . . ."

"Every act of kindness, every bid for your loyalty, it was all for one purpose: to hone you into the blade that would rid me of that curse. Aye, and in murdering an innocent girl, destroy yourself as well."

Conn gazed out over the crowd and sighed. "But now, because of Magnus's babbling, some of my people know much of the truth. They will soon guess the rest. Can you not see them, amidst the crowd, Niall? Their doubts? Their suspicions? Even with all my power, I will never be able to find them all, silence them before the rumors spread. Rumors are hard to silence. The truth, impossible once it escapes. The curse, it seems, will come to pass. The girl doomed my rule. There is only one thing I can do in the face of all you have cost me."

Before Niall could move, the chieftain snatched the sword from Niall's numb hand. "You die by your father's sword?" Conn murmured. "It is the perfect end to this sordid tale. Ronan's son will never rule in my place!"

He drew back the sword, his voice a roar. "Niall killed my son! It is my right to take his life!"

Niall searched for another weapon, stumbled to his knees. "Caitlin!" He screamed her name, helpless, loving her.

Caitlin saw the sword flash high above Conn's head—knew in a heartbeat what the chieftain intended. Not even the finest warrior could help her love now! Nay, it could not end this way after all Niall had suffered!

She tore from the grasp of the stunned warriors, wrenching a spear from a burly hand. Desperation and hopelessness clawed through her. Every time she had aimed a shaft before, she had failed.

This time, she closed her eyes, groping through time and space for a hand she had never held, a love she had never known, though both had been there all her life.

"Father, help me!" she cried out as she hurled the spear into the darkness. A guttural cry rent the night, and she opened her eyes to see Conn crumple, the spear buried in his heart. Niall's sword clattered from the chieftain's hand to the wood of the dais.

Clutching up the folds of her leine, Caitlin plunged through the shocked crowd. She clambered onto the dais, gathered Niall in her arms.

Blood. There was so much blood. A sob tore from her throat as she clutched him close.

"You are safe now," Niall said, with a tortured peace in his face. "Declan will take care of . . . of—"

"Take care of me yourself! You promised me a home! Family! Promised me babes!"

Death-pale lips curled in a shadow of the smile she loved so much. "Pray there may be one. When you look in his eyes, remember how . . . much I loved you, Lily Fair. But the cup. Conn gave me . . . poison."

Sick horror jolted through her. "Nay! Nay, Niall, it cannot be true! Help him!" she screamed, clutching him tight. "Someone help him!"

The bard slipped forward, his face grief-stricken. How much had this wise man heard? "There is nothing to be done if he was poisoned. No magic that can bring him back."

Caitlin shook Niall, desperate. "You promised not to leave me alone!"

"Wish we had forever. Tell Fiona she was . . . right about Father. Conn . . . told me the truth. The treachery was his. Father was innocent. Tell her. Nothing . . . girl likes more than proving me wrong. And Mother— tell her—how sorry—for pain I . . . caused her."

"She loves you, Niall. She always has."

Niall's hand curled in the waves of Caitlin's hair, his eyes suddenly fierce, pleading. "Take me back to Father. Bury me beside him. He sacrificed everything for us. M-Mother, Fiona, and—and me. Beg . . . his forgiveness."

"There is nothing to forgive! Oh, Niall! He knew— he always knew you were too fine a man to be corrupted by Conn. He trusted you would find the truth someday, know he had always loved you."

"Love . . . I forgot wh-what it was until you. Think my—my father sent you to remind me?"

"Aye! Just as my father sent you to love me, protect me! You have to get well! Conn is dead. You know the truth about your father. No one can hurt you anymore."

Niall reached up, cupping her cheek in one trembling hand. "All my life, I wanted bards to sing . . . of battles fought. Honor won. Live . . . forever. Now, I only wish to live in your heart."

"You will." Tears coursed down Caitlin's cheeks. "Until the end of time."

Niall's hand fell away.

She cradled him in the terrible silence, stroking his dark hair, marking each rise and fall of his chest. Death—it seemed impossible that its dark night could fall upon this man, rob him of his strength, his honor, all the laughter and love that might have been.

She wanted to rage, wanted to scream, wanted to lie down across his chest and let her own life force ebb away, traveling with her love to whatever land awaited heroes when they fell—fairy-kissed Tir naN Og, the Land of the Ever Young, with its magic and its merry wars, or heaven, with its soul-deep serenity. She would travel any distance, through any danger, if only she could still hold him close.

"If you will not stay, take me with you, Niall," she pleaded. "Do not leave me all alone."

She felt something brush her back, glanced behind her to see a frail hand upon her shoulder. She looked up into a face older than the sea, druid robes flowing around a body brittle as old bones. "Why do you weep, child? You, above anyone, should know a legend never dies."

"Wh-what good is a legend to hold?" She clung to Niall, bitter. "All your words could never give me my father's hand to hold. Can it bring Niall back into my arms?"

"Your father's love carried that spear into Conn's black heart. But you will have to breathe life back into this man you love with magic of your own."

"Magic? Is that not what has destroyed us? Your prophecies of doom, when I care not if Glenfluirse sinks into the sea? Leave us in peace! I have heard enough tales of enchanted quests and Tir naN Og to choke me! I want Niall alive! I want him in my arms, in my bed!"

The druid chuckled with astonishing tenderness.

"You may have your mother's face, but Fintan's fire burns within you, a fire beyond the powers of heaven and earth to extinguish. Tell me, Caitlin of the Lilies, do you deserve happiness just as Fintan did so long ago? The glory of a love so great it will live until the mountains turn to ash?"

"I do not know if I deserve it, but Niall does! He has suffered so much, been so strong and noble and brave and good. I would take the poison from him if I could. Drink of it myself. But it does not matter. It is too late."

"Are you so certain of that?"

"Wh-what?"

"Magnus spilled the cup. I saw him do so. Watched him refill it. We cannot know how much of the poison remained, or how much it would take to kill a man the like of Niall—a warrior stronger than any other in body with a love strong in his heart."

"Then there might be hope! If only I could ask Reverend Mother what to do! She healed people when it seemed impossible." But it was five days' ride to the abbey, five days' ride back. By then, it would be too late.

She would have to trust in herself. Had she watched the nun closely enough? Listened and learned anything that might help Niall? She had to try. "But where can I begin? I know nothing about the land surrounding this fortress, where to gather things I might need."

The druid tucked his frail hands deep into his sleeves and nodded. "There are herbs aplenty in a clochen hut I once dwelt in, beside a standing stone. Take what you need from that place. Tend your beloved one, Fintan's daughter. He has suffered much, this man. He deserves the future I see shining in your eyes."

Laying Niall gently on the dais, she rose, stood before the white-faced crowd. "I am Fintan's daughter, Caitlin of the Lilies!"

A ripple of wonderment and awe cascaded through the stricken crowd as they stared up at her.

"Take your new chieftain to his bed," she commanded. "Declan will guard him until I return."

"Return?" Declan pushed forward, his scarred face puckered with grief at Niall's desperate state, yet also with worry, the crushing responsibility for his friend's vulnerable lady. "Where are you going?"

"A clochen hut where the druid keeps herbs that might save Niall. I must find this place if Niall is to have any hope."

"Niall would want me to go with you!" Declan protested.

"You must stay with him," Caitlin objected. "You are the only one I can trust to watch over him."

"I am the only one you can trust to guide you to the place you seek." Declan flushed. "I know the way well, rode it often even in darkness. It was there, in the shadow of that standing stone, your father put you in my arms. From that clochen hut I carried you to the abbey."

"You?"

"Aye. And mine are the hands that brought the lily to you each year, your father's token, a symbol of Fintan's love for you."

"Declan . . ."

The bard stepped forward, his power seeming to awe them all. "There is no time to speak of this now. You must hasten. I will guard Niall. No one would dare harm him in my care. Go, Caitlin of the Lilies. Only you can give this hero tale a joyous ending."

She knelt, crushing Niall to her one last time. Rising, she reached out, clasped Declan's hand. Together, they rode into the night.

Chapter
23

CAITLIN SAT in the silent chamber watching Niall's haggard face, marking each precious breath that slipped between his pale lips. Four days had passed since she first pressed an elixir of herbs between his lips, struggling to purge the poison that flowed through his body.

She prayed she had blended the right mixture, prayed that too much time had not passed for the healing powers to work. Yet with each sunset he did not awaken, she grew more frightened, felt more alone.

She could hear the abbess's gentle voice as she bent over a novice who had lain senseless for days. *It seems the longer they sleep, the closer God draws them to eternity. I fear she will never awaken.*

Never awaken . . .

Nay. She could not bear it. And yet, if Niall must slip away, she was glad he had clung to life this long. If he could stay with her a few more days, his mother and Fiona would come, would have the chance to tell him good-bye.

Declan had sent riders to Daire, men he trusted, men who cared for Niall, though Niall had never known how deep their loyalty ran. Yet she feared even one more sunset was too much to ask of the fates now.

He looked so pale, so still. His face like marble, translucent, as if captured in some wicked spell. She had decked the chamber with elderflowers to remind him of his mother, talked endlessly late into the night as if stories and tales, cajoling, and commands could reach him in the mist world where he wandered now, alone. She had sung the melody they had danced to at the bonfire and told him how much she loved him, until her throat ached and her voice rasped in exhaustion.

Yet still his eyes would not open.

She heard a soft sound in the doorway, turned to see Declan peering in, the warrior worn out from keeping his own vigil, standing guard outside the door.

Caitlin tried to smile, motioning Declan into the room. "Would you care to sit with him awhile?" she asked. "I know it gives him comfort that you are here watching over us."

"Do you think he knows? Knows that I . . . I would die for him. Not only as my chieftain but as my friend."

"I am certain he knows."

"Caitlin, there is nothing more to guard against beyond this door. Few would challenge Niall now. If you could only step outside, look about you, listen to the people, what they are saying. The truth has spread through Glenfluirse swiftly. The tales of Conn's treachery with Niall and his father gave other men courage to step forward, tell how Conn schemed and plotted against them, trapped them into doing things that shamed them."

"How many other lives did he corrupt the way he did Niall's?" Caitlin said sadly. "Poisoning with half-truths and secret fears?"

"More men than you can count have suffered under Conn. Of any gift, any strength Niall could bring to

Glenfluirse as chieftain, this is the greatest of all. He freed them from the chains of Conn's lies, opened their eyes to the truth for the first time in so very long. Aye, and opened their hearts with his courage against Conn's evil. He showed all of us that his first loyalty was not to his own gain but to what was right."

Caitlin reached over, touched Niall's cheek. "He is the finest man I have ever known." She surprised herself with a ragged laugh. "He would say I have not known enough men to judge, having grown up in the abbey. But it would not matter if I had known every man in Ireland, would it, Declan? He is the finest of them all."

Declan nodded, swallowed hard.

"It is still so strange to know that you were the one who carried me to the sisters."

"You must despise me for my part in taking you from your parents. But I wish you to know I did not abandon you. Whenever I was near Saint Mary's, I would climb the tree that looks over the wall. I would watch you at your play."

"I remember telling the sisters I thought a giant lived in that tree. I always thought I had imagined you."

"You were such a beautiful child, and it comforted your parents to know the sisters loved you."

"My parents knew?"

"It was the only thing I could do to ease their pain. Carry tales about you back to them. Images of a little girl to hold in their hearts. Conn forbid me to tell anyone where you were hidden or ever to return there. Made certain I knew the penalty was death. But I have babes of my own, could not bear the grief in your father's face. He wanted you to sense his love, though he could not be there to hold your hand. That is why he sent you the lily each year on the day of your birth."

"The lily was from my father?"

"Aye. After he died this last winter, I could not bear to bring one to you when the time came. I should have, I know, and yet . . . every time I thought of Fintan, every time I thought of you, knowing you would never have the chance now to touch your father's face, hear his voice . . . the pain of it, aye, and my own guilt, was nigh unbearable. I tried to banish you from my mind, and your father as well. There was nothing I could do to change what had gone before."

The warrior swallowed hard. "Forgive me. For leaving you there. For refusing to tell your father where you were. I believed Conn's vow that you were safe. If I had ever suspected what he planned for you, I would have snatched you from the abbey myself, taken you to safety."

Caitlin slipped her hand into Declan's big, battle-scarred paw, saw surprise widen the warrior's eyes. "I thank you, for all your kindness to my father, to me. You gave my parents pieces of my childhood to hold by the tales you told. Maybe when Niall is well, you would grant me one last favor as well. You could tell me what they said, what they thought, tell me if they laughed or cried when you spun stories about me. Then it would almost be as if—as if we shared those times together, like a real family."

Declan's eyes watered. He cleared his throat gruffly. "They never stopped loving you, longing for you. Every day, I heard them speak of their little daughter."

A ruckus sounded beyond the door, someone yelping in pain. Declan's hand went to his sword, Caitlin rising, facing the portal just as a warrior staggered in, clutching his shin.

"We are under attack! Beware—"

The surge of alarm in Caitlin dissipated into relief

and what was almost amusement as a slender girl with bright red hair charged into the room.

"Try to stop me again, and you will be crawling for a week, you puling worm! 'Tis my brother in there!"

The girl rushed in, cheeks flushed and travel-stained, eyes wide with terror.

"Fiona! It is too soon for the riders to have reached Daire! However did you get here?"

"We were already riding like fire, Owaine and I. He awoke, told me when he went to deliver Niall's message Conn tried to kill him! Owaine knew something was wrong and guessed Niall was in danger."

"He was."

"I left the others behind because I had to know. Caitlin, the warriors said that Conn . . . Conn poisoned him."

Caitlin stepped away from the bed. Hated the horror contorting Fiona's small face.

"Is he . . . ?" *Dead?* Fiona could not speak the word, but it hung there between them.

"He lives. If he would only awaken."

"He will. He has to," Fiona choked out. "He—he always comes back for me. Even this time, after so very long . . . he came back."

Caitlin brushed a lock of hair from Fiona's stricken face. "He asked me to tell you that you were right about your father. Conn confessed Ronan was innocent before he died. Niall said you loved nothing more than proving him wrong."

"Then he can just wake up and give me the pleasure of gloating! Niall!" Fiona shook him by the shoulder. "Niall, I came all the way to Glenfluirse to find you again. Tell you—I . . ." Her voice roughened. "I love you, curse you to hell!"

Caitlin peered into the girl's face, with its anguish

and devotion. Surely, even the cruelest fate could not steal her brother away.

Caitlin knelt at Niall's side, touched his cheek. "Niall, please, you must awaken now. I know Fiona has never said those words before. It took so much courage . . . but then, she learned courage from you. We cannot lose you now, Fiona and I. Aye, and your mother."

Her breath caught. Had she seen his eyelashes flicker? His lips move? Or was it her imagination? Nay, he was trying to say something!

"Now I have to stay . . . dead."

"What? Niall?" Caitlin gasped.

"He said something!" Fiona cried.

"I said, now I have to stay . . . dead. If I live, Fiona will never forgive me for . . . hearing that." His eyes drifted open, bloodshot, weary, but sparkling with wry humor. "Say it . . . again . . . wee one."

"Niall!" Fiona sobbed, flung herself across his chest.

"Help!" came a muffled yelp. "I really will be dead. You are smothering me!"

Caitlin tugged Fiona away, and the girl fell into Declan's arms, the two of them hugging, laughing.

Caitlin dropped to her knees beside Niall's bed. "You came back to us. Fiona knew you would."

"I was so . . . so tired. Wanted to let go, sleep. It hurt so much, lady. But every time I thought I could not hold on, I saw my father shimmering before me with something in his hand."

"What was it?"

His lips curved in a bewildered smile. "A lily. He said there were no lilies where he dwells. Laid the flower on a standing stone so I had to trudge farther, farther, out of the mist to reach it. So far that at last I could hear you calling me."

Caitlin gathered him in her arms. "I never stopped calling you, loving you. I never would have, even if you had stayed in the mist with your father. I would have spoken to you as your mother spoke to him, in all the places you loved me, knowing you could hear me."

"And I would have listened. Whispered back to you. As my father whispered to me for so long, even though I refused to listen. He forgave me, Caitlin, for every wrong I did him. I pray that when our babes come, I will be half the father he was to me."

"You have already proved you will be. The most loving of men, the bravest of warriors, the most honorable of heroes."

His brow creased, troubled. "And what kind of a chieftain will I make? I never wished to rule. I have spent all my life avenging a lie. Believing what was wrong. Angry. An outcast. Trusting no one but the man who had already betrayed me. I know nothing about how to be a chieftain."

She had wished to remain at Daire, wished for a simple life with this man she loved. And yet, after all she had witnessed in Glenfluirse, could her own dreams have changed? So many people Conn had hurt, so many lives destroyed. Such terrible power in the hands of a man who had not deserved the trust his people had put in him. Trust Niall would hold as sacred.

"Everything in your life shaped you to be the finest chieftain Glenfluirse has ever known," she said. "You are brave, aye, and just and strong enough to rule. But you carry something in your heart more valuable to your people than any of those things."

"And what is that, Lily Fair?"

"Compassion. You will never forget what it feels like to be alone and afraid and helpless. You will not value only the mighty and the powerful, you will cherish the weak, protect them. These people need you, Niall, almost as much as Fiona and your mother and I do. Show them that strength can be good. Power can be trusted. That there are men who dare to shine with real honor instead of shape-shifting to suit their own purpose."

A shadow glided across the bed, so slender it seemed to be dissolving into mist. The druid, frail and wise. Was he not the one who had begun this when he had placed his hand upon her mother's womb?

"It would seem Fintan's daughter is as wise as she is beautiful," the aged holy man said. "I heard that you have awakened, Niall of the Seven Betrayals. It is good. I did not understand the truth until you lay half dead at my feet. The truth—'twas not that the old ones were silent, 'twas that I was too fearful to listen, knowing I was the man who condemned this girl to death with my prophecy. I did not want to know, did not want to listen—realize I had condemned those whom the old ones had chosen."

"Chosen?" Niall breathed. "I do not understand."

"You and Fintan's daughter are the ones the ancient writings spoke of—rulers destined to take the old ways and mingle them with the new, the ancient magic Niall battled in his quests and the sacred echoes from the abbey Caitlin was nurtured within. Ireland will change, give itself to the Christian God, but the birth pangs of this new age in Ireland will not suffer blood and violence, killing and hatred, as in the rest of the world. A gentle blending will blossom under your care, a sweet layering of new wisdom over the old."

Caitlin stared, stunned, remembering her own thoughts that day she had dashed through the woods to the druid altar, that very thought running through her head—before she had found Niall, begun to love him.

"Niall," Caitlin whispered. "Remember the writings

on the stones, the standing stone at Daire, the druid altar near the abbey where my lilies once lay? The symbols were the same. It is true, what the druid says."

"Can you doubt it, Lily Fair?" Niall said, reaching up, kissing her. "From the first moment I saw you, splashing in the sea waves, the first moment I touched your hand, I knew—we were destined to love each other from the beginning of time."

"A new age is coming, when the abbeys and saints will rule. There are those who claim the old voices will fade, but you—you both know the truth." The druid smiled, a gentle, secret smile. "Ireland will always have a pagan heart."

The white wind sang of courage, of faith, of a future newborn. Caitlin curled herself tighter into the strong hollow of her husband's body, the rhythm of the horse's gait so familiar, the strong bands of Niall's arms about her waist keeping her safe. Chieftain he might be, hero of bard song, but Caitlin knew the most precious kingdom in Niall's eyes was the one he ruled in her heart.

"It seems impossible the seasons have passed only once since I took you from this place," he said softly, reining the horse to a halt in the druid glade. "I was so angry, sent to fetch some convent-bred woman. I was a warrior, destined to fight wars, perform great feats of valor. I never guessed I was about to fight the most important battle of my life. Learning to love. Learning to trust. Learning to face truths I could scarce have imagined."

"But you fought for them and won. Daire thrives under Fiona's care, and your mother blossoms more certainly than the flowers she loves."

Niall grimaced. "It would be perfect, if only there were a merry little war I could send Owaine to fight. It has been far too peaceful for our budding hero, and since he cannot grow tales of valor, I fear he is growing something else—calf's love for my sister."

"I can only hope she finds as much happiness with her warrior as I have with mine."

"Are you, Caitlin? Happy? I know it is not the life you wished—imagined. Wife of the chieftain, when you wanted simpler things."

"I watch you rule each day with wonder, bring honor where there was deceit, compassion where there was cruelty. I see the love in your people's eyes and see the peace and plenty you have brought them. How can I have any regrets? I am proud to have won the heart of a man so wise, so merciful. It is a better world our babe will know, because of you, Niall."

"You are wrong, Lily Fair. I have much to learn. But I will fight with all in my power to live up to the trust you offer me."

His eyes glistened overbright as he swung down. Careful of the tender burden she had carried from Glenfluirse, he cradled her in his arms and set her feet gently in the grasses she had run across as a girl. He touched her rounded belly where their child grew strong. "You are certain you are not tired? This journey might not have been wise. How can you even be certain anyone will come here, find—"

"It is my special day. I know she will come."

"I could have brought your gift myself."

Caitlin shook her head with a heart-full smile. " 'Tis my gift to offer. I knew the day I left the cloister I could not return. I can never enter the abbey, curl up at Reverend Mother's feet as I did when I was small. Perhaps I can never tell her with words how happy you have made me. But when she sees these, Niall, I am certain she will know."

Niall slipped his arm around her, guiding her through fields of wildflowers, guarding her as if she were a treasure, more rare and beloved than a fairy's wings.

Tears of joy welled over Caitlin's lashes as she laid her offering upon the druid stone: an armful of lilies perfect as the love she had won in Niall's valiant heart.

Kimberly Cates

945-10